For:
Linda Ricken
with my very best
wishes.

The broad plains of the Punjab
roll northward into the sudden thunder
of the Himalayas, "Home of the Snow,"
whose melting ice caps perpetually
replenish the five rivers nourishing
the fertile fields far below

Melvin A. Casberg M.D.

Dr. Casberg is also the author of
DEATH STALKS THE PUNJAB
first of the Prem Narayan stories.

FIVE RIVERS TO DEATH

Melvin A. Casberg

illustrations by Matt Gouig

Strawberry Hill Press
2594 15th Avenue
San Francisco, California 94127

Manufactured in the United States of America

Edited by Donna L. Osgood
Proofread by Stephen LaPorta
Typeset by Donna L. Osgood and Cragmont/ExPress
Cover illustration and design by Matt Gouig
Printed by Abbey Press, Oakland, California

Library of Congress Cataloging in Publication Data
Casberg, Melvin A., 1909—
    Five rivers to death.

    I. Title.
PS3553.A78975F5   813'.54   82-5814
ISBN 0-89407-051-7   AACR2

To my wife, *Olivia*

"For her price is far above rubies."

Proverbs, 31:10

Cast of Principal Characters

[In Order of Their Appearance]

Raj Kumar Singh—*American surgeon, descendent of a line of Sikh kings, narrates his hazardous encounters with the Naya Ghadr anarchists in northern India.*

Madan Singh—*Paternal uncle of Raj Singh, and last of a line of Sikh kings.*

Prakash Singh—*Renegade relative of Raj Singh, and leader of the Naya Ghadr anarchists.*

Pat [Patricia]—*Wife of Raj Singh. She died two days following the birth of their daughter, Leilani.*

Major Daljit Singh—*Maternal uncle of Raj Singh; killed in an ambush in the Himalayas.*

Karam Chand—*Hit man of the Naya Ghadr anarchists; hired to trail and destroy Raj Singh.*

Soli Dorabji—*Parsi banker in Bombay. Former fraternity brother of Raj Singh in their undergraduate days at Stanford University. Wife: Indira.*

Captain Prem Narayan—*Crack sleuth of the Indian Criminal Investigation Department (C.I.D.); assigned the task of bringing the Naya Ghadr anarchists to bay.*

Douglas Gordon—*American Consul in Bombay; born in India. High school classmate and long-time friend of Captain Narayan*

David [Ahmed Khan]—*Muslim employee of the C.I.D.. Captain Narayan rescued him from a crazed Hindu mob in Delhi during the early weeks of the Indian independence.*

Biba [Ranjit Kaur]—*Canadian pediatrician, and second cousin of Raj Singh. She is visiting India with her father, Balak Singh.*

Bubli [Tara Kaur]—*Daughter of Madan Singh, and first cousin of Raj Singh. She is engaged in clandestine meetings of a highly suspicious nature.*

Gurdial Singh—*Husband of Bubli. He is employed by All India Radio; he is also being blackmailed by the Naya Ghadr.*

Jay Clemens—*American doctor currently directing a population control research program in the Punjab. He was a classmate of Raj Singh at Stanford. Wife: Joan.*

Ganga Ram—*Sweeper at the Clemens' bungalow.*

Ramdas—*Youngest son of Ganga Ram.*

Ranga Prasad—*Would-be cook from Ambala. He has sinister designs on certain occupants of the Clemens' bungalow.*

Captain Karan Singh—*Superintendent of Police, Ambala District.*

Aggarwal—*Proprietor of the Quality Shop, Ambala. Highly suspicious.*

Samuel—*Recently-hired cook at the Clemens' bungalow.*

Lieutenant Ian McVey—*Chief of the Chandigarh branch of the C.I.D. An Anglo-Indian greatly respected by his fellow officers. Wife: Joyce.*

Saha Masih—*Professor of Medicine at Ludhiana Medical College.*

Anandi Khosla—*Vivacious students nurse at the Ludhiana Hospital.*

Sergeant Major Sardar Khan—*Retired from the Indian Army; currently in the employ of the C.I.D.*

Shivaram—*Leader of the outlawed ultraconservative Hindu secret society, Rashtriya Swayam Sewak Sangh (R.S.S.S.), one of whose members assassinated Mahatma Ghandi.*

Pratap Singh—*Professor of Medicine at Amritsar Medical College*

Imam Muhadin—*Muslim priest; respected community leader in Amritsar.*

Chotu—*Gardener at the Clemens' bungalow.*

Sergeant Gaikwad—*With the C.I.D. in Bombay.*

Doctor DeSa—*Bombay neurosurgeon.*

Sister Lakshmi—*With the C.I.D. in Bombay.*

Singh, or Lion, is a name shared
by Sikhs, hence its frequent
occurrence in the relating of
these actions centered in
the Punjab, homeland of the Sikhs.

Chapter One

"Man overboard!" The words were hoarse croaks which I hardly recognized as my own. Again and again I shouted into the roar of the storm.

Racing to the nearest life preserver, I lifted it off the bracket and hurled it into the turbulent wake of the ship. It quickly receded into the darkness, sliding from crest to trough of the waves as if seeking out the hapless passenger, if that term can be applied to a would-be murderer. The noises of the crashing ocean and the wind-snapped canvas awnings overhead drowned out my shouts. I ran toward the small bar on the aft deck. The weather had driven all passengers inside, leaving the area deserted. A lone bartender, welcoming the excitement, snatched up the telephone, shouting into it, gesticulating wildly. Within seconds the ship vibrated to a shuddering stop.

Shouting officers and scurrying seamen took over. The few curious passengers, roped off from the action, huddled in shivering groups. Restless searchlights swept the waves, their cones of light frail against the backdrop of tossing whitecaps and blowing spray. No longer under the stabilizing propulsion of the propellers, the deck pitched and rolled at the mercy of the ocean swells. An hour later, without even having discovered the life preserver I had thrown over, the quest was abandoned and our ship again moved forward.

Captain Alberto Rossini of the *M.S. Orient*, a sleek white vessel which was the pride of the Neopolitan Maritime Lines, sat behind his meticulously neat desk and waved me to a seat directly across from him. From the moment I stepped inside the Captain's quarters, he studied me intently through eyelids narrowed to slits. A highly-polished brass chronometer rested on the table between us, obstructing a clear view of my host. I shifted in the chair until our lines of vision were improved. He was a short man, nattily dressed in a well-tailored uniform which minimized his ample proportions. The full mustache, trimmed and waxed to a point, accentuated his official bearing.

A cabin boy placed a cup of coffee before me. In helping myself to the sugar, I spilled several grains on the gleaming mahogany desk, compromising its spotless surface. After cautiously stirring the hot drink I raised it to take a sip. My hand trembled slightly. It was evident that the Captain noted my tremor, which I hoped he would attribute to the proper cause, the fact that I was chilled. I was beginning to consider the repercussions which might be spawned from the events of the evening.

"This...this happening...a horrible thing, yes?" Captain Rossini's smile was synthetic. Without permitting me a reply to his question, he continued, "Doctor, you will kindly tell me what did happen on the deck...all you saw. I am preparing a report of this most tragic affair for the authorities. You will appreciate the fact that all passengers are the Captain's responsibility." There was a touch of annoyance in his voice.

"Yes, sir. I fully understand your difficult situation and shall cooperate in every way."

Realizing the inevitability of this interview, I had been assessing the evening's disaster, trying to sort out the facts into those to be revealed and those best kept to myself, at least for the time being. To tell all would result in endless interrogations and at the same time might jeopardize my personal freedom. Also, to share the whole truth could play into the hands of my unknown enemy. To the best of my knowledge there had been no other witness to the bizarre drowning.

Captain Rossini shifted restlessly in his chair, "You were saying?"

"Sorry." I set my cup on the table. "Just trying to collect my thoughts. Now let me see...I was standing on the short catwalk that juts out from the deck in the stern..."

"Port or starboard?" the Captain interrupted gruffly.

"The starboard...the right side?"

A flicker of amusement crossed his face. "Yes, yes, the right side."

"I had been leaning on the rail in the stern near the flag..."

"The taffrail...that is called the taffrail," he broke in again, drumming his fingers on the desk.

"If you say so, Captain, we'll call it the taffrail," I retorted bluntly, irritated by his obvious efforts at intimidation.

Rossini dropped his eyes and nodded me on.

"Well, I moved from the taffrail around to the catwalk and stood at its outside end looking down into the ocean." I paused to take a sip of coffee.

"And?"

"Suddenly out of nowhere this man rushed directly at me, knocking me to my knees on the deck. The sheer impetus of his charge carried him over my body and over the railing into the ocean."

My interrogator pursed his lips and frowned. "That simple, eh?"

"May sound simple to you but it was a damned harrowing experience to me. The whole thing happened so suddenly that I didn't even get a look at his face."

"Yes...poor man," he murmured with an unctuous sigh, making the sign of the cross.

"You've identified the fellow?"

"He was of Indian registry and you are an Indian, are you not?"

"Of Indian ancestry, but an American by birth."

He cleared his throat authoritatively. "You will be available for further questioning." It was an order.

"At your convenience, Captain."

Captain Rossini stood and indicated with a wave of his hand that the interview was over. I stepped out onto the wind-swept deck and headed back to my cabin.

My roommate was an Italian Jesuit priest, Father Milani. His knowledge of English was inadequate for conversation and my familiarity with Italian or Latin was equally wanting, so our exchanges were primarily smiles and short salutations. The Father's activities were limited to brisk walks on deck, cassock flying in the wind, and to reading in the ship's library. When I let myself into our cabin, the priest was sleeping sonorously in his lower bunk. I undressed and climbed into the upper berth.

My nerves were taut and my mind raced as I lay awake in the darkness. Slowly the steady vibration of the engines and the ship's rolling eased the tension. As I relaxed I reached into the past for facts that might shed light on my situation. The first indications of a threat to our family came in a communication from India. I remembered watching my father gravely studying the telegram in his hand.

"Your uncle Madan just died," he told me in a barely audible voice.

Madan, a younger brother, had assumed the responsibilities of the eldest son of a princely family when my father embraced Christianity and left India with his bride for America.

"I'm really sorry, Dad. I know the two of you were close..."

Through the years I had sensed bouts of homesickness in my parents. A prosperous and progressive farmer, Father delighted in and had grown to love his adopted country. Yet the flat dry lands of the Imperial Valley made green by irrigation reminded him of the Punjab of his birth, and the mountains rising from the plains called to mind the foothills of the Himalayas. Still, he and my mother had adjusted well and were liked and respected in their community.

My reminiscent searchings were cut short by a particularly forceful wave smashing against the side of the ship, rattling the glasses and water carafe in their wooden slots on the wall. Father Milani climbed out of his bunk and staggered across the rolling floor toward the toilet, moaning. With a sudden pitch of the ship, he was slammed against the wall across from our bunks and slumped to the floor. I jumped down to help. With lips tightly pursed, he pointed frantically toward the bathroom, moaning pitifully. I managed to steer him to his destination where he fell on his knees before the toilet bowl and vomited with loud retchings. When the siege had subsided, I eased him back to his berth. He mumbled something which I took to mean that he felt better.

With the cabin returning to its normal rolling quiet, I again reached into the past for clues that might interpret the very deliberate attempt on my life. My thoughts returned to Father and the telegram.

"Dad, at breakfast you said something about land...an inheritance. Is there some problem with it?"

"Quite a bit of land, Raj, willed to me by Madan. He's asked that I dispose of it in any way that seems best to me. The pressing problem is that unless a member of our family signs the deeds in the Punjab in person, it reverts automatically to the next of kin, a nephew named Prakash."

"Name rings a bell...isn't he the..."

"The renegade,"Father broke in, "The black sheep of the family."

"Well, here's your chance to see the Punjab again, Dad." Over the years neither of them had returned to India.

A knowing look passed between my parents."No, Son, we feel that you should go," my father proposed quietly.

"But why?"

"Several reasons really. Among them the fact that you've never seen the Punjab. Besides that, your mother and I feel you should get away for awhile...travel..." his voice drifted off.

The suggestion that I take a traveling vacation was not new. My parents had been urging this diversion ever since Pat had died. A massive clot...a postpartum embolus in medical terms...had taken her from me two days after Leilani was born. This all happened during my surgical residency at the Los Angeles County Hospital two years before. I had treated my depression, with moderate success, by spending long, hard hours in surgery. My mother and father took over the role of foster parents, and it was heartwarming to see how my baby daughter became the queen of my boyhood home. Two months out of residency, I was looking for a place to start a surgical practice.

"Now about the land..."Dad began, beckoning Mother to join us in the front room, "Major Daljit Singh was your maternal uncle. He was killed somewhere along the Kashmir border."

"I remember when you got the news."

"Daljit's widow and two sons are not in the best of financial circumstances. Your mother and I have decided to turn this land over to them."

"Sounds good to me." I stood to stretch my legs. "So, when should I leave?"

"As soon as you can...say in a couple of weeks?"

"That soon?"

"Son, there are reasons we must move quickly."

"I don't quite understand." I searched his face for an answer.

"Over the past two weeks I've received several anonymous letters...threatening letters."

"Threatening? Why didn't you tell me?"

"Raj, you've had your share of problems and we didn't want to burden you further.''

"But what are the threats?"

"Someone doesn't want us to have the land." Dad waved his hands deprecatingly, but I noticed a hint of worry in Mother's eyes.

"Just what do they threaten...I mean are they explicit?"

"No, just general threats of dire consequences if we return to the Punjab."

"What were the postmarks on the letters?"

"All the way from Delhi to Los Angeles."

"How would they find out about the land?" I raised my voice in exasperation.

Dad smiled at me patiently. "They've read the will. Courts practically make them public property once they've been recorded."

"Prakash behind the letters?"

"Shouldn't be surprised. I've heard that he's become a ringleader of some disreputable underground gang in the Punjab."

Mother, who had been knitting and quietly listening to our conversation, left momentarily to return with tea and biscuits. Leilani, my little chatterbox with endless energy, helped her grandmother...at least that was what she thought...passing out the biscuits individually in her chubby little hands. I would miss her, but I had no misgivings as to her welfare during my absence.

The multitude of travel details were soon worked out. I would stay with a Stanford medical school classmate of mine. Jay Clemens and his wife were in the Punjab to conduct research into population control. Just a few weeks ago I had received a letter from Jay and Joan describing their enterprise and urging me to visit them in India. Their warm invitation was to be honored sooner than any of us had anticipated.

I flew directly from Los Angeles to Paris and from there proceeded to Genoa by train, boarding the *M.S. Orient* on the night of my arrival. Several times while traveling overland, particularly while changing trains in Milan, I had an uncomfortable feeling that someone was watching me, though I could never catch anyone at it.

At breakfast, the first morning out into the Mediterranean aboard the *M.S. Orient*, I noticed a swarthy, middle-aged man, whom I took to be an Indian, staring at me from time to time. He sat at a table across the dining saloon from my regular seat. A steward, motivated by a generous tip, brought me the information that the man's name was Karam Chand. This verified my surmise that he was an Indian. He deliberately evaded close contact but kept me under his watchful eye. During routine shipboard activities, I would discover Karam Chand in the background guardedly watching me. His efforts in sleuthing were clumsy and rather obvious.

At Naples I went ashore and took a bus trip to visit the ruins of Pompeii. My Indian sleuth quite deliberately boarded the same bus. I made it a point to remain with the crowd of sightseers. These same tactics prevailed from Naples on to Port Said and Aden. It became a rather puerile game of cat and mouse. My disadvantage was that I knew neither the rules nor the stakes of these hide-and-seek capers.

The ship was two days out of Aden when the rough weather broke. Southwest monsoon winds and waves howled and pounded from across the Indian Ocean. After dinner that night I decided to take a stroll on deck before turning in to enjoy a biography of Jawaharlal Nehru.

The final lap around, I paused on a catwalk jutting out from a deck in the stern. Grasping the rail firmly in my hands I did some quick knee bends and took a series of deep breaths. The next instant I was grabbed around the waist by some assailant from behind who tried desperately to force me over the rail into the churning sea below. My firm grip on the rail and the narrowness of the catwalk saved my life. Thrusting one leg under the railing to the side, I wrestled with the strength of one fighting for survival.

Karam Chand was older than I and soon the struggle was taking its toll of his limited physical reserve. Breathing in noisy gasps and momentarily losing his hold on me, he stepped back, blocking any possible retreat. This gave me a chance to shout for help. The cry, just barely heard in the fury of the storm, drove my assailant into another attack. Giving a quick look around for any possible witness, he bellowed into the gale and rushed at me like an enraged bull. The advantage of surprise no longer was his. I quickly crouched down at the blind end of the cul-de-sac and braced myself for the impact.

It really was not my intention to kill Karam Chand. I was concentrating on staying alive. The sharp collision of our bodies pushed me up from a crouching position and vaulted him over the rails. A scream of fear replaced his roar of anger. I turned just in time to see his body hurtle through a beam of light coming from a porthole and then plunge into the convulsing ocean below.

Father Milani's chanted prayer interrupted my thoughts. I raised up on my elbow to watch the morning sun, shining through a porthole, focus a shifting circle of light on the far side of our cabin wall. From the continued tossing of the ship it was evident that the monsoon had not abated. In spite of a sleepless night, I remained wide awake. Although the rules of the game were not clear yet, the late Karam Chand had demonstrated that the stakes were high.

Chapter Two

The *M.S.Orient* docked at dawn and I stood at the ship's rail eager to catch a first glimpse of the city. Bombay was just waking up. Winches rumbled, pulling taut the thick hemp ropes securing the ship to Ballard Pier. Scurrying dock workers pushed gangplanks into gaping doors in the vessel's side.

A black crow, sitting on the rail nearby, eyed me curiously with head cocked first to one side and then the other, punctuating each rapid twist of his neck with a raucous "caw." His small sharp eyes looked me over, asking whether I would dispute his right to perch on the rail. Assured of my peaceful intentions, his looks and tone changed to those of a begger and scolder.

The southwest monsoon had been in full swing for almost a month. A steaming humidity combined with a generous perspiration glued clothes and skin together. Puddles of water on the dock were mute evidence of recent showers. Low lying dark clouds scurried toward the rising sun, leapfrogging the city.

Breakfast was a hurried affair, the last meal together for a band of people who had been living in that peculiar shipboard intimacy of those isolated from their normal routine. Several times during the meal, I glanced over at the empty chair which had been Karam Chand's and felt a tingle of apprehension. As I prepared to disembark, my mind turned back to that stormy night two days out of Aden. There had been a sense of protective security on board the vessel since the death of my assailant. Now I was stepping into an environment, familiar and dear to my parents, which seemed strangely ominous to me. There were people out there who opposed my coming to India. Would they go to the same lengths as had Karam Chand to prevent the fulfillment of my duties in the Punjab?

The ship's lounge presented a bustle of activity as the Port Authorities methodically checked passports, immunization records and other documents. As instructed by the Los Angeles office, I solicited the services of an agent of the American Express, who took me into his protective custody. It surprised me that at no point in the formalities of disembarkation were questions raised concerning the death at sea. I was expecting a thorough interrogation by the authorities. Were they accepting my story? Possibly they were prepared to play the surveillance game. This was a standard police procedure and certainly there was no problem as to my identity. Although innocent, I couldn't help but feel entangled in a sinister web.

My fears were submerged temporarily by the waving arms and expansive smiles of Soli Dorabji, who stood on the dock end of the ship's main gangplank.

"Raj, Raj!" he cupped his hands to shout above the din. "Welcome to India!" And then, much to the annoyance of the passengers as well as those directing the human traffic, he began to push upstream to meet me halfway down. Pedestrian movement by this particular route was halted temporarily as we hugged each other, suspended between ship and pier, oblivious to the commotion around us. Soli, the son of an influential Parsi banker, had been my fraternity brother at Stanford. Although he had majored in business administration and I in science, we had roomed together in the dormitory. He had spent many a vacation at my home, and Mother and Dad had accepted him as another son.

Soli had changed little over the eight years since I had last seen him. Perhaps he had put on a little weight, although he always had been modestly plump. His ample frame gave him an opportunity to distribute extra poundage inconspicuously. A handsome, round face gave the impression of benign affluence. He walked and moved slowly, almost ponderously, as suited a financier addicted to banking and the stock market. As in his undergraduate days in America, he was dressed immaculately.

The American Express agent expertly guided me through customs. It was quite early in the day as Soli and I threaded our way through the heavy rush hour traffic. Bombay, gateway to India and confluence of the East and West, swallowed us unceremoniously into the stream of her millions. This new environment held a strange and hypnotic fascination for me. The sights, smells and sounds...all so different and yet hauntingly familiar. Associations, like a weaver's bobbin, shuttled back and forth between the past and present to knit variant factors into a single fabric.

Women in colorful saris, walking with the stately carriage characteristic of this part of the world, reminded me of my mother. Delicate odors of spices and cooking food stimulated gustatory memories. Snatches of conversation in Marathi and Gujarati, heard at random, sounded familiar. Although neither the Punjabi nor Hindustani of my understanding, the dialects reflected their common Sanskrit source.

"Raj," Soli said, throwing a quick glance in my direction, "does this trip of yours involve an element of personal danger?"

"Why?"

"Well," he coughed nervously, "day before yesterday I checked down at American Express on the time of your arrival and the manager asked me to step into his office."

"And?"

"He wanted to know about our relationship. Asked a lot of questions about you."

"Seems a threatening telegram arrived addressed to you in care of American Express."

"Threatening? How did they know it was threatening?"

"Posts and Telegraphs, seeing the viciousness of its content, notified the police."

"Soli, I really hadn't planned to bother you with my problems but certain complications have developed. Hope they don't get you involved."

"My involvement be damned!" Soli exploded so vehemently that our car almost ran down a motorized rickshaw.

"I'll tell you all about it later. Please don't let this worry you."

He drew in a quick breath as if to relax and turned to throw me a grin.

"That's better," I responded with a laugh, slapping his shoulder.

"The manager of American Express told me the police had been in to question him. So when I turned up asking about you, it really was quite natural for me to become a suspect."

"You mean they thought..." I burst out laughing.

"Oh, I've a clean bill of health. They must've checked around pretty thoroughly."

"You mean the police?"

He nodded. "Several of my friends and business associates who'd been contacted by the police have been calling me to find out what it's all about." Soli grinned sheepishly.

"Did you see the telegram?"

He shook his head. "You might be interested to know that a C.I.D. inspector dropped in to see me just last night."

"Asking about me?"

"Uh-huh. Told him all I knew about you. All about our association at Stanford. The chap's on our side."

"International intrigue!" I laughed in spite of myself. "And what happens next?"

"They want to meet you down at American Express in the morning." Soli punctuated his remark with a loud blast of the car horn.

We braked to a stop at an intersection where a white-gloved policeman in a smart turban, standing on a small platform, directed traffic. Soli looked at me solemnly and said, "You'll be seeing the C.I.D. tomorrow."

"And who is the C.I.D.?"

"Criminal Investigation Department. They've gotten interested in the case, possibly because of the international implications."

"Sounds ominous. A police record before I even land in India."

"Raj, could be worse, you know. I mean these chaps' real interest is in your welfare, your safety.''

The traffic cop waved us ahead. We moved into a broad boulevard adjoining Malabar Hill. I caught the name Marine Drive and recognized this as the road on which the Dorabjis lived.

Soli cleared his throat and announced, ''For your information, Raj, you've already been under the scrutiny of the C.I.D.''

''You're kidding!''

''No, my dear chap, I'm not kidding. The Captain who visited me last night came off the gangplank behind us and hovered in the background while you went through customs.''

''You're sure? I mean with all those people milling about us...''

Soli gave an emphatic nod. ''I'm certain. The Captain has an identification one just can't miss. You'll see what I mean in the morning.''

The Dorabji family lived in an upper story apartment condominium on Marine Drive, facing the Indian Ocean. The view from their balcony embraced a wide inlet from the ocean, peppered with small fishing boats, sails flapping, lazily plying back and forth over the water. A chain of imposing buildings, mostly apartments, fringed the landward side of the boulevard which curved gracefully in a sweeping concavity extending from the base of Malabar Hill on the far right to end on a blunt peninsula on the distant left.

Indira, Soli's wife, was a charming hostess who immediately made me feel at home. She was quite aware of her husband's affection for me, so nothing was too good for Soli's American college classmate. To make my adoption into the family even more complete, the six year old twin girls addressed me as ''Uncle Raj.''

After dinner on this first night ashore, Soli and I moved out onto the balcony overlooking the bay. It was dark and the boulevard lights along Marine Drive sparkled cheerfully below us. Soli lit a cigarette as we settled into our chairs. I recounted everything which might have a bearing on the threats to my life. He smoked in silence throughout my story.

''That's about it,'' I concluded soberly.

Soli leaned back in his chair, hands clasped behind his head, and stared out into the cloud-filled monsoon sky.

''You know, Raj, I just find it hard to believe that Karam Chand was acting on his own.''

''Agreed.''

''The bugger must have been a hired agent...'' Soli stopped to draw on his cigarette, ''and the motive just isn't clear yet. Must have something to do with that land...but what?''

I rose from my chair to lean against the porch railing. ''The land is valuable and there's quite a bit of it. But, you know, for my nickel's worth there's more to this land business than just the rupee value.''

"Might there be something in the soil you don't know about?"

"You mean oil or coal?"

"Yes."

"I just don't know and neither does my father."

Soli lit another cigarette and we watched it glow in the dark.

"That renegade cousin of mine..."

"Prakash?"

"Uh-huh. That character must be tied into this in some way."

"Don't worry, Raj, the C.I.D. is working on the Karam Chand matter. And I'll bet they are quite aware of your cousin."

"You seem to think they're sharp, the C.I.D."

"Quite sharp, really. Something like your F.B.I."

"Sounds reassuring."

"They'll keep close tabs on you if for no other reason than to satisfy themselves that you didn't push Karam Chand overboard."

"Come on, Soli, you're talking out of both sides of your mouth...you intimated that I had a built-in safety factor with the C.I.D. protecting me."

"Damn right they'll protect you. Their reasons for doing it really don't matter, do they?"

"Just sounds cold-blooded, that's all."

Soli grinned, his face barely visible in the glow of his cigarette. "Come on, Raj, let's not get down."

"O.K., I'll accept their protection, regardless of their motives." I laughed self-consciously.

"Karam Chand's death introduces another potential motive." Soli sounded grim. "Although he brought this on himself, his relatives will take it for granted that you killed him."

"An eye for an eye and a tooth for a tooth," I muttered more to myself than to my companion.

Soli hesitated a moment, drawing deeply on his cigarette. "You know, Raj, in this country revenge is a matter of personal as well as family honor."

I knew.

"This responsibility is considered by some to be so binding that it's even passed on from generation to generation. Certain tribes, in the event of there being no male issue, actually will select a man to carry out the act of revenge in the family's name. There was a particular case published recently in the newspapers of a daughter being given in marriage for no other purpose than to help in wreaking vengance on the bridegroom's family." Soli wiped his face with a handkerchief. "Don't mean to sound gruesome, but I want you to treat the matter of revenge seriously."

We sat in silence for a while looking down on the Marine Drive traffic. The lights from a couple of fishing craft bobbed around on the bay, pointed up by serpentine shafts of reflection on the water.

"Well then, we've identified two sources of trouble," I broke into the quiet. "Two passions, greed and revenge."

"And the greed may be for power or money or a combination of both."

I was awake the next morning earlier than the Dorabjis, and lay in bed contemplating the events of the past twenty-four hours. It was reassuring to have Soli's counsel and friendship. As my roommate at Stanford he had told me about his family in India. In some ways it had seemed to me that he was beyond his years in a sensitivity to the philosophical aspects of life. He had attributed this to the teachings of his Parsi mother.

The Parsis, religious refugees of the seventh and eighth centuries fleeing Muslim persecution, left their native land of Persia and were given sanctuary by a king of Western India. Followers of Zoroaster, they believed in the sacredness of the elements of fire, water and earth. They expose their dead on the tops of circular buildings called "Towers of Silence," so the bodies are dissipated without defiling the earth. In these towers are three circular tiers: the outer for men, the middle for women, and the central one for the children. Their method of interment, so different from those practiced by other religions of India, stems from the veneration in which the Parsis hold the three elements. Unlike the Hindus, they think fire is too holy to be polluted by burning the dead, and unlike the Muslims and the Christians, they consider the earth too sacred for the purpose of burial.

In large part the Parsis follow the professions and in spite of their minority status have contributed greatly to the land of their adoption. Philanthropy is an integral part of their religious practice. The large cancer hospital in Bombay, for example, was built as a Parsi gift to their fellow citizens of India.

After breakfast, Soli dropped me off at the American Express building where I met Mr. Taylor, the manager, who in turn introduced me to Captain Prem Narayan of the Criminal Investigation Department. For several minutes, under the astute direction of the Captain, we engaged in social pleasantries. Such amiable conversational tactics relaxed my initial apprehension of this confrontation with official India.

I soon found myself becoming an admirer of this Captain Narayan, who presented more of an academic than a military bearing. In his early forties, he was of medium stature and slender frame, with a head of closely cropped graying hair adding to the dignity of his appearance. Long tapering fingers, heavily stained with nicotine, moved restlessly, exploring objects close at hand. His eyes, dark and deep-set, were alive with curiosity, equally capable of reflecting steely determination or warm compassion.

The Captain spoke slowly, almost hesitantly, seeking out words with the same care one might use in selecting stepping stones to cross a swift mountain stream. As a result he spoke a precise English, perhaps a bit stuffy at times, refusing to cut grammatical corners for the sake of brevity or simplicity.

His uniform consisted of a khaki bush jacket without insignia of any kind, and shorts to match, with knee-length stockings and brightly polished brown shoes. Across his knees he balanced a black wooden swagger stick.

Although the Captain's movements were unhurried and methodical, he gave the distinct impression of one who could react physically with an unusual swiftness should the occasion demand. In spite of his professorial deportment, he could not entirely hide his military background—even in mufti, or civilian clothes. He walked, stood and sat with the erect posture born of service with the armed forces.

Having been seated on Captain Narayan's right side, I was not completely prepared for a sudden exposure to the left part of his face. I was glad of my surgical discipline, which had inured me to the disfiguring results of wounds. I did not start at the sight of the deformity, a fact which he noted as his eyes searched mine for any reaction.

An ugly scar slashed across the left side of the Captain's face from temple to the angle of his mouth, pulling his upper lip into a permanent sneer and distorting the outer angle of his left eye. The result of this unfortunate state of affairs was that he presented two quite different facial expressions, depending on which profile happened to be in view. Seen from the left, he gave the impression of savage anger, whereas by turning his head, he reflected an amiable calm. Surely a plastic surgeon could do something for him, I thought, but perhaps in some strange way this blemish might be an advantage. Before the interview was over, this became a rather grotesque game of comparing a dual identity. Many others must have shared this same grim fascination.

"This message arrived for you, Doctor Singh," Mr.Taylor said, interrupting my reflections. He reached across the desk and handed me a standard telegram envelope.

Captain Narayan cleared his throat and added, "It is our duty to inform you that the message has been read by my office. The Department of Posts and Telegraphs sent us the missive because of the nature of its content."

I slipped the form out of the envelope and unfolded it. It was addressed to me in care of the American Express, and the date of receipt was the third of August, two days ago. The telegram had been sent from Amritsar in the Punjab. It read, "THE PRICE OF MURDER IS DEATH STOP A JUST REWARD AWAITS YOU." It was signed, "Brother of Karam Chand."

I shot a puzzled look at the Captain, who merely studied me thoughtfully. I reread the telegram and pondered its content. The accomplice who sent the telegram probably got the news of Karam

Chand's death when the *M.S.Orient* docked at Karachi, the last stop before Bombay. From that point he might have contacted someone in Amritsar by wire or traveled there in person. At any rate, the fact of the drowning was known to the victim's relatives. Soli was right, the motive of revenge had entered the picture.

"Doctor Singh, please do believe me, I'm sorry that your visit has been marred in this unfortunate manner," the Captain apologized. "May I add that your friend, Mr. Dorabji, has been most cooperative in assisting us with information."

"Just one of those things, can't be helped," I observed with a shrug.

Captain Narayan studied me soberly for a minute, then smiled and asked, "Would you join me at our C.I.D. offices where we might discuss these matters in the privacy they warrant?"

"Why not?" I nodded in agreement, and watched a look of appreciation cross his face.

"As you may be aware, my office knows of the unfortunate accident at sea."

"Any breakthrough? That is, did you find out any facts about the fellow?"

He shook his head. "We interrogated several of the ship's officers and certain passengers, including your cabin mate, Padre Milani."

"And?"

"Unfortunately little came to light, at least from those on the *M.S.Orient*. The questioning was significant in a way, I suppose, because it brought out practically nothing."

"Shouldn't the American Consulate here be notified?"

"Yes, I've contacted them and someone from the Consulate will join us."

We rose to leave. The interview, although brief, gave me a degree of confidence in Captain Prem Narayan. I marked him as a man of professional competence, firm in his convictions and imbued with a sense of personal integrity. Actually, it was with a feeling of relief that I walked out with him and climbed into the back seat of his car, driven by a uniformed chauffeur.

Flora Fountain is an ornate architectural showpiece with statues and decorations mounted on top like sugar frosted figures on a wedding cake. It stands in the center of Naoroji Road in front of the American Express offices at the confluence of several streets, like the hub of a great wheel. The driver of our car cut through a line of oncoming traffic and careened toward the left side of the fountain. As we sped forward I noticed a man dressed in Western style who seemed familiar. He was seated on the cement wall enclosing the pool at the base of the statuary. On our approach he stood and quickly moved around to the other side of the masonry. In the distance he looked and walked like Soli Dorabji.

At the C.I.D. offices, doors opened, as though automatically controlled, before the Captain and me. The office servants, known as *chaprasis*, sprang from their seats to facilitate our passage through the corridors. Our entourage moved along in a continuous flow, unhampered by such obstructions as doors or screens. There were *chaprasis* all through the building, some seated on chairs and benches along the hallways and verandahs, others standing quietly outside office doors, awaiting the beck and call of the men within.

Captain Narayan motioned me to a chair in front of the desk and sat down. I noted that for the most part his benign profile was turned my way.

"Cigarette?" He opened a beautiful cloisonne case and held it out before me.

"Thank you, no."

"Ah, you doctors," he murmured in mock seriousness, "trying to frighten us away from some of the basic pleasures of life."

The Captain laid his swagger stick down at the side of the desk and clasped his hands before him. His dark eyes studied me closely. Slowly his face broke into a friendly smile and he asked, "A spot of tea, eh what?"

I returned the smile and replied, "Sounds good to me."

"Bhaskar!" he called out and almost immediately one edge of the hanging bamboo curtain was pushed aside admitting a young *chaprasi*.

"*Ha ji*—Yes sir," Bhaskar responded politely.

"*Do cup chay lao*—Bring two cups of tea," the Captain ordered, in Hindustani. As the fellow left, my host turned to ask, "You are of Indian ancestry, Doctor?" This was more a statement of fact than a question.

"Yes, both of my parents came from the Punjab."

Captain Narayan nodded and paused to look out of the window before saying, "Doctor, I hope you will realize that it not only is my responsibility but my sincere personal desire as well to protect you from harm."

"Thanks, I believe you...and...and I'm most grateful."

Another *chaprasi* pushed aside the curtain to inform us that a gentleman from the American Consulate had arrived.

"*Us-ko andar ane do*—Let him come in," the Captain ordered, rising to greet the visitor.

"Doctor Singh, this is Douglas Gordon, the American Consul here in Bombay."

We shook hands, each of us quietly sizing up the other. "Thanks for coming," I said, surprised that the Consul himself would attend this session.

Another chair was pulled up beside mine. Mr. Gordon was about ten years my senior, neatly dressed, and obviously an American. He moved and conversed easily, breathing the confidence of one who accepts his own capabilities without vainglory or arrogance.

"Doctor Singh," the Consul turned to me, "do please remember that I'm here as your representative as well as that of our government. May I urge that you take us...Captain Narayan and me...into full confidence."

"I'm certain it'll be in my best interest to do so," I replied, having come to the conclusion that the presence of Consul Gordon was warranted by the serious nature of my problem.

Bhaskar interrupted the conversation by stepping in with a tray bearing a teapot and three cups. He had noted the addition of another member to our party. Pleasantries were exchanged as the Captain poured.

"Sugar and cream for you, Doug?" Our host pushed the pitcher and bowl across the table toward us.

"You know me, Prem, plenty of sugar and cream with a little tea. Your man Bhaskar brews the blackest and strongest pot of tannic acid in Bombay."

Prem Narayan pointed at the Consul and announced with a chuckle, 'He's one of us—a *pakka* Indian."

"Mr. Gordon, you must have attended school here in India?" I asked, studying the American over my cup of tea.

He nodded. "Went to grade school at Woodstock...up in the Himalayas...an American boarding school."

"Good old Breeks," the Captain broke in. "Doug and I attended high school together there. Up in the Nilgiri mountains in South India. Both of us were on the school soccer team. Same dormitory together for four years."

"And after that?" I directed the question at both men.

"I went back to the States to college," Doug Gordon replied, "while Prem here went to Military Academy in North India, Dehra Dun. My alma mater is Occidental College."

Bhaskar came in and removed the tea dishes leaving the three of us alone. For a few moments the only motion in the room was the slow turning of a ceiling fan, which emitted a grating squeak at a certain point in every revolution. Looking past the Captain through a window into the yard beyond, I could see a gardener squatting on his haunches digging soil about the roots of a large hibiscus bush. An ample turban on his small head gave the man a disproportionate, even a grotesque, appearance. His ear lobes were pierced and a large silver ring hung from each. The man must have had a cold with a running nose, a problem which he handled with finesse simply by compressing one nostril with a finger and giving a quick forceful blow, repeating the same procedure on the other side. Not really a bad idea, I thought, considering the ease with which the cold virus is spread. Instead of carrying around a soiled handkerchief full of contagious organisms in one's pocket, throw the excretion out on the ground exposed to the sterilizing rays of the sun.

Suddenly Captain Narayan straightened in his chair. For a few seconds his eyes probed mine speculatively, then he spoke. "Now Doctor, please relate all the information you have that may have any bearing whatsoever on the problem at hand. Please do not feel rushed."

It appeared that the only record to be kept of our session was whatever the Captain chose to jot down on a pad of paper before him. His dark eyes studied me closely as I presented my story. The sudden interruptions of my narrative for clarification showed that he was carefully analyzing my story. Only occasionally did he write anything down. Douglas Gordon also evinced a keen interest in my recitation. His familiarity with Southern California made it possible for him to follow the geographic landmarks of my report.

"That's the story, gentlemen." I spread my hands before me.

Captain Narayan rose slowly from his chair and walked to the window behind the desk, staring outside with his back toward us. Gordon and I watched him expectantly.

"Those bloody anarchists!" He spat the words with a vehemence that startled me. "There's much more to this than just the monetary value of the land. . ." He stopped as suddenly as he had started and turned to face us. All the humor had drained out of his eyes.

"Anarchists?" I was incredulous.

"Yes! Anarchists! Located in the general area of the land in question." Captain Narayan selected a cigarette from his cloisonne case and lit it, then drew in slowly and deeply to exhale the smoke from his nostrils.

"Captain, I've brought with me certain documents, such as a copy of my uncle's will. Perhaps we should check these out together."

He thought a moment. "Join me here this afternoon with your papers, say about four o'clock."

Douglas Gordon looked uneasy as he watched Prem Narayan. "How do things look? I mean as to the Doctor's safety?"

"Doctor Singh's life is in danger," he said quietly.

I studied the Captain's face briefly. "And just how do I face this danger?"

"Be damned careful. Don't go out alone. Don't expose yourself unnecessarily. Be suspicious of everyone and of everything."

"That's a tall order," I groaned.

"One learns to live with it, sort of becomes a habit," Captain Narayan muttered, walking over to shake our hands. He stopped before me, smiling wryly, and said, "Doctor, be assured the C.I.D. will back you up."

Douglas Gordon offered to drive me to the Dorabji residence. We rode in silence in the back of the Consular limousine for several minutes until he asked, "Well, Doctor, what do you think of the Captain?"

I thought for a moment. "He's a solid citizen. I must say I'm impressed."

"Trust him. He's a man of impeccable integrity. Believe me."

Chapter Three

Tara Mahal, the apartment building where the Dorabjis lived, appeared deserted. Even the elevator boy was not at his post. I climbed the stairs to the fourth floor and knocked on the door. The cook let me in, explaining that the *memsahib* was out shopping.

When I saw my open suitcase, with its contents strewn on the floor, I knew that the documents would be missing. After verifying the loss, I walked into the hall and called the cook from his clattering in the kitchen.

"Who's been in my room?" I asked sharply.

His eyes were drawn with worry and he twisted a towel nervously in his hand. "Only the sweeper who cleans the floor and the servant woman who makes the beds."

The man obviously was withholding information, but I knew better than to try to pursue the matter with him.

Indira let herself into the apartment shortly. She was shocked and angry to hear of my loss and asked whether she should contact Soli. I told her that would be unnecessary. I stepped out onto the balcony and sat down while she interviewed the cook.

"He lied to you," Indira confided as she came out to join me later. "He slipped out after I left and visited for a time with the cook on the floor below. On returning he saw a stranger run out of the apartment."

"Did he get a look at the fellow?"

"I asked him that. The man covered most of his face with the tail of his turban."

"Did the thief say anything?"

"Yes. Shouted out in Hindustani, '*Mai jata hu. Mujhe jane do*—I'm going. Let me go!'"

"How about his size or any identifying thing about him?"

Indira called the cook out. He came and stood in the doorway to the balcony. "How large was the man?" she asked.

He shuffled his feet a moment before replying, "About as I am."

I smiled kindly at the cook, trying to ease his agitation, and continued the questioning, "The Hindustani...was it like that spoken in Bombay?"

"No. Like the Uttar Pradesh or Punjab."

From what he said, the cook had run out after the thief but the lack of light in the corridor and the speed of the culprit had made escape easy. It appeared quite unlikely that the cook was an accomplice.

Early in the afternoon we had tea on the balcony overlooking the bay. The cook was nervous. He rattled dishes and spilled hot water, embarrassing all three of us. If the man is innocent, I thought, why is he so disturbed?

Indira seemed to sense my question, and explained, "This robbery will mean an inquiry by the police and under such circumstances the servant is usually suspect. The investigation can be quite rigorous. So the chap's a bit anxious."

Douglas Gordon picked me up shortly after tea. On the way to the C.I.D. offices I told him of the loss of my papers.

"Complicates things, doesn't it?" he asked with a frown.

"Perhaps not too much. These all were copies of the originals with my dad. I'll call him tonight and have them sent out air mail."

"Think they might have learned anything from what they stole?"

"Not much. They already know the contents of the will."

Bhaskar ushered us in to Prem Narayan's office and arranged our chairs. The Captain had stepped down the hall for a moment. On his return we stood to shake hands. I must have displayed my worry, for he looked at me enquiringly and asked, "Something has gone wrong?"

"Yes...someone stole the documents from my case this morning." His dark eyes revealed a hint of worry as I recounted the details.

"Was he not a Sikh, the intruder?" the Captain asked.

I shook my head. "Although the man wore a turban, it was not Sikh and he wasn't bearded."

Captain Narayan stared thoughtfully at his hands folded before him on the desk, then looked up quickly to say, "Never mind. Every move, even such as this one, gives us some information." He smiled at both of us.

"I'll call my father and get more copies by air."

"*Accha*—Alright. And let me add that one of my men is on his way to the Punjab at this moment to investigate the will."

"Good. Maybe he can smoke out more information."

"By the way, Doctor Singh, have you contacted any of your relatives in this country and informed them of your purpose here?"

"No, we've corresponded only with the lawyer to my late uncle's estate."

"Where is he, your solicitor?"

"Chandigarh." I pulled out my small address book and read the notation to him.

The Captain jotted down the information on his note pad and then stared at me. His eyes appeared to focus at a point some distance beyond my face. I felt uncomfortable under such scrutiny, though I eventually realized that this was an unconscious habit of his when deep in thought. Finally, he took a deep breath and exhaled slowly, blowing out both cheeks.

"There obviously are several facets to our problem." He spoke with more than his usual deliberation. "The factor most crucial to your physical safety is that of revenge." His eyes probed into mine. "The other factor has to do with the land willed your father. The matter of revenge is not a complicated one. In fact, it presents a simple and understandable motive, one lending itself to logical analysis. Now the land, here we have an enigma. In my estimation there is involved, how shall I say it, there is a motive beyond the simple greed for land."

"Well, a cousin of mine, Prakash Singh, is known by our family to be a renegade, and I . . ."

"Yes! That's one of the pieces to the puzzle of the land," he replied.

"Our family knows precious little about this man Prakash, just vague rumors about his being involved with some underground society."

The Captain either did not hear me or preferred not to comment. He picked up his swagger stick and began tapping it on the desk.

"For God's sake, Prem, let us in on it!" Douglas Gordon said in exasperation.

"Righto!" Prem Narayan rose and walked back to the window before turning to address us. "Let me throw something together and see if the ruddy thing holds water. The anarchists, and we shan't identify them for the moment, have in their top echelon one Prakash Singh, who comes from a family of rajahs. It so happens that the financial status, and possibly the prestige, of this underground organization is, let's say, a bit shaky. Suddenly, here comes an opportunity to acquire funds and even some prestige through legitimate channels if the legal inheritors do not consummate their proper obligations."

"So far so good," Gordon observed.

"Here's where the hired killer, or hit man as you Americans say, comes into the picture. When Karam Chand failed in his mission—a failure of which they're fully aware—what recourse do the anarchists now have?"

"They've an ally in the family of Karam Chand," I volunteered soberly.

"Exactly!" The Captain slapped the swagger stick into his palm. "The damned anarchists could just sit back and let others pull their acorns out of the fire. But I doubt they'll stand idly by."

"Meaning?" I asked.

"They'll use their options, as they've done before, which may mean further attempts on your life or scare tactics to try to drive you away."

"You're suggesting then, indirectly perhaps, that I should get out of India?" My voice sounded strange to me, almost mechanical.

"Not at all. You're the one to make that decision, Doctor Singh. My duty is to keep you in possession of the facts, serious as they might be, upon which your decision can be made."

"Prem, you knew about Prakash Singh?" Gordon asked.

He nodded. "He was apprehended about three years ago on a technicality, a minor thing really, and since then has disappeared. Probably went underground. At the time of his arrest, there was some question of his association with an anarchist band. Now we are certain that he's an important figure in this pseudo-political underground in the Punjab."

Bhaskar entered with a chit which the Captain read. He excused himself and left the room.

"Wheels within wheels. . . ." I laughed mirthlessly.

"It is a bit mixed up," Gordon said, adjusting his glasses. "You know it's difficult to appreciate the force of emotional currents still flowing along the border between India and Pakistan, particularly in the Punjab. The demographic upheaval of partition still carries the wounds of hatred. As a result of this continuing turmoil, there are political and religious forces which retard and even threaten this country's progress. Misguided patriotism, provincialism and communalism present far greater threats than any from outside India's borders."

Captain Narayan returned, followed by Bhaskar with a tray and the ubiquitous tea service. We sipped our drinks quietly, each wrapped in his own thoughts.

"Doctor, have any of your father's or mother's relatives lived in Canada or the United States?" Captain Narayan questioned.

"Dad has spoken of a great uncle who moved his family to Canada shortly before World War I."

"Where in Canada?"

"British Columbia."

"His business?"

"Lumber. . . owned and ran a large lumber mill."

"Did he move down to the United States?"

"Yes, down to San Francisco."

"Why did he leave Canada?"

"Something to do with loyalties, Indian independence."

"Did he ever go back to Canada?"

"Yes, got into some kind of trouble with American authorities over the same problem, the matter of Indian independence."

"Ghadrites," the Captain observed quietly.

"What was that?" I leaned forward to catch his words.

"Ghadrites, one of the early intrigues to free India from the British."

"Captain Narayan, a frank question. In your own estimation, should I go on up to the Punjab?"

"Really, Doctor, I can't answer that question. But I might say, as one who carries the burden of responsibility for your personal safety, the simplest thing to do would be to place you on the next plane out of India."

I had given serious thought to my personal options in the face of recent developments. Oriental revenge, according to my understanding, knew no national boundaries. I decided to stay in India and face the threat in the land of its origin. If I were to flee the country now, my future would be clouded with uncertainty.

The Captain studied my face closely.

"I'm going ahead with it."

"You will go to the Punjab?"

"Yes."

"Righto, jolly well thought you would." He smiled approval.

"My plans call for leaving Bombay tomorrow night by the Frontier Mail." We stood to leave. "As I've told you, my headquarters in the Punjab will be with the Clemens in Nilapat."

"Compartment D in the air-conditioned coach," the Captain added.

I looked at my ticket and really was not surprised to find that Prem Narayan was correct. It was reassuring to realize that I was under close surveillance.

"There's only one air-conditioned carriage?" I asked.

"Only one. The Railroad Department has been instructed that the entire two-berth compartment has been reserved so you will travel alone. Under no circumstances let anyone under any pretext get into these quarters with you. We will provide you with a companion on the coach."

Douglas Gordon invited me to his apartment for lunch the next day. His wife was visiting up in the Himalayas where their two children were attending school at Woodstock, the same institution in which he had been enrolled a few decades ago. I accepted the invitation gladly, hoping to have an opportunity to discuss my problems more fully in the privacy of his home.

Around the dinner table I recounted the events of the day. Soli expressed his embarassment at the pilfering of my suitcase. After the meal the two of us moved out onto the balcony above Marine Drive where I told him of the afternoon's deliberations. We sat in silence for a moment just enjoying the cool breeze blowing in from the Arabian Sea. Soli lit a cigarette and inhaled slowly.

"Raj, I'm worried...and I wonder if you're wise to pursue this matter further here in India."

"Soli, I've got to see this thing through, and I'm sorry to bother..."

"Please, please, old chap, no apologies," he cut in.

"At least some type of pattern seems to be evolving...we're making a bit of progress."

Soli nodded.

"What do you think of Captain Narayan?" I asked.

"Works damned hard. Stays in the background. Not one to get into the limelight." He drew thoughtfully on his cigarette. "The man's got an excellent reputation. Been involved in some heavy cases."

We stepped back into the living room. Indira sat knitting before the television set. The children had gone to bed. After a few pleasantries I excused myself to retire. Soli followed me to my room to see that all was in order. As he turned to leave, I commented, "Funny thing, but I thought I saw you by the Flora Fountain this morning."

Soli looked at me in surprise, but said nothing.

Chapter Four

I was awake before I knew why. In that hazy borderland between sleep and wakefulness, I was trying to identify something...was I dreaming?

I began taking inventory of my surroundings. The bolted door opening onto the balcony was solid wood without glass panes and the large window next to it was locked. That side of the room was dark. A fine haze of light filtered through the bathroom window, barely outlining the communicating doorway beyond the foot of my bed. The soft grinding of the overhead fan and the chorus of crickets outside made a background of sound. Opening my mouth, I held my breath to hear more clearly.

I began to pick up a sensory stimulus too subtle to identify immediately. For a few seconds I was not even certain which of my senses was involved. There...it was an odor...faint and somehow familiar. Every instinct warned me of danger.

A cold sweat broke out on my face. The palms of my hands were moist. I wracked my memory to identify the smell. The faint and sickening wisps of aroma ebbed and flowed while I sniffed cautiously. Suddenly my thoughts fled back to a day in Arizona...a field trip...a cave infested with bats...and a peculiar, musty smell.

A soft rustling sound attracted my attention. It was coming from the bamboo matting in the center of the room. Holding my breath again, I listened intently.

Suddenly I knew. It was a large snake slithering over the matting. An icy chill coursed through me. I lay in a dark room, out of reach of the light switch, with that snake on the floor. I knew from the sound that it was large. That the creature was poisonous I took for granted.

The door to the apartment was bolted on my side, so any shout for help would be useless. Just how the snake had gotten into the bedroom was an academic question for the moment.

The snake moved faster as it tried to escape. It slithered along the baseboards, seeking an outlet. I could identify its position only when it was crossing the matting or when its body slapped against the floor after exploring up the walls. The reptile, most likely a cobra, was large and fast. A viper would have been much smaller. There was no place in the room I would be safe. Could I be certain there was only one snake? Did I dare wait for daylight? How much longer might I expect to be safe on the bed?

The cot was against the inner wall across the room from the balcony. The door into the apartment was opposite the foot of the bed. The light switch was at the far side of this door, between it and the entrance to the bathroom. The bathroom door had been removed and a curtain hung in its place, so I could neither trap the snake nor barricade myself in the smaller room. To escape into the apartment, I would have to throw back the bolt and open the door, which would expose me to an attack, and would endanger the Dorabji family.

I needed a weapon and light. It was essential to reach the switch. In the dark my adversary had an advantage over me.

I lay motionless on the bed, trying to visualize the room and anything in it which could be a weapon. There was a chair in the far corner of the room, at the foot of the other cot. Too far away, I decided, and too clumsy. What about the iron rods supporting the mosquito netting at each corner of the bed? Were they loose, or were they welded into their sockets?

Cautiously I rose to my knees and felt for the inner bedpost near the head. I twisted...thank God, it moved freely!

The sound of my movements brought an ominous quiet. Not daring to move, I listened for any sound. The tense silence was broken by a loud hiss. I froze and waited for the blow. The snake struck the edge of the mattress with such force that it shook the bed. A few inches higher and it would have buried its fangs in my leg.

The battle was on. Even the bed had become a combat zone. I rose to my feet, using the wall to steady myself, and grasped the rod. The snake came at me again, and again struck the mattress a resounding blow. Then all was quiet. The cursed reptile, somewhere in that darkness below, was watching my every move. At least there seemed to be only one snake.

I tried to guess the number of steps to the light switch. Was it really where I remembered it? Two steps from the bed should put me at the wall, I decided.

What about timing? Four seconds should do it...if I had judged the distance right and if I found the switch instantly. Turn on the light and swing the rod up, ready. Five seconds would be better. My eyes really should have more time to adjust to the sudden light. Wonder if the snake would suffer the same disadvantage? I could buy a couple of seconds more by some sort of diversion. The pillow, yes, throw the pillow, I thought.

Reaching down cautiously, I picked up the pillow and made last minute calculations. If I were to throw it across under the other bed I might gain some time. The cobra would have to rise off the floor to strike effectively. The restricted space under the bed might confuse the creature for a second or two.

The pillow hit the matting and I heard it slide on beyond somewhere. Waiting a couple of seconds, so as not to distract the snake with my movement, I stepped off the foot of the bed. For one horrifying instant I thought I had lost my balance. Stumbling heavily against the wall, I grabbed for the switch. The next instant the room was flooded with blinding light.

Grasping the rod in both hands, I spun around to face my enemy. The pillow and the sudden light had disconcerted the snake enough to give me the precious couple of seconds to adjust. It was a cobra, a large one, waiting on the far side of the room. Its hood was spread, its dark eyes reflecting the light as pinpoint diamonds. The reptile rose a foot from the floor and its body stretched behind in undulating coils.

I made a practice swing to be certain the rod would clear the furniture. How fast would the snake be moving, I wondered?

The cobra lowered its head and started toward me. I braced myself for the attack, and remembered to think that the snake, in sinking its fangs into my mattress twice and then into the pillow, must have emptied the venom sacks partially. Somehow that wasn't much comfort. About halfway across the room it hesitated for a couple of seconds, probably disturbed by the fact that I was standing my ground. It hissed again and frothy foam collected about its mouth. Its slender forked tongue flicked in and out, sensing the air.

My thoughts were cool and deliberate. I was elated to realize that I felt no fear. The snake started forward again, a little more cautiously, and moved within my range. I brought the rod down with all the force I could muster, bending the rod. The wounded creature writhed violently, thrashing about the floor. I sprang back on the bed.

I had struck the snake diagonally just below the hood. Surveying the damage from the safety of the bed, I pulled another rod and dealt a swift *coup de grace*. My watch read a quarter to three.

Unbolting the door to the balcony, I pushed the cobra outside. Checking the bathroom, all appeared to be in order, except that the window still was open. I borrowed the pillow from the other bed and lay down. The Dorabjis had slept through the entire encounter. As the light of dawn etched the details of the bedroom fixtures, I finally fell asleep.

My return to consciousness was abrupt. I sat up with a start. My pillow still lay under the other bed. There were two puncture holes in the pillow case, soiled by venomous stains. The metal rods, both bent grotesquely, lay in the corner

I warily stepped onto the balcony. The snake was gone! It was not in the courtyard below. I studied the side of the building. The plumbing of the *Tara Mahal*, following Bombay sanitary codes, was exposed on the outside wall with pipes spreading from the ground up, resembling carefully groomed espaliers. A main trunk of the sewage system climbed the wall past the edge of the balcony. Someone could have scaled this branching structure, using the enlarged joints of the pipes as footholds.

I mentioned nothing of the night's encounter until after breakfast when Soli and I stepped out onto the living room balcony with our cups of coffee.

"My God! A cobra!" Soli spoke in a hoarse whisper. His face was ashen as he sat down in the nearest chair.

"Well, the reptile's dead," I muttered, reaching over to pat his arm.

"A hellish scheme. Makes me sick in the pit of my stomach."

I knew that Soli was thinking of his family. He fumbled briefly with a cigarette. We sat in silence watching a small fishing craft being poled along the shallow edge of the bay. My visit to Bombay was proving to be anything but pleasant for the Dorabjis.

"For God's sake, Raj, quit this bloody mess while you're still alive and get back to the States." There was fear written in Soli's eyes.

"Look, it's probably difficult for you to understand my position, but. . . but listen, old fellow, I'm just too deeply involved in this thing to turn back now."

"If you insist on pursuing this thing up into the Punjab you may. . . well. . . you may pass the point of no return."

"What do you mean?"

"What do I mean, dear God. . ."

"Soli, are you hiding something?"

He bit his lip nervously without replying.

"There's one thing I don't want to do and that's to endanger your family. My problem is very real, but it's my problem. And as far as I'm concerned, the point of no return has already been passed."

Further conversation on the subject was interrupted by the twins, coming out to kiss their daddy before leaving for morning classes. We both stood at the balcony rail and waved to them as they ran onto the sidewalk below, holding the bearer's hands.

A haunting, high-pitched and undulating music attracted my attention. Looking across Marine Drive, engorged with the morning rush of traffic, I saw a turbaned man squatting on the far sidewalk facing us, his back to the sea wall, blowing on an instrument fashioned from bamboo flutes inserted into an elongated gourd. Around him were several reed baskets, round and shallow. I stiffened and Soli drew a quick breath as a large cobra rose out of the basket before the snake charmer's wailing instrument. The spread of the snake's hood was plainly visible from where we stood.

"See how simple it is to transport snakes," Soli said in disgust.

"What's your idea as to how the cobra got into the bedroom?"

"Lowered the bloody thing into the bathroom in a basket."

"Climbed up the pipes on the outside wall?"

"Most likely. I've seen kids climbing all over them in play."

The shrill note died down like a deflating bagpipe. We watched the turbaned man cover his cobra with the lid of the basket and begin collecting his equipment.

I grabbed Soli's arm and pointed. "Look! He's staring at us!"

"The bugger sure is," he muttered.

We both watched closely. He was rearranging the contents of one of the baskets, lifting out a long coil of rope and setting it aside, then slowly pulling out a large snake, obviously dead.

"That's got to be the snake!" I exclaimed. "Let's get him!"

Soli stepped in front of me as I turned to dash out, placing both arms around me in restraint.

"Take it easy, old chap, remember the Captain's warning about security. The bugger's probably just trying to get you out into that crowd."

Walking over to the rail, I looked down again on Marine Drive. The snake charmer's baskets, balanced high on the head of an accomplice, were swallowed up and fast disappearing in the throng of moving people.

There was the faint odor of seaweed and the taste of salt in the breeze coming from the Arabian Sea. It gently rattled the leaves of the potted palm on the balcony beside me. I took a deep breath and turned back into the apartment.

Chapter Five

Doug picked me up at noon. I soon found myself in an apartment that tastefully blended the Orient and the Occident. Brightly colored curtains, picturing Rajasthan dancing girls, fluttered in the breeze of an oscillating fan. Indian paintings, statues, screens and furniture lent a living beauty to his home.

A rosewood coffee table of particular beauty drew my attention. Jungle scenes of elephants and palm trees covered the top, all intricately inlaid with ivory. A wooden screen with five tall hinged panels elaborately carved on both sides zig-zagged between the front room and the dining room. In the center of each panel brass and copper overlays of wild roses alternated with lotus blossoms. The design was Muslim or Persian, and it was carved from the shisham tree, a hardwood of India. According to Doug, the screen was created by a Muslim artisan in the city of Saharanpur, north of Delhi.

Noting my interest in the pieces of art, my host showed me a marble side table with a delicate inlay of semiprecious stones. The marble, he told me, came from the same quarry as that used for the construction of the Taj Mahal over three hundred years ago. The pattern reproduced that of the carved marble walls within the Taj, surrounding the inner tombs of Shah Jehan and Mumtaz, his queen. The geometrically-precise designs were carried out with pieces of carnelian, lapis lazuli, jade and mother-of-pearl.

"That water color is by Paul Matthai." Doug pointed out a large picture of women at a village well. "He's from South India."

"Looks just like the rural India mother talked about. The trees stand out in three dimensions. Just look at the sun's rays penetrating that dust—I can almost smell it."

"Paul Matthai is of the Mar Thoma Church, a branch of the Syrian Christian Orthodoxy, said to have been founded by the Apostle Thomas in the first century."

"Mar Thoma, Church of Thomas."

"The earlier Christians of India," Doug continued, "and through the centuries these people have risen to positions of national prestige and respect."

"What you might call the indigenous Christians of India, eh?"

Doug nodded and stepped across the room to point out another painting, an ornate and detailed oil. "Now here is the work of an artist from North India."

"Sobha Singh," I read the artist's name, then stepped back to study his work.

"Hill Woman. That's the title. She's really alive, isn't she?"

The picture was of a woman dressed in a skirt of reds and yellows and greens, with an equally colorful blouse. A shawl turbaned her head. She was sitting on the ground on the mountainside cradling a basket in one arm. Jewelry of precious metals graced her arms, ankles, neck and ears. A large silver ring pierced her nose. Even more interesting than the striking attire and jewelry was the expression on the woman's face. The artist had brought to life a blending of serenity, pride, and physical strength. Her dark eyes laughed as they looked down on me. I felt almost self-conscious as I stared at this woman of the Himalayas.

"Is the artist still living?" I asked.

"Not only is he living, but I happen to know him personally. He's a patriarchal, white-haired Sikh with long flowing locks and beard. We first met at an art show which I'd been asked to inaugurate. Since then he's been in our home several times. He's quite a philosopher, as well as an artist."

"Where does he live?"

"Away from the rush of the world, up in the Himalayan foothills, in the Kulu Valley."

The ring of a gong announced lunch. As we sat down the bearer hovered in the background. He was a tall young man of rather striking appearance, with friendly brown eyes and an aquiline nose. His long white coat was gathered at the waist by a broad belt buckled in front with a large bronze clasp. He wore a turban which might be described as flamboyant, a long white strip of cloth wrapped firmly around and around his head. One end of the turban hung loose and tail-like down his back and the other end stuck up out of the top in a pleated fan like a cock's comb.

We ate our *polau* and curry in silence for a few minutes, then I launched into the details of my encounter with the cobra. Doug listened quietly until I finished my account.

"So you think the snake was poisonous?" Doug's forehead wrinkled in thought.

"A cobra? Are you kidding?"

"Snake charmers frequently pull the poison fangs. Makes them quite harmless except for the puncture wounds of the teeth."

I looked at Doug long and hard. "You mean to tell me that the snake might have been harmless, just put into my bedroom to scare me?"

"Wish I could believe that."

"Meaning?"

"That cobra most likely was the real McCoy and could have killed you."

I thought of my venom-stained pillow and decided he was right.

"Changing the subject, Doug, what happened to Captain Narayan—I mean the scar on his face?"

He leaned back and pushed his glasses up on the bridge of his nose. "It was back in 1947, the year of partition between India and Pakistan. The times were seething with emotional turmoil. Psychological wounds of race and religion cut deeply. Gentle people were swept into the maelstrom of hatred and devastation. Indians of different faiths, who had lived peacefully as neighbors and friends for centuries, suddenly were caught up in a bitterness and an anger which led to mob rule, pillage and wanton murder. Religious intolerance in moderate doses is bad enough, but when fanned to white heat it can be hell."

The bearer came into the room to clear the dishes. Doug fell silent until the kitchen door closed. I had a visceral sensation that the bearer was aware of the content of our conversation

"Prem was stationed at Delhi at the time and was charged with maintaining order in a particularly sensitive area known as Subzimundi, a meeting point of Hindu and Muslim residential blocks. One morning, quite early, word came to the Police Headquarters that trouble was brewing in this particular section of Prem's jurisdiction. A band of Hindus were invading a Muslim street in revenge for a killing during the night. He alerted the riot squad, and rushed to the scene. Elbowing his way through the crowd, he found it spearheaded in a large enclosed courtyard. Several bodies lay sprawled over the ground. In one corner a ring of rowdies, led by slogan-shouting Hindu fanatics, were taunting a Muslim lad not yet in his teens. The boy, stripped to the waist, was backed up against the mud wall of the compound. He was terrified. . .the swords and knives pricked his bare skin, and the blood ran down his chest to mix with the rivulets of sweat."

Again the narration was interrupted as the bearer brought in dishes of ice cream and cups of coffee.

"Prem Narayan pushed his way to the boy and stood in front of him. Drawing an automatic, he faced the mob and ordered them to disperse. The bloodthirsty crowd continued to press forward. Prem shouted above the din, 'If you want to kill this Muslim, you must first kill this Hindu!'

"The rabble hesitated, taken by surprise by the courage of the young Lieutenant, but surged forward again, angered by this denial of their blood lust. As the grim human circle tightened, a hush fell, broken only by the gentle sobbing of the boy.

"The flash of a sword and the simultaneous report of a gun shattered the quiet. The swordsman crumpled before the Lieutenant. But the sword had taken its toll. Blood covered the left side of Prem's face, blinding the left eye and flowing down over his shoulder and chest. The sight of this fearless symbol of law and order, bloodied but resolute, was too much for the mob. They broke and fell back, leaving their dead at the feet of the police officer.''

A dish of fruit was set in the center of the table and finger bowls were placed before each of us.

"Good gosh! What a story!" I murmured.

Doug reached for a tangerine and began to peel it. "Prem is reticent about the episode. I've been able to piece together the story bit by bit over the years. That's how he got the scar.''

"What about the Muslim boy?" I asked, helping myself to the fragrant mangoes.

"The boy's name was Ahmed Khan.''

"A good Muslim name," I observed.

A smile hovered about Doug's lips. "Raj, the bearer's name is Ahmed Khan.''

"You've got to be kidding!" I shook my head in astonishment.

We left the table and moved into the living room. Doug nodded toward the dining room and lowered his voice. "He's actually an employee of the C.I.D., trained under Prem, and one of his favorites.''

"That's easy to understand. Must be quite a bond between the two.''

"Raj, Ahmed Kahn will be accompanying you to the Punjab—Captain Narayan made the decision last night.''

"You mean as a sort of a personal bodyguard?''

"After a manner of speaking, yes. A great fellow, devoted and fearless. He's brainy as well. You'll like him.''

"So, I've got myself a bodyguard," I said quietly.

"His name will have to be changed—in the Punjab Muslims aren't all that welcome.''

"Well, there are plenty of good Hindu names to choose from.''

Doug shook his head. "No. Muslims in their social habits are more like Christians.''

"The name change was the Captain's idea?" I asked. He nodded. "What about Ahmed? Does this idea of masquerading as a Christian bother him?''

"No problem. David will handle it.''

"David?''

"Prem and I selected it. And, Raj, the first syllable is pronounced as in 'dark' rather than 'day'.''

"Does sound more Indian, doesn't it?''

"Our office here will forward a resume of your case to the Delhi Embassy.'' Doug studied my face thoughtfully. "Raj, keep me informed, will you?''

"Will do. You know, I've been wondering about the security of mail, particularly the correspondence between Captain Narayan and me.''

"Be careful about it. Let Ahmed...er...David handle it for you. You can trust him implicitly. And Raj, if you're in trouble, let's say life-and-death trouble, the code word is 'Kansas'.''

"Just the single word?''

"Right. Get the word to any American Consulate or the Embassy. Give your location and contact."

Our conversation extended well into the afternoon. I had an opportunity to become better acquainted with him. Doug understood and loved India. He was a part of this land, more so than I could ever be, although my ancestors for generations had inhabited the Punjab.

The consulate car whisked us back to the Tara Mahal. David was seated very properly in the front beside the driver. I reclined in chauffered luxury. David's luggage consisted of a small metal trunk, painted a garish yellow, and a bedding roll. These had been deposited in the car boot.

Indira met us at the apartment door, and evinced no particular surprise as I casually introduced David as my newly-hired bearer, hired on the recommendation of Mr. Gordon. I was interested to see that David fell right in with the cook. In fact, shortly after our arrival, he was scurrying around fixing the sandwiches and setting the table for afternoon tea. I watched him critically, realizing that this young man might make the difference between life and death for me.

Taller than average and of slender build, David's movements were lithesome and precise, making even difficult physical maneuvers seem simple. A long and distinctive stride carried him over the ground quickly. His craggy, good-looking features were built around a thin, straight nose. David gave the appearance of enjoying life, smiling frequently and often. It was evident that he made friends easily. He appeared sure of himself, in the simple assurance of one who had mastered a technique and enjoyed its application. Looking into the uncertain future, I was glad that David was going with me.

The evening meal was unusually sober, except for the happy chatter of the twins. Attempts to maintain a conversation failed. Our friendship was being tested by pressures beyond our control. Suddenly I felt an overwhelming desire to leave before these unknown evils enveloped the Dorabji family.

I insisted that a taxi be ordered to take David and me to the railway station. Soli had planned to chauffeur us to the depot, but under strong pressure from me finally agreed to my plan. Standing on the threshold of the apartment as we said our farewells, Soli's eyes filled with tears. My vision blurred in a moist response.

Chapter Six

Sheer bedlam reigned on the platform of the Bombay Central Station. The Frontier Mail...an immobile mass of carriages in the center of this noisy turbulence...patiently engorged a motley assortment of passengers. Red-turbaned coolies with numbered metal armbands balanced tiers of baggage stacked high on their heads and gracefully dogtrotted their way through the shifting patterns of human flow. Vendors guided their pushcarts, moving cautiously about the platform in search of potential customers. Most transactions were negotiated through the carriage windows. Cups, glasses and cones (fashioned from old newspapers) conveyed the drinks, sweetmeats and spicy foods. The bargaining and banter of conversation between salesman and consumer carried the friendly overtones of a holiday atmosphere.

Passengers, singly or in groups, explored the compartments by peering through the windows. Once ensconced within the carriage, those inside controlled overcrowding by stacking baggage against the doors, which opened inwards. Even these tactics did not stem the onslaught, however, for where windows were not barred, would-be passengers, abetted by friends, pushed their way into the train.

David had taken our safari in hand and, led by two coolies bearing our baggage, we headed for the single air-conditioned carriage of the Frontier Mail. The cool air within was a relief from the heat of the station platform. A corridor ran the length of the coach along one side, with the individual compartments opening into it. At one end of the hallway were the toilet facilities and at the other was a room which not only stored the excess luggage but also housed two attendants.

I must confess that it was not a complete surprise to find Captain Narayan seated on the lower bunk of my compartment. In fact, had he not contacted me before my departure from Bombay, I would have been disappointed.

"How nice of you to see me off," I greeted him.

He rose and gripped my hand. "A couple of things to clear up before you leave...a few more words in private."

"Anything new?" I asked, a little anxiously.

The Captain smiled and shook his head, "No...as of the moment things are jolly well under control."

"That's good."

"And we'll try to keep it that way. Shan't let our guard down."

"I'm going to be dependant on your advice."

Under David's surveillance the coolies deposited my bags in the compartment. I caught a quick exchange of looks between the Captain and his protege. Having completed his task, David discretely stepped out into the corridor.

Captain Narayan slid the compartment door closed and pulled the curtain across the outside window. "Hope you're finding Ahmed...I mean David... quite satisfactory."

"I'm impressed. Of course, I've only known him a few hours."

"You'll find him absolutely trustworthy." We both sat on the lower bunk. "You don't mind?" He tapped his cloisonne cigarette case.

I shook my head. "Please, go ahead."

He lit a cigarette, drawing deeply and exhaling slowly. "David will stay with the attendants at the end of the carriage." He stabbed his cigarette in the direction of the baggage room.

"What about the Dorabjis? Are they in danger?"

"Yes, after a manner of speaking, they are."

"And I've brought it on them," I muttered, more to myself than the Captain.

"Your departure from their home should ease matters."

"That's what I thought."

"Soli Dorabji visited me this morning and told of your encounter with the cobra. A bit nasty, eh?"

"That's putting it mildly."

"He confessed that he'd received a couple of threatening letters. Threats to him personally as well as his family."

"Because they were housing me?"

The Captain nodded soberly. "You're a Jonah. Isn't that what you call it?"

"Did you learn anything from the letters?"

"They're being studied. Rather difficult to trace. All were written on the same typewriter."

I stood to stretch my legs while the Captain smoked thoughtfully. After a moment of silence he observed quietly, "Soli Dorabji has been cruelly torn between fear for his family's safety and his friendship for you."

"Yes, I've become aware of this."

"He even took to following you around, to see that you came to no harm, until he was convinced that the C.I.D. was protecting you. You'll be interested to know that we will be keeping the Dorabjis under protective surveillance, at least for the time being."

"I appreciate that."

"He's upset that you're pursuing this matter up into the Punjab."

I nodded. "He's tried his best to dissuade me."

Walking over to lean against the washstand, Captain Narayan exposed his scarred cheek and distorted left eye. In the coalesced lights and shadows of the compartment I thought I was facing another man, a man of ferocious cruelty. His calm voice came as a relief, breaking the spell of involuntary revulsion.

"Doctor Singh," he said, his eyes fixed on mine, "you must be aware that your life is in danger. One who accepts the fact of danger is in a far better position to survive."

I nodded, waiting for him to continue.

"You must train yourself to suspect people," he warned. "Be suspicious of everything. Your survival depends on suspicion."

"I'll have to work on it...it's not my nature."

"David will help you in this." He stepped over and placed his hand on my shoulder. "He's been given instructions concerning your safety and only under exceptional circumstances should you ever disregard his advice. He's been briefed on the details of your problem, from Karam Chand to the present. David will be intensely loyal...please don't expose him to danger needlessly."

"Don't worry, I won't."

He smiled and continued, "One word of caution. You Americans have little respect for class distinctions. An admirable trait, I must say, but please remember that David in his present capacity is functioning in the role of a servant, a personal bearer. The distinctions of this relationship must be observed. The master and servant association is essential for the success of his duties and even the safety of you both."

"I understand."

The shrill whistle of the guard broke into our conversation. David knocked on the compartment door and announced *"Capitan ji, samay ho chuka*—Captain sir, the time is up." We walked down the corridor to the carriage exit and shook hands. Prem Narayan stepped off the moving train onto the platform, waving his swagger stick at me. The station slid by like a moving conveyor belt covered with people. I stood at the door briefly as the train snaked its way through the suburbs of Bombay. The metallic rattle and squeal of wheels and tracks ricocheted off tawdry apartment buildings forming a man-made canyon. Vignettes of intimate family life flashed past, framed in the doors and windows of the multistoried dwellings.

Walking past the baggage room I caught a fleeting glimpse of David. He smiled, a contagious grin which was to be his trademark through the months ahead. I moved on toward my quarters knowing that, leaving Bombay, another chapter of my India adventure was closed.

I bolted the door to my compartment and surveyed the layout of the room. On one side were two bunks, the lower one serving as a seat, and the upper with my baggage stacked on it. Across from the berths in the corner next to the hallway stood a closet and set of drawers. Adjoining that was a metal washbasin with a hinged wooden top. Further along that side of the room was a door opening into the next compartment, closed and locked from the other side. The latch on my side was broken. An inspection of the door hinges showed that it swung open into my quarters. As a precautionary measure I placed my heavier bag against the door.

Above the noise of the train I could hear the voices of a man and a woman conversing in the adjacent compartment. The words were indistinct but identifiable as Punjabi. The couple had boarded the train just ahead of me and were Sikhs about my age. Their dress and bearing bespoke refinement. Neither of them appeared to pay me any attention as I walked by their compartment.

I rang the buzzer for an attendant. He responded with unusual alacrity. Stepping to the door I admitted the young man and requested that he make up my bed. The lower berth was prepared in short order with many a covert glance thrown in my direction. Having completed his duties, the bearer bade me a goodnight and stepped out into the corridor.

David informed me later that my American luggage, with an American address, all under an Indian name, had created considerable curiosity among the attendants.

Just as I was getting into bed I heard a quiet knocking on the compartment door. Cautiously pulling aside the curtain covering the glass section, I peered into the dimly lighted hallway. David was standing directly under a light a few steps back from the compartment door so that I could identify him with certainty. Once inside he lifted down my bags from the upper bunk.

"What gives, David?"

He turned and looked at me questioningly. "What gives? I am sorry sir, do you need something?"

"Nothing. Just some American slang." I laughed and after hesitating a moment, he joined in my laughter. "I wondered why you were taking my things down from up there."

"Oh," he exclaimed, grinning broadly, "safer for you up here to sleep."

David's English really was quite good. His sentence construction sometimes was patterned after the grammer of his mother tongue in which the verbs came last. Although our conversation could have been carried out in Hindustani, I opted for English, primarily for David's benefit. And I must say that he became an apt language student, though tainted by American idioms and accents.

Having completed the berth above, he stepped close to me and announced in a low voice, "Sir, from now I shall answer all calls."

"Good!"

"The compartment door will keep bolted, yes?"

"Roger."

David turned at the door and looked back at me with a tolerant smile, whispering, "You forget, sir. My name is David. May you rest well."

"Yes, David, rest well yourself." This was not the time to explain American language idiosyncrasies.

The rhythmic vibration of the train speeding across the plains of Northern India offered a degree of relaxation. Suddenly, overcome by sheer exhaustion, I set aside any further probing of the mysteries of Karam Chand and the anarchists. Instead of resting, as I had hoped, my thoughts flowed inwardly, leading eventually to a desolate loneliness. Home, father, mother, my little Leilani, all seemed an eternity away. Waves of homesickness swept over me. Finally, in deep fatigue, my mind slowly submerged into a subconscious sea of fantasy from which the past reached out into the present.

"Pat," I whispered wretchedly, "I miss you...dear God how I miss you." The wound created by her death two years ago had not healed. A mysterious sense of her presence crept into my half-conscious reverie. I recognized her delicate perfume and felt once more the softness of her body against mine. The threshold of my emotions crumbled, ravishing again the anguish of the past. I finally fell into a fitful sleep to awake some hours later weeping quietly.

Switching on the reading light at the head of the bunk, I surveyed the compartment. All appeared in order. It was after two in the morning. The train was slowing down to enter a station and soon the platform noises were filtering inside. Passengers boarded and left the carriage. Coolies jostled baggage in the corridor. As the sounds stilled, a shadow paused at my doorway. The station lights on the far side silhouetted the outline of a head. The profile unmistakably was David's. With a deep sigh, I lay down again in my bunk and pulled the covers high.

Chapter Seven

Shafts of early morning light squeezed past the edges of the window shades. The train had stopped at a station. Hearing a knock, I jumped down and unbolted the door for David. He was carrying a tray with tea, toast and marmalade.

"*Chota hazri,*" he announced with a broad grin, setting up the dishes on a table whose hinged top lifted from the outside wall of the compartment, just under the window.

"*Chota hazri* "

"Yes sir. Means 'little breakfast,' like this. And you sleep well?"

"Fairly well, David, only fairly well."

"Very sorry." His glance was sympathetic.

I stepped over to the basin to wash up. On the hinged wooden cover of the washstand was a small package and an envelope, each addressed, in a dainty hand, to "Dr. Raj Kumar Singh."

I examined the intercompartmental door. It, and the baggage barricade, had been shoved inwards about six inches. Obviously someone had reached through and placed the package and letter on the washstand.

I opened the envelope and read the message inside. The daintiness of the script and the faint perfume of the stationery led me to believe that the author was a woman. It read, "Dear Dr. Singh: In the package is a bracelet. Wear it at all times on your left wrist. This may save your life. Truly a friend." There was no signature or identification of any kind. Did this come from the young Sikh lady in the next compartment, I wondered? She would appear to be the most likely source. The Captain's warning to trust no one came to mind.

Lifting off the lid of the elongated box with great caution, I saw a bracelet which gave an immediate impression of age. The wrist band was made up of oval links of silver-like metal about an inch in their widest diameter and hinged together with tubed sheaths of the same material. In the center of the chain was an oval solid silver piece somewhat wider than the links. On the base of this piece were two hemispheres of highly polished transparent gems, dark red garnets with swirling veins of lighter red.

The antiquity of the bracelet was evident, even to me. The links and stones were fitted together firmly, albeit somewhat crudely. The metal was smooth and polished from years of use. On the back of the silver mount for the gems was a delicate etching almost obliterated by wear.

After careful study, I made it out to be the head of a lion. Under the animal were a few Sanskrit characters unknown to me.

The bracelet unlatched to a larger size and fit my left wrist snugly. It must have been worn last by a woman or a child. Blazing like angry eyes, the crimson garnets flashed an aura of mystery. I stared at them in fascination, and they returned the stare in cryptic silence.

The train was moving through low rolling hills of luxuriant green richly watered by the monsoon. Munching without enthusiasm on cold toast spread with unmelted butter and marmalade, and sipping lukewarm tea, I reflected on the latest turn of events. Occasionally I could hear the muffled conversation of the couple next door. Was the lady the donor of the bracelet, I wondered again? Should I ask her? Could they be linked in some way to my future? Again I remembered Prem Narayan's warning and decided to keep my silence.

David's knock interrupted my thoughts. While I finished the last slice of toast, he took up the bedding in the upper bunk and stacked the sheets, blanket and pillow.

"By the way, David, who're my next door neighbors?" I showed him the bracelet and note, which he examined closely.

"Sikh gentleman and wife." David lowered his voice to a whisper. "They very much rich and high class too. I think they from kingdom. You know what I speak?"

"Yes, perhaps one of those kingdoms dissolved after partition."

"Dissolved. That is it. Dissolved," he repeated, savoring the word as an addition to his vocabulary.

"You have spoken to them?"

He shook his head. "Very early this morning, while it was breaking into daylight, the gentleman get off at station and send a telegram."

"You saw this?"

"Oh yes. I removed myself from the train and watched and then I spoke words with the telegraph clerk."

"And?"

"Telegram sent to Aggarwal, Quality Shop, Ambala Cantonment, Punjab."

"*Sabas*—Well done!" I complimented him in Hindustani. "And by any chance did you learn the message?"

David grinned mischievously and nodded. "It say 'Arriving Frontier Mail'."

"Did anyone enter their compartment during the night?"

"No. I keep watch. Midnight the train stopped and one air-conditioned coach passenger remove himself. Coolies and attendants going backward and forward in the hallway."

Faithful David, I thought. "How far are the Sikh couple going?"

"Delhi, Sir." He scowled. "The lady spoke with anger to the man, before he remove himself to send the telegram."

I made a mental note that David's understanding of the word 'remove' had to be clarified some time. "You heard what they had to say?"

"Not all, sir, no. She did not want him to send the message. That much I am hearing."

"And why the bracelet, I wonder? That is, if it came from her."

"I shall look into it, sir." Picking up the dishes, David asked what my order for lunch would be. There was no dining car on the train, so orders for meals were telegraphed to a station ahead and the courses picked up to be eaten enroute.

"What's the menu?"

"European, Indian vegetarian and Indian non-vegetarian."

"Let's try the Indian non-vegetarian."

"Sir, you like chicken curry and rice?"

I nodded.

Balancing the tray of empty dishes in one hand, he excused himself and stepped out of the compartment, with a thoughtful glance at the communicating door.

A day of leisure lay ahead and I anticipated the pleasure of reading without distractions. David had collected a supply of newspapers and magazines and stacked them neatly in the closet. Turning first to yesterday's copy of *The Statesman*, one of India's prestigious English language newspapers, I browsed from page to page. The Prime Minister was welcoming a representative of one of the Third World nations at Palam Airport in Delhi. An Indian mountain climbing team was being feted in Dehra Dun at the Military Academy for its successful conquest of a seven thousand meter Himalayan peak. Monsoon floods in a province to the north had taken a toll of thirty-four human lives and also destroyed many homes. Another column noted that the same storm had caused the deaths of thirteen cows housed in a special shelter for homeless cattle. Certain of the local citizenry were highly incensed at the death of these holy animals and a delegation was proceeding post haste to the chief Provincial Minister to demand an investigation. I scanned the paper but found no evidence of any proposed inquiry into the loss of human lives.

To one not familiar with the social customs of India, the matrimonial advertisements made interesting reading. Mother, in describing her marriage to my father, explained that most marriages were contracted through a variety of matrimonial brokers. I glanced down long lists of proposed nuptial contracts. It was evident that the adjective "homely" equated to "home loving" rather than "plain." The matrimonial specifications usually were very much to the point.

A handsome Jat Sikh engineer, Govt.
service, income Rs. 700/p.m., 28 yrs.
5'8" with family members in high posts
wants very pretty, homely, educated,

*vegetarian, light skinned bride, maximum
height 5'4'', caste no bar.''*

Noting that the train had stopped, I called David and suggested a stroll along the station platform. The air-conditioned carriage was in the forward section of the train so we first walked up toward the engine. A bright green metal picket fence enclosed the station from the outside world. At each end of the platform, at right angles to the tracks, large signs mounted on solid metal posts proclaimed in English and Hindustani that this was Phulgaon. The station was typical of those I had seen—a standard construction plan used by the Department of Railways.

From the main building, a roof of corrugated sheet metal extended out over the platform. Under this cover, down the station a ways, I noted the Sikh couple browsing in front of a newsstand. Jutting out from over the many doors leading into the station building were a series of signs. Walking the length of the platform I read them: Station Master; Assistant Station Master; Post and Telegraph Office; 1st Class Waiting Room—Gentlemen; Dining Room—1st and 2nd Class; 2nd Class Waiting Room; 1st Class Waiting Room—Ladies; 3rd Class Waiting Room, and finally the Baggage Room. Somewhere near the middle, a heavy iron gate opened to the outside where clamoring rickshaw and horse tonga drivers loudly fought over the customers. Guarding this exit was a white-uniformed officer of the railway collecting tickets from the passengers recently disembarked from our train. I paused to watch the people funnel through.

"All of the tickets are collected here?" I asked, pointing at the exit gate.

"Yes sir," David acknowledged with a nod.

"In America the tickets are collected on the train."

"Why?"

"There the guard, or conductor as we call him, can walk the length of the train, but not so here."

The guard was blowing his whistle and waving a green flag. We hurried to our coach and arrived at the entrance just ahead of my Sikh neighbors. Stepping aside I waved them ahead of us, deliberately extending my left hand toward the carriage steps. Both of them threw quick glances at my left wrist, then courteously acknowledged the deference I had extended. The lady was lovely—stunning in fact—and dressed in a beautiful sari. The man was handsome and imposing, wearing the fashionable *acckan,* a long dark coat reaching to the knees and buttoning up the front to the neck. White cotton pants, tight fitting from ankle to knee, completed the outfit.

They must know who I am, I thought. Was there a message of warning in the glance she threw my way as she walked up the steps? Was her perfume the same as that of the letter? I could not say.

David was right. The non-vegetarian dinner was chicken curry and rice. The meal was stacked four dishes high, tied neatly in a napkin. Pulling up the folded table leaf, he undid the bundle and set out the food. The thin flat wheat cakes, called *chapatis*, and mango chutney were set out onto smaller side plates. The pot of tea was covered by a colorful tea cozy.

David arranged the dishes, then leaned down to whisper, "I have learned that the Sikhs have a friend in this compartment." He waved his hand toward the rear of the train.

"Next to me on this side?"

"Yes, sir." David smiled before adding, "She is very beautiful Indian lady."

"So?"

"She comes from the W.C. right now and watch me go to your compartment with luncheon."

"And?"

"The Sikhs visit her last night."

"You saw this, eh?"

David nodded soberly.

"How was she dressed?" I asked.

"Last night, sir?"

"No, just now."

His forehead wrinkled in thought. He was quite familiar with the clothes but not with their description in English. "You know the Punjabi *salwar* and *kamiz*?"

"The *kamiz*, like a dress coming down to the knees, and the *salwar*, pantaloons tight around the ankles?"

"That is it."

"A scarf around the front of the neck and draped to the back over the shoulders," I continued my description.

"Oh, yes. A scarf."

"Anything else?"

"Foreign baggage. She has American baggage."

"Yes, go on."

"Last night, getting on train at Bombay, she is wearing a lovely blue sari with gold border and..."

"Anyone with her?" I broke in.

"Old gentleman comes with her, father maybe."

"Where is she going?"

"Amritsar, last stop Frontier Mail."

"David, you're an amazing source of information." We laughed.

With the hiss of escaping steam and a series of jangling jerks the train started out of the station. I again directed my attention to the chicken curry. The Indian dish was highly seasoned compared to the European version, with red peppers and other spices. Soon a prickling sensation crept over my skin as the perspiration broke through. David moved out into the corridor and closed the sliding compartment door after him.

The Frontier Mail, its slackening drive shafts clanging like broken temple bells, pulled into the New Delhi station fifteen minutes ahead of schedule. After a brief stop the train continued on to Old Delhi.

"We remove from here and take a walk, alright?" David suggested, poking his face inside the compartment.

"Roger!" I called out, welcoming his invitation and jumping up to join him.

A perplexed look replaced his grin. "But, sir, I am David. You must not forget."

I laughed. "Sometime I'll tell you about Roger. Don't worry, David, I know your name."

He looked relieved and I watched the grin slowly return to his face.

Taking the line of least resistance, we flowed along the platform with a stream of jostling passengers. After a few minutes, not wishing to be swept on out through the exit gate, I turned suddenly and almost collided with the Sikh couple. The confrontation surprised us all. For a second we stood motionless, staring at each other. The man's eyes narrowed and revealed a hint of fear. He turned quickly and grasped his wife's arm. Throwing him an angry look, she pulled away and took an impulsive step in my direction, her lips forming soundless words. Then, just as I was about to say something, she dropped her eyes self-consciously and moved away. The couple pushed forward to the exit gate and disappeared with the crowd. I stared after them, wondering what she had tried to tell me. She had looked worried—was she trying to warn me?

David, who had observed the encounter, joined me and suggested that we return to the train where my dinner would be waiting. Although there were dining rooms in the station, Captain Narayan had instructed me to take all my meals in the compartment.

The food was European, a thin broth soup, mutton chops, boiled potatoes, cauliflower and a cup of custard pudding. By contrast with my noon lunch, the meal tasted flat and unseasoned. My future meals would exclude European dishes.

"Sir, one half hour before Nilapat, you shall be awaked," David announced.

"Thanks, and have a good rest."

"Same for you, sir." He slipped out of the compartment.

Chapter Eight

I had just dozed off when the noise of a train pulling into a station awakened me. A large sign outside my window identified the station as Subzimundi, a suburb of Old Delhi. The name immediately brought to mind Doug Gordon's story of Captain Narayan and the Muslim lad, now my bodyguard. I wondered just what might be going through David's mind at that moment. The bond of affection between the two must be as deep as that between father and son. My responsibility for the young man's safety rested all the more heavily on me. The Captain was sharing with me someone far more important to him than merely another C.I.D. employee.

Picking up a copy of *Newsweek*, purchased in Delhi, I was reading the section on National Affairs when David knocked.

"Come in. Something the matter?"

"Sir, it is the Indian lady." He nodded toward the compartment behind mine.

"And what about her?"

"She wishes to see you."

"How do you know?"

"She ring buzzer for the attendant and ask him that I speak with her."

"And?"

"When I come she ask if I am your bearer. Then she tell me to tell you to come to her compartment for a visit."

"And should I visit her?"

"She speaks Hindustani with accent like you."

"That badly?"

Flashing an embarrassed smile, David nodded.

"You mean she's an American?"

"A foreign Indian like you, sir."

"Well, you haven't answered my question. Shall I go and see her?"

"If you wish, sir."

"David, it's not what I wish. I'm asking you what you think."

He frowned thoughtfully and scratched his chin. "Yes. Yes. See her. I will stay very close and please do not take food or drink from her."

She stood at the open door of her compartment, holding aside the curtain. "Doctor Singh, thanks for accepting my invitation." After David's description, I was not surprised to hear English spoken with an American accent.

"It's my pleasure, believe me."

"What say we leave the door open in deference to the niceties of society," she suggested with a twinkle in her eyes.

"And the curtains drawn in deference to the niceties of our privacy," I added.

"Touche!" She joined in my laughter. "I'm Doctor Ranjit Kaur." We shook hands.

"I'm Doctor..."

"Doctor Raj Kumar Singh," she broke in with a broad smile.

"How come you know who I am?"

"A long story really. But that's why I wanted to see you."

Waving me over to be seated at the foot of the lower berth, she kicked off her slippers and folded herself into the other corner of the bed, clasping both legs in her arms and resting a dimpled chin on her knees. She was wearing the classic Punjabi *salwar* and *kamiz*, just as David had said.

To have described her simply as beautiful would have been an understatement. She was much more. She was petite without giving the appearance of frailty, and blessed with a form whose delicate contours painters and sculptors have been trying to capture through the centuries. Her rich contralto voice lent her words a special charm. I found a particular fascination in the vivid animation of her conversation and her contagious laughter. An olive complexion, fairer than usual for an Indian, was set off by coal-black hair and a pair of bluish-gray eyes.

I came to my senses with a start, embarrassed by the realization that I had been staring at my hostess.

"Do you like what you see?" she teased.

Grinning sheepishly, I apologized, "Excuse my manners. I really know better."

"No excuses needed." Ranjit Kaur waved her hand in absolution. She turned to adjust a pillow at her back and I noted the perfection of her profile.

"May I ask what part of the States you're from?"

"Not the States. Canada, British Columbia."

"And here I'd taken you as a fellow countryman—I mean, country-woman."

"Doctor Singh, I shan't sail under false colors. I know quite a bit about you. In fact we're related. We're second cousins."

"You've got to be kidding!'

She shook her head, and her hair, which was loose about her shoulders, moved as a black curtain framing her face. "No, it's the truth. Your grandfather and my grandfather were brothers. Atma Singh, my grandfather, went to..."

"I've heard my father speak of him."

"So you see, we're second cousins." Her eyes danced teasingly as she added, "Kissing cousins."

"And here we are on the Frontier Mail, meeting for the first time."

"Getting back to my grandfather. I guess he'd be your granduncle, Atma Singh. He went to British Columbia shortly after the turn of the century and entered the lumber business on Vancouver Island. Then in 1915 he joined a party of Indians known as Ghadrites. This band of nationalistic revolutionaries, headquartered in San Francisco, had as their goal the independence of India. With the outbreak of World War I, the Ghadrites allied themselves with German interests and received financial assistance from them. In 1917, when the United States declared war on Germany, some seventeen Indians, including my grandfather, were arrested and tried in the Federal Court of San Francisco. During the trial, which dragged on for six months, a break in the Ghadrite ranks spilled bitter accusations of misappropriation of funds. These dissensions finally culminated in a dramatic courtroom murder. One of the defendants, Ram Singh, pumped five revolver shots into a codefendant named Ram Chandra. Ram Chandra fell dead by the witness box. The marshal of the court shot Ram Singh, killing him instantly." Doctor Kaur drew a deep breath and grimaced with distaste.

"You know, just yesterday I was asked if my granduncle was named Atma Singh."

"Captain Prem Narayan?"

"You know him?"

She nodded. "Yes, I know the Captain. He's with the Criminal Investigation Department."

"He's sort of become my mentor."

"From what little I've seen of him, he seems quite sharp."

"My sentiments also. Hope we're right."

Ranjit Kaur settled back and continued her story, "Grandfather and the rest of the defendants were given jail sentences. Atma Singh became disillusioned and disgusted with the Ghadr movement. He got out of jail when the war was over. His Canadian citizenship had been revoked, so he placed his lumber holdings in trust with a friend until his son—my father—came of age. Balak Singh, my dad, was born in British Columbia. My brother and I were born, raised and educated in Canada. I went on to medical college at McGill and continued after graduation in a pediatric residency at the University Hospitals in Vancouver."

"So you're a pediatrician?"

She nodded. "Did a stint in child psychiatry as well."

"Going back to the Ghadrite movement...Captain Narayan did mention them in one of our discussions. First time I'd ever known of their existence."

"Since the independence of India, the old Ghadr cause has come into its own. In fact, not too many years back some sort of a monument to them was dedicated in San Francisco by the Indian Ambassador."

"That's funny. I gathered from the Captain's tone of voice that he wasn't exactly enamoured..."

"Oh," she interrupted, waving her hand, "he was referring to something entirely different...the Naya Ghadr...but more about that later."

The train had pulled into a station. Someone knocked discretely at the compartment door. Doctor Kaur jumped up to admit David.

"Doctor Sahib, may I serve tea?" He studied my face.

I looked over at my hostess for approval and she smiled her acquiescence.

"Yes, David, we will take tea."

"That man sure keeps an eye on you! But then...I'm glad he does."

"Go on with your story," I urged, to change the subject.

"Well, as you've gathered by now, our lives are sort of linked to this past history."

"And, *mirabile dictu*, here we sit in the Frontier Mail in India."

She gave me a long thoughtful look. 'The reason for all this detail is that I feel it will help you."

"How?"

"The solution of your problem, I'm convinced, is in some way linked to our family background..."

"I'm sure you're right," I broke in. "Not much doubt of it."

David brought our tea. While Ranjit Kaur poured, David passed the cream and sugar. I watched with interest as he unobtrusively scanned the compartment as well as my hostess, and gave me a satisfied smile on his way out the door.

We sipped our tea in silence for a moment. I caught her studying my face intently and she dropped her eyes self-consciously.

"You do know quite a bit about me," I observed.

She smiled enigmatically. "Yes, I do."

"If it's none of my business just say so, but what are you and your Dad doing in India?"

"Mother died two years ago and, with my brother doing so well in the lumber business, Dad just decided to come back to India. He persuaded me to accompany him. He's a consultant to a Bombay export-import firm. As for me, I'm teaching pediatrics in a medical college there."

My hostess filled our cups again. "Dad and I knew of your coming to India through the grapevine of family gossip. Our family, yours and mine, is rather an extensive one, numerically and geographically. Day before yesterday that Captain of the C.I.D. called on Dad and me."

"Prem Narayan?"

She nodded and frowned. "One could hardly forget that scar with the staring eye and curled lip."

"But how in the world did the Captain know that we were related?"

"Don't ask me." She shrugged, and her scarf slipped off onto the floor. Picking it up, I returned it to her. The delicate scent of her perfume was pleasantly exciting.

"Of course the C.I.D. probably keeps a pretty good dossier on foreigners," I suggested.

"Especially when my grandfather was a revolutionary."

"Then you must know why I'm here?"

She set her teacup down slowly. The pull of worry showed on her face. "This is the reason I wanted to see you. If there's any way I . . ." Her voice drifted away.

"Thanks. You've already helped," I said quietly.

"The C.I.D. Captain, Captain Narayan . . . he's concerned about you?"

"Somewhat, I guess."

Again and again I searched Ranjit Kaur's face. Had she been telling the truth? Was she really my second cousin? The Captain had warned me to trust no one. I wanted very much to believe her. Either she was a sympathetic and charming young lady or a deceitful and clever antagonist in league with my enemies. How could I be certain? The stakes were high. God, they were high!

"A penny for your thoughts."

"Sorry. There I go again, staring at you."

"And again, you're forgiven." Her laughter was comforting. She suddenly became sober and fixed her eyes on mine. "You haven't asked why I'm on this particular train and in this compartment next to yours."

"So, I'll ask. Why are you?"

"I was planning a trip to visit a classmate who's teaching in the Amritsar Medical College. She and I knew each other in Vancouver. It wasn't difficult to find out that you had booked on this train. I wanted to meet you and here we are."

"That simple, eh? And how long will you be in Amritsar?"

"Oh, not much more than a couple of weeks."

"Do you happen to know the young Sikh couple who occupied the compartment on the other side of mine?"

She frowned and bit her lower lip. "Yes, I do. But let me tell you about them later."

"Sure. Go ahead. I'm listening."

"With the independence of India the princely states or private kingdoms accepted their dissolution and were absorbed into the new democracy. Some bowed to this change voluntarily, while others were pressured with military, political, financial and social coercion. The members of ruling families, of which both of us are a part, were thrown out into a world for which many of them weren't prepared."

Ranjit Kaur picked up her teacup and sipped thoughtfully, watching me quizzically through the rising steam. I stood and leaned against the compartment wall, waiting for her to continue.

"True, the Central Government subsidized them to a degree, but as a matter of fact they were pretty much on their own. Most of them struck out bravely into the more mundane ventures of business, politics and government service. A few tried to hang on to the empty husks of regal trappings, subsisting on the crumbs which fell from the government table, and a few entered the various fields of social and health services. This last group in some part was motivated by a desire to make amends for the privileged status of the past, a guilt reaction, a psychiatrist would say. However, among this group were a handful of mixed-up souls who pushed their social interests to an extreme position and embraced various brands of radicalism."

My hostess slipped out of her bunk and moved across the floor to my side. Looking up at me seriously, she asked, "Is this boring you?"

"No, of course not!"

She smiled as she reached for my hand and led me to sit beside her on the lower berth. She continued, "The vacuum created by the loss of wealth and position, compounded by a guilt complex, led some of the activist elements into the militancy of anarchy."

"Communism?"

"After a manner of speaking, yes. Some organizations are Marxist aligned, but in a nationalistic context."

As the discussion continued, I became more and more surprised at her fluent and intelligent presentation. She's really done her homework, I mused.

"These misguided neophytes believe the end justifies the means. They adopted the credo that man was made for the government and not government for man. To these zealots, truth is flexible, to be distorted or denied at will in order to serve their objectives. Individual man is of little value except as life's blood to a particular brand of fanaticism. In such a context murder, blackmail, thievery and lying all become righteous acts." She paused, frowning.

"I take it you think I'm up against such an organization?"

"Yes. We're facing a particularly vicious underground..."

"We are?" I cut in. "You're including yourself?"

She tried to smile, but ended with a grimace, not answering my question.

"Do go on," I urged, reaching out to pat her hand.

"This anarchist group is said to receive assistance from their friends in the northwest, the Russians. Some of its top members are relatives of ours."

"The Ghadr movement that Prem Narayan talked about?"

"The Naya Ghadr, or New Ghadr, claiming historical connections with the Ghadrite revolutionaries of World War I days."

"And are they connected?"

"No, only the name is similar."

"You're hinting that my threats are coming from the Naya Ghadr?"

"More than just hinting. I'm convinced that you're in real danger from them."

"Really?"

"Yes. Dad pressed Captain Narayan on this matter and he intimated that the Naya Ghadr was involved."

"They've. . .they've been after you?" I asked incredulously.

"Dad and I have felt their pressures. With my grandfather having been a Ghadrite revolutionary, they thought it would lend their cause prestige if Dad would join them. He refused, of course, and they've tried all kinds of threats, including blackmail. Dad kept the Canadian High Commissioner and the C.I.D. informed."

"This is beginning to put sense into some of the Captain's questions."

"There were times when I was scared, really scared, and urged Dad to take us both back to Canada," she admitted with a wry smile.

"And?"

"He is a stubborn man, refused to budge. Wanted to pack me off home, but I balked. So here we are." She shrugged.

"And what's the current situation between you and the anarchists?"

"For almost a year now we've not had any contacts with them. That's why Dad's willing to let me travel alone."

"Sort of fought it out to a standstill, eh?"

She looked worried. "They've scented other quarry." I felt her hand creep into mine and hold tightly. My fingers responded.

"Guess they want that land pretty badly." I muttered, more to myself than to her.

"They feel, particularly those related to us, that the land rightly belongs to them. Another thing, even though your father abdicated his rights by leaving the country, you're directly in the royal line, ideal as a leader for the deposed aristocrats. . ."

"But, my dear," I interrupted, "they've been trying to murder me!"

"True, but don't be surprised if they change their tactics."

"Just doesn't make sense." I said in exasperation.

"Doctor Singh, listen to me, anarchists just don't make sense!"

"O.K., O.K.," I shrugged and laughed. "Doctor, I'll bet you deliver a well-packaged lecture in pediatrics."

"And what brings that compliment?" Her eyes twinkled.

"Your persuasiveness."

"Just one final thought," she said, holding up an index finger, "the young intelligentsia in this land are in a personnel pool from which the anarchists like to recruit. It will be a bitter pill for our Naya Ghadr relatives to swallow, to have you around when they're constantly preaching about the decadence of American capitalism. End of lecture."

"May I bring up again the matter of the Sikh couple who had the compartment next to me?"

Ranjit Kaur drew a long breath. "They're related to us."

"What!" I exploded.

She laughed at my response. "Let me explain. In fact the couple are related to each other—third cousins, I believe. This isn't at all unusual in India, the marriage of second or third cousins. Tara Kaur, or Bubli as we call her, is the daughter of the last rajah, your father's brother, who succeeded your grandfather on the throne. So, Bubli's your first cousin."

"I've heard my parents talk of Bubli. She's Uncle Madan's daughter."

"She used to rate the title of *Raj Kumari*, or princess, but those days are long since gone. She visited me in Canada several years ago, before she was married, and spent the summer at our home. An intelligent and strong-willed but very personable young lady."

"And beautiful," I added.

"So you did notice that."

"What about her husband?"

"Gurdial went to England after finishing at Bishop Cotton's in Simla, a school run by the Anglicans. Took advanced courses in communications and now holds an important post with All India Radio. He works in Delhi."

"And Bubli?"

"All her education in India. Wanted to go on the stage but her parents objected."

"Gurdial must have problems. He looked very unhappy there on the Delhi platform tonight."

"Unfortunately during Gurdial's younger days he was involved in a compromising act of some sort which was known to a relative who is now with the Naya Ghadr. Poor fellow's being blackmailed and lives in constant fear of losing his position. The trouble is that his association with such a propaganda potential as All India Radio is important to the anarchists. They'll destroy the man rather than let him off the hook."

"No wonder the poor guy looked so disturbed."

"One final bit of information, and then I think you're brought up to date on all the important background references. Your mother's brother, a major in the Indian army stationed near the border in Ladakh, was killed in an ambush about a year ago. I don't remember his name."

"Daljit Singh."

"That's it, Daljit Singh. Well, he was a distant relative of Gurdial's. There is a strong suspicion that he and his party were killed by the Naya Ghadr."

"I thought it was a border clash of some sort with the Chinese."

"The early news releases intimated that, but the scuttlebut is that the anarchists really were to blame and that the Russians masterminded the clash to bring discredit on the Chinese."

"Now that's quite a motive, eh?"

"That limbo of international boundaries where Pakistan, Russia, Tibet and Kashmir all meet is a hotbed of intrigue. Your uncle, the major, knew of espionage and arms smuggling in this area and was gathering information for the Ministry of Defense. Not a single member of the party survived to describe the assailants. In large part the arms smuggled into India are Russian."

All during the evening as I listened to the narration of facts and events so lucidly presented by Ranjit Kaur, a nagging suspicion was building up in my mind. Why should she be in possession of all this information? I watched her closely, almost impolitely, as she presented the story. Try as I might, I failed to observe any signs of duplicity or deceit. Could I be undergoing a meticulous brainwashing at the hands of an efficient and beautiful young woman? Captain Narayan's warning kept ringing in my ears.

"Doctor," I addressed her soberly, "I'm amazed by your knowledge of all these facts as well as your apparent political awareness. May I ask how you've come by all of this?"

Ranjit Kaur winced at the sudden formality.

"Doctor Singh," she replied cooly, "for the most part, all of what I've shared with you relates to my...to our...family. My father has many friends and relatives in the Punjab, and for that matter in India. Also he has a keen investigative mind. In our discussions with Captain Narayan we shared information which substantiated certain of our suspicions. Furthermore, we..."

"Mea culpa!" I interrupted, raising both hands.

She shot me a puzzled look. "I am to blame."

"Yes, I'm sorry. My heart and mind are at odds. My mind just took over and quoted me the Captain's warning last night in Bombay. 'You must train yourself to suspect everyone. Your very survival depends on this.'"

For a moment she sat motionless, staring into my eyes. I watched as a tear grew and then rolled down her cheek. Without brushing it away, she started to speak, not much above a whisper, "The Captain is right...absolutely right. By entering the Punjab you'll become Public Enemy Number One to the Naya Ghadr." Ranjit Kaur took my hand in hers. "Raj, please be careful." She had used my first name and it struck a warm note.

The look of those blue-grey eyes, moist with tears, melted my mental reservations. I lifted her hand into my lap, squeezing gently, and she made no attempt to withdraw it. Her head dropped and she wiped the tears away. Suddenly she stiffened and turned, throwing me an enquiring look. She pointed at my left wrist. "That bracelet. Where did you get it?"

"This may sound funny, but I really don't know," I replied, showing her the wrist band.

"How long have you had it?"

"Someone slipped it, with a letter, into my room last night." I pulled the note out of my pocket and read her the message. She studied the writing.

"Bubli," she said, dropping her voice to a whisper. "Bubli wore it all the time. I first saw the thing when she visited us in Canada. It's an heirloom handed down through the royal line. Bubli's the last of that line—an only child."

"But why did she give it to me?"

She stared at the floor moodily. I waited in silence. She drew in a long, catchy breath and said, "To protect you. According to Bubli the amulet has protective powers."

"Then the note was from her?"

She nodded. "And Raj, please do follow her instructions. Don't take it off."

I unlatched the bracelet and turned it over. She leaned forward, holding her hair off her face, and studied the lion's head and the Sanskrit letters. 'Bubli told me the characters meant *Rajkumar* or 'Prince'." she murmured, touching the garnets. "Of course, that's your name. *Singh* means lion. So there you have it all, Rajkumar Singh."

"Hadn't really made the connection, I mean the lion part of it."

"Bubli and Gurdial both visited me here last night. We had run into each other unexpectedly on the platform of the Bombay Central station."

"Did they know who I was?"

"I told them..." she sighed, biting her lip nervously. "Really shouldn't have, I guess."

"No matter, really. Bubli did give me this." I held up the wrist band. She smiled and nodded.

"Gurdial sent a telegram to Ambala from some station our first night out of Bombay." I recited the address and the message, as well as the details of the confrontation with the couple in the Old Delhi station.

"Under the pressures of blackmail, I don't see how Gurdial can be trusted." Her eyes were troubled.

We sipped our tea in quiet for a moment.

"What about Bubli? Can I trust her?" I broke the silence.

She shook her head in uncertainty. "I...I really can't say. Blackmail's such a vicious thing. We've heard that she disappears for days at a time. God only knows what she's doing."

"My gosh, it's almost midnight," I exclaimed, rising to my feet. Taking my hand, she gently pulled me down on the bunk.

"Raj, tell me something about yourself," she asked quietly.

I sketched my life's story, starting with my parents settling in Imperial Valley, then shared my recollections of childhood, college and medical school days at Stanford, and my surgical residency. Almost unconsciously I told her of Pat, our courtship and marriage, Leilani, and Pat's sudden death. It seemed natural and easy to bring this comparative stranger into the intimacies of my life. In fact, in this sharing I felt a gradual easing of the oppressive loneliness which had burdened me the past few days.

My audience was most attentive. Tears wet her cheeks as I recounted the events surrounding Pat's death. We laughed together at my tales of Leilani's capers.

"Well, that's about it," I concluded, self-consciously studying her eyes for a response. "Thanks for listening."

"And thanks for sharing." She smiled and dried her cheeks with her scarf.

"Will I see you again?" I asked.

"Raj...excuse me, but if you don't mind I'm going to call you that. After all we're cousins."

"But will I see you again?" I persisted.

"Why absolutely!" Her eyes sparkled.

"And how can I reach you?"

"Department of Medicine, Topiwalla Medical College, Bombay. We're planning to move, Dad and I, so our home address is a bit fluid at the moment."

"You can reach me in care of Jay Clemens, M.D., Research Bungalow, Nilapat, Punjab."

"Raj, I'll give you a call from Amritsar."

"Great! And Ranjit..."

She broke in with a bubbling laugh. "My family and friends call me Biba, my nickname since the days I was crawling on all fours."

"Biba," I started again, "couldn't you stop in Nilapat for a couple of days on your way back to Bombay?"

"And why not?"

I stepped toward the door. She walked beside me.

"Till we meet again," she said softly. Our eyes fixed on each other in quiet exploration. Then with a quick move she placed her arms around my neck and kissed me squarely and lingeringly on the lips. Caught by surprise in the unexpected warmth of this farewell, I hesitated briefly in my response. She cozied her head on my shoulder. The soft perfume of her hair exploited my senses. The next instant we were locked in each other's arms. Biba sighed softly as I pressed her pliant body close. She lifted her lips to mine and we kissed again.

"Goodnight, Raj," she murmured, her eyes dancing.

I stepped out into the hallway, pulling the door closed behind me. David was keeping watch a discrete distance down the corridor, squatting on his haunches, back against the wall. He stood and smiled.

"You are alright, sir?" he asked sleepily.

"Yes. Quite alright, thank you, David."

"A good time you are having?"

I nodded. "A good time. In fact, a very good time."

Stretched out on the upper bunk, I lay awake thinking about Biba. My emotions were spinning giddily. She was a stunningly beautiful woman, utterly charming. There was something in that farewell embrace that went beyond the formalities reserved for cousins...even second cousins. The visit with Biba had been heady nourishment for a starved heart.

Chapter Nine

Nilapat station at four in the morning was wrapped in drab low-lying mists and fine drizzle. I stood at the door of the carriage surveying the dull scene as the Frontier Mail ground to a stop. The subdued picture was a far cry from the frenzied and noisy Old Delhi station of the night before. Glowering monsoon clouds clutched the landscape. The station lights fluctuated in the blowing curtains of mist and rain.

Jay Clemens, umbrella lifted high above a cowboy hat, pushed his way up the platform, presenting the picture of an animated palm tree tossed in the storm. His tall, angular frame in motion gave the impression of progress by a sort of pumping action.

"How's Joan?" I asked after the handshaking and backslapping of a boisterous welcome. Jay was a demonstrative person, after the open manner of those from the Rocky Mountain states. He had been raised on a Wyoming cattle ranch.

"Rustling breakfast," he replied with a scowl.

"How come? I mean what about the cook?"

"Quit last night. Gave no warning. Just left like that." Jay had a habit of expressing himself in clipped sentences. At Stanford we had nicknamed him 'The Riveter'because of his bursts of conversation.

"Gee. Sorry to hear that."

"Beats the hell out of me. Thought he was happy. Good wages and quarters. No explanation. Damn fool just up and quit."

"Forget it, Jay. David here's a multitalented bearer. Just for your information, he's a good cook."

"Jay swung around and grabbed David's hand to shake it, breaking into a broad grin. "Oh boy, will that woman of mine ever be glad! Not much fun being a cook in this country. She's all in a dither to see you."

Eyes squinted and forehead wrinkled in concentration, David hung on Jay's words in a determined effort to follow this variant of the English language. Occasionally his lips moved silently in an effort to form words so quickly spit out by Jay. I anticipated many future private lessonsEEE-corrective lessons. . .in grammar and diction.

Soon we were packed into Jay's jeep out of the rain. We headed out of the railroad compound and onto a modified macadam road flanked on either side by a single file of shade trees. Clods of mud and gravel, flung off the tires, splattered noisily against the car. Fingers of rain drummed incessantly across the canvas top of the jeep, as the windshield wipers permitted quick intermittent peeks at the road ahead.

Our headlights picked up the reflections from the eyes of a yoke of bullocks plodding slowly toward us pulling a creaking cart. We navigated past with care. The driver lay bundled up and fast asleep, stretched out on top of his sacks of grain. A double sloping roof of reed matting protected him and his cargo from the rain.

Hunched over the steering wheel, which he encircled with both arms, Jay launched into a monologue. Only the key words in a sentence counted in his system of communications. A newspaper headline technique.

"Four-wheel drive jeep. Best vehicle there is. Monsoon, floods, mud, this buggy beats them all..." he laughed and patted the dashboard affectionately. "Most important equipment in my research program."

"The ubiquitous jeep, all over the world." I agreed.

Embracing the road ahead with a sweep of his hand, Jay continued, "There it lies, soaked with centuries of history. The Grand Trunk Road. Runs from Delhi up into the Northwest Frontier. Kipling wrote about it." He paused to wipe off the fogging on the inside of the windshield. "All early major invasions of India came right along here. God, what stories are hidden in the mud and rocks we're driving over. Portugese, French and British invaded by sea. The rest marched right along here. Great battles. Foot soldiers and cavalry, camels and elephants. Panipat, south of here a ways. Site of a collosal battle a few hundred years back. Muslims came down from Afghanistan. Muslims won."

We were stopped at a railroad crossing by a lowered gate. The blue-shirted and blue-turbaned gatekeeper leaned sleepily against the wall of his little brick house by the side of the tracks. We could hear the whistle of a locomotive in the distance.

While we waited, Jay picked up his narration. "Just a few miles north of here's the Beas river. One of the five major tributaries of the Indus. 'Punjab' comes from the Sanskrit-*panch* means five and *jab* means river. Alexander the Great and his army marched down from the north as far as the Beas. Soldiers refused to come any farther. Built barges and floated down the Indus river and on down into the Arabian Sea. Some of Alexander's men settled around here. Foothills of the Himalayas."

The roar of the passing train interrupted Jay's discourse. The rain prevented the usual swirl of dust. We bumped across the tracks as the gatekeeper pumped the cross arms into upright positions.

"Nilapat." Jay included the entire scene ahead with another sweep of his hand, as if formally introducing us to each other. "Population a bit over a thousand. Trading center for the surrounding rural villages. Name means Blue Town. Supposed to have been blue shale outcroppings around here."

Our passage through town went unnoticed for the most part. A few people drifted along in the shadows of the shops running on either side of the highway. Two cud-chewing cows raised their heads as we skirted them lying on the road. A skulking pariah dog howled a mournful welcome.

Driving on to the southern edge of town we came out into open countryside. The jeep slowed to turn and cross a ditch running along the border of the Grand Trunk Road. Jay straightened in his seat and pulled the vehicle up short before a metal gate set in a brick wall about seven feet high. The wall surrounded the entire compound. A diminutive but stiffly erect man wearing a khaki uniform opened the gate.

"Home," Jay announced, pointing ahead. "Old but substantial. Guest house for government officials in years past. Also known as a Dak Bungalow. *Dak* means mail. Now it's home to Joan and me...all thirteen rooms."

The half-light of dawn outlined a ponderous building lying directly ahead. Irregular in shape and partially covered with climbing vines, it rose out of a shroud of shadows. A verandah, symmetrically etched in arching pillars, fronted the bungalow. The driveway, bordered by a thick low hedge, circled at the front of the building under a covered porch whose supporting pillars were hidden by vines. Large leafy trees hovered over us, barely discernable except for their massive overcast. Perhaps their shadows contributed to my feeling of foreboding about the place.

The excitement of meeting Joan erased the nagging aura of apprehension. Jay, who had been a little older than the average medical student, married Joan, a nurse, after his junior year. 'Craggy' and 'rawboned' best described Jay Clemens. He stood just over six feet tall. To watch him walk and to hear him talk raised images of cattle trails, rolling plains, horses and saddles. His straight-lined chiseled features were molded around high cheekbones, suggesting the enrichment of American Indian heritage somewhere in the past.

Jay's father managed a large cattle ranch in the range lands of Wyoming. He grew up amidst sweating horses, bellowing cattle and the pungent profanity of cowboys. We met and became fast friends as undergraduate students at Stanford. The raw language and manners of the ranch were tempered gradually on the University campus. Under duress the cowboy in Jay would break out in accent and expression that could be devastating. Joan, petite, pretty and socially graceful, was a perfect foil for his toughness. She unobtrusively smoothed the abrasive edges of this granite character, her husband. Jay was fully aware of this transformation, which he described as being "marinated in high society."

Much to Joan's delight, David took over in the kitchen. Within an hour we were gathered around the table enjoying a hearty breakfast. The meal was a blending of East and West, with fresh papayas, a hot cereal of cracked wheat, known locally as *dhalia*, scrambled eggs, bacon and *chapatis*. After the inadequate food on the train, I tackled each course with a keen appetite.

After breakfast we gathered in the living room. The gentler rain of the early morning hours had turned into a downpour. I reviewed for the Clemens all the details of my trip, holding nothing back.

"It's outlandish! Downright outlandish!" Joan burst out.

"Things have changed a bit since I invited myself to be your guest," I said, leaning my elbow on the fireplace mantel. "Wherever I've gone here in India this thing has followed me. I'd hate to expose the two of..."

"Now look here," Jay broke in, "any old cowpoke can afford to be a friend when the goin's good. It's when things get tough that you can count on your real friends. Now you wouldn't let some little old thing come between us, would you pardner?"

"No, Raj, we aren't going to change our plans. Please don't pursue this any further." Joan added, with a reassuring smile.

"This is serious business..." I began.

"Don't give a goddamn, Raj," Jay cut in. "You're a stranger in a strange land. Hell, man, in these parts you're an unbranded maverick. I'll be damned if we're going to turn you out. Never done anything like that to one of my poor bastard dogies on the range. No son of a bitch anarchist outfit's going to change my mind!"

"Jay, your language." Joan shook her head and frowned. Then she looked at me and announced firmly, "Raj, I agree with what Jay has said. The Clemens just don't treat friendship casually."

My throat tightened painfully. I had just received a most practical lesson in friendship.

The first day at Nilapat passed quickly. I was installed in a large bedroom in the southwest corner of the bungalow. An adjoining bathroom opened outside into the compound. The only other door to the bedroom led to a spacious common front room. A large barred window looked out onto the front compound garden. The thick whitewashed walls rose a sheer eighteen feet to the ceiling from whose center, supported by a long metal rod, hung an ornate three-bladed fan.

There was cold running water and a flush toilet in the bathroom, both introduced by the Clemens. Hot water for bathing and shaving was supplied as needed in buckets which were filled from large metal containers heated on an open charcoal brick stove protected from the elements by a lean-to against the kitchen. Waste water from the shower drained out through a pipe to an open tile trough leading to a sand pit. A wire mesh cork in the pipe kept snakes out.

The plan of the building was simple and similar to the many thousands of guest bungalows scattered throughout India, all made from the same mold by the Public Works Department, virtually unchanged since early colonial times. Four bedrooms, two on the west side and two on the east, opened centrally into an ample front room. Each of these quarters had its own communicating bathroom, opening to the outside, affording easy access for the sweeper who, before indoor plumbing, removed and cleaned the commodes and replenished the water.

Jay and Joan occupied the master bedroom next to mine. The other two rooms were unoccupied, Jay's assistant in the research project having moved out recently. The dining room, lying to the north of the front room, was boxed in by the kitchen and a large storeroom.

I unpacked my bags into a large and ornate piece of furniture which the French would call an *armoire*, known locally as an *almira*. Joan's touch was evident in the neatly papered shelves and colorful window curtains. By midmorning I was unpacked and comfortably settled. Stretching out under the ceiling fan, I fell asleep.

The luncheon bell startled me. I had slept three hours. As we ate, Jay explained his research project. It was a combined effort by an American foundation and the Indian Ministry of Health, collecting data on population control in the rural areas. The research team included an anthropologist, a sociologist, a biostatistician and Jay as the physician. Six villages were included in the study, all within a five-mile radius of Nilapat. The program had been going on for a year, and would extend over another year. The first step had been to win the confidence of the villagers. Although this had been difficult, they had made progress, so that now when the jeep entered a village, it was welcomed by all, young and old. The present phase involved the collection of data on the prevalence of family planning, contraceptive techniques, infant mortality rates and the average family size in the population.

After lunch Jay and Joan took me on a tour of the compound, in spite of the continuing rain. A rehabilitated carriage house now served as the workshop for the research project. The servants' quarters, a long building of four rooms with a common verandah, lay west of the bungalow, outside my room. David was housed in quarters which had been evacuated precipitously by the cook just the night before. As we made the rounds, I was introduced first to the Nepalese Gurkha ex-soldier who served as gateman and watchman, the *chowkidar*. A short man, he wore his old army uniform, and saluted me smartly. The large curved knife, called a *kukri*, hanging from his belt gave him an air of fierceness out of proportion to his diminutive size.

Despite the inclement weather, the elderly Hindu gardener, or *mali* was out checking the potted plants lining the bungalow verandah. Rising from his knees, he placed the palms of his hands together at his forehead, greeting me with the Hindustani "*Namaste*". He wore a large turban, a frayed sweater and loose fitting drape skirt pants known as a *dhoti*.

Ganga Ram, the sweeper, boasted a family of five children, four of them boys. Lucky fellow, Joan told me with a laugh, he has to worry about a dowry for only the one girl. The verandah in front of the sweeper's lodging was enclosed with reed matting, creating another room for his clan.

A steady rain was falling as I retired to my room after dinner. I drew the window shades and lay down to read. Sudden gusts of wind thrashed the sides of the bungalow with rain, and I could hear the steady runoff of water from the eaves. Tired and finding it difficult to concentrate on my reading, I bolted the doors and turned in for the night.

I had barely drowsed into sleep when a tapping on the windowpane woke me. Taking a flashlight, I cautiously explored the darkness outside. It was David. I beckoned him toward the bathroom door. He stepped inside quickly and I waved him to a reed stool called a *morah*.

"Sir, a report I am making. Things today have happened."

"Yes?"

"The sweeper, one named Ganga Ram, he is visiting with me in my room this afternoon and just now again he is visiting. The man is friendly and also wise. Both Hindi and Urdu he is reading."

"Go on."

"The sweeper is not understanding why you are here. To him you are just a guest and visitor to the Clemens Sahib and Memsahib. Many people are coming and going from here."

"David, I don't quite understand what you mean."

"I am meaning, sir, it is good for the servants not knowing why you are coming to Nilapat."

"You're talking about security?"

"That is it, sir, security."

"Good!"

"Ganga Ram giving me information about the cook leaving and he knows about..."

"Can he be trusted, this sweeper?"

David stared at his hands for a moment then looked up to say, "Sir, I think yes. But I shall careful be."

"What about the others, the *mali* and the *chowkidar*?"

"I think good men, sir, both men. They do not speak. May be afraid."

"Afraid of what?"

"This message, sir." David reached into his pocket for a crumpled note.

"You've read this?" I asked.

"I know Urdu," he nodded.

"Alright, go on."

"I think this to the cook was given, last night."

"What does it say?"

"It warns him, very much harm, unless he leave Nilapat right away."

"Who sent it? I mean is there a signature?"

David pointed to the bottom of the page. The words were in red ink. "It say 'Naya Ghadr'."

"You know about the Naya Ghadr? Captain Narayan told you, didn't he?''

He nodded, adding, "From Ambala it is sent.''

How do you know?''

"Ganga Ram. He tells me. He spoke to messenger.''

"How did you get the note?''

"I found it, sir. On the floor of cook's room.''

"*Sabas*—Well done!'' David's face lit up at my compliment.

"Sir, you remember the Sikh gentleman on Frontier Mail and telegram he is sending?''

"Yes.''

"Sent to Ambala, sir.''

"By gum, you're right, David.''

"There is relation between Sikh gentleman and Naya Ghadr, I am thinking.''

"Looks mighty suspicious,'' I muttered.

"Sir, there will be man wanting to cook for this bungalow, perhaps coming tomorrow.''

"From the Naya Ghadr?''

David frowned and nodded.

"I'd better alert the Clemens first thing in the morning.''

"I shall cook until the proper person is coming.''

"Great! I know Mrs. Clemens will be relieved. But remember, David, this may mean trouble for you.''

His eyes narrowed and I watched the muscles of his jaw form hard knots. "Trouble for them, too.''

I let David back out the bathroom door, and watched him disappear toward his quarters into the rain-drenched night. Back in bed, I gave thought to the Naya Ghadr note of warning. My lovely hostess on the train last night had been correct in her assessment of the source of my own dangers. Poor blackmailed Gurdial Singh must have warned the anarchists in Ambala of my impending arrival. I found no rancor in my heart against him, realizing that he was being ground under the heel of our common enemy. Knowing the actual source of my peril came as a relief of sorts.

Captain Narayan had warned me to lie low in Nilapat until I heard from him. He was awaiting the report of his agent on the status of the land. In the morning I would write him the details of the trip from Bombay and also forward the Urdu note. Then too, I was anxious to ask him about Biba.

The rain continued to fall unceasingly. The steady pattering on the roof, like a muffled rolling of drums, and the softer dripping from the bungalow eaves made a monsoon symphony. Suddenly I felt tired, and sleep came quickly.

Chapter Ten

Opening the curtains of my bedroom window I looked out onto a garden washed by the night's showers and sparkling in the early morning sunlight. Straggling clouds raced towards the Himalayas in the northeast as gentle gusts of wind sent the bushes and trees into quivering dances, showering the ground with glistening drops.

Breakfast was a cheerful occasion of food and conversation, mostly the latter, as David assumed his new role with admirable aplomb.

"My gosh, what a relief! That man must be a jack-of-all-trades," Joan said, nodding toward the kitchen.

I recounted the last night's conference. Jay and Joan listened soberly as I outlined the probable implication of the Naya Ghadr in the sudden disappearance of their cook.

"You know, Joan, it would be a good idea to have David about when you interview this applicant. He's pretty damned sharp."

"Egad," Jay drawled. "Situation may liven up around here. Alright with me. We need some excitement, especially in a good cause."

"Now, cool off, Jay. Let's not ask for trouble," Joan cautioned, winking at me.

"I'm a bit rusty. Haven't tried out my battle cry since coming to this country." He pushed his chair back from the table.

"Oh no! Jay, please, for God's sake take it easy. These people won't understand what's happening." She clapped her hands over her ears.

Prancing around the table, stepping high, bending and straightening, Jay was well into the ritual war dance of the Indian brave. Then it began, low at first and rising slowly in a fierce crescendo, the spine-chilling war cry of the Sioux tribe.

My memory touched back to our fraternity initiations at Stanford. These same cries had blanched the face of many a neophyte pledge. This part of the initiation had become a tradition but no one had ever reproduced the authentic Sioux war cries since Jay's graduation.

The piercing and undulating shouts had mobilized the entire compound. David dropped his pans in the kitchen sink and dashed into the dining room to stand and gape in amazement. Behind him, peering through the screen door, was a retinue of servants, wide-eyed with stark astonishment. Jay, in a grand conclusion, let out a particularly ferocious cry.

Joan, who had ridden through the wild waves of sound with her ears protected, implored, "Raj, you'd better give some rational reason for this to David and the servants or we'll have mass resignations on our hands."

"You mean this is the first time here? He's not done it before?" I asked incredulously.

"First time." Joan groaned.

"How come?" I glanced at Jay, who had quietly returned to his seat.

"No cause, not until today. Decided we should get the message across to the anarchists," he said with a grin.

"Clemens Sahib comes from a part of America," I explained to David, "where there is a tribe of people known as the Sioux. He was demonstrating their war cries and dance."

Slowly David's look of astonishment melted, turning into an understanding smile. He went back to the kitchen and nonchalantly waved the servants away. I gave him credit for weathering a crisis which, to him at least, must have been nerve wracking. I was answering an accumulation of mail when Joan knocked on the door. "Can you manage minor surgery?" she asked. "I mean do you have the equipment?"

"What's the problem?"

"Ramdas, the sweeper's boy, fell and gave himself a nasty cut in the thigh—broken glass."

"Sure, bring him in." It was my habit to carry with me a small suture set with vials of local anesthetics and a modest assortment of medications.

David carried the boy in from the compound. We washed the wound and placed him on my bed with a couple of large bath towels under him to absorb the blood. Fortunately the cut was to the muscle only and not serious, although it looked bad.

Ramdas faced the ordeal bravely, his dark eyes following my every move. A final touch was the tetanus antitoxin, procured from a stock in the Clemens' refrigerator. Ganga Ram and his entire family were squatting on the ground outside the bathroom door awaiting the patient's return. They rose as we emerged and a triumphant parade followed David as he carried the boy back to his quarters.

This episode was the beginning of a fast friendship. Ramdas was a bright lad, quick of wit and always cheerful. Outside the bungalow, he became my shadow, silently trailing me, barefoot and wearing cotton shorts overhung by shirttails fluttering in the wind. At first, David was annoyed by the boy's devotion, because it complicated his task of watching over my safety. However, in a short time the two were staunch friends.

True to David's prophecy, a cook appeared at the bungalow two days after my arrival. He presented an ancient cardboard folder, carefully tied together with string, containing an assortment of letters of recommendation dating back over the past several years. Joan read a few of the enclosed chits purely out of curiosity. The man's previous employers included government officials, a member of the World Health Organization in Delhi, a missionary family and, most recently, a manufacturer of bicycle accessories. The would-be cook waited unctuously while Joan browsed through the information. After a few moments, she closed the folder and, handing it back to the man, informed him that she had another cook in mind. Seeing the adamant look on her face he turned with a churlish frown and headed for the compound gate.

I stepped from the kitchen as the interview ended. "How'd it go?"

"Alright." Joan smiled wryly. "He's a bit smug and sanctimonious."

"Sir," David volunteered, "his clothes much too good for cook."

"Living beyond his means," Joan observed.

"Yes, living beyond his means," David repeated, savoring the phrase as an addition to his vocabulary.

"What was his name?" I asked.

"Ranga Prasad," Joan replied.

A registered letter from Captain Narayan arrived in the morning's mail. The agent investigating the land had telephoned him from Chandigarh. The property was located between the Sutlej river on one side and a large irrigation canal on the other. He reported the soil to be fertile and arable. In addition, the agent had uncovered a recent Ministry of Mines survey report revealing substantial glass sand deposits along the river suitable for the manufacture of high-quality glass.

There were two postscripts to the letter. In the first he assured me that the Dorabjis were well and had received no further threatening notes. Secondly, he apologized for not having informed me that a fellow passenger on the Frontier Mail was a Doctor Ranjit Kaur, a distant relative of mine who could be trusted. This bit of information profoundly relieved my mind.

Before dinner, in the cool of the evening, Jay and Joan invited me to join them in a stroll through the garden. The rain of the day before had refreshed the plants and cooled the air. Tender care was evident in geometric beds of roses, cannas, zinnias, marigolds and even pansies. An oval lawn was edged by rows of potted palms. Neatly trimmed oleander hedges bordered the compound road. Brightly colored bougainvillaea clambered in profusion over the walls of the compound and the arches of the verandah. The light perfume of a variety of night-blooming jasmine, known in India as *rat-ki-rani*, or queen of the night, titillated our senses. Scattered about the bungalow were a variety of shade and fruit trees, among them the medicinal *neem*, the mango, the fine-leafed *gul mohr* with its brilliant red flowers, the guava and clumps of papayas.

We sauntered in silence for a while, until Joan turned to ask me, "Your family came from these parts, didn't they?"

"Right. Actually our ancestral home was a small Sikh kingdom quite near here."

"Great people, those Sikhs," Jay put in. "Straightforward, seem to know what they're doing."

"Contrary to what some people think, the Sikhs aren't a race. I mean they're not an ethnic entity. Sikhism is a religion," I explained. "Actually their beliefs lie somewhere between Hinduism and Mohammedanism. In fact the *Granth Sahib*, holy book of the Sikhs, has the writings of several Muslims in it."

"Really!" Joan lifted her eyebrows in surprise.

"The great majority of Sikhs are from the same racial stock as the Punjabi Muslims. The Jats, who form a substantial ethnic part of the Sikh community, have been known through the centuries as tough fighters. So the military tradition of the Sikhs reaches back into the early history of India."

We sat on a bench to watch the wild parakeets noisily feed in the trees.

"The Sikhs never cut their hair?" Joan asked.

"That's true of the majority but the beard and long hair aren't a part of the Sikh religion. It's possible to be a member in good standing without the long hair, as for example the Sindhis and Sahajdhari. But without these external symbols, a Sikh can't belong to the Khalsa community."

"Well, there's something I didn't know," Jay said.

"The Khalsa community lists five symbols to be used by their members, each beginning with a "K," and they are *kes* or hair; *kanga* or comb; *kaccha*, the soldier's shorts; *kara*, the steel bracelet worn on the right wrist, and the *kirpan* or saber which may be worn in miniature form."

The mosquitoes were becoming a nuisance so we moved inside to prepare for dinner. The Clemens had adopted the European custom of dining at eight. In large part our conversation around the table was a recounting of what had happened in the years since we left Stanford.

Finally, excusing myself to devote a couple of hours to catching up on correspondence, I retired to my room. Hardly had I finished my first letter, before a babble of shouts broke out in the back compound. I arrived just in time to see someone dashing past with David in hot pursuit. With a shoe in his hand, my young bearer was headed toward the outside gate, his quarry barely ahead of him. Following in a disorganized, shouting group were the servants, young and old. The shouts and insults were the kind best not repeated in mixed genteel company. The essence of the derogatory calls focused on incestuous relationships.

"Sir..."David stopped to get his breath,"that *goonda*, this note he handed me."

Stepping under the compound light, I scanned the paper. It carried the red signature. Again it was the Naya Ghadr. "What does it say?" I asked, handing the message back to David.

"Same thing, same as to the cook," he spat out the words between gasps.

"Leave immediately or the Naya Ghadr will harm you?"

"Yes, sir."

"Did you recognize him?"

"Ranga Prasad," he replied through clenched teeth.

"You beat him with a shoe?"

He nodded.

I learned later that the Gurkha *chowkidar*, on seeing David in pursuit of the intruder, had stood in the gateway holding a flashlight in one hand and brandishing his *kukri* knife in the other. Seeing this forbidding obstacle ahead, Ranga Prasad had taken off on a tangent through the flower beds and scaled the compound wall. This diversionary tactic had made it possible for David to deliver a few final blows with the shoe to his adversary's posterior.

Ganga Ram and his children gathered around listening to our conversation. Even young Ramdas, using a stick as a crutch, limped over to eavesdrop. Encircling us, the children, heads tilted back and mouths open, looked like little birds waiting to be fed.

"*Wo admi bara badmas hai*—That man is a big rascal," Ramdas chimed in excitedly.

"Ranga Prasad comes from Ambala," David said.

Jay and Joan joined us and I recounted the details of the skirmish. After looking over the scene, we stepped indoors. Joan heated water on a petromax stove and made some tea.

"David's beating that Ranga fellow with a shoe has a deeper significance than might appear on the surface," I commented. "To beat a caste Hindu with a leather shoe is to defile and degrade him."

"That David was mad. His eyes were throwing sparks," Jay said. "The damned Naya Ghadr'll be gunning for him now. Hope he carries a side arm."

"He does."

"How about you, Raj, you're carrying one aren't you?" he asked.

"Yep. Captain Narayan issued me one. Instructions are to have it on my person at all times."

"Know how to use it?" Joan asked, grinning at me. She knew that Jay and I had captained small arms marksmanship teams during our college days.

I winked back at her.

"My armory consists of one rifle, three hundred magnum with a telescopic sight, and that's it," Jay said. "Use it to hunt antelope. Mutton and chicken can get mighty tiresome. Have to go out and forage for food, just like the old New England pilgrims."

"Any objections to shooting the antelope?" I asked.

"None, absolutely none. A dozen of these creatures can destroy a farmer's grain or peanut field in one night. Beg me to come out and hunt.''

"What say we postpone this discussion, you two. It's time to hit the hay," Joan suggested with a yawn.

Next morning after breakfast I had a visitor. As I entered the front room, a Sikh in uniform rose and stepped forward to greet me with a firm handshake.

"Doctor Singh, I am Captain Karan Singh, District Superintendent of Police, Ambala," he announced in a clipped British accent. "Nilapat lies in Ambala District."

"I'm pleased to meet you, Captain."

"Captain Prem Narayan of the Criminal Investigation Department has requested that I confer with you," my visitor informed me. "There are matters of mutual interest that we must discuss."

Joan came in, followed by David with a coffee tray. Our conversation followed the usual line of social inconsequentials. We found that the Captain was born and raised in the area once ruled by my forbears. Also he informed us, quite proudly, that he had spent one year at California State University, Long Beach, studying police administration. As we finished our coffee, Joan and David withdrew, leaving the Captain and me alone.

My visitor looked about cautiously and lowered his voice. "I have instructions to give you every assistance, every protection. You understand, I am sure. To facilitate this matter, please keep me informed, all unusual events..." He studied my face thoughtfully.

"Don't worry. I'll keep in close touch."

The Captain smiled reassuringly as he pulled out a notebook from his pocket. Would you bring me up-to-date on your activities since leaving Bombay?"

I related all those incidents which seemed to be of consequence, concluding with the episode of the previous night.

"The chit handed to your bearer by Ranga Prasad, do you have it?" he asked.

I stepped into my room and brought back the note. The Captain studied it, frowning and pursing his lips. He acknowledged, "There is a cell of the Naya Ghadr in Ambala."

"And you can't apprehend them?"

"Very nebulous. The goondas move about."

"As I've just told you, the telegram, Gurdial Singh's, was sent to..."

"Quality Shop," he interrupted quickly. "Aggarwal is the proprietor."

"That's the cell you were mentioning?"

He nodded. "Probably...nothing definite...they keep barely within the law. Bloody chaps are clever." He sounded bitter. "People are afraid to testify against the buggers."

"I take it you're convinced that this is the Naya Ghadr?"

"You mean this chit?" He held up the note.

"Right."

"Evidence points in that direction. This isn't the creation of just cranks..." he paused to study the note again. "They're fanatical zealots and a menace to the security of our national boundaries to the north. In my estimation several mysterious, and as yet unsolved, murders are of their doing. It is most difficult to deal with them. A bloody underground organization working out from their home territory."

"They must have local support to carry on like this."

"Blighters pose as modern Robin Hoods and for the most part are concerned with the rural areas, the farmers."

"How many members are we talking about?"

The Captain paused thoughtfully, fingering his beard. "No accurate count. But we consider their strength to be not more than a couple dozen hard core. Of course there are many hangers on."

The Captain rose to leave and extended his hand in farewell. "Thank you, Doctor Singh, for your candid account. We shall keep in contact, eh?" Suddenly I felt a tightening of his hand. He was staring at my left wrist. The bracelet was visible below my shirt cuff.

"That...you know what it is?" His voice was tense.

"Yes. Do you?" I asked, deliberately casual.

He swallowed nervously and whispered, "The royal bracelet."

"Right. But how did you know?"

"I have seen it before, many years ago." Karan Singh had regained his composure. "As a young man I served as a member of the late Rajah's palace guard, your uncle's."

I nodded. "So that explains it."

"In many parts of the Punjab that bracelet is remembered and, I might add, respected."

Before leaving the premises, the Captain met with David, and later invited the Gurkha *chowkidar* into the discussion. David told me later that Karan Singh had urged a constant vigilance. Particularly, the *chowkidar* had been instructed to be on the alert for strangers. Immediately on the departure of the Police Captain, the Gurkha was seen sharpening his fearsome knife. The *kukri*, a curved and heavy bladed steel knife, has won a gruesome reputation among those unfortunate enough to come into close combat with Gurkha soldiers. Initiation into certain of their regiments requires that the recruit decapitate a buffalo with one stroke of the *kukri*.

The following week moved forward without excitement. A letter from my father included copies of the documents stolen from me in Bombay, which I forwarded to Captain Narayan. The C.I.D. agent who had been checking on the land drove down from Chandigarh, the Punjab capital. He estimated that in a couple of weeks all the papers would be ready for final signatures. I gathered from this man that the value of the property was greater than we had thought. Furthermore, the land was located in the heart of the Naya Ghadr's territory. This explained the importance of the inheritance to the anarchists.

Also that week Joan hired a cook. Samuel had been working for an American family in Ludhiana who were returning to the States after a two-year term as members of the Technical Cooperation Mission advising in the organization of the Punjab Agricultural University. He was a portly man with a waxed moustache and, in his apron and white hat, looked the part of a chef from the heart of Paris. Samuel cooked well. He spoke good English, better than David's. He soon won the friendship of all the compound and he and David became fast friends in a matter of days. Although officially relieved of his cooking responsibilities, David continued to help in the kitchen and dining room. The two bantered and joked as they worked, their laughter carrying through the bungalow.

"You really like to cook, don't you?" I asked David one evening.

He nodded with a quick grin. "Good way to do the necessary."

"What do you mean?"

"Security, sir. Close to you without...without...." he groped for the right word.

"Without being so obvious." I broke in.

"Ah, yes, so obvious," he repeated.

"Killing two birds with one stone, working as cook and security guard."

"Two birds and one stone." He laughed and nodded at me knowingly.

A letter from Prem Narayan arrived, adding something new to our exchanges of information. He hinted at the possibility of my being of great assistance to the C.I.D. in the destruction of the anarchists. My role might be considered as the bait to draw out and trap the Naya Ghadr ringleaders. He dwelt on the fact that one of the top persons, if not the actual head of the organization, was a relative of mine. The Captain intimated that my coming to India had resulted in a surfacing such as had never happened before. The entire presentation was couched in terms which would not cause me embarrassment were I not to accept the challenge. Concerning my own safety, the Captain reasoned that in a joint action involving the C.I.D., the actual hazard would be no more, if as much. I gathered that the matter had been discussed with the central office in Delhi and had received its enthusiastic support. Narayan had emphasized that such joint action would be contingent on stricter security measures.

"Cheese for the mousetrap, eh?" Jay asked.

The three of us were sitting in the front room with our after-dinner coffee while Samuel and David cleared the dining room table. Outside in the darkness a chorus of frogs croaked an unremitting background of sound.

"I guess you might call it that," I answered, throwing a quick glance at

Joan to catch her reaction.

"Raj, you haven't committed yourself on the matter," she said quietly.

"Perhaps I haven't made up my mind yet. I'd just like to get your reactions." I surveyed my companions' faces.

"And why not?" Jay shrugged.

"Well, let's start with the basic fact that I'm in danger as long as I remain in India."

They nodded.

"But then the revenge factor...Karam Chand's family...might well reach out beyond the borders of India."

"That's true." Jay agreed.

"Alright, I have two alternatives. I could settle the land inheritance matter and then get the hell out of the country. That would accomplish what I came here to do. Or I could combine that with assisting the C.I.D. in nailing down the Naya Ghadr."

"Just where in all these propositions is any attention given to the matter of your personal safety?" Joan asked.

"They'll beef up security, so they say, and I'm quite willing to trust Prem Narayan's word on that."

Joan obviously was worried. "Raj, why tangle with the Naya Ghadr any more than absolutely necessary? This wasn't a matter of your making."

"I'm not so sure you're right, Joan. One of the things that really bugs me is that a relative of mine is running the damned outfit. I feel sort of locked into the crazy situation. And again, Joan, if I don't settle the matter here, what's to keep them from extending their pursuit to the States?"

"Raj, you've answered your own question, haven't you?"

Chapter Eleven

September arrived, bringing cooler and drier weather. Occasionally the clouds parted and revealed broad-angled panoramas of the snow-tipped Himalayas rising sheer from the distant rim of the horizon in the northeast. Gentle mountain breezes carried the freshness of glacier-fed streams and the chill from lofty snow-capped peaks.

One morning at breakfast Jay announced that the elders of Bhirgaon, a village included in the population control study, were planning a social afternoon for his research team. As a guest of the Clemens, the village had extended me a warm invitation.

It took two trips in the jeep to transport the entire group from Nilapat. Jay, Joan, David and I made up the final shuttle. Leaving the Grand Trunk Road about a mile north of the railroad station, we branched off onto a rutted dirt trail through a sea of green fields. Our vehicle struggled through the mud, propelled by its faithful four-wheel drive. We passed sugar cane, standing high in thick plots, giving the impression of solid blocks of green. Corn, planted more sparsely, stood not quite as high. The wheat was still immature and the peanut fields looked like shaggy green lawns.

The ubiquitous Persian well punctuated the countryside. Its endless chain of small buckets dipped down into the water and poured a steady flow into sluices radiating through the fields. Power for the process was provided by a yoke of oxen or a lone camel tediously plodding around a circular track. The beast's outside eye was blindfolded to screen out distractions.

From a distance Bhirgaon, built on an escarpment, looked like a fairy tale island rising out of a green ocean. Scattered mango trees surrounded the base of the village, like waves rolling up to dash against a rugged shoreline. Drawing near, the honeycomb geometry of houses came into view. I wondered whether the houses originally were erected on a hill or if, through the centuries, successive crops of buildings had been built on the ruins of their predecessors, until the crumbling mud walls created the rise.

Our arrival was heralded by the shouts of children and barking dogs. Jay put the jeep into low gear and crawled along for fear of injuring one of the enthusiastic greeters. Narrow streets, barely wide enough to drive through, brought us close enough to share the intimate sounds, sights and odors of the surrounding houses. Built of mud bricks and plastered over with more of the same mud, they reminded me of our adobe construction in the southwestern United States. There was the same squareness of design with wooden ceiling beams incorporated in the walls and rounded mud shoulders following the edges of the roofs.

Our host's house was easy to identify, even from a distance. A general convergence of villagers around it completely blocked our approach. We left the jeep and walked the final few yards. Long chains of flowers and colored paper were strung over the gateway. As we stepped inside the threshold, each of us was garlanded with marigolds.

The compound was made up of three parts, with easy intercommunication. First was the open courtyard, the only roofless area, which was cloistered from outside noise and flurry by high mud walls. The family residence opened freely onto this yard. Next to the family living space a section housed the buffaloes, their feed and the farming equipment. Dogs and chickens roamed throughout the compound unnoticed and undisturbed.

As our party moved into the courtyard we saw all about us the evidence of gala preparations. Crisscrossing over our heads were streamers of multicolored flag bunting gaily gyrating in the breeze. Clay pots of flowers were set up along the tops of the courtyard walls. Much larger clay urns with flowering shrubs were arranged along a low mud parapet which bordered the residential roof jutting out over us.

Wooden frame beds with woven rope springs were arranged in a semicircle along the inner section of the courtyard. Bright homespun blankets covered these pallets, on which we were to sit. For the most part, the women modestly remained in the background, their faces partially veiled with thin scarves.

We were ushered through the crowd toward the host, an elderly Sikh. Recognizing us across the compound, he started in our direction. Jay moved ahead to meet him.

"*Namaste, Kuldip Singh, ji. Ap kaise hai*—Greetings, Kuldip Singh, sir. How are you?" Jay had mastered the Hindustani of social niceties.

"*Mai bahut accha hu*—I am very well," he returned, and added, "*Apse phir milkar mai bahut khus hu*—I am very glad to meet you again." Our host used the widely understood Hindustani rather than his dialect of Punjabi.

Jay turned to introduce me to Kuldip Singh. His dark eyes probed mine and I detected a shadow of apprehension. He must have been aware of my identity. If only I could have read his mind!

When we were seated, an older woman served us strong black tea, steaming hot. This was followed by pastries stuffed with vegetables and deep-fried in a batter of lentil flour. These hot, crisp and peppery snacks were called *pakoras*. Then came sweetmeats, *barfi* and *laddu*, made from milk, sugar and honey.

With the tea dishes cleared away, a troupe of turbaned young men dressed in their Punjabi outfits of short vest-like red jackets and white pantaloons, with anklets of bells, jangled into the courtyard. Seated cross-legged on the floor in one corner were two men with drums of various sizes balanced against their knees. This was to be the *bhangra* dance, so well known throughout the rural Punjab. The entire performance pantomimed farming activities.

A hush fell on the courtyard chatter as the drums began to speak. The rhythmic intonation captured and entranced the audience as well as the dancers. I sat near the swaying, gesticulating bodies of the performers and yielded every fiber to the hypnotic rhythm of motion and sound. Intrinsic to the dance is the smell of dust and sweat as well as the enthusiasm of the dancers. The arm swinging, body flexing, knee bending pantomimes gradually increased in vigor and tempo, urged on by the drums throbbing like ecstatic hearts nourishing the corporate body of the dancers. One persistent motion traced throughout the dance—the rotation of both shoulders timed to the measured cadence of the drums. In a grand finale the drumbeats rose as a powerful wave to crash in a climax of action and sound, followed by a sudden silence.

Applauding, Joan dropped her handkerchief. I quickly moved forward to pick it up. As I reached down, one of the large urns on the parapet overhead crashed into the exact spot where I had been sitting, splintering the wooden frame of the bed. David instinctively leaped across from his seat and was by my side before the broken pieces of pottery had come to rest. Joan, who had been seated beside me, found herself on the floor. The bursting effect of the earth-filled vessel had thrown me forward to my knees. David and I helped Joan to her feet. Her face was so pale that her freckles stood out like crumbs on a white table cloth. Jay looked grim, the muscles of his jaws knotting rhythmically. Having assured himself of my well-being, David disappeared into the crowd.

Our venerable host bade us farewell with the salutation of the Sikhs, *"Sat Sri Akal."* I repeated the words, looking into his troubled eyes. He must have appreciated the significance of the 'accident' in his courtyard. I found it difficult to believe that Kuldip Singh was in any way related to the Naya Ghadr. But then Prem Narayan had warned me explicitly that I should trust no one.

The beauty of the green fields gave a sense of peace as we drove home, the setting sun at our backs. For the most part we rode in silence. Herds of buffalo lazily lumbered along narrow paths leading to the village, followed by small boys or old men prodding the lagging ones with long sticks. Here and there graceful peacocks stopped to cast wary looks in our direction or ran for the shelter of sugar cane clumps, necks stretched out ahead and long tail feathers following in undulating waves.

"Well...a bit of excitement, eh?" I drew in a long breath.

"Excitement, yes. But accident, no!" Jay's voice was hard.

"That urn couldn't have fallen off without a lot of help from someone," Joan observed with a frown.

"Thank God you weren't hurt." I threw her a relieved look.

Jay groaned, "Damn whoever did it, but that seating was carefully arranged."

"Sir," David broke in, "I explore on roof. Person can crawl behind bush, push pot, and crawl away quickly. No one can see him."

"Be to their advantage to make my death look like an accident."

David continued, "Young man is leaving courtyard when *bhangra* dance is starting and is not coming back."

"Could you recognize him again?" I asked.

David nodded. "I think I am able, sir. He was Sikh and his face with smallpox marks is covered."

"*Sabas*—Well done!" Jay complimented.

"Sir, in two days we are receiving two men from C.I.D." He smiled at me encouragingly.

"That'll give us around the clock security." Jay sounded relieved.

"Around the clock," David repeated slowly, pleased to collect another English phrase.

"The seating on those beds..." Joan scratched her head thoughtfully "you know that woman made me move over. She insisted quite firmly. That whole thing was planned very carefully."

The next day's mail brought a letter from Biba. She had tried to telephone without success. Her train would arrive in Nilapat at five-thirty on the afternoon of the twentieth, just two days hence. She planned to stay overnight. Joan's eyes sparkled with excitement on hearing my news. We sat around the dinner table discussing ways to entertain our visitor.

"Raj, it's in your eyes. You kinda like the gal, now don't you?" Jay teased.

I grinned self-consciously.

"Aw, come on, Raj. You're among friends..."

"Hon," Joan cut in, "for gosh sakes quit pestering Raj!" She winked at me. "My husband's the most romantic fellow in the world and he'll..."

"That's a compliment to your marriage," I interrupted with a laugh.

Nilapat station bustled with excitement as the Delhi-bound express arrived from Amritsar. David first spotted Biba through the window of the compartment and the three of us converged on her as she stepped down onto the platform.

"Biba, this is Jay Clemens," I introduced them.

Jay, putting on his homespun Wyoming charm, bowed and doffed his cowboy hat. "Howdy, Miss. Welcome to Nilapat."

Smiling mischievously, Biba replied in an equally Western enunciation, "Howdy pardner. You all sure do make a stranger feel mighty comfortable.'' We broke up into gales of laughter.

I had almost forgotten the pleasing tone of her voice and the rich vibrancy of her laugh. She was dressed in a sari of light orange which contrasted pleasantly with her black hair.

"Raj, how nice to see you again." She extended her hand, and as our fingers touched, a wave of excitement passed through me.

David called her aside a moment to identify certain pieces of baggage. Jay put his arm around my shoulder and whispered, "Stunning! Raj, she's lovely. Will Joan ever love her!"

Dinner was a festive affair, with lighthearted conversation. Samuel had risen to the occasion with a main course of delicious antelope Swiss steak, followed by homemade apple pie-a-la-mode for dessert. The ice cream had been handcranked in an old-fashioned freezer brought from the States. By the end of the meal Jay and Joan had accepted Biba as a member of the family. I was delighted to see that an easy communication flowed between the two women.

We moved into the front room for coffee, taking with us our dinner conversation. Looking through the window onto the verandah I was startled to see the shadow of a man. David was pouring our coffee, and I nodded him over to my side.

"Ko admi admi bahar hai—Some man is outside," I whispered.

"*Ha, ji. Wo hamara admi hai*—Yes sir. He is our man," David replied.

So, the extra assistance from the C.I.D. had arrived. This would be protection for Biba as well, at least during her stay in Nilapat.

During a brief lull in the conversation I intercepted a message, spelled out in sign language, from Joan to Jay. Shortly thereafter the Clemens rose and excused themselves.

Biba and I stepped out into the garden and walked along the paths meandering through the flower beds. The night was quiet and clear. A half-moon hazily outlined the shrubs and plants. The perfume of the jasmine scented the air. Biba slipped her arm through mine and leaned her head against my shoulder.

"Cold?" I asked, feeling her shiver slightly.

She looked up into my face and smiled. "No, just happy."

"How was the Amritsar visit?"

"A good time. Fun renewing an old friendship."

"No problems? I mean with the Naya Ghadr?"

"Not a ripple—very quiet." She paused a moment. 'I did keep my eyes and ears open, though, and asked some questions."

"And?"

"Nothing really new, just confirmation of the things we discussed on the train."

I told Biba of the two attempts at intimidation of the cooks as well as the recent incident in Bhirgaon.

"You said David spotted a young Sikh who looked a bit suspicious?" she asked, suddenly grave.

"Right."

"Any identification?"

"His face was pock-marked."

Biba gripped my arm and exclaimed in a whisper, "Pockmarked! Raj, our cousin in the Naya Ghadr, he's pock-marked."

I whistled softly. "Prakash?"

She nodded. "He's probably the fellow who pushed that urn off the parapet, the black sheep of our family."

We stood in silence a moment, absorbed by the shadows about us. I could see the vague outline of the Gurkha *chowkidar* moving around the compound gate. In the other direction, leaning motionless on the verandah wall, was the C.I.D. guard. Somewhere to the north a jackal howled mournfully and the Nilapat pariah dogs replied in sporadic barking. Again I felt Biba tremble. I put my arm around her waist and drew our bodies together. She turned quickly and came into my arms, burying her head under my chin.

Holding her close, I whispered, "My sweet, my dearest."

"Raj, I'm afraid for you." There was a catch in her voice.

"Now, darling, let's not cross any bridges." I stroked her cheek tenderly. We stood thrilling in each other's embrace. The softness of her body pressed close to mine and the perfumed fragrance of her hair against my face, raised again the flame which had burned low these many months.

A brief pang of conscience assailed me as my thoughts turned back to Pat, but in that same instant I sensed her understanding. For the first time since Pat's death I felt a healing warmth reaching into my lonely emptiness. Biba raised her face to mine and in the dim moonlight I could trace the faint outline of her smile. Our lips met, sealing an understanding of our hearts.

Next morning at breakfast Jay and Joan sensed the changed relationship between Biba and me. Our faces told the story.

"She's lovely, Raj, so sweet," Joan confided while Biba and Jay strolled out to the jeep which was to take the investigating team to a village.

"Thanks, Joan. She is, isn't she?" I grinned.

"Serious?"

I nodded.

Joan leaned over and kissed my cheek. "I'm so happy for you, Raj." She dabbed her eyes with a handkerchief.

The day passed far too quickly, but I knew of no way to slow it down. That night Jay, Joan and I, accompanied by David, drove Biba down to catch the Frontier Mail for Bombay. After seeing her settled in the air-conditioned carriage, the rest of our party withdrew to the station platform.

"Raj, when'll we see each other again?" Biba clung to me.

"As soon as the land is transferred legally. I should be back in Bombay in a couple of weeks."

"Sweet, please take care of yourself," she murmured.

"Even more reason to be careful now," I whispered into her ear.

"You must think me terrible," she said between sniffs. "I don't seem to be able to keep my eyes dry."

"'Give smiles to those who love you less, but keep your tears for me.'"

"How sweet," she said. "Was that Byron?"

"No, Thomas Moore. Can't remember the exact poem." I placed my hand behind her head and gently brought our lips together. We held close a moment and then stepped back, holding each other's hands. Biba's face broke out into a smile as I bent forward to kiss her wet eyes.

The guard's whistle announced the time of departure. The train was moving as I jumped down onto the platform. I caught a quick glimpse of Biba waving and then she was gone.

Returning to the bungalow, we found Samuel setting up dishes on the dining table. He disappeared briefly into the kitchen, returning with a freshly baked cake and coffee. We decided to take our snacks and drinks into the front room where we drew up chairs around the crackling fire. There was a chill in the air that made us appreciate the hot coffee and the warmth of the blaze. We sat watching the flames leaping up into the chimney.

Joan broke the silence. "Raj, I know Pat would like Biba," she said quietly.

"Thanks."

David signaled for my attention. Excusing myself, I stepped to his side. "The Gurkha is seeing a man walking outside the compound," he reported in a low voice. "it is a man who is...is..." he groped for the proper word.

"Suspicious?" I suggested.

"Yes, suspicious. A suspicious man."

"In what way is he suspicious?"

"He is walking many times on Grand Trunk Road and is looking hard at compound."

"Perhaps he is just a curious villager," I countered casually.

David shook his head. "No, sir, excuse me please. It is not just a villager. You will keep good security, yes?

"*Bilkul*—Absolutely!" I assured him.

Our trio broke up for the night and as I moved into my room my thoughts were unsettled. The elation of Biba's visit persisted in waves of delightful memories. And yet behind these happy reveries, a disturbing shadow of foreboding lurked in my thoughts. I checked my automatic and slipped it under the pillow. The night seemed unusually quiet.

Blanketed in this stillness, I fell asleep.

A train headed south noisily picked up speed after the Nilapat stop. I stirred reluctantly and bemoaned the fact that my rest had been disturbed. A veiled moonlight reached down into the compound through the trees. My hand reflexively reached under the pillow. The touch of steel gave a sense of assurance. Dogs from the village suddenly broke into a chorus of barking. The train moved on into the distance. Again there was quiet and I relaxed. In that vague state between consciousness and unconsciousness, a sound reached out seeking identification. It knocked persistently on my attention and forced me into wakefulness. Just a prowling cat, I thought. But this explanation was not convincing. I could not go back to sleep. As it came closer, the sound seemed more human than animal. Quickly getting into my slippers, automatic in hand, I unbolted the outer bathroom door and cautiously stepped outside. A figure ran out of the servant's quarters and dashed toward me. I slipped the safety catch off and held the gun tensely.

"Doctor!" The voice was David's and he sounded relieved.

Sensing that something was wrong, we moved quickly to the shrubbery under my bedroom window. The sounds, half groans and half whimpering cries, were coming from there. We heard the running footsteps of the Gurkha approaching from the gate. All three of us arrived at the shrubbery together. Parting the bushes, David reached down and lifted up Ramdas, the sweeper's son. Ordering the Gurkha to alert the C.I.D. guard and search the premises, we carried the gasping and blood-covered boy into my bedroom.

The pathos of the next few minutes haunts me to this day. Little Ramdas, with an ugly and gaping slash in his chest, struggled for each breath. David sat on the bedroom floor cradling the dying boy in his arms. He removed the torn and bloody shirt with all the tenderness of a grieving parent. His tears, the first that I had seen, fell to mix with Ramdas' blood now staining David's supporting arm. A last catching and sighing breath and the struggle for life was over. I rose from my knees and stood in silence. For an instant David raised his tortured eyes to mine. I reached down and placed my hand on his shoulder. He stared ahead in silence, still clutching the dead lad in his arms. Perhaps he was thinking back to that early morning in the Delhi suburb, where as a boy of Ramdas' age he stood alone facing a bloodthirsty mob.

The police arrived the next morning. Even Captain Karan Singh drove up from Ambala. Interrogations included everyone on the compound.

"My police detective tells me the boy was attacked just inside the compound wall, on the east side, and made an effort to reach you. A trail of blood and overturned potted plants mark the path he crawled," the Captain explained.

"Probably to warn me. . ." I began, unable to finish as my throat tightened.

"Bloody cad! Murdering a child. But they have no conscience." Karan Singh stroked his beard and scowled.

"Then you feel this was the Naya Ghadr?"

The Captain nodded soberly.

"Your men probably have reconstructed the murder?"

"From what we can gather, the victim crept out from his room, as he had done many times recently, on an escapade playing detective."

"Probably heard something suspicious and went out to investigate," I surmised.

"Quite," Karan Singh agreed. "Knowing every inch of the compound, he was able to explore without alerting either the Gurkha or the C.I.D. agent."

The entire compound went down to the burning *ghats* on the outskirts of town that afternoon to witness the funeral of Ramdas. I had given David some money to buy wood for the cremation. A sandaled Hindu priest, or *sadhu*, chanted from the *Upanishads* as flames began to consume the wet-sheeted body. The holy man's words soon were lost in the crackling of the fire. I watched as the wind played with the priest's saffron robe and a ray of sunlight penetrated the overhanging pipal tree to accentuate the white ashes spread across his forehead. Tears flowed unashamedly in memory of the cheerful little boy who had won his way into our hearts.

As we returned to the bungalow, I noted David's unnatural stillness. "We suffer, but we cannot let this blunt our senses," I warned him. "Do you understand what I mean, David?"

"I am understanding." His voice was mechanical.

"Our enemy is cunning, and if we lose our minds in anger, we play right into their hands."

David stared at the floor. I had not reached him.

"Deep grief is known to me also," I confided quietly. He looked up at me, and the hurt on his face was eloquent. I recounted Pat's story. His eyes slowly filled with tears. He understood. We had met on the common ground of human loss and loneliness.

"Sir, I shall do no foolishness," David promised as he stepped out of the room.

The registered letter from Captain Narayan expressed his appreciation of my decision to assist the C.I.D. in their efforts against the Naya Ghadr. In light of this decision, greater security measures were to be invoked. Besides the two agents already assigned, Lieutenant Ian McVey from the Chandigarh C.I.D. office would be arriving shortly.

Prem Narayan also mentioned in the letter a possible change of tactics to be used against me. Information picked up by a double agent within the Naya Ghadr hinted that they might attempt to win me over to their cause. Apparently there was not a consensus among the anarchist leadership as to how my case should be handled. The Captain intimated that this rift in their ranks might present an opportunity for exploitation. That night around the dinner table I shared this information with Jay and Joan. "Sorry about this extra boarder, Ian McVey," I apologized.

Jay waved his hand in a generous approval. "No problem. When the goin's tough we can always take on another pair of hands."

We moved into the front room, taking our after-dinner coffee along. Burning logs in the fireplace cast a welcome warmth over us. We sat quietly for a time.

"You know, something worries me," Joan broke the silence. "When your widowed aunt gets the land, what's to keep the Naya Ghadr from making her life miserable. . .or even murdering her?"

"Good question. In fact I confronted Captain Narayan with that same problem."

"What did he say?"

"Her family, the Daljit Singh family, is highly respected in the area. The two grown sons, each with families of their own, have considerable influence, political and social, in their village. Also, it is in the best interests of the government to keep the land out of the anarchist's hands."

Samuel stepped into the room to stir the coals and add a couple of logs to the fire. David followed him in with a pot of coffee.

"Almost forgot to tell you—Biba says that our cousin working with the Naya Ghadr has a pock-marked face."

"Knew it! Just knew it!" Jay broke in. "That was no accident at Bhirgaon."

Joan drew a deep breath and exhaled with a sigh. "So the C.I.D. will use you as cheese in the trap," she said wryly. "Raj, run that matter of your being prime bait by us again, would you? Enlarge a bit on your role."

"Alright." I took a drink of coffee and set the cup down. "Like a fly on a trout stream, I've already attracted several passes. Some of their key members apparently have surfaced at me in a way they haven't used against the C.I.D. The clincher is that a small tight group at the reins of the band comes from my own family and being related to them makes me a more attractive target. Also, it's probably significant that I'm an American."

"But my God, Raj, this is so damned impersonal. God Lord, man—bait in a trap!" Jay exclaimed.

"Granted that governmental agencies—such as the Criminal Investigation Department—may be impersonal, but I have a feeling that Captain Prem Narayan is interested in me, in a personal way. At any rate, I'm willing to gamble on him."

Joan put her arm around my waist. "Raj, be careful. We can't let anything happen to you."

"Thanks." I kissed her cheek. "You're a sweetheart."

Chapter Twelve

A military vehicle drew up to the bungalow. The single passenger vaulted out and ran up the verandah steps. He was dressed in civilian clothes.

"Lieutenant McVey, madam, Ian McVey," the newcomer announced formally, extending his hand to Joan as she met him at the front door. Jay was out on his village tour, so I joined Joan and our guest for tea in the front room. His luggage had been deposited in my quarters since, in accordance with Captain Narayan's orders, he would be my roommate. The driver and jeep returned to Chandigarh.

Ian McVey would have made a fascinating subject for a caricature artist. Bushy eyebrows jutted out like awnings shielding inquisitive blue eyes in a face framed by thick sandy hair. A square jaw pushed forward as if challenging someone to punch it. Thick set and muscular, he stood just under six feet. His swarthy skin portrayed a dual heritage—European and Indo-Aryan. The suggestion of solemnity and dourness about his features was misleading, and concealed an underlying shyness. Later, after weeks of close association, I came to the conclusion that his reserve, in part at least, was the expression of a social vulnerability related to his Anglo-Indian status.

British colonialism, in creating a two-part society—the ruler and the ruled—was discomfited by the hybrid offspring of the union and tended to ostracize a singular class of people. Not to be outdone by the British, the Indians followed suit. In spite of this, the Anglo-Indians survived as intelligent, loyal and contributing members of their society

In his letter Captain Narayan had written that the Lieutenant, son of a Scottish soldier and his Indian wife, had often demonstrated a cool bravery and intelligence in action which had earned him the respect of the Department.

"Doctor Singh, we should take a quick run up to Amritsar in the next day or so," McVey proposed.

"No reason why not. My schedule's quite flexible, really. Why don't you just pick the time?"

"A bit of a botheration, don't you know, but some of those land documents need to be signed—preliminary signatures—by you and your aunt. I'll contact the parties and we can all meet at the District Commissioner's office." He drew heavily on his pipe. "Our agent will bring the documents from Chandigarh."

"My docket's clear and I'm anxious to get this finished."

"Wait, let me suggest something," Joan broke in. "Jay's been waiting for an excuse to check a family planning program in a village just outside Amritsar. He could drive you up."

"Jolly good!" McVey responded.

We discussed the proposed trip that night at dinner. Jay offered to drive us to Amritsar, but said he really should spend more than a day there.

"We can drive up with you and return by train," I suggested.

After a leisurely breakfast, we piled into the jeep and pulled out of the compound, headed for the holy city of the Sikhs, Amritsar. The car curtains were snapped into place to protect us from the cold wind, curtailing our view of the passing countryside. We drove up the Grand Trunk Road, arriving at the District Commissioner's office around noon. Lunch was served as we waited for everyone involved to arrive. Mrs. Daljit Singh, my late maternal uncle's wife, was a quiet but proud Punjabi woman who spoke good English. We visited and exchanged news about our families. Finally, the several documents were signed and notarized. There would be further signatures needed in a couple of weeks to complete the transfer of the property.

We barely made the train, finding our way into a second class compartment just as the engine and guard were whistling their departure warnings. After jerking and clacking over the rail connections in the station yard, we were out in the open plains rolling along at a surprising speed. A few minutes later the train slowed to cross a long bridge over the Beas river, the southern limit of Alexander the Great's invasion. I stood and moved over to the window for a better look at the flood sculptured banks winding across the plains. The muddy water indicated rains somewhere toward its source.

The shadows of the trees were lengthening as the train slowed to a stop at Jullundur. A passenger left and another took his place. Ian McVey surveyed the change unobtrusively and seemed to be satisfied, turning his attention to the ritual of pipe lighting. A railroad sweeper entered the compartment and checked out the water closet.

A young man staring through the window at us attracted my attention. Disconcerted by my return stare, he turned self-consciously and walked away. I caught a quick glance from Lieutanant McVey, who had been watching closely.

The railway guard, in his white uniform and cap, stood on the platform beside our carriage. A red and a green flag, each neatly rolled on a short-handled stick, were tucked under his left arm. He glanced nervously at a large watch taken at intervals from his coat breast pocket.

Suddenly, with an air of finality, he closed the timepiece cover with a snap and pulled out a whistle from another pocket, which he blew with practiced efficiency. He unfurled and waved the green flag.

The people on the station platform surged in a pre-departure ferment, accentuated by noisy blasts of steam from the engine. McVey, who was seated across the aisle next to the door, bolted the entrance to our compartment. The train was pulling out of the station when the young man who had been peering into our compartment jumped onto the outside step of the carriage and pounded on the door for admission. Lieutenant McVey chose to ignore the would-be passenger. Making a nasty face and an obscene gesture, the intruder jumped off his precarious perch.

"Bandits and *goondas* use that trick," the Lieutanant muttered out loud for all to hear. He calmly drew on his pipe before adding soberly, "Isolated compartments such as this are most vulnerable to robberies." We all nodded in acquiescence.

McVey had suggested before we arrived at the Amritsar station that we should travel as strangers to each other. We boarded a few seconds apart and once inside, sat separately with no indication of our relationship.

"Just another safety factor," he had explained with a grim smile. "Gives me a freer hand for security measures."

Thinking back to our departure from Amritsar, I remembered watching with curiosity as my companion had opened the lavatory door and inspected inside. In the light of the attempted boarding episode with its potential for banditry and mayhem, the precautionary measure now appeared quite reasonable.

Over the countryside twilight shadows were fading into the obscurity of dusk. Farmers, some on foot balancing assorted bundles on their heads, others driving produce-laden carts and farming equipment, all were converging on the villages, their progress marked by trails of dust. Here and there the swifter flow of men and vehicles was dammed back by plodding cattle being herded toward their stockades for the night. The outlines of the houses and trees were blunted into softness by the failing light and the haze of smoke from the evening fires.

The station lights were being turned on as we pulled into Ludhiana, the last stop before Nilapat. A man whom I judged to be in his early sixties entered our compartment and sat down beside me. He was well dressed, with a professional bearing. McVey scrutinized him closely. Turning to look at me, the passenger nodded and smiled. I responded in kind. As the train started out of the station, he removed a medical journal from his valise and adjusted an overhead reading lamp.

"Excuse me, I'm a physician, too." I said. "My name is Raj Singh."

"Saha Masih here," he replied, extending his hand.

"You live here in Ludhiana?"

"Yes. Actually I'm on the faculty of a medical college here." Doctor Masih replaced the journal in his valise and studied me, asking, "Your accent, it is American?"

I laughed and nodded. "From California."

"Aha, I thought so. You see I took my residency in internal medicine in Dallas, Texas."

"Southwestern Medical?"

"No, Baylor, before the school moved down to Houston."

"My field is surgery. Took my residency under U.S.C. auspices at Los Angeles County General Hospital."

"You're not Indian then?"

"American by nationality, of Sikh ancestry but of Christian persuasion."

Ian McVey, who had been listening surreptitiously to óur conversation, evinced restrained surprise at that last comment.

"Ludhiana is quite an educational center," Saha Masih volunteered, turning in his seat to face me. "Two colleges, an agricultural university and two medical colleges."

"And how large is the city?"

"About six hundred thousand."

"Really! Hadn't realized it was that large."

"I'm a faculty member of the Christian Medical College, founded in 1894 by an English lady, Doctor Edith Brown, as the first medical school for women in Asia. The founder later was honored by the British with the title of Dame Edith Brown."

"The faculty are all Indians?"

He shook his head. "No, besides the Indian nationals there are Americans, Canadians, English and other Britishers."

"And the students?"

"Indians, of all sects, and the college is coeducational."

"Teaching is in English?"

He nodded. "Medical education in India is almost all in English. Really the only common language here."

"Do you follow the British system—that is, function under the academic umbrella of a university?"

"Right you are. The medical college is under the aegis of the University of the Punjab. Technically, our degrees are issued by that institution."

The vibration of the carriage indicated that the train was approaching normal speed. The passing lights outside suggested that we still were on the outskirts of Ludhiana. Doctor Masih, apparently enjoying our chat and not planning to read further, reached above his head and switched off the lamp. As the light went out, a window on the far side of the compartment slid up and a hand gun shoved in.

Behind the automatic was a shadowed face, crowned by a knitted khaki stocking cap pulled down low. Cruel eyes were intermittently visible in the changing lights and shadows.

All eyes were focused in horrified fascination on the shiny muzzle of the gun. Time froze. Like helpless quarry hypnotized by the beady eyes of a snake, we were benumbed—all of us except Lieutenant McVey, who leaped toward the open window with a shout.

I remember the startling sounds of shots, and a mild, not particulaly painful stinging in my left arm and at the nape of my neck. Then there was a vague recollection of falling forward onto the floor amidst a bedlam of shouting and moving bodies. The fleshy impact of the bullets threw me into a slow-motion sequence in which time wound down. My fall was a gentle drifting, my thoughts seemed to be disassociated from my body. At the moment I touched the floor action stopped like a run-down mechanical toy, and my memory came to an abrupt halt.

Chapter Thirteen

The first stirrings of consciousness...frail shafts of cognizance...began to probe my mind. The hazy indefiniteness was distressing, like the tingling of a numb limb regaining sensation. I struggled with the knowledge that I was passing back and forth between consciousness and unconsciousness.

I strove to remember the recent past. I remembered the beginnings of the conversation on the train with Doctor Masih, although sketchily, but nothing after that. My head ached fiercely.

With the first breakthrough into consciousness, I realized that I had been enroute to Nilapat from Amritsar and did not reach my destination. Then came a series of questions. What interrupted the journey? Where was Ian McVey? I had no answers, so I set aside those problems and began to explore my surroundings.

It was obvious that I was in a hospital and lying on a firm bed with the head slightly elevated. The side rails were up. An empty chair with knitting material beside it probably indicated a special nurse who had stepped out for a moment. The window curtains were partly drawn, leaving the room dim. The door into the hallway was slightly ajar. My left arm was sore and bandaged, and my head was swathed in a turban-like dressing.

I noted that I could think and move, so there was no critical neurological damage. Knowing neither the extent nor the cause of the injuries, I could not assess the symptoms.

Deciding that my condition was not critical, I returned to an exploration of the room. Although Spartan and frugally furnished compared to an American hospital, it had all the essential facilities, and was clean and neatly arranged. On top of the bedside table were a sphygmomanometer and stethoscope as well as a handbell for summoning the nurse. This last item, I thought to myself, might prove disconcerting to patients in nearby rooms. The shelves in the table held a bedpan and metal handbasin, with a towel and a bar of phenol-scented soap, and a pair of woven jute slippers.

My investigation was interrupted by a young face haloed with a white nursing cap peeking around the door.

"Oh, Doctor Singh, you are awake!" she whispered in surprise, and without further comment turned and ran down the corridor. The clatter of her sandals on the tile floor was sweet music to my recovering senses.

As her steps faded into the distance, the squeak of a chair and the soft scuffle of shoes brought my attention back to the door. A khaki-turbaned head and uniformed shoulder pulled back into the hallway. There was a guard seated just outside my room.

A minute or two later I heard the approaching steps of two people, moving sedately. The door opened and the nurses, or sisters as they are called in British hospitals, quietly entered. The young lady whom I had just seen brought up the rear.

"How do you feel, Doctor Singh?" the older woman asked. Without waiting for a reply, she added, "I am Sister Mary Matthai and this is Sister Tara Muttra."

"I feel pretty good, Sister." I acknowledged the introductions with nods to each of them.

"Do you need anything, Doctor?" Sister Matthai asked as she looked my bandages over.

"Yes," I replied with a smile, "the answers to a lot of questions."

"Ah, yes. Doctor Masih instructed me to notify him immediately on your regaining consciousness—an orderly was sent over to his bungalow just a minute ago."

"He must live close."

"Just across the street from the hospital," Sister Tara Muttra chimed in.

"Many people have been asking about you," Sister Matthai remarked.

"Such as?"

"Doctor Kundan Lal, the surgeon, has placed you strictly off limits," she countered, choosing to ignore my query.

Doctor Masih entered the room, his face wreathed in smiles. The two nurses greeted him and left quickly.

"Am I ever glad to see you." I grasped his extended hand. "There's a big gap in my memory which needs filling up."

He pulled a chair up to the bedside and sat down with a sigh. "Let me narrate the events from our first meeting on the train. Then you can ask questions, alright?"

"Great. But first, was anyone else hurt?"

He shook his head. "Not a soul."

"What about Lieutenant McVey?"

"Fine, just fine. You know you've quite a group of worried friends, and they're all here."

"All here?"

"Especially a Doctor Ranjit Kaur who appears to be vitally concerned with your welfare." There was a teasing look in Saha Masih's eyes.

"But she was in Bombay!"

"The Doctor flew up to Delhi yesterday and then took the train to Nilapat. She drove here with the Clemens and the three of them stayed overnight in the guest quarters next to the Director's bungalow."

"What a relief!" I murmured.

Saha Masih brought me up to date. The night of the shooting, Doctor Kundan Lal, the Professor of Surgery, had been called in to handle my case. He had concured with Doctor Masih that the trauma was not serious. Tetanus immunization and antibiotic therapy were instituted immediately. The wounds were debrided and cleansed in surgery.

"It's hard to believe that at that range no one was killed," I mused quietly.

"The Lieutenant said that my turning out the overhead light just as the assassin raised the window probably confused him just enough to spoil his aim," Doctor Masih observed and added in Hindustani, "*Bhagvan ki kripa hai*—God is very good."

"What about the gunman—did they catch him?"

"I'll have the Captain and the Lieutenant brief you on that later today, if you feel up to it."

"The Captain? You mean..."

Doctor Masih grinned. "Yes, Captain Narayan. He flew up to Delhi with Doctor Ranjit Kaur. An amazing chap that. Had him over for dinner last night." The doctor walked over to open the window curtains, then returned to check me over.

"And how do things look, from your exam?"

"You're doing just fine," he replied, straightening up.

"What's the E.T.D.?"

"E.T.D.?"

"Estimated time of discharge."

He scratched his chin thoughtfully. "Oh, let's see. I'd say about ten days or so."

"Sounds good." I studied his face a moment. 'What about company? Say I invited in a couple of friends for a quiet dinner here tomorrow night?"

"Alright, but be sensible, Doctor."

A quiet knocking interrupted our conversation. Sister Matthai peeked through the door and reported in a stage whisper, "Doctor Ranjit Kaur is at the nurses' desk, Doctor Masih."

"I'll be right out, Sister," he replied. Turning to me, he said, "You may dangle your legs if you wish, but let's hold up bathroom privileges until tomorrow morning." With these admonishments, the Doctor waved and stepped out into the hall.

With a soft, almost timid knocking, the door opened slowly. Biba stepped inside quietly, standing for a few seconds as if poised for flight, her eyes fixed on mine. She first looked at me through the eyes of a physician assessing a patient's condition, followed immediately by the embracing glance of a lover. Biba was even more beautiful than I had fantasized over the days of our separation. Her hair, fastened high on her head, contrasted with her olive complexion. The lovely feminine curves of her body refused to be hidden by her graceful sari.

I called her name. With a low cry she ran to the side of my bed, where she hesitated and cautiously reached forward to touch the bandage around my head. Then she came into my outstretched arms and I felt her warm tears wetting my cheek.

"I'm sorry for the tears, Raj, but I'm so relieved...you'll never know what I've been through these past couple of days." Biba pushed herself to a sitting position on the edge of the bed and sighed contentedly as she looked down at me.

"Biba, just when I'd give anything to break out with a poetic verse, all I can think of is an old cliche—I love you."

"What do you mean a cliche? They're beautiful words...beautiful words."

I laughed and pulled her close. After lying quietly against me for a moment, she raised up to ask seriously, "Raj, was that a proposal?"

Taking her face in my hands, I asked, "Darling, will you marry me?"

She grinned down at me through eyes still wet with tears. "This silly crying..."

"Darling, answer my question. Will you marry me?"

She studied my face solemnly before replying, 'Yes, Raj, I'll marry you." She leaned forward and her lips found mine, sealing our troth.

We discussed the time since our separation. I found that, on hearing from Ian McVey of the shooting, Captain Narayan had called Biba immediately and arranged for their flight from Bombay to Delhi.

"That chap's really something." I commented.

"Yes...looks hard on the outside...that awful scar...but he's really thoughtful and warm."

"Just remember how he got that scar." I reminded.

Biba jumped off the bed, pushing her hair into place and straightening her sari. "I promised Doctor Masih not to stay with you too long, and just look at the time."

"By the way, I'm making reservations for four tomorrow right here at the *l'Hopital Parisien Cafe.* Sort of a reunion, you know, for Joan, Jay, you and me."

"*Oui monsieur. Quelle heure?*" Her eyes sparkled.

"*Oh, vers sept heures.*"

"Don't worry, we'll all be here!" Kissing me on the tip of my nose, she walked toward the door, turning as she grasped the doorknob. "I take it that this room will magically turn into *l'Hopital Cafe* tomorrow night?"

"*Oui, mademoiselle.*"

She laughed and stepped into the hall.

I slept for an hour and awoke refreshed. My headache had improved. Soon after I woke up, Captain Narayan and Lieutenant McVey, both in uniform, were ushered into my room by an obviously impressed Sister Matthai. The preliminary greetings were brief but warm.

Gesturing to the two men to be seated, I addressed the Captain. "Really hadn't expected to see you again so soon."

"Thank God you escaped serious injury," Prem Narayan countered, sitting down.

"Did you catch the fellow?"

"Let Lieutenant McVey give you the details of the shooting," the Captain suggested, pointing at him with his swagger stick.

Ian McVey sat forward in the chair and clasped his hands before him. "Fortunately, no one else was wounded. I pulled the emergency chain to stop the train. Doctor Masih examined you, and said that you weren't seriously injured. On the southern outskirts of Ludhiana, where the train had stopped, the Grand Trunk Road closely parallels the railroad. The guard on the train helped us commandeer a truck to use as an ambulance. We drove you to the medical college hospital, cushioned on the Doctor's bedding roll." He paused to draw several times on his pipe.

"A ride of which I have no recollection."

"With you safe in the care of Doctor Masih," the Lieutenant continued, "I ran back along the tracks toward the Ludhiana station and found the assailant's body. In his jump from the moving train, he struck a signal post and broke his neck."

"Has he been identified?"

McVey nodded. "Karam Chand's brother."

"The responsible members of the family were rounded up in Jullundur yesterday and brought down here," Captain Narayan picked up the narration. "They claim there are no more males in the immediate family."

"And where do we go from here?" I scanned their faces. "The shooting was purely a matter of revenge?"

The Captain nodded. "Probably not masterminded by the Naya Ghadr...pure personal revenge."

"Then that should at least clear up the matter of revenge, with no more male members of the family...or will it?"

"Possibly," Narayan responded. "We're tightening security even more. In fact, as an extra precaution, Doctor Ranjit Kaur also will be kept under constant surveillance."

"That's great!" I was relieved at this decision.

"Douglas Gordon called me this morning from the Bombay Consulate inquiring about your welfare and asked me to convey his good wishes for a quick recovery," the Captain reported.

"You've all been more than kind. Thanks so much."

"I shall be leaving for Delhi on the Frontier Mail tonight. Shan't be needed around here with Ian carrying on." He tapped his associate's shoulder, and the two rose to leave, each shaking my hand cordially on the way out.

At midnight the nursing sister awakened me as I had requested.

Placing an intercontinental telephone call to my parents, it was less than ten minutes before Mother and Dad were on the line.

"Just wanted to let you know I'm convalescing even better than the doctors expected," I reassured them.

"Thank God!" Mother exclaimed. "We've been so worried ever since Consul Gordon called us from Bombay."

"And. . .and I've an announcement to make." I drew a deep breath. "I met a lovely young woman whom I've asked to marry me."

There was a pause at the other end of the line before Dad cautiously interjected, "You did."

"Ranjit Kaur. You know the family. Balak Singh's her father. They're from British Columbia. Her nickname's Biba."

"Yes! Yes!" Dad responded excitedly. "They're related to us. Let's see. She's your. . .your second cousin." I detected a note of relief in his voice.

Mother asked about the circumstances of our meeting, which I related briefly. Just before hanging up the phone I heard a sound, half sob and half laugh, punctuating her goodbye. I knew Mother was happy.

The next evening Tara Muttra prepared my room for the dinner party, barely concealing her excitement. With several little suggestions from me, the room took on an aura of celebration. By the time linen tablecloths, napkins and silverware had been added, we had created a reasonable facsimile of a Parisian sidewalk cafe. The sister added a final touch with small vases, each containing three pansies.

"Tara, you're very artistic," I complimented, "and just where did you find the flowers?"

"The *mali* is getting them for me from the hospital gardens," she replied, rewarding me with a dimpled smile.

The reunion was a tribute to our friendship. Our conversation moved about on a wide range of subjects. Just as Jay was pontificating on the formation of a new coeducational combined sorority and fraternity to be called the Nilapat Neophytes, the door opened and Sister Muttra led in an entourage of three bearers, each carrying a covered tray. While the guests were being served, Tara fussed about arranging my bowl of consomme and dish of rice pudding. Completing their duties, they all marched out with Sister in the lead.

Jay watched the exodus with a broad grin. "Bunch of ham actors."

"Now really, Jay," Joan interjected with a chuckle, "she's a cute little nurse."

"And you know who she has a crush on?" Jay pointed a finger in my direction.

Biba grinned and winked at me.

On the spur of the moment, I waved for attention and announced, "Biba and I have something to share with you, and I'm going to ask her to divulge our secret."

Caught by surprise, she drew a quick breath. "Raj has asked me to marry him and I...I... So you see, this is our engagement dinner."

Joan jumped up from her chair to hug each of us. Her eyes were wet with happy tears.

Jay rose solemnly and began prancing around the room in the initial steps of his famous Sioux war dance.

"Oh my dear God...and in a hospital," Joan groaned, staring apprehensively at her husband. "Jay, please, in the name of all that's decent...this is a hospital!"

Fortunately for the patients as well as our reputations, the usual blood curdling whoops were subdued, though not sufficiently to prevent the guard at the door from coming in to make sure that his ward was safe. Again I had to explain to the confused onlooker, as I had in Nilapat, that this was an American ritual of no dangerous significance. Perplexed but convinced that Biba and I were not being massacred, the uniformed man withdrew.

"When and where shall we have the wedding?" Joan asked. "After all, what more important subject could we discuss during an engagement dinner?"

"Joan," Jay implored, "give them a chance..." he grinned apologetically at us. "That wife of mine's such a romantic."

Oblivious to his admonitions, Joan continued, "The Clemens offer their bungalow in Nilapat."

"Offer accepted!" Biba broke in with a laugh.

"Second the motion," I added.

"Well," Joan sighed as she pulled Jay to his feet, "such a lovely evening. But, Raj, this business of scaring us to death has got to stop. From now on please behave."

"Will do," I promised.

After a grand round of hugs, handshakes and congratulations, the Clemens stepped out into the hallway and quietly pulled the door closed after them.

"What a pair, those two," Biba said, sliding a chair up beside my bed.

"Salt of the earth," I agreed.

She reached over and took my hand in hers, holding it in her lap. "Raj, we're really engaged, aren't we?" Her eyes smiled into mine.

"According to my calculations, darling, we most certainly are. Hope I didn't jump the gun on the announcement."

"Absolutely not. The timing was perfect."

A few rapid knocks on the door and Doctor Masih entered. "How does the patient feel?" he asked, nodding pleasantly at us both.

"Improving by the hour. Headache's cleared and amnesia improving a bit at a time."

"Just how recent is your recollection of events?"

"Still drawing a blank on the actual shooting, but I think I now remember most of our conversation on the train."

"Good! And how was the party tonight?"

"Out of this world," Biba replied enthusiastically. "I hope there were no complaints. We tried to be..."

"None whatsoever," Doctor Masih broke in with a grin. "Should you need me, please call at any time. My quarters are within a stone's throw of here. Goodnight to you both." He slipped out of the room.

Biba stood looking down at me. A gentle smile played hide-and-seek about the corners of her mouth. "Don't worry," she reassured me, "my room's right next to Jay and Joan's, and the guard will pick me up at the door here and see me to my quarters."

As she leaned over to kiss me goodnight, I pulled her down into my arms. She sighed and nestled against me. Then, whether by intent or not I'll probably never know, her hair loosened and the jasmine-scented tresses cascaded around our faces, offering us a cloistered intimacy for a moment's tryst.

Chapter Fourteen

I awoke to the sound of rain on the leaves outside. The air smelled earthy and pleasant. My head felt clear and the wounds were less annoying. The turban bandage had slipped off during the night and a couple of blood and serum spots stained my pillow case. This caused me no worry, since small wounds usually are sealed within a few hours.

"Good morning, sir," a feminine voice addressed me. I surmised from her uniform that the little wisp of a girl who stood at the door was a student nurse. "Did you rest good?" Her English was permeated with an Indian enunciation.

"Slept well, thank you. And your name, young lady?"

"Anandi Khosla," she replied, smiling with her entire face. "I shall assist you wash and shave. Then I shall take your blood pressure, pulse and temperature. Also, Doctor Masih has ordered for you the bathroom privileges."

The measured and mechanical rhythm of her words reminded me of the lines from *My Fair Lady,* "The rain in Spain stays mainly on the plain." She busied herself setting up the paraphernalia necessary for my morning toilet, hovering around like a mother getting her youngest off to school. The friendly harassment culminated in the recording of my vital signs. It was evident that she was enjoying the experience, particularly the opportunity to practice her English.

"My home is in Nilapat. My father is teaching in the Ambala middleschool." She was responding to my questions. "I shall receive my cap and pin next June."

"Do you know the Clemens in Nilapat?"

"Oh yes," she replied, breaking out into a broad smile. "My father is *pundit* to them in Hindustani lessons."

"And where did you learn your English?"

"Middleschool. Also, Mrs. Clemens is teaching..." she looked at me questioningly with her large sober eyes. "I speak English good?"

I nodded and smiled encouragingly. "Very well indeed. You won't mind if I make a suggestion or two from time to time?"

She straightened quickly from dusting the side table and stepped over to my bed. "Oh no, Doctor Singh, please. I am asking, you will correct, yes?"

"Alright, then, you have used the word 'good' when you should have said 'well'. Now repeat that sentence, please."

"Do I speak English well?" She grinned self-consciously.

"Splendid!"

Suddenly she frowned and pursed her lips. "Did you get...did you..." she struggled for a word. "Did you discover English hard?" She shook her head in frustration.

"Anandi, listen. 'Did you find English difficult?' That's what you're trying to say, isn't it?"

"Did you find English difficult," she repeated, nodding vigorously. "I shall remember that!"

"Well done, young lady. You're speaking good English."

She looked confused. "Doctor, you told me to say 'well' instead of 'good', but now you make my mistake."

I smiled. "Anandi, in your case we were using an adverb and in my case an adjective."

She studied me shrewdly a moment before she conceded, "I shall study more my adverbs and adjectives."

A hospital bearer brought in my breakfast. After arranging the tray on the bed, Anandi waved and left the room.

In the midst of the meal Biba walked in, wearing a raincoat with a hooded cape which framed her face. As she stooped to kiss me some of the rain sprinkled over my head. Taking the napkin from my tray she brushed the moisture off my face and quoted, "Into each life some rain must fall."

"Whittier?" I queried hopefully.

"No, Longfellow," she corrected, playfully tweaking my nose, "from 'The Rainy Day'."

"And I got good grades in English Lit," I groaned.

We were laughing as the door slowly opened to admit Ian McVey. He hesitated on the threshold, cap in hand, with an embarrassed look.

"Am I intruding? he asked self-consciously. "I'll return later."

"Not at all. Do come in, Ian." I beckoned him to join us.

Handing his raincoat and cap to the door guard, he walked in.

"Biba, this is Lieutenant McVey, and Lieutenant, may I present Doctor Ranjit Kaur."

He stepped up and took Biba's extended hand, bowing from the waist. "Delighted to meet you, Doctor."

Pointing to an empty chair, I urged, "Do be seated, Ian."

"You're sure...I mean...I'm not interrupting..." he studied our faces.

"Not at all. In fact, it's quite important now that Biba is included in our discussions. Ian, we're going to be married."

"Now that's what I call a bit of alright," he said, with a shy smile. "You've informed Captain Narayan of this?"

"Not yet. But we will shortly." I promised.

"Jolly good."

"Ian, I've been worried about Biba's safety. Although the Naya Ghadr's attacks are aimed primarily at me, our impending marriage may change things."

He began filling his pipe. "Yes. The C.I.D. has been exploring this matter. You must remember that Doctor Ranjit Kaur and her father have been up against the anarchists even before you. We are fully aware of..." he struck a match and drew forcefully on the pipe..."the danger we face. Also, a close watch has been staked out on the Karam Chand family." He puffed on his pipe thoughtfully as we waited. "Even with the death of this last adult male member, we daren't ease up on security."

"Revenge still remains a real danger, doesn't it?" Biba leaned forward in her chair.

"Definitely so, and neither can the anarchists be disregarded."

I tried to reassure Biba with a smile. There was a hint of alarm in her eyes, but she smiled back.

A knock interrupted our discussion and Biba rose to open the door. Little Anandi swept into the room with a tray, ceremoniously setting it down on a small table. In the center was a teapot, snugly covered with an embroidered tea cozy, surrounded with all the necessary adjuncts. Biba sat down and began to pour, while I diplomatically talked our student nurse out of the room.

Ian leaned forward, cup in hand, to say in a lowered voice, "Hope you'll not consider me a snooping cad of some sort, having to keep a constant eye on both of you."

"Not at all, Ian...if I may call you that?" Biba replied with an understanding chuckle.

"Oh, do." He seemed pleased by this touch of intimacy. "In order to develop and maintain good security for the both of you, I should know something of your plans."

"Well, to begin with, Biba and I plan to get married here in India before we return to the States."

He gave an approving nod. "Could you say as to the time and place?"

"We haven't decided on the date as yet. The place..." I studied Biba's face.

"Nilapat. The Clemens," she said quickly, placing her hand in mine.

"Very good!" There was a touch of excitement in Ian's voice and under the bushy eyebrows his eyes twinkled.

"Raj, let's get married soon," Biba entreated. "Can't we at least give Ian an approximate date?"

"That would help, don't you know," Ian offered, then blushed bashfully. "A bit cheeky of me, I mean, sort of butting in on your affairs."

"Oh Ian, not at all, not at all." She patted his arm.

"Well, to begin with, my folks can't make it here from America," I explained.

"No problem about Dad," Biba countered. "He'll hop the Frontier Mail from Bombay, and besides. . . " she winked at me, "he'll be glad to get me off his hands." Ian and I joined in her laughter.

"What're we talking about, honey, maybe a couple of weeks?" I asked.

She stared out the window trying to calculate our timetable. "None of our guests will be more than forty-eight hours away, and that'll be Bombay."

"Let's see, from Bombay there'll be the Dorabjis, the Gordons, Prem Narayan, and of course your Dad."

Biba shot a quick glance at Ian and asked, "There is no Mrs. Narayan?"

He shook his head. "The Captain is a widower."

"Say," Biba pointed her finger at Ian, "of course you are to be a guest and do you realize that yours is the first direct invitation to our wedding?"

"Splendid, jolly good, I must say!"

"By the way, where is your home?" Biba asked.

"We live in Chandigarh."

"You're married?" she continued her questioning.

"Yes. Joyce and I have two girls, Doreen and Kathleen."

"And of course, this invitation includes Joyce as well."

"Thanks, I know Joyce will be very happy to accept."

"Getting back to the date, two weeks from today would be on. . . " I turned to look for a calendar.

Ian walked across the room to a picture calendar on the wall. "Here it is. That would be the first of November," he said, tracing the dates with his index finger.

"Will the wedding be a serious security problem?" I asked.

"It can be handled. Actually, the bungalow and compound lend themselves quite well to the establishment of good security."

"I hope the security matter won't inconvenience our guests too much," I wondered out loud.

"They'll just have to understand," Biba shrugged.

"You know, Ian, something bothers me about the shooting incident on the train. Although I still can't recall the actual events, Doctor Masih recounted some to me."

"Yes?" He studied my face intently.

"How come that window could be shoved open?"

He looked embarrassed. "That was a mistake on my part. When we boarded at Amritsar, besides looking into the W.C., I checked the windows and they were locked."

"Then how did. . . " I shook my head, puzzled.

"Two things happened, both at Jullundur, either of which might answer our question. You will remember the passenger who sat beside that particular window got off the train there. He might have disengaged the latch before leaving. But more likely, the railroad sweeper who stepped in and inspected the W.C. did the unlatching.''

"Yes, I remember the fellow. He entered the compartment on the station side and left through the opposite door past the window.''

"Could this sweeper have been the gunman?'' Biba asked.

Ian shook his head. "No. I saw his face and they were not the same person.''

"The sweeper might have been bribed to unlatch the window,'' I suggested.

"Quite possible,'' Ian nodded. "And the assassin in all likelihood squatted on the carriage steps until the shooting, just waiting for it to get dark.''

"You don't think the young fellow who tried to board the train at Jullundur was involved in the conspiracy?'' I asked.

"I doubt the bugger had anything to do with the shooting.''

The guard opened the door and beckoned for the Lieutenant. The Clemens were standing in the hallway beyond. Biba jumped up and ran past Ian and the guard to throw her arms around Joan.

"We accept! We accept!'' she exclaimed.

"Accept what?'' Jay's question rose in the background.

"Your invitation to be married in your bungalow.''

"Well, I'll be damned! And just when does all this take place?'' Jay boomed.

"The first of November, two weeks from today,'' Biba announced.

Ian, all smiles, excused himself and left the room. The two women immediately began talking of wedding dresses, bridesmaids and other details of the ceremony. I knew that the planning was in good hands. Jay winked a benediction. Biba gave me a quick kiss and left with the Clemens.

About an hour later, while I was in the bathroom cleaning up, Doctor Kundan Lal came in, Anandi in tow. While waiting for me, he positioned his rather ample body in one of the chairs. On my return the Doctor jumped up with an agility that belied his size and pumped my hand vigorously. After checking the wounds, he appeared satisfied and sat down again in his chair. Anandi was dispatched to fetch the surgical cart.

"You are fortunate, Doctor Singh.'' He spoke in a bass voice that reverberated through the room. "Fortunate in surviving a point blank shooting.''

The surgical cart, powered by energetic Anandi, wheeled to the side of my bed. Doctor Kundal Lal deftly cleansed the wounds and changed the arm bandage.

"We'll leave the back of the neck exposed without any dressing. I'll ask the sister to use sterile pillow cases.'' He surveyed his handiwork critically, flashed me a smile and boomed his farewell.

Doctor Masih entered as the surgeon departed. He moved the tea tray off the side table to set down his instruments. Suddenly he reached forward and picked up a slip of paper.

"Doctor Singh, had you noticed this?" Saha Masih handed me the small envelope. "It lay under the teapot in the center of the tray."

I studied the address, typewritten and in English, "Dr. Raj Singh and Dr. Ranjit Kaur." The letter within also was typewritten and in English, on paper of poor quality. My pulse pounded as I scanned the crude drawings below the message—two prone bodies, each with a dagger in the back. Above the gruesome sketches were the words, underlined with red ink, "You cannot escape the Naya Ghadr." At the bottom of the page was the signature in red.

"Doctor Masih, please call Lieutenant McVey. The guard at the door will help you find him."

For the first time Biba had been brought into the picture. A knot tightened in my stomach.

Ian sat in silence studying the envelope and its contents. "Blithering cads!" I heard him mutter as he tucked the document into his pocket. "A couple of telephone calls to make," he announced, abruptly heading for the door.

I had just finished telling the kitchen bearer to leave the tray of dishes alone, when Anandi came in. She was out of breath and obviously had been running. She stared into my eyes for a moment.

"You are sorrowful," she observed sympathetically.

I shrugged, not wishing to explore the problem of the moment with her.

"I may helpful be?" she persisted. "Something has happened. Officer McVey was here."

"Thank you Anandi, for your offer of help, but suppose we let the Lieutenant solve the problem, eh?"

She stepped over to the dishes on the table and studied the tray, then looking up quickly at me, asked, "Here is the wrong?"

The discussion was tabled by the entry of McVey, who unceremoniously whisked the student nurse out of the room and firmly closed the door after her.

"I've contacted Delhi and they're sending up a crime laboratory specialist. Captain Narayan's enroute to Bombay and there's a message waiting for him there to call me on his arrival. I've a detective investigating all possible contacts in the hospital kitchen." Ian nodded encouragingly, and paused to fill his pipe.

The guard at the door looked in to inform us that Sergeant Major Sardar Khan had arrived. Ian beckoned the Sergeant into the room. He looked the epitome of military spit and polish. Stiffly starched khaki turban, bristling waxed and pointed mustache, uniform, campaign ribbons, and posture, all attested to years in the armed forces. After the introductions, he used the napkin on the tray and his handkerchief to pick up the load of dishes, and disappeared down the hallway.

Ian sat down slowly, stretching his legs out before him, and drew deeply on his pipe. "Those bloody bastards!" he muttered, scowling.

"Remember, Ian, you're to keep me informed, right?"

He nodded soberly. "I will. Need we tell Doctor Ranjit Kaur about the note?"

"Perhaps not, but let me be the judge of that," I suggested.

"Jolly good."

"You know, Ian, it just might be best and in the interest of all concerned if the two of us left India as soon as possible."

"I appreciate that this turn of events places her in serious danger. Please believe me, I understand your real concern for her safety."

"When I was the bait, so to speak, that was my own voluntary choice. With Biba involved we're in a different ballgame."

Ian nodded, studying my face.

"Let me talk the thing over with her this evening."

The Sergeant Major returned and Ian left with him. I sat alone struggling over this new dilemma and just how much, if any, of it to share with Biba. After a few moments of reflection I decided to tell her everything. Anything less would be unfair, particularly if it involved an immediate departure from India.

My recorder of vital signs, little Anandi, went about her business of taking blood pressure, pulse and temperature. She hummed a cheerful tune.

"There is much trouble in the hospital kitchen." It was difficult to tell whether Anandi was simply relaying a fact or interrogating me. She continued, "All people are going to the Director Ram Singh's office for questions."

"And just how do you know?"

"Everyone is talking. They study who put the letter on your food tray."

Word travels about hospitals as fast in India as in America, I thought. Wonder if the content of the letter is known? Anandi left me, smugly satisfied that she was in on an event of mysterious proportions. Later I dozed off, to awake with a start, looking up into Biba's face.

"You look troubled, even in your sleep," she said, her face drawn with worry.

Clearing my throat I conceded guardedly, "Well, sweet, something has come up which complicates things a bit." I tried to sound casual. Apparently some inkling of the day's problem had come to her attention, for she nodded as if she were aware of it.

Biba sat down on the edge of the bed and picked up my hand, holding it in her lap. I caught a hint of foreboding in her eyes.

"Raj, I know something's up. Jay was over..."

"Then you know about the letter," I studied her face closely.

She nodded. "Jay was here in the hospital earlier this afternoon and saw the police running about the place. By the way, Jay and Joan drove back to Nilapat just a while ago. Said to say 'aloha' and that they'd be dropping in regularly."

I recounted to Biba the events surrounding the note. She listened quietly. I mentioned my discussions with Ian about us leaving India immediately.

Biba frowned in thought, turning to stare out the window into the hospital garden.

"Darling, what would you do if I weren't involved?"

"What would I do? That's kind of hard to say."

"Now, Raj," she turned and faced me squarely. "Let's have out with it, honestly."

"I guess I'd see the thing through here in India. But honey, that's not quite a fair question, is it?"

"Why not?"

"Oh, because..." I hedged, trying to think of a convincing argument.

Biba moved herself into a more comfortable position on the edge of the bed. "Darling, let's go through with the wedding here. I know there's a risk, but..." she hesitated and looked at me wistfully.

"Hon, you're sure? I mean, you've really given enough thought to it?"

"You know, Raj, in a way this is my problem also. I mean, our relatives are involved. Prakash, Gurdial and perhaps even Bubli. This may not be the safest way, but if we can help the C.I.D. resolve the problem...well, I'd just feel better."

"You're a brave little wench, my darling, and I love you for it." I pulled her down into my arms. As we lay close together she knew, without my saying, that our wedding would be in Nilapat.

We walked over to the window arm in arm. The clouds had withdrawn and the sunshine accented the freshness and color of the landscape. In the center of the hospital compound, beyond the row of *neem* trees, stood a large tree whose leaves fluttered tremulously in the wind.

"Gee, that must be at least a hundred feet tall." Biba said, pointing. "What kind is it?"

"Haven't the faintest."

"Let's ask Ian. I'm sure he'll know." We stood quietly for a moment. Biba nestled her head on my shoulder.

"What about your room, now that Jay and Joan are gone?"I asked.

"The guard was doubled this afternoon. One was sitting on the verandah just outside my door and the other squatting under a tree not far from my back window."

"Great! That eases my mind. Remember Prem Narayan's warning not to trust anyone.''

"Oh yes! Ian told me there would be a police woman sleeping in my room at night.''

A knock at the door announced Ian's arrival. Seeing us together, his face eased into a smile.

"Speak of the devil. We've just been talking about you,'' Biba warned him with a chuckle.

"Kindly, I hope.''

Biba pulled three chairs into a circle and we sat down. Ian settled with a sigh and stretched his arms toward the ceiling. We looked on as the kitchen bearer brought in a tray with the usual tea things.

"The wedding's on,'' Biba announced, handing Ian his cup. "We're going to be married in Nilapat.''

"Bully for you both!'' he beamed.

"You haven't heard from Captain Narayan?'' I asked.

He shook his head.

"When he calls remember to tell him he's expected as a wedding guest.''

"Righto. By the way, don't discuss the specifics of your plans before curious ears. Later maybe, but not this early.''

As Ian stood to leave Biba took his arm and led him to the window. She pointed to the large tree and asked, "What do you call that?''

"That's a *pipal*. . .holy tree of India. Also known as the *bodhi* tree. It is said that Gautama Buddha received his inspiration while seated under the *bodhi*.''

"Look at those leaves,'' Biba exclaimed. "They flutter as if they were alive.''

We watched the foliage gyrate in the breeze. Ian continued, "The Buddhist monks actually paint on them. The leaf is prepared to eliminate all but their fine skeleton of veins, which form a framework on which they paint colored pictures representing proverbs. Variations in the angles of lighting produce fascinating changes in the shades and intensities of colors.''

"You're a walking encyclopedia, Ian,'' Biba complimented.

"Must get on with it,'' the Lieutenant apologized as he turned to leave the room. "Cheerio. See you again.''

Chapter Fifteen

The days of hospitalization slipped by, one on top of the other. Doctors and nurses continued to make their repetitive and interminable rounds. My convalescence was progressing quite satisfactorily, both by Doctor Masih's pronouncements and my own self-assessment. There were no further threats, probably because of the close C.I.D. surveillance. David had been added to the hospital guard and visited me frequently.

Anandi Khosla, or the Nilapat Wonder as I nicknamed her, appeared to have been assigned as my personal nurse. This placed a certain obligation for her continued education on my shoulders. She consulted me quite frequently about her nursing class lecture notes. A few times after her duty hours she brought a couple of classmates to meet her "professor." She would pass on hospital news while carrying out her duties in the room. Her romantic nature was enraptured with Biba's and my courtship, tidbits of which she probably recounted in vivid stories to her dormitory mates.

"Anandi," I addressed her as she was making my bed one afternoon, "Doctor Ranjit Kaur and I are to be married next week in Nilapat." No doubt she knew all about our wedding, but I felt that a personal announcement would thrill her. "As my nurse you shall receive an invitation to our wedding."

This precipitated a paean of joy, a wild mixture of word and song. She could hardly contain herself and finally dashed out the door and down the hall squealing short unintelligible phrases.

"What in God's name happened to Anandi?" Biba stood in the doorway looking down the corridor. "Why she almost ran me down, and talking such gibberish."

Controlling my laughter, I said, "Darling that's just a little bit of our surplus happiness."

"I don't get you, Raj."

"I just told her that she would receive an invitation to our wedding."

"And that happened?" Biba turned to stare again in the direction of the disappearing nurse. "Real potent, our love, eh?" Plumping herself into my lap she put her arms around my neck and hugged.

A knock on the door brought Biba to her feet again. One of the guards looked in and then stepped back to admit Ian McVey and an attractive lady. Ian proudly introduced his wife Joyce. She had just driven down from Chandigarh. More outgoing than her husband, she conversed freely and without restraint. Her complexion showed the dual ethnic background of the Anglo-Indian.

"Where do your daughters attend school?" Biba directed her question to Mrs. McVey.

"Woodstock, up in the Himalayas," she replied, nodding toward the mountains. "Up around seven thousand feet elevation, in Landour, about two hundred miles by car."

"Actually, Joyce and I both attended Woodstock," Ian broke in. "Essentially an American institution, founded over a hundred years ago."

"That's where Ian and I met," Joyce said, smiling self-consciously.

"We understand that the Gordon's children are enrolled at Woodstock and that Doug himself was a student there," I interjected.

"Oh yes, we know the Gordons," Ian replied.

After a few minutes of chit chat, Joyce rose and excused herself. She had errands to run and people to meet before returning to Chandigarh in the morning. The Lieutenant escorted his wife to the door and kissed her goodbye.

"Anything new?" I asked Ian as he settled into his chair.

"Talked with Captain Narayan in Bombay. He sends his best to you both and accepts the invitation to your wedding."

"That's wonderful!" Biba exclaimed.

"Did the crime lab experts have anything to say about the Naya Ghadr message?"

"Nothing as yet," Ian replied. "Trouble is that just about every village has its letter writer or scribe, and many of them these days have typewriters. Something like this can be damned hard to trace."

"No leads then?"

"Yes. Actually we have turned up something," he muttered through teeth clenched on his pipestem. "A woman, probably a resident of Jullundur, worked her way into the hospital kitchen the morning you found the note. She posed as a vegetable vendor and actually sold a sizeable supply of fresh cauliflower and carrots."

"Whom would she be working for, the Naya Ghadr or the Karam Chand family?" I asked.

"Can't say yet, but regardless, we're on the alert." Ian banged his pipe on the edge of the ashtray. "Witnesses claim she was lame in the left leg. One of the girls preparing the food trays reported that a lame woman speaking in hoarse whispers appeared interested in her work. We're fairly sure the intruder had access to meal trays."

"Why didn't she just poison the food instead of placing the letter?" Biba asked.

"God only knows. Scares the bloody hell out of me!" Ian scowled. "Might not have had a chance to reach the dishes after the food was added."

"Are you tailing her?"

"Disappeared into thin air." He threw his hands up as if to emphasize her evanescence. "She wore her sari over her head while in the kitchen, an effective disguise, and even her limp may have been faked. I have a man checking out Jullundur, her home town." Ian rose and shook our hands, explaining that he and Joyce were invited to a friend's for dinner.

Left to ourselves, Biba and I sat reflectively. I broke the reverie."And how are the wedding plans going?"

"Copesetic!" She grinned happily. "Joan is wonderful! She knows so much about everything social. The decorations, with lots of greenery, are in the hands of the *mali*, Chotu. According to him this is the greatest thing that's happened since the coronation of Queen Victoria as Empress of India. He claims that his father took him as a small boy down to Delhi to witness the great event. He called it a *'Barra tamasha*—Big show'."

"Now, Biba, just a minute. That was a long time ago. He'd have to be at least..."

"He sounded truthful," she interrupted with a shrug.

"Well, I guess anything's possible," I admitted without much conviction.

"Joan's going to be my matron of honor and Jay your best man, and it's just possible we'll have an extra person or two," she added with a wink.

"You must know something I don't."

"Just perhaps," her eyes sparkled.

"Biba, what about the ceremony? How do we handle this? You're a Sikh and I'm a Christian?"

We faced each other, our knees touching. Leaning forward she grasped my hands and looked into my eyes solemnly. "Raj, in the beginning this bothered me, but no longer. We both should be of one faith, not the least of reasons being the harmony of our family. When your father accepted the Christian faith and left for America, your mother adopted his religion and emigrated with him. So, if you're agreeable, we're planning a Christian wedding."

"Darling are you sure? I don't want to...to...coerce...."

She rose to her feet and pulled me up beside her, then cuddled within the enclosure of my arms. I peeked down at her and watched the smile wrinkles play about the corners of her eyes and lips. Moving to the window we stood silently and looked on as a beautiful twilight slowly dissolved into night.

"Raj?"

"Yes?"

"Just one compromise? I mean about the wedding."

"Yes, hon."

"A Sikh priest to stand by the minister and bless us. Sort of a double blessing?"

"Why not? By all means!"

"I'll get Dad to help us select a priest."

"Then I guess it's up to me to find a minister, right?" I hesitated. "I really don't know any."

"Joan and I have a suggestion."

"Who?"

"Doctor Masih's brother is a minister of the United Church of North India. He's the padre of the Ambala church. Jay and Joan know him. In fact they occasionally drive down to attend his services."

"Sounds great." I conceded with a sigh of relief. "Say, you and Joan are quite a team, aren't you?"

Anandi and an orderly brought in two trays and arranged them on the *morahs* beside our chairs.

"She looks awfully sober tonight...her eyes are red and I'll just bet she's been crying," Biba whispered as we moved toward our seats.

Anandi barely greeted us and then began puttering about the room, putting fresh water in the flower vases, changing bathroom towels and adjusting the lights. We tried not to notice her unusual behavior but watched out of the corners of our eyes.

"Anandi, why so serious tonight?" Biba asked, tugging at her sleeve as she brushed by in her bed-making efforts.

The question touched off a cloudburst. She threw herself into Biba's arms, sobbing loudly. The comfort of caring arms slowly calmed her.

"Here, sit down, Anandi." I pulled up a chair so she could be between us. "Now tell us what is the matter."

With an occasional residual sniff, she began her story. "To the dormitory I was walking, this afternoon for rest period, and a woman comes out from bushes by the path and takes my arm. I was greatly frightened. I try to pull away but she hold me strongly." Anandi paused to regain her composure, sighing deeply in catchy bits, and continued, "She promise me one hundred rupees if I put something in your food."

She began crying again and Biba hugged her. Gradually her turmoil subsided.

"Did you recognize this woman?" I asked.

"No, never before am I seeing her." She shook her head emphatically. "And I cried out in much fright when she would not let go. Then she release me and quickly go back in bushes." Anandi's large frightened eyes sought our support.

"Alright, my dear," Biba leaned over to say soothingly, "don't worry. The woman's probably a long way from here now."

Anandi seemed perplexed. She kept looking back and forth between us, her face puckered in a frown.

"Whatever is the matter?" I asked, patting her hands.

"I do not think she was, she was..." Anandi stopped.

"Go ahead, dear," Biba urged. "You don't think what?"

"Her feet were large. Her voices are heavy. I do not think she was a woman."

"A man!" Biba and I exclaimed in unison.

"A man," she repeated quietly.

Stepping over to the door I asked one of the guards to call Lieutenant McVey immediately. The bedside bell summoned Sister Tara Muttra to the room. We explained that it would be necessary for Anandi to remain beyond her regular hours.

When Ian McVey arrived, we recounted the details of the story.

He swore softly. "They know the inner workings of the hospital, that this nurse is assigned to you. Authenticates the note you received as the real thing."

"What about Anandi's theory that it was a man?" Biba asked.

"Could jolly well be a man. The sari is a good disguise. Fits in with the hoarse voice described by the kitchen personnel."

Anandi was crying again, this time more quietly. With Biba's consolation the weeping subsided again into a series of hiccoughs.

"Did this person actually give you something to put into the food?" Ian's voice was gentle.

Anandi shook her head as she wiped her face with a handkerchief. She dropped her eyes to confide, "I tasted your food tonight."

"You did what?" I asked.

She looked up at me and repeated in a barely audible voice, "I tasted your food."

"Why?" Ian cut in abruptly.

"To be sure," she replied.

"To be sure of what?" Ian persisted.

"Poison," she countered, with a touch of defiance.

"My God! The lass has courage!" Ian looked down at the diminutive nurse with a mixture of surprise and admiration.

Biba hugged Anandi tighter and kissed her on the cheek.

"Speaking of poison, what's the usual technique in these parts?" I tried to sound casual.

"Cyanide, potassium cyanide. Not difficult to get hold of. Salty in taste. Usually put into highly seasoned foods. Powerful and sudden. A matter of a few seconds," Ian reported convincingly. After a reflective puff on his pipe, he continued, "As physicians, you may be interested to know that recently we investigated a case where the poison was used deliberately in a cough mixture, substituting potassium cyanide for potassium chloride."

"How horrible!" Biba groaned.

Pointing his pipestem at Biba, Ian suggested, "Doctor, would you please have all your meals here with Doctor Singh? Makes our security task simpler and more effective."

"I'll love that, Ian." She winked at him.

"What about Anandi here, her security?"I asked.

"Leave that to me," he proposed, stepping over and patting her hand. "If you'll excuse me, I'll get back to the dinner party."

"Give our apologies to Joyce for hauling you away."

"Will do and cheerio."

"Tomorrow's the day." Doctor Masih smiled broadly as he delivered the verdict. With my chart held firmly in one hand and his glasses in the other, he surveyed me with apparent satisfaction. "I take it you'll be going directly to Nilapat?"

"Yes, with the Clemens."

"Doctor Clemens can keep an eye on you. Just watch for any neurological changes. Don't expect any, but take care."

I shook his hand. "You know, it's impossible to put into words my appreciation of your help, professional and otherwise. Please accept my profound gratitude and extend this to your colleagues as well. And I'm sorry you missed the medical meeting in Delhi."

He laughed. "It was my real pleasure to have been able to help you, Doctor Singh, and may I add, I missed little or nothing in Delhi. As you know, the papers come out in medical journals later."

I had signed the documents on the land transfer the day before, settling the negotiations, the whole purpose of my trip to India. Mrs. Daljit Singh and her two sons were present. The official hospital photographer was kind enough to take pictures to show my parents. My aunt and cousins regretted their inability to attend the wedding, because of other commitments.

Biba and Joan had sent out the invitations, all forty-seven of them. Having agreed with surprising equanimity to his daughter's Christian wedding, Balak Singh had made all the arrangements for a Sikh priest to participate, a priest from the Ludhiana Gurdwara. We received acceptances from Doug Gordon and Prem Narayan of Bombay, as well as several of our new friends in Ludhiana. Soli and Indira were unable to come but were setting up a party for us on our way through Bombay. Jay and Joan had called personally on the Reverend Masih of Ambala, and he had accepted the honor, as he expressed it, of performing our wedding. Furthermore he had welcomed the Sikh priest as his associate in the ceremony.

The guard knocked and admitted Ian, whom we invited to join us for a cup of coffee.

"Just returned from Nilapat," he announced, sipping his coffee with relish. "Bungalow and compound check out quite well for security. Servants appear to be reliable chaps."

"What about our plans for tomorrow, the trip to Nilapat?" I asked.

"The Clemens will be fetching you both at nine in the morning in their car. I shall precede you, just in front. We shan't be taking the direct Grand Trunk but a rural back route."

The noonday sunlight reflected brightly off the newly-whitewashed bungalow and compound walls in Nilapat. Our entourage filed slowly through the gate past the *chowkidar* who came to a rigid attention for our benefit. Once within, the sudden green of the garden and trees presented a pleasant contrast to the stark white. An evacuation of the servants' quarters and bungalow confronted us as we approached the building.

After acknowledging the chorus of *salaams*, our group moved up onto the verandah, followed by a safari-like retinue of volunteer baggage carriers. Our room assignments had been worked out in detail as a matter of security, Ian informed us. As we stepped into the front room, Jay was standing like a traffic cop, controlling the flow of people and their belongings to their proper destinations. The Clemens had moved out of the master bedroom, turning it over to Biba. Joan informed us that after the wedding this would be the honeymoon suite as it boasted the only double bed. Jay and Joan were taking the smaller room just across from theirs which had been vacant since the departure of Jay's assistant, Doctor Ramesh. My quarters, the same as I had used before, would be shared with Doug Gordon. Ian, who would be joined later by Prem Narayan, was to have the room directly across from mine.

"Nothing scheduled tomorrow except breakfast and dinner," Joan announced as we sat around the fireplace drinking our after-dinner coffee. "Samuel will prepare tiffin or luncheon for anyone who is here."

"A couple of villages to visit, so I'll be skipping lunch," Jay reported.

Biba patted my arm and said, "Hope you don't get too lonesome, Raj, but Joan and I'll be driving back to Ludhiana to arrange for the rented folding chairs for the wedding luncheon."

"I shan't be here at noon, either," Ian chimed in. "A trip to Ambala to discuss security matters with Captain Karan Singh. Incidentally, he's promised to help cover the wedding."

"Well, Raj, that leaves you here alone for tiffin," Joan observed.

The blazing wood fire took the chill out of the high-ceilinged room. Our socializing continued into the night, supported by frequent replenishments of tea, coffee and hot chocolate. Finally, the congenial party broke up and we began moving toward our rooms. I escorted Biba to her room and, while she watched, carefully barred the windows and doors, then checked out the *almirah*.

"There you are, hon. Just lock the door behind me and you'll be as safe as the Crown Jewels in the Tower of London," I announced with a laugh.

"Oh, Raj, just think, soon we'll be able to live without this constant fear."

I took her in my arms. "My sweet Biba, that day can't come too soon for..." My words were smothered in her lips.

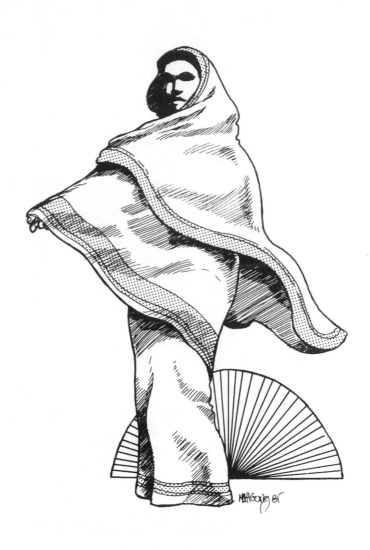

Chapter Sixteen

Consciousness returned slowly in interrupted segments like a series of clear pockets in a bank of moving fog, focusing on a point of severe pain in the back of my head. My attention fixed on the fact that both wrists and ankles were bound firmly and painfully. At first these tortures made me welcome the respite of unconsciousness, but the will to survive kept forcing me to return to wakefulness.

I began to assess the situation. I was in the back of a moving truck, surrounded by loosely stacked crates which, from the smell, contained fresh vegetables. It was night. Shafts of light from an occasional passing car flitted through the truck interior, verifying my sense of smell. I lay in the center of boxes of cauliflower, onions, and lettuce. The pain of turning my head brought a groan. Immediately a hand forcefully grasped my leg. It was then that I saw the shadowy outline of a guard sitting at my feet with his back against the truck tailgate.

With the background rhythm of a throbbing headache, the events of the past hours slowly linked themselves into a chronological chain. I had been alone in the bungalow. David had just left on foot for the local post office, leaving me with one of the guards. I was reading on the verandah when a jeep driven by a man in military uniform pulled up to the compound gate. There was one passenger in the rear seat and he engaged in a brief, spirited conversation with the Gurkha, who finally saluted and waved the vehicle on toward the bungalow. The C.I.D. guard reached the jeep as its passenger stepped out. After a short exchange he escorted him to the verandah. It was Gurdial Singh. His eyes were deeply troubled and I noted a tremor in his handshake.

"Bubli is in grave danger, Doctor Singh," he said, swallowing nervously. "You must come! She desperately needs your help!" Fear was written all over his face.

"Why didn't you bring her with you?" I was parrying for time, aware of an impending crisis which would require a quick decision.

Gurdial glanced about furtively and lowered his voice, "We were on our way here. My wife has an important message for you."

"What is this grave danger? Is she sick?"

"Yes, yes," he nodded. "She is ill, very ill!"

"And why can't you give me the message?"

"Bubli insists it must be delivered in person."

"Where is she?" I continued to play for time, trying to check out the truth of what he was saying.

"In Ambala. We were on our way here when the car broke down and she became violently ill. I took her to the home of a friend."

"Why this military vehicle?"

"An acquaintance, an officer in Ambala Cantonment, loaned it to me."

"Sounds a bit irregular, picking up a military jeep, doesn't it?"

"An emergency, Doctor Singh, it was an emergency," he repeated, his voice desperate.

"If she's that ill, why in God's name didn't you take her to the Ambala hospital?"

"Bubli refused, kept saying that it was imperative she see you first," he pleaded, mopping his forehead with a linen handkerchief.

My memory led me back to the train trip from Bombay, and my conversation with Biba. "Gurdial, I know of your problems with the Naya Ghadr," I dropped my voice to a whisper, "and you certainly must be aware that they've tried to kill me."

He winced when I mentioned the anarchists, and stuttered, "I. . .I. . .I promise. . ."

"But damn it, man, how do I know this isn't just another trap?"

His mouth moved but no words came out. He tried to speak again but made no articulate sound.

I stepped off the verandah to confer with my C.I.D. guard who confirmed that the jeep and driver were in fact from Ambala Cantonment.

Returning to Gurdial I agreed to accompany him, much to his relief. "My bearer will come with us," I announced, pointing at the guard.

I scribbled a note explaining the situation, and left it with Samuel. The jeep's motor was running when I came out of the bungalow. I jumped into the rear seat beside Gurdial and we sped out of the compound. As we drove down the Grand Trunk Road I realized that my guard had been left behind.

"What happened to my bearer?" I shouted through the noise of the wind.

He turned and looked at me vacuously without replying.

"My bearer?" I repeated loudly.

"Oh, sorry, must have forgotten him." His voice sounded strange, mechanical. I wondered if he was under the influence of drugs.

In the interludes of consciousness, my head throbbed with a bursting pain accompanied by a dry wretching. This head injury, following so soon on the gunshot wound, could be serious, I thought anxiously. A bitter wind whistled through the truck and chilled me into fits of uncontrollable shivering. Either our speed had increased or the road had become rougher, for the vibration of the vehicle worsened, aggravating my pain. A crate of vegetables tumbled down onto my legs as the car swerved to miss something, probably a bullock cart. The guard swore lustily and crawled forward to lift it back on the stack beside me. My legs, numbed by the cold, hardly felt the injury.

My amnesia was clearing rapidly. I recalled the polite but perfunctory conversation with Gurdial as we drove down toward Ambala. Our stilted dialogue soon faded into an uneasy silence. He was nervous and almost incoherent at times. It was dusk when we reached the outskirts of the city. A military convoy headed into the Cantonment held us up for several minutes, causing my companion to mumble nervously under his breath. Then we were moving again down a narrow street in the bazaar district. Our driver slowed to a crawl, carefully skirting stray cows, playing children and loitering pedestrians.

We stopped in front of a cloth shop, one of many crushed together side by side. There was no door at the entrance but on either side of the storefront stood folded metal screen barricades which, when pulled into position, secured the premises. Two broad wooden steps admitted the customer from street level directly into a small room with open shelves on either side on which were stacked a variety of textiles. The shop section was separated from the living quarters in the rear by a hanging curtain. Sitting crosslegged in the center of the floor, the proprietor was surrounded by his wares, all within easy reach.

Gurdial approached the shopkeeper. He stood under a hissing petromax lamp conversing briefly but intensely, finally turning and beckoning me to join them.

"How's Bubli?" I asked anxiously.

"She's inside, in the back of the shop." He pointed to the interior.

The proprietor looked up at me and grunted as he stuck his feet into thonged slippers. He stepped over a bolt of cloth and led us toward the curtain in the rear. Gurdial spoke hurriedly, "This is Mr. Aggarwal."

I looked up at a sign on the lintel above the curtain. It read "Quality Shop." A bursting pain at the back of my head put a sudden end to all thoughts.

The lorry careened around a series of sharp curves, causing the stacks of crates to lean and shift. My attendant struggled to prevent an avalanche of vegetables. Frequently now the engine changed in and out of low gear, and the chill of the air intensified. It was apparent that we were climbing.

In spite of my aches and pains, I managed to stay calm. After all, I was alive! They could have killed me in Ambala. The anarchists had chosen to preserve my life, at least for the present.

After a couple of hours of a slow and grinding ascent, our journey was over. Barking dogs and the smell of wood smoke announced our arrival in an area of human habitation. The lorry slowed to an unsteady stop. A door creaked open next to our vehicle and footsteps moved toward the truck. I heard the crunch of shoes on cold earth as the driver and his companion climbed out of the cab. Tantalizing fragments of conversation drifted my way. I recognized the voice of Gurdial Singh. He must have been sitting up front with the driver. A sense of betrayal, mixed with pity, saturated me.

"I've lived up to my promise," Gurdial spat the words in English. "He's alive as stipulated."

"Yes, yes. You have done the necessary," a man's voice responded scathingly, "we shan't forget." The enunciation was that of a person with more than an ordinary education.

A hoarse and rasping voice, which I took to be that of the driver, urged them to get me out of the truck quickly. He muttered something about getting back down the mountain to Hoshiarpur and delivering the load of vegetables before sunrise. He climbed back into the cab, cursing the delay.

"Gurdial, you will need our protection." The words were cold. "The entire Punjab will be looking for you."

"I know it," Gurdial choked.

"Our underground will protect you. For the time being you will remain here in Dharamsala."

"Where do I go?" He sounded defeated and tired.

"Follow that man." The voices drifted away. Footsteps crunched on the cold gravel and moved into the distance.

So this is Dharamsala, I thought. At least I knew where I was. In one of our weekend trips, Jay and Joan had driven me up into this area. A small hill town of some five thousand feet elevation, Dharamsala was a trading center for the surrounding hill people. Tea plantations skirted the lower slopes below the town giving the appearance of quilted patchwork aprons showing varying shades of green. Even more significant in my memory of the previous visit was the fact that the Dalai Lama, spiritual and political leader of the exiled Tibetans, lived here in a guarded isolation, the guest of the Indian Government.

My thoughts were interrupted by the sound of scuffling feet as several people joined our entourage, all of them apparently under the direction of the man who had been conversing with Gurdial.

"*Jaldi calo. Us admi-ko andar lao*—Hurry along. Take that man inside," he commanded impatiently.

Three men came to the rear of the truck and, with the assistance of my guard, lifted me out. A narrow flight of stairs swayed a little under our combined weight. At the top landing a solid wooden door opened and the four men deposited me unceremoniously on a bed in the center of a cold room. A small, barred window was dimly outlined by the scanty light of early dawn. I squirmed to ease myself into a more comfortable position.

Having delivered themselves of their burden, the men left quietly. One of them bolted the door from outside, then the creaking stairs punctuated their exodus. Although the window did not open directly over the main street, I could hear the lorry door slam and the engine struggle wearily. Finally, the noisy and erratic firing of the truck's cylinders outraged the quiet of the mountain air. With grinding gears, the truck started on its return. Soon the barking of dogs in the distance heralded the passing of the load of vegetables beyond the lower boundaries of Dharamsala, on its way down to the Hoshiarpur market.

The passing minutes drew into a seeming eternity. My hands and feet were numb from the binding ropes and the increasing cold. The icy mountain wind blew through the open window, sending me into bouts of uncontrollable shivering. It must have been an hour later that I heard the bolt cautiously pushed aside and the hinges squeak as the door opened. A gust of wintry air pushed over me. The door closed and a figure stood just inside. As I watched, the intruder began to approach my bed stealthily. I kept my eyes barely open, just enough to watch the approaching form. He was bearded and turbaned after the fashion of the Sikhs. Feigning unconsciousness might work to my advantage, I thought, so I lay still and breathed sonorously.

He came close, stooping low to study my face. I could feel the warmth of his breath. Suddenly I opened my eyes and looked directly into his. He drew back startled, but not before I noted that his skin carried the scars of smallpox.

"*Sat Sri Akal,*" I greeted him calmly.

He coughed self-consciously and replied, "*Sat Sri Akal.*" His voice was brusque. This was the same person who had spoken with Gurdial outside the truck.

"You're Prakash Singh, aren't you?" I decided that a direct approach might gain some respect.

"Uh-huh," he grunted, slowly stroking a knife across the palm of his hand. Almost as an afterthought, he added, "We are cousins, you know."

"That's right. And you are the leader of the Naya Ghadr." I tinged my voice with contempt.

Prakash nodded and grinned slyly, manipulating the knife before my eyes. I recognized his obvious attempt to intimidate me.

"Your behavior falls short of what one would expect of our royal lineage," I taunted.

"What do you mean?" he growled.

"Flourishing a knife at one who is bound hand and foot is not terribly courageous."

He scowled and studied me shrewdly a moment. "Royal lineage means nothing today," he sneered.

"You've tried to kill me before. Why capture me alive?"

"Our tactics have changed, at least for the time being."

I was prepared to make a desperate lunge with hands and feet if he threatened me with the knife. However, Prakash very deliberately reached over and cut the ankle and wrist bonds. The restoration of circulation was exquisitely painful and I rubbed my tingling hands and feet frantically.

"Your cause is a disgrace to our royal ancestors." I decided to push my advantage by attacking.

Prakash drew a sharp breath. I must have been on target. Could this renegade be sensitive to the fact of his disloyalty? Perhaps this was a chink in his armor.

"We may give you cause to change your mind." His voice was cruel.

"Brainwashing or torture?" I asked derisively.

"Perhaps both," he snapped back.

The anger in his voice was uncontrolled. I decided to blunt the point of my attack, lest his reactions reach beyond reason. Slowly and painfully I pulled myself up to a sitting position. We stared at each other silently.

"Would you please close that window and bring up a seat," I said calmly. "There are matters of concern to each of us which we should discuss."

My order caught him by surprise. He hesitated briefly, then pushed the window down. Picking up the stool he came over and seated himself beside my bed. The hatred in his eyes slowly changed to a sly inquisitiveness.

"Do you know what that is?" He pointed at my left wrist.

"This bracelet?" I pretended indifference, holding up my forearm between us.

"Yes." For the first time his eyes showed a hint of fear.

"It's a family talisman."

"And where did...who gave it to you?" he burst out, unable to restrain himself.

"A long story, really." I shrugged, deliberately evasive.

Prakash Singh frowned. "It is the royal bracelet, protective to those who wear it."

"You don't say?" I feigned ignorance. "And you believe that about the protective power?"

"Perhaps..." He stared at me.

This acknowledgement brought me a sense of relief. And yet there was an Achilles' heel to this psychological armor of mine. Could he forcibly remove the talisman? I must find out.

"If this is so powerful," I said, holding out my wrist, "why don't you take it from me?" I spoke quietly, trying not to sound defiant. "After all, I am your captive."

Prakash recoiled, his eyes narrowing in apprehension. "It brings only tragedy to those who acquire it by force," he admitted.

I felt a little more secure. Bubli was right, I must never take off the bracelet. I understood now why it had not been removed while I was unconscious. As the circulation restored its warmth to my hands and feet, I sensed an inner warmth as well, a renewal of courage.

My captor, his face distorted in a scowl, strode out of the room without further comment. He had lost the first round. I must take care to determine the temper threshold of my opponent and not push him beyond the point of no return.

A Sikh servant entered shortly. He brought in an open charcoal brazier and set it down in the middle of the floor. Its heat, though pitifully inadequate, was welcome. His second trip supplied me with a brass washbowl, a bucket of hot water, a bar of phenol-scented soap and a clean bath towel. All of these were placed on the table by the window. Hobbling over, I enjoyed the primitive luxury of a hot sponge bath, soothing my contused wrists and ankles. My spirits continued to rise as the warm beams of morning sunlight peered between the bars of the window. The pounding headache was subsiding to a more tolerable level.

An inventory of the room revealed a simple Indian bed, known as a *carpai*, with tightly woven hemp springs on which I had been lying, a wooden table and a single stool set up by the barred window and a high old-fashioned toilet bowl with water closet above. This sanitary complex was placed, like a canopied throne, in the corner of the room across from my bed.

There was a musty smell as if the room had been unoccupied for some time. Wafted intermittently from outside were samples of bazaar odors ranging from the pleasant aroma of cooking spices to the more pungent scent of manure freshly deposited on the street by produce-laden hill ponies.

The servant brought a tray of tea and toast. The sugar for the tea was a tattletale gray, and closer inspection revealed large granules mixed with insect legs and wings. My attempts at conversation with the young man were fruitless. He had been instructed well. Any effort to communicate only brought quick glances from eyes shaded by fear.

Seated at the table eating breakfast, I surveyed the world through the barred window. My room was on the second floor of a two-storied building. The view over the adjacent single-storied house showed the mountains and wooded hillsides beyond. By placing my face against the window bars, I could look to the side between the stone walls onto a narrow segment of the main street of Dharamsala. The morning life of the town was in full swing. An elderly goatherd, long staff in hand, trudged behind a dozen or more meandering goats led by a large and amply bearded buck with a hollow-sounding wooden bell around his neck. Hill folk plodding in from the surrounding villages to sell or exchange their wares carried cannisters of milk, bundles of charcoal, fresh vegetables and other products for the local market. Some of these items they balanced gracefully on their heads, while others they carried on stooped backs supported by woven rope straps passing under the burdens and up over their foreheads. An occasional lorry with horn blowing almost constantly ground up or down the steep road.

As I reflected on the life outside, many questions surfaced. Poor tormented Gurdial now was at the mercy of the anarchists. If only Biba could know that I was alive and. . . at least for the moment. . . unharmed. By now Captain Narayan must have initiated investigations throughout the Punjab. All of this because I had reacted to emotions rather than common sense. The only consolation I could muster in support of my stupidity was that the Naya Ghadr had surfaced.

The grating of the door bolt interrupted my somber thoughts. Prakash strode into the room and surveyed the empty dishes on the table. I remained seated while he stood, legs apart and hands on hips, staring coldly at me. His face was stamped with cruelty, but there were facial lines that might once have been handsome. The ravages of a virulent form of smallpox had peppered his skin with scars, but a full Sikh beard and mustache softened the impact of the blemish.

"Pardon my lack of courtesy. I should rise to greet you but my feet are still numb," I explained with a touch of sarcasm. "Your henchmen aren't blessed with attributes of gentleness."

He scanned my face quizzically, unable to fathom the intent of my comments. I sensed his disappointment that I did not appear to fear him. He addressed me condescendingly, "It is not our intent to make your stay here a physical hardship."

"Quite thoughtful of you, I must say, and please accept my appreciation." I smiled up at him wryly. "But I would like to ask why you're using plural pronouns?"

"Plural pronouns?" he repeated, perplexed.

"You just said something about 'our intent'." I was enjoying his confusion and embarrassment.

Prakash scowled and retorted, "There are others. . . that is. . . there are other leaders of the Naya Ghadr."

My captor stalked to the other side of the room and then abruptly swung around to face me. I sensed a touch of the ham actor on a stage. He was trying desperately to recoup his dignity.

"You will instruct the servant as to your needs."

I nodded and threw him a good-humored smile. "By the way, Prakash, may I have some warmer clothes?" Struggling to my feet, I steadied myself against the wall while both of us surveyed my crumpled and dirty suit.

"Do you mind wearing my clothes? We are about the same size."

"Not at all. . . any port in a storm," I replied with a laugh.

"Just what did you mean by that. . ." By this time my cousin was getting a bit paranoid trying to interpret the nuances of my comments.

I shrugged, choosing not to answer, and limped over to the bed.

"Do you have any questions before I leave?"

"Yes, I do. Exactly what is my particular role in this cloak and dagger drama of the Naya Ghadr?"

The question surprised him for a moment, then he said patronizingly, "This is a matter for the Naya Ghadr Council to decide."

"And when will they meet?"

"Soon, quite soon, Doctor Singh, and you will be there."

"Prakash, you should be intelligent enough to realize you can't possibly succeed in this kidnapping," I countered bluntly.

That triggered a monologue which lasted some ten minutes, delivered in an artificial and repetitive exhortation, most of which sounded like the regurgitation of memorized dogma. According to Prakash the people of India were to be delivered from the decadence of its current democracy. This delivery would of necessity be accomplished through violent revolution. As his presentation progressed I noted an ambivalence of thought, almost schizoid, which made me consider the possibility of a serious psychotic disorder. As he railed on, it became quite evident to me that Prakash Singh was a disturbed man.

Sometime during the night I awoke to the sound of a car stopping in front of the building, followed shortly by the sounds of footsteps climbing the creaking stairway. The hinges of a door directly across the hall grated open, then closed. Whisperings followed, unintelligible at first. As heated voices rose in anger, words and phrases became recognizable. Apparently two men were conversing in English, Prakash and another whom he addressed as Shivaram. Wrapping up in a blanket, I crept over to the door. By placing an ear against the keyhole, I could hear the dialogue. Shivaram's voice was forced and wheezing, as that of an emphysematous person, and his moist coughing spells frequently disrupted the conversation.

"*Rashtriya Swayam Sewak Sangh,*" Prakash pronounced each word sarcastically. There followed a pause during which the visitor's harsh breathing was the only sound. Then Prakash continued, "Yours is a fanatical fascist organization fighting for a pure Hindu society which would eliminate all minorities, including me. Now that's what I call a bloody bit of rot!" Prakash was shouting.

"Come, come, my dear chap, not so loud. Better control that temper..." Shiviram breathed wheezily for a moment. "Under present circumstances neither you nor I can afford to be so bloody independent." He broke into a prolonged seizure of coughing before picking up the conversation again. "We might consider this as a marriage of convenience, and dash it all man, we have a common enemy...the C.I.D."

"Granted we do...what the hell can you offer the Naya Ghadr?" Prakash sounded skeptical.

"Small arms, vital information, and a place to hide out in Bombay and its environs. If things get too bad here, we can help. Don't underestimate the R.S.S.S. my good fellow. After all our man, Nathuram Godse, assassinated the coward Gandhi,'' he boasted.

"So you assassinate him and bring down on your heads the wrath of all India, not to mention the world. And where are you now? The C.I.D. netted your conspirators and sent Godse and his cohort, Narayan Apte, to the gallows. And ever since then the R.S.S.S. has been forced underground."

Shivaram broke into another prolonged coughing spell. Finally, clearing his throat, he wheezed, "An informal collaboration, that's all we ask."

"Righto, then, an informal collaboration," Prakash agreed in a more amicable tone.

I heard chairs scraping over the wooden floor as the men broke up their negotiating. Returning to my bed, I feigned sleep with gentle snores, while the couple descended the stairs and stepped outdoors. The harsh sound of a motor broke the night's stillness and then gradually moved down the mountain into silence.

Over the next few days I did not see Prakash and came to the conclusion that he must have left town. My only contact with the outside world was through the servant. After breakfast he would busy himself about the room, cleaning, dusting and making up the bed. The man obviously was curious about me. I often caught him eyeing me covertly, and in an attempt to break down the conversation barrier, I would talk out loud in a soliloquy which, although not requiring his participation, did include him. This monologue was carried out both in Hindustani and in English. His interest was evident from the fact that he would deliberately quieten any noisy action whenever I spoke. Several times he actually opened his mouth as if to speak, but stopped just short.

One morning, several days after my incarceration, I spoke out to nobody in particular, bemoaning the lack of reading material. I suggested that someone might wrap the laundry or line the bottom of my meal tray with sheets of newspapers. He looked up from sweeping the floor and stared at me. Then I distinctly saw him nod. Fortunately my personal belongings had not been appropriated in the course of the abduction, so I was able to tuck a rupee note under a dish on the breakfast tray. Portions of *The Times of India*, published in Delhi a day or two earlier, began to appear in a variety of guises.

"*Akhbar mez par hai*—The paper is on the table," he whispered, looking about apprehensively. Sections of the paper were tucked under the dishes.

The communication barrier had lifted. However, attempts to enlist his aid in carrying a message to the outside always ended in failure.

The first two days of reading elicited no news relating to my disappearance. I interpreted this to be a deliberate blackout by the C.I.D.

to curtail the likelihood of panicky action by the Naya Ghadr. On the third day I found a small paragraph on the back page stating that an All India Radio executive had disappeared without trace. In the following issue an obscure item datelined from Simla, a hill resort in the Himalayas southeast of Dharamsala, gave the tragic story in a few words. Gurdial Singh's body had been discovered by a shepherd in the mountains near that town. The cause of death was referred to as foul play.

Gurdial had paid the ultimate price in spite of his efforts to appease his blackmailers. Bubli might have saved her husband's life if she had given him the bracelet instead of passing it on to me that night on the Frontier ail. But for her, mine could have been the body found by the shepherd. Why did she give me the amulet? I lifted my wrist, as I had done many times, and studied the enigmatic reflections of the two transparent garnets, their rich red beauty shining in silence, enshrouding the past and refusing to divulge the future.

Sitting at the window became a pastime, pressing close to the bars for brief glimpses of the traffic on the street. It curbed my loneliness just to see the people. By standing and looking directly down, the ground was visible. About three feet separated the walls of my building from those of the next. This blind inlet from the roadway, littered with trash, ran into a vertical granite bank in the rear. Should anyone venture into this narrow passage, there was a chance that I might attract his or her attention. Just in case, I prepared a note on a piece of wrapping paper and kept it folded in my pocket. Addressed to the Superintendent of Police, Dharamsala, the contents were brief:

> I am a captive of the Naya
> Ghadr. Please notify the C.I.D. Also
> telephone or cable the word 'Kansas' to
> the American Embassy in Delhi. The one
> delivering this chit can direct you to
> the site of my imprisonment. Dr. Raj Singh.

Chapter Seventeen

It was early afternoon, two weeks from the day of my arrival in Dharamsala. I was pacing back and forth in the room, not only for exercise, but also to warm my chilled body. Approaching the window, I caught a flash of color below and immediately stood on my toes to get a better view. A Buddhist monk, shaven-headed and dressed in saffron-colored loose flowing robes, had stepped into the alley beneath. He squatted to urinate. Quickly reaching for my note, I banged a knife handle against the bars, attracting his attention. A youthful Tibetan glanced up in surprise. I smiled and he returned the smile. An attempt to communicate in Hindustani and English ended with a firm shake of his shaven head. Reaching through the bars I dropped the note. He picked it up and stared at the writing. I pointed toward the street and repeated the word "police" several times. With a final puzzled look in my direction, he walked out to disappear into the stream of passing people.

At first I was disappointed that the lone wayfarer could speak neither Hindustani nor English, but I reasoned that the monk would probably carry the note to his superior. This thought lifted my spirits. Darkness began to soften the outlines of the objects below. I continued to watch at the window.

Suddenly the gait of a pedestrian caught my attention. The distance and the covering shadows of dusk hid the features, but the stride—a lithe, quick step, a certain rhythmic pace—all belonged to one man. David! The blood pounded in my temples and I clenched the window bars. He was in view for a couple of seconds at the most, and that on the far side of the street. Then once again he passed, on this side of the thoroughfare, his form barely recognizable through the smoke and darkness. There was no doubt that it was David. Plans for my release must be afoot, waiting only for the cover of night. My excitement was difficult to contain.

The servant entered with my evening meal and I welcomed his intrusion to nudge creeping time to a faster pace. A petromax lamp sitting on the edge of the table hissed gently as I picked halfheartedly at the curried lamb and rice. My ears strained to pick up any sound.

A rattling of the door latch tightened nerves already taut. I watched as the door slowly swung open. Prakash strode to the center of the room, glancing about nervously.

"Hello, stranger," I greeted him, carefully controlling my voice.

He fixed me with a cold stare. "We leave in a few minutes, a bit of a long trip."

"You've got to be kidding!"

"I've what?" He scowled at me.

"Forget it." My heart sank.

"Just a few minutes," he warned, and marched out of the room, bolting the door behind him.

I peered out the window, but all was dark. Putting on my shoes, I pulled the charcoal brazier close to the side of the bed and sat down to warm myself. The door opened and Prakash stepped in, followed by a burly henchman. Both were dressed warmly with overcoats and woolen mufflers. I was handed a heavy military coat and a scarf which Prakash himself carefully wrapped around my neck and head to conceal my face.

"This man has orders to shoot if you attempt escape," Prakash warned.

"I'm outnumbered, two to one," I countered.

"You had better bloody well remember that!" His face twisted into a sardonic leer.

The man's raving mad, I thought to myself, resolving not to goad him rashly. We walked down a flight of steps in the back of the building. The noise of a lorry grinding to a stop nearby drew my attention. There were sounds of a confrontation. Shouts and commands broke out.

"Diversionary tactics," Prakash whispered, with a mirthless chuckle.

The only person I saw in the building was my room servant squatting on the dimly lit kitchen floor scrubbing a brass cooking pot. Slipping out through the back door, we took a narrow, winding and steep path up the mountain slope. In the background the confusion and shouting continued. In a few minutes we were looking down on the far lights strung along the main street of Dharamsala. It was cold and the sky above was clear. A crescent moon and bright stars gave enough light to identify the trees and massive rocks on either side. There was no sound of pursuit. It seemed inconceivable to me that Prakash and his cohorts had outwitted the C.I.D. I chose not to ponder these issues for the moment and directed my attention to the sheer trails and the matter of personal survival.

In less than an hour, out of breath, we came to a narrow mountain road, just wide enough for a car. From here the going was easier for we no longer were climbing. In about ten minutes we reached a parked Landrover. A large and bundled man, whose face was wrapped in a muffler, stepped forward and greeted Prakash.

"*Motar taiyar hai, ji*—The car is ready, sir," the driver reported obsequiously.

"*Accha, jaldi jane do*—Alright, let's get off quickly," Prakash ordered.

Without further conversation we all climbed into the vehicle, Prakash sitting in the back with me. Our heavy coats fitted us into the seat snugly, which proved to be a blessing as the night grew colder. We rode in silence. The car seemed to be headed downgrade in a northeasterly direction as nearly as I could tell. We rarely saw the lights of habitation and passed no vehicles. The road bed was rough and often our driver slowed to ride over deep chuck holes washed out by mountain rains.

"A damned long trip ahead of us." Prakash muttered, breaking the silence.

"Uh-huh" I grunted.

"You will be permitted your present freedom as long as there's no attempt to escape."

"Thanks for the consideration." I reflected on the painful restraints of my ride from Ambala.

The car hit a particularly deep hole, jostling us about roughly.

"*Hasti, hasti calo*—Carefully, go carefully," Prakash barked angrily, then muttered under his breath, "Bloody bastard!"

I waited for a moment after the outburst before asking, "This long trip, just where does it lead?"

He scanned my face, probably wondering just how much he should tell. I waited, looking back directly into his eyes.

"Kashmir, the northeastern part known as Ladakh," he responded, dropping his voice to exclude the passengers in front.

"Ladakh," I repeated, happy to see the channel of communication open. This was the place where my uncle, Daljit Singh, had been ambushed and killed.

"A damn barren waste, Ladakh. Four to five thousand meters elevation." Prakash looked disgusted.

"Then why Ladakh?"

He pulled his scarf up around his face. "There's to be a strategy meeting of the Naya Ghadr leaders and that part of the country offers good security for us."

"Isolated, eh?"

He nodded with a chuckle. "You will see for yourself."

"What part do I play in all this?"

"The Council has requested that you be at this meeting. You are to be interrogated. Besides, we had to move you from Dharamsala because of the C.I.D."

"Is that right? They were on our trail?" I pretended ignorance.

"Aggarwal was taken in by the police at Ambala several days ago. The blighter probably talked." Prakash cursed under his breath.

It appeared that my captor was being quite factual in his replies to my questions. Meeting with the Naya Ghadr leaders would commit me to joining their ranks or being executed. They would not release me after a session with the inner circle of the organization. Even at this early stage, Prakash could not let me escape alive. I knew too much. So why shouldn't he be frank?

"You're forcing me into a difficult decision," I admitted.

Prakash laughed and taunted, "Not much choice, Doctor Singh." He was reveling in my discomfiture.

"By the way, how is Gurdial Singh?" I probed.

"Ah, terrible news! Poor chap is dead!"

I feigned surprise.

"Some bandit blokes in the mountains near Simla, they robbed him and then killed him." He sounded edgy.

"How was he killed, shot?"

"Goatskins."

"Goatskins? I don't..."

He drew in a breath noisily and exhaled slowly before explaining, "Take two freshly-skinned goat hides and sew them very snugly around the victim's body, from armpits to groin. Then stake the person out in the sun, spread-eagled." He paused for effect, relishing the gruesome story. "As they dry, the goatskins slowly shrink and, over a period of a few days, crush out the victim's life."

"Good God!" I whispered in disgust. There was no doubt that Gurdial's murder was engineered by the Naya Ghadr. I was seated next to a psychotic killer, a sadistic homicidal maniac. My chest tightened and a fleeting nausea swept over me.

Prakash rested his turbaned head on the back of the seat and drowsed. The two men in front conversed sporadically in low voices. I had time to worry. Why hadn't the C.I.D. contacted me in Dharamsala? Prem Narayan must have known my whereabouts. I had seen David just outside. Had the Tibetan monk delivered my note?

While Prakash slept, I wrestled with my thoughts. A persistent reflection repeatedly directed me to the Captain's letter. I tried to recall the document sentence by sentence. Suddenly the problem focused into clarity.

"That's it! My God, how obvious!" I blurted out loudly enough to cause Prakash to stir uneasily in his sleep. Even the driver gave a quick glance to reassure himself that all was in order. My optimism grew. The fragments of the puzzle were beginning to fall into place.

Joan had used the phrase "cheese in a trap" to describe my new role. That was the key. Prem Narayan had not used these exact words but his letter had described my anticipated function in more delicate terms. The apparent official blundering in Dharamsala now made sense. My continued captivity was permitted by the C.I.D. Not only permitted but encouraged. The lack of guards to prevent our escape was a planned omission. The C.I.D., with a double agent in the inner circle of the Naya Ghadr, would be aware of the time and place of their meeting in Ladakh. I was the bait.

It was up to me to act out the last scenes of this drama. Also it was essential that I be on stage at the final curtain. I would not attempt to escape. A sense of confidence and direction followed in the wake of these decisions. Soon I too laid my head back against the seat for intervals of fitful sleep.

During the night we dropped down to a lower plateau for a short time then climbed again over precipitous roads. At dawn we stopped at a roadside teahouse from which the driver procured a few *chapatis* and a large copper kettle of hot tea. We sat in the car and enjoyed the thin wheatcakes and steaming drink. As the day progressed we continued to climb and the weather got colder. The car had no heater and I stamped my feet at intervals to keep them warm.

It was the barren wasteland Prakash had described. Drifting snow was packed behind boulders strewn over the inhospitable landscape. Our road rose and fell, steeply in some sections, climbing steadily from one plateau to the next, hugging precipitous banks above rushing streams. As the Landrover ground its way to higher levels, the valleys narrowed to gorges cutting through the earth like deep incisions.

At one point we detoured through open countryside where recent monsoon rains had washed out all semblance of a road. Under the direction of an Indian in uniform, a team of Tibetans labored patiently repairing the damage. The military lorry which had brought them to work stood idly nearby. Dressed in their ankle-length garments, they dug and carried dirt and rocks sedately. As we drove by, their sober eyes followed our vehicle in goodnatured curiosity, some of them smiling at us shyly. Prakash watched me closely when we passed the military person supervising the repair.

The scenery was massive and severe. Craggy peaks, covered with snow, rose sheer from our road, thrusting headlong into a blue sky. A bitter cold wind gusted about, carrying with it the cutting and brittle edge of ice fields. Small fragments of clouds scooted by as if in a hurry to get somewhere. An occasional glacier, highlighted by its bluish-green translucence, pushed the debris of rocks and boulders down granite-walled canyons. High above our trail, a few of the Himalayan pinnacles were plumed with blowing snow, like white banners flying from mastheads. Soon dusk was settling softly about us. The snow on the peaks was caught in the last pink blush of the setting sun.

Prakash began to show signs of restlessness and irritability due to fatigue and cold, and the building tension of our nearing the conference site. The Landrover's progress was slowed both by the darkness and the deteriorated state of the branch road we had turned onto just before sunset. Two or more hours had passed since we had seen human habitation of any sort. The elevation must have been well over ten thousand feet, for I estimated my respiratory rate at twice the normal. Our driver slowed to a crawl and lowered the window to inspect a large rut in the road. A blast of icy wind gusted through the car, infuriating Prakash.

"*Khirki band karo*—Shut the window!" he bellowed.

"*Accha, ji, accha. Gav kitni dur hai?*—Alright, sir, alright. How far is the village?" The driver's voice sounded flat and tired.

"*Abi milege*—We'll arrive shortly," Prakash replied impatiently.

"We're all tired," I offered quietly. "Any idea of our quarters? Tents, stone huts?"

"Oh," he said abruptly, "an abandoned Buddhist monastery. Raiding brigands made the monks so miserable that they just fled to safer territory."

"I take it you've been here before?"

Prakash chuckled coarsely. "We were the ones who made them miserable."

We drove on in silence through the dark, our lights tunneling ahead. After another thirty minutes of driving, the faint outlines of a building appeared before us.

"There it is." Prakash pointed. His voice was touched with excitement.

As we drew nearer, I discovered that the monastery did not look as I had expected. Instead of clinging precariously to the sides of the mountain, the rather ordinary building had been built on the gradually sloping border of a narrow valley. A continuous single story structure surrounded a large central compound, the entire structure occupying about a city block. No other habitation was visible. A turbaned guard carrying a rifle admitted us through the gate after identifying Prakash. We drove into a large enclosure and parked at the far end beside several other vehicles. The monastery, which encircled three sides of the compound, was composed of a series of rooms like a motel, each opening onto a covered verandah bordering the central courtyard. The gate end of this complex was occupied by a larger structure which appeared to be a chapel for the monks. All in all the whole thing looked more like a fort than a monastery, probably a necessary design for the barren wilds of these parts.

Our arrival seemed to create little interest. It was late and apparently most had retired. A few of the servants stood or squatted around a fire in the center of the enclosure. The pleasing incense of burning wood permeated the area.

Prakash huried me to a room at the end farthest from the entrance. An armed guard, who had been leaning against the door, straightened as we approached.

"You will not leave this room without my permission," Prakash admonished curtly. "Food will be served in a few minutes." He scowled at me, then turned abruptly and strode down the verandah.

The guard looked me over curiously as I stepped into my quarters. A kerosene lamp burned dimly on a low stool in the back. My bed was a simple wooden cot pushed up against the outside wall of the room. Three rough-woven wool blankets were stacked on the foot of the bed and a metal commode had been placed underneath. No other furniture was evident. A narrow and barred transom high on the outside wall above the bed was the only opening besides the door. The walls and floor were of stone and the ceiling, which was the roof, consisted of dark shale. Patches of living green moss spotted the room. A dank odor, like that of a seldom-opened cellar, saturated the air. Even in the dim light of the lamp the heavy condensation of my breath was visible. I began some stationary jogging to warm myself.

My keen appetite was accentuated by the tantalizing odor of cooking coming from somewhere in the compound. We had eaten nothing since the few *chapatis* early that morning, so I welcomed the brass plate of steaming food brought in by the guard. Placing a folded blanket on the floor I sat and enjoyed the spicy mutton curry and rice. Having eaten amply, fatigue suddenly overcame me. I crawled between the blankets and succumbed to the slumber of exhaustion.

Chapter Eighteen

I opened my eyes to find the subdued light of early morning exploring the room. The courtyard outside vibrated to the sounds of chickens clucking and crowing, goats bleating and servants bustling about their duties. In spite of the wool blankets my body was stiff from the cold. I crawled out of bed slowly, groaning. The guard stuck his head in the door and looked me over critically.

"*Kuch cahiye, ji?*—Do you want anything, sir?" he asked politely.

"*Ha. Garam gusal pani aur sabun cahiye*—Yes. I would like hot bathwater and soap."

He stepped out onto the verandah and passed my order on to a servant. Shortly a bucket of steaming water and a bar of soap were delivered. Before I finished bathing, breakfast arrived. The menu was meager but adequate.

While eating, seated on the floor, I tried to anticipate the challenges which faced me. The critical problem was my lack of knowledge as to the strategy of the Naya Ghadr and the plans of the C.I.D. These reflections were interrupted by Prakash, who sullenly ordered the guard away from the door.

"A friend of your wishes to visit with you," he announced.

"A friend?" I asked, astonished.

He nodded and pointed toward the door. A woman stepped inside, her face partially covered by a thin scarf. She removed the veil as she stepped forward.

"Bubli!" The vehemence of my exclamation startled her. She stopped a second then moved toward me again, her face breaking into a wan smile.

"Yes," she acknowledged in a low voice.

"My God! They've captured you too!" I reached out and took her hand, leading her to the bed where we sat down. Prakash had stepped out onto the verandah, just outside the door.

"It's good to see you again, Raj." Her voice sounded so much like Biba's.

"What a tragedy, Gurdial's death." I took her hand. It was cold. She did not reply, staring ahead, her eyes showing neither grief nor fear. Had she been drugged, I wondered? Or perhaps the sheer magnitude of her misfortunes had pushed her into a state of shock. A wave of pity engulfed me.

"Bubli, I'm terribly sorry." I put my arm around her shoulders. She sat motionless, neither responding nor rejecting my gesture.

"Listen," I whispered, "I'm sure the C.I.D. are..."

Convulsively she stood, shaking herself free of my arm, and contemptuously spat, "Damn them! I don't want to hear any more!" Her voice was harsh and loud, bringing Prakash to the door to assure himself that all was well.

My utter surprise at her response must have been quite evident. "Bubli, what is..."

"You mean you don't know?" she cut in, her words steeped in sarcasm.

The horror of the situation dawned on me. Bubli was one of them, a member of the Naya Ghadr! I looked up into the chill of her eyes. And I had almost warned her of the probable C.I.D. attack on the monastery. My pulse pounded.

"Oh my God," I groaned.

"So, now you know," she taunted, breaking out into a wild laugh. Then suddenly, effortlessly, Bubli changed her personality. Once again she was the demure and gracious lady, the gentleness of her smile contrasting strikingly with the savage heartlessness of the preceding moment. It was difficult to steady my thoughts.

"Raj, we need you," she pled quietly.

"For what?" I decided to play along with her mood.

"You must join the movement. Your American background would be a great asset." She threw me a disarming smile.

"Join the Naya Ghadr?"

"Why not?" Bubli sat down on the bed beside me again.

"And if I don't?"

She stiffened and drew a quick breath. For a moment the coldness returned to her eyes. Then she relaxed and forced a smile. "Remember, Raj, we are both of royal lineage." She reached over to place her hand on mine and I felt her fingers tremble.

"Bubli, why the bracelet?" I held up my left wrist.

"To protect you." Her voice was intense. "Karam Chand's relatives were bent on revenge. I wanted you spared for our cause." She spoke loudly enough for Prakash to hear.

"But, but why not Gurdial?" I looked directly into her eyes.

She stared down at her hands folded in her lap. A strange mixture of pity and revulsion swept over me.

"Bubli, either you're mad or devilishly clever and heartless," I muttered, shaking my head.

Slowly she raised her eyes and looked at me. Her face was ashen. I watched in surprise as tears slowly formed and rolled down her cheeks. Then she rose without a word and hurried out of the room.

I sat bewildered for a few moments, trying to pick up the pieces of our conversation and fit them together. I had a strong suspicion that Bubli was psychotic. Her rapidly changing personality and emotional vacillation were consistent with schizophrenia. This awareness assuaged my earlier disgust, particularly about her husband's murder. As abhorrent as the act had been, she could not be held fully accountable.

The very real possibility of a psychotic leadership in the Naya Ghadr made my position even more precarious. A logical presentation before the Council probably would not be persuasive in an environment of mental instability. My only weapon would be procrastination, buying time for the C.I.D.

Around midafternoon Prakash appeared in the doorway. He nodded and stepped inside.

"The Council will meet tonight, after dinner," he said.

"So soon? I thought it might be tomorrow."

"All but two of the members have arrived and they are expected shortly." He sounded impatient.

I shrugged and nodded. "I'll be there."

"You were foolish not to agree."

"Agree to what?"

"Tara Kaur's request, you know, to join the Naya Ghadr."

"Well, I didn't flatly refuse, did I? After all, you eavesdropped on the whole conversation." Prakash turned and stamped out of the room.

Following the evening meal I stretched out on the cot and tried to relax. The air was chilling rapidly and I pulled a blanket over me. In the distance a mountain wolf howled into the brittle night air and a few seconds later there was a reply from someplace much closer. It was a lonely sound. Thoughts of my parents and little Leilani crowded in. In memory I again felt Biba's soft body close to mine. Thank God, they were all out of harm's way. I sent up a quick prayer for my own safety.

Heavy footsteps terminated my reverie. Prakash strode into the room and approached me. No words were exchanged. We stepped out of the door and walked down the verandah toward the auditorium. I had the fleeting sensation of the condemned being escorted to execution. Again the howl of a wolf, even closer, undulated over the compound. A dog in the courtyard responded dolefully. Then a heavy silence, broken only by the sound of our weather-stiffened leather shoes on the cold stone floor along the verandah.

I saw that the compound gate was closed, with a blanketed and shadowy sentry leaning against it. Only three or four guards appeared to be on duty about the premises. In fact the seeming lack of security surprised me. They must have felt certain of the secrecy of their gathering. Seeing us approach, the gate sentry came alive and began to pace back and forth. The draped blanket shrouded the soldier completely, but those strides? Could it be David? The tensions of the moment were playing tricks on me. Wishful thinking, I thought to myself. But then again, perhaps the trap was closing.

The guard at the council room door pulled aside the curtain, and Prakash led the way inside. I paused to let my eyes adjust. Two kerosene lamps sat on the floor near the center of the room, one on either side. There was no furniture and the Council members were seated on blankets or rugs against the walls. My escort led me directly to a small rug in front of the assemblage, facing the far side of the auditorium. A raised dias revealed a lone occupant, sitting back in the shadows. Prakash strutted forward and mounted the dias to sit in the remaining place. The draft of his passing threw the lamp flames into flickering dances. The room must have been the chapel of the monastery and probably a statue of the Buddha once occupied the center of the platform.

I felt all eyes focused on me and, save for the occasional sputtering of the lamps, there was an ominous silence. It was bitterly cold with no source of heat, and those present, except for me, were draped with blankets. The flickering of the lanterns gave the illusion of shadowy stirrings against the walls. I looked about and counted thirteen human forms and one dog, the latter stretched on the floor beside the dias.

"Raj Kumar Singh." The words startled the silence of the room. It was Bubli's voice.

"Yes," I responded firmly.

"The Council of the Naya Ghadr has convened to persuade you to join our ranks." She emphasized the word "persuade" in a way that brought to mind the hideous murder of her husband.

The directness of the statement came as a surprise, for I had expected a more delicate oriental approach with verbal niceties and subtle feinting in preparation for the final thrust. My plans for delaying things were threatened. Somehow I had to fight for more time. Should I be forced into a prompt answer, I might maneuver and cast my lot conditionally with the Naya Ghadr. But this could cause serious problems. In an anarchist group a convert could be pressured on short notice to prove his or her loyalty by violence.

The Council showed signs of restlessness as I paused. Breaking the embarrassing silence, Prakash spoke up. "Brothers, I have presented the aims of our organization to Raj Kumar Singh and our president also has approached him concerning this matter."

This confirmed my suspicion that Bubli was the head of the group and Prakash probably the second in command. Rising to my feet, I addressed her. "Tara Kaur, the channels of our blood ties reach back through many centuries. As cousins we have a common and splendid heritage. Your father, the last rajah of a long line of great men, was my father's brother. However, due to circumstances not of our choosing, we have been raised in different cultural environments, you in the East and I in the West. Now you ask me to make two difficult decisions, precipitously and under coercive threat. In the first..."

"Wait," Prakash broke in. "I shall translate for those who may not be familiar with English." He stood and spoke in Punjabi.

I continued, 'As I was saying, in the first place you wish me of the West to revert suddenly to the East. And secondly you desire to force me to espouse a cause not only foreign to my personal principles, but actually outlawed by the very nation whose citizenship you claim." I sat down and waited.

There were whisperings and movements among the shadowy forms encircling me. Bubli and Prakash were involved in a dialogue whose emotional overtones spilled out into the auditorium. Although the words were unintelligible, a clash of opinion was evident. The wailing of a wolf again lacerated the stillness of the night outside. I shivered, not so much from the eerie call of the wild or the cold of the room, as from the realization that my fate seemed to rest in the hands of two mentally unstable people.

Clearing his throat, Prakash pontificated, "A total loyalty to the Naya Ghadr will be the price for your life." I was disturbed by the poor logic which failed to appreciate the utter inadequacy of a conscripted loyalty.

I waited quietly a moment before rising to my feet. An oppressive silence suffused the room as I slowly turned and surveyed my audience. "Members of the Council," I began in a firm voice, "you most certainly shall receive a reply. However, I have a single request and that is for a delay in order that there be an opportunity for me to deliberate. I ask for a postponement, until tomorrow at this time. You must all agree that mine is a difficult decision. Whatever my reply, the future will not treat me with kindness." Prakash interpreted my statement while I sat down on the floor rug, awaiting the Council's reaction.

A persistent, unusual sound caught my attention. Barely audible, the sound seemed to be coming from the outside wall and roof. Perhaps the wind, I thought without conviction. More likely the beginning of Prem Narayan's raid, I thought hopefully. In any event, the sound would alert the others in the auditorium. I needed an immediate diversionary action.

Rising from the floor and facing the dias, I called out, "Would someone kindly clarify for me the relationship, if any, of the Naya Ghadr to the Indian Communist Party?"

Prakash jumped to his feet and moved to the front of the platform to accept my challenge. Without hesitation he launched into an emotional harangue, thrashing the air with his arms and raising his voice in political demagoguery. The ruse was working well, blanketing out the noise from outside.

As the seconds pushed ahead, my muscles tightened, anticipating conflict. I tried to listen for signals. There was only one entrance, and that was the door directly behind me. Having no weapon, I decided to remain immobile in the first moment of the attack. As Prakash droned on, my throat tightened and my mouth became cottony dry.

A stooped and blanketed figure stepped noiselessly past me. He moved very deliberately toward the dias, his outstreached hand holding a sheaf of papers. No one appeared to pay the messenger much notice. As he reached the center of the floor, just in front of me, the intruder exploded into action. Throwing aside his blanket, he grasped the kerosene lanterns and hurled them against the wall, leaving us in pitch dark. I heard footsteps rushing in from behind. Someone tackled me hard enough to throw me to the floor and then another deliberately covered me with his body.

"Do not move, sir!" The voice was David's. He was breathing heavily.

Pandemonium broke out in the auditorium with the sounds and shots of hand-to-hand fighting. I heard the clamor of combat from the compound outside. Then, almost as suddenly as it had started, the noise subsided. A single shot, like a punctuation mark, brought the drama to a close.

The ensuing silence was almost distressful. Beams from flashlights probed nervously in the darkness about us. Lanterns were brought in from outside. David helped me to my feet and we flung our arms about each other like long-lost brothers. The room was a shambles. Blankets strewn around assumed a variety of bizarre shapes in the lantern light. Two immobile human forms sprawled misshapenly against the wall. Prisoners were being sorted out and manacled. Voices were low, some still in whispers. The only loud sounds were the groans of a wounded man lying on the floor under the surveillance of a guard.

"Jolly good to see you again," Captain Narayan called out from where he was standing on the dias, automatic in one hand and a flashlight in the other."

"Good show, as the British say," I shouted back, waving both arms in welcome.

The Captain stepped down to join David and me. In spite of the broad smile, his face looked haggard and his voice was tired.

"Sorry to be so ruddy slow in releasing you," he apologized, shaking my hand with an iron grip. "Damned good show yourself, Doctor, playing along with these bloody bastards."

"Not much choice. They held the trump cards until tonight."

"Forced to move slowly, your safety you know. Worried that the cads might do you in if we pushed them." Prem eyed me grimly.

"What about Bubli and Prakash?"

The Captain turned and pointed at a blanket-covered form against the wall. "Prakash was shot resisting. Sorry, really. Now we shan't have him as a witness at the trials. Your cousin, Tara Kaur, was captured unharmed and without resistance."

I caught myself sighing with relief at the news of Bubli's safety.

Ian McVey stepped up grinning widely, shook my hand and dashed off again. Prem, David and I stepped over to a quiet corner and discussed the past fortnight. They had picked up my trail at Dharamsala within hours of my arrival. A message from the agent within the Naya Ghadr told them I was being held to appear before the Council of the anarchists. This information eased Captain Narayan's mind as to my immediate safety and he placed a close watch around the house where I was held. Following further intelligence reports that a special meeting of the Council was to be held in the Ladakh monastery, they decided to prepare for a raid on that isolated spot.

Listening to Prem's recounting of the two week's of surveillance and planning, I confessed, "Now that it's all over and the good guys won, let me congratulate you, but in all frankness there were times when the C.I.D. stocks were mighty low in my portfolio."

"Did the buggers abuse you?" the Captain asked.

I shook my head. "Not really, except for that ride in the lorry from Ambala to Dharamsala."

"Glad you didn't try to escape. We were worried to the last minute that you might just try."

"An escape really would've thrown a monkey wrench into your machinery."

"Monkey wrench?"

"A spanner, a spanner in your machinery."

"Blooming right you are," the Captain laughed.

"Did you get the note I dropped out of my window to the Tibetan monk?"

"Did we? Did we ever," he groaned. "Stopped the police just in time. The chaps were all for an immediate raid. In the interest of security we informed no one of the stake-out around you, so the local police were ignorant of our plans."

"How did you get into this compound?"

"Our agent inside and a little bribery." He smiled knowingly. "Managed to slip in two infiltrators, David at the gate and another chap at the assembly room door. We knew the exact layout before we entered the auditorium. David threw a chit over the gate giving all the positions, particularly yours, so our men knew exactly where to go and what to do. The darkness was essential for the first few seconds, hence the elimination of the lanterns."

"Worked like a charm. Headquarters in Delhi should be mighty happy." I patted the Captain's back.

"They will be. Very, very happy. Mission accomplished, as you Americans say." He grinned self-consciously.

"How did Bubli react to all this?" I asked.

"Quiet, quiet as a mouse. Actually seemed relieved at her capture. Delhi has been repeatedly instructing us that Tara Kaur should be captured quickly and unharmed."

"Poor girl, mental problems, you know," I volunteered sadly.

"She asked about your safety as soon as she was taken into custody."

"She did? That's strange."

We left the auditorium and walked along the verandah toward my room. The compound looked like a military cantonment. The bonfire had been replenished and was showering sparks high into the air. Prisoners were being loaded into two lorries parked in the courtyard.

"Biba and the Clemens, have they been informed?" I asked anxiously.

"Rather, almost daily messages, no details because of security, but sufficient to reassure them."

"Thanks. That relieves my mind tremendously."

"We've been in close touch with the American Embassy in Delhi as well as Doug Gordon in Bombay. The code word was sent the day you landed in Dharamsala."

"You knew about that, the code Kansas?"

He nodded. "Doug gave me the information."

"And my folks?"

"Doug has kept them informed."

"Prem, you sound terribly efficient."

He waved a hand in deprecation. "At this moment there's a messenger on his way to Post and Telegraph in Srinagar to inform Delhi and our friends of the success of tonight's operation."

We entered my quarters where several stools had been set up. David left us, promising to return with some hot drinks. Prem sat down with a groaning sigh and stared at me in silence for a moment.

"Raj, you know..." he broke into a smile. "I think each of us has earned the right to first names. We've been through a helluva touch-and-go situation together. Your cooperation has been crucial in our success tonight." He pulled out his cloisonne case, thoughtfully selecting and lighting a smoke. "Particularly your role as a lure. This is the first time in years that the whole Naya Ghadr Council has met together. You, my good chap, were the reason." The Captain played with his flashlight, spotting various objects on the floor.

"You've been under more than your share of pressure," I sympathized.

"Haven't had much sleep since your abduction," he admitted with a smile.

This man has nerves of steel, I thought. He had gambled for dangerous stakes. True, it was my life on the line, but if anything had happened to me, his career would have been destroyed. A lesser man would not have taken on such a hazardous job and might well have forfeited my life to the anarchists.

David returned with two large brass tumblers of tea too hot to handle without a wrap of pieces of newspaper. Prem slowly lifted his tumbler and studied me over its top through the rising steam. I sensed he wanted to say something.

"What's on your mind?" I asked.

He took several noisy sips of his drink before responding, "There was an attempt to kidnap Doctor Biba, about three days ago, possibly to bring her up here for the Council meeting."

"She's..."

"She's alright. No need to be alarmed," Prem assured me.

"What happened?"

"One of our agents tipped us off so we were prepared."

"She wasn't touched?"

"Actually she didn't even know of the attempt until we informed her. No one was hurt...of our folk...except the Gurkha who bruised his shoulder."

"Did you get any information out of the man?"

An odd look crossed Prem's face as he replied, "The Gurkha took care of the intruder with one blow of his *kukri*. A bit messy it was."

Ian McVey stepped into the room to announce that he would be leaving to escort Tara Kaur to Delhi. A military plane would fly them out of Amritsar and the Lieutenant would return to join me there the next day so that he, David and I could travel by train to Nilapat.

Memories of Bubli and the Frontier Mail returned to haunt me, as I watched Lieutenant McVey walk out the door. I thought back to my first glimpse of the royal bracelet and the soft-scented note of instructions; the striking young couple as they strolled the station platform; the distraught Bubli who visited me in my room just a few hours ago, and now she was leaving under guard for an undetermined future. I tried unsuccessfully to shed the oppressive melancholy enshrouding me.

Chapter Nineteen

For the rest of that night and most of the next day we drove down the narrow, steep and winding roads of northeastern Kashmir onto the Punjab plains. For the first few hours the rough roadbed and the darkness kept our speed to a crawl. A few times we lost our way and had to retrace our trail with a flashlight. The confining trip provided an unusual chance to discuss our situation.

"Just about a year ago the C.I.D. was able to plant an agent within the inner circles of the Naya Ghadr," Prem confided as we bounced along the road.

"And I must have seen this person."

"You did."

"Who was it?" I asked.

"In due time, my dear fellow, in due time." He reached down to flick cigarette ashes into an empty can on the car floor. "Raj, before you landed at Bombay we were aware that someone of considerable interest to the Naya Ghadr was arriving."

"This agent passed on the information?"

"Yes. Of course Karam Chand's death did bugger up things a bit." We rode in silence for a few minutes until he continued, "From this source we learned of the exact site of your incarceration in Dharamsala as well as the proposed assemblage in Ladakh."

"You know, I'm still a bit confused about the role I've been playing the past couple of weeks. Why recruit me when you already had an agent planted with them?"

"Damned good question that. It has a damned good answer."

"I'm ready to hear it."

"Over the past several months our agent's credibility with the anarchists had been deteriorating rapidly. Prakash had become increasingly suspicious, so much so that he placed severe restrictions on this person's comings and goings. In fact communications from the agent had come to a virtual standstill, until two chits were slipped out, at the risk of our informant's life, giving us the two locations, the site of your confinement and the Ladakh assembly."

"You're beginning to make some sense," I agreed with a nod.

"There was a period of several weeks when we feared our agent had been done away with," Prem confided.

"You must have known him well," I pressed my questioning.

"Yes. A very good friend and precisely because of this friendship, I've worried my way to hell and back several times over."

"Then my arrival from America stirred up the hornet's nest."

Captain Narayan nodded. "Our anarchist friends had pretty well gone underground until you drew them out again. After a bloody hard mental battle, I decided on the gamble."

"Using me as bait."

"Yes, precisely. Not exactly my cup of tea, but I had my back against the wall."

"Did my kidnapping come as a surprise to you?"

Prem drew heavily on his cigarette. "Bloody well right it did." He shook his finger at me. "Raj, you did a damned foolish thing and broke our agreed upon regulations."

"*Mea culpa*," I confessed with an embarrassed laugh.

He smoked quietly for a while, then stubbed out his cigarette in the can on the floor. "Prior to the arrival of the Naya Ghadr entourage in Ladakh, two of our agents dressed as Buddhist pilgrims explored the old monastery. From this information we developed our plans for the assault last night."

"How in God's name did you get all your men into that area without alerting the Naya Ghadr?"

Prem pulled out a kerchief and wiped his eyes, brimming with tears from the bitter wind. "Tibetan refugees work the roads all through these parts of the Himalayas, road building and repairing."

"We passed just such a road gang on the way up from Dharamsala."

"Precisely. Government supervises these activities and transports the workmen in military lorries. So we came up yesterday morning masquerading as Tibetans, bivouacked out of sight, then crept up on the monastery by moonlight."

"Did you lose any men?"

Prem shook his head. "Three of them killed, Prakash being one. Only two escaped. They ran for a jeep and got away with it in the dark."

Prem rested his head on the back of the seat and shortly was fast asleep. Following suit, I dozed fitfully. The lower elevation moderated the temperature and the dawn began extracting details of the passing scenery from the shadows. We had dropped below the timber line and scrubby trees began to appear along either side of us. A rain-carved rut bounced us into a rude awakening.

"There's one thing I want to share with you," I mentioned as we settled back into our positions.

"*Accha*." He waved me on.

I told him of the conversation I had overheard in Dharamsala between Prakash and Shivaram.

"We've suspected some collusion between the two organizations," Prem admitted wearily. "Hard to believe that two such diametrically

opposite societies would join forces. But then the pressures of government prosecution can create strange bedfellows.''

"Have you any informants within the R.S.S.S.?" I asked.

"We used to have, but no longer. At present they're mostly a nuisance
factor, with a deep hatred for the C.I.D. Bastards tried to assassinate me
a couple of years ago, but the bloody fools funked out and buggered the
whole thing up.''

"I keep thinking of your plant within the Naya Ghadr. What in the
world is the incentive for a person to take on such a hazardous job?''

"The motive, at least in large part, was revenge.''

"Revenge for what?''

"A family disgraced by the Naya Ghadr.''

"The hierarchy, thirteen of them, they're all accounted for?''

Prem nodded. "Twelve captured and one killed—our man Prakash.
Two second echelon fellows escaped. They're on the lam as you say.
Both were close friends of Prakash so we'll have to run them both
down.''

"Gurdial...''I broke off and stared at Prem.

He frowned in disgust. "Sewn in fresh goatskins and staked out to die
a slow suffocating death." I heard him mutter under his breath, "Bloody
bastards.''

"This was done by the Naya Ghadr?''

"They suspected his loyalty. Poor blighter just knew too much so they
liquidated him.''

"Then Bubli must have been involved in her own husband's murder.
Seems incredible...''

Prem chose to keep his silence and turned to stare curiously at a large
black Himalayan crow circling our vehicle and scolding raucously as if
trying to frighten us away.

"Bubli appeared to be trying to protect me," I admitted, studying the
bracelet.

"You're quite right, she didn't wish you physical harm. Prakash on
the other hand wanted to destroy you. He almost succeeded on several
occasions. This was contrary to Bubli's wishes, and unknown to her
according to our informant. Karam Chand was what you would call a hit
man.''

"Why did Prakash want to do me in?''

"Bloke probably thought you just might be persuaded to join up.
You'd become stiff competition.''

The sun was still up when our car broke into the flatlands at the base of
the mountains. Dusk was settling as we approached Amritsar, the holy
city of the Sikhs. After the partition of India, this would have been the
logical capital of the Punjab, except for one fact—it lay only a few miles
from the Pakistan border. Thus an entirely new capital city, Chandigarh,
rose in the open lands against the foothills of the Himalayas, a hundred

and fifty miles to the southeast of Amritsar.

Among the communications forwarded from police headquarters in Srinagar last night was one to a dear family friend, Doctor Pratap Singh, head of the Department of Medicine at the Amritsar Medical College. The message announced our estimated time of arrival and requested overnight lodging.

Lights were coming on as we entered the outskirts of Amritsar. The heavy veil of smoke from countless evening fires cooking meals and providing warmth, lent an aura of oriental mystery to the city. Figures moved about us in a flowing pattern, almost illusory but for the brash cacophony. Various odors of charcoal and wood smoke blended pleasantly with the savory aroma of Punjabi food. A nervously shifting pattern of vehicles passed along on either side of us. Modes of transportation centuries old blended freely with those of more recent vintage. Each pedestrian or driver challenged the boldness of the others. The nerviest of the lot, the bicycle and motorcycle rickshaws, plowed daringly through the humans, animals and conveyances. A train of camels plodded along in single file, their noses held high in haughty disdain, just as they had on these same plains thousands of years ago.

Doctor Pratap Singh and his wife Sundar met us at the entrance to their home. Greetings were warm. Ushering us into the guest bedroom, we were urged to relax with a hot bath. Dinner would be served in about an hour. David and the driver brought in the luggage. My belongings were limited to the clothes I was wearing. Something of our predicament must have been conveyed to Pratap Singh in the call from Srinagar, for neatly folded on my bed were clean clothes which fit me surprisingly well.

Refreshed and presentable, we moved into the living room where our host and hostess were waiting.

"Would it be possible for me to make a phone call to Nilapat?" I asked the Doctor.

"Certainly! The extension cord will reach to your room." He carried the instrument into the bedroom and made the connections before leaving.

"Joan, this is Raj." I fought to keep my voice calm.

"Raj!" she exclaimed tremulously, then I heard her call Biba. Again she was speaking into the phone, "Oh, if you only knew!"

"Knew what, Joan?" My heart sank for a second.

"Just knew how we all feel that you're safe. That telegram from Srinagar this morning. Oh God, what a relief."

I heard her hand the phone to Biba.

"Darling..." I ran out of words as a racing pulse pounded in my ears.

For several seconds all I could hear was Biba's deep breathing on the other end of the line. Then her words rushed out like water through a collapsed dam. "Raj, dear God, how I've prayed to hear your voice again..." she broke off with a sob.

"I understand, my love, I know. It's the same for me."

"They didn't hurt you?"

"Feeling fine, Biba. Get the wheels turning again for our wedding."

She broke into a mixture of laughing and crying, the laughter finally winning out. The phone connection suddenly became poor.

"See you tomorrow, darling," I called out before the communications broke down completely. Joining Prem and the Pratap Singhs, I arrived just as the bearer framed himself in the door to the dining room. He quietly nodded toward Sundar and she escorted us all to the table.

The unique aroma of Punjabi food was by no means strange to me, for my mother had taken with her to America the many little subtleties of Indian cooking. In the typical fashion of this land, the table was crowded with a variety of dishes, each contributing in its special way to the overall fragrance and taste so peculiar to the food. Spices are the foundation of this cuisine, a careful blending of ingredients so that the variety, amounts and even the order of addition are meticulously correct. Combinations of freshly ground spices are known as *garam masala*, the sine qua non of Indian cooking.

In the center of the table was a large platter of barbecued chicken know as *tandoori murg*, named after the *tandoor* or clay oven in which it was cooked. Encircling the center plate were many supporting servings, such as a large bowl of saffron rice; *muttar pannirf*—peas and cubes of white homemade cheese; *kheera ka rayta*—yogurt with cucumber and tomato; *pakoras* and *samosas*—deep-fried pastries filled with vegetables and meats; *naan*—thick leaf-shaped bread, and finally, *puris* or deep-fried unleavened whole-wheat bread. On a side table were the sweets and desserts, including *jalabis*—deep-fried pretzel-shaped syrupy candy; *barfi*—an almond-pistachio sweet somewhat like divinity fudge, covered with a thin edible silver leaf and cut into diamond-shaped sections; *gajar halva*—a sweet desert made of cooked wheat and finely grated carrots, as well as an assortment of fresh fruits.

The sumptuous meal completed, we settled again in the living room. Our hostess passed around a beautiful compartmented silver dish with betel nut, cloves and other spices as after-dinner condiments.

"I hope you don't think my appetite tonight was in any way typical," I said. "Not only was the food superb, but over the past fortnight my menu's been rather mediocre."

"*Mujhe-bhi. Khana bahut accha tha*—I too. The food was very good," Prem interjected, punctuating his words with a discreet belch, an acceptable postprandial tribute to the excellence of the meal.

"Ah, and don't worry about indigestion for that is why we serve the betel nut and cloves. They settle the stomach," Pratap explained.

"Coming from the Professor of Medicine, your words are most comforting," Prem laughed.

The Naya Ghadr had been the principal matter of discussion around the dinner table. Our host was better informed on this subject than either Prem or I had expected. In fact Pratap contributed some important background information about them. The Doctor confessed, quite modestly, that mountain climbing was an avocation of his and that he was familiar with the topography and demography of the Himalayas directly to the north. His last venture, just this past summer, had taken him into the area of shadowy boundaries where the interests of India, Pakistan, Afghanistan, Russia and China converge.

"Arms smuggling has become an important economic factor in the lives of many of these mountain folk," Pratap reported. "When I was last there it was an open secret that Russian supplies were finding their way into the northern borders of India, Pakistan and Afghanistan."

Prem leaned forward in his chair and pointed his cigarette at our host. "Doctor, were you able to verify these...these open secrets?"

"You sound like a scientist," Pratap replied with a laugh. "On one of our more rugged trails in Northern Kashmir, not far from the Karakoram Pass, we overtook a train of mountain ponies laden with boxes which the drivers, on our questioning, openly admitted contained small arms and ammunition."

"The Karkoram Pass is about fifty-five hundred meters in elevation, if I remember," Prem commented, raising his eyebrows.

"Quite right." Pratap nodded and frowned. "Bloody cold, little oxygen, tough climbing and wild terrain. Practically impossible to patrol."

"Boundaries in that area are ill-defined and fluid," Prem mused, reaching forward to select a piece of betel nut. "It was up there that Raj's uncle, Major Daljit Singh, was ambushed and killed as he led his patrol investigating arms smuggling."

Noticing the yawn I couldn't hide, my host suggested we all retire. With warm expressions of our appreciation of their gracious hospitality, Prem and I turned in for the night.

"*Accha*," Prem mumbled, half asleep, and then with a sigh pulled his covers up. In less than a minute he was snoring softly. Neither of us had slept for over forty-eight hours, except for occasional cat naps.

The outside door of our bedroom opened onto a small roofed verandah where David sat covered with a blanket. Although the raid in Ladakh had captured the ringleaders and scattered their followers, Prem had insisted on continuing strict security. He had bolted both doors as well as the windows and then positioned his bed between me and the outside.

I tossed restlessly, my muscles refusing to relax. In a college psychology class one of my assignments had been a paper on sleep. I remembered my final sentence, "Ah, sleep, sweet mistress of the night, whose fond embrace soothes the souls of mankind." Instead of counting sheep, I began repeating those words, like a Hindu priest chanting his mantra. It worked.

Chapter Twenty

A shout and the sound of running feet startled me awake. Jumping out of bed I ran to the door where Prem was loosening the bolt. He shoved me back into the room, slammed the door behind him and disappeared outside. Ignoring his implicit order, I made my way into the dimly lit compound just in time to see the Captain sprinting toward two men rolling on the ground, locked in combat. Coming to an abrupt halt, Prem hovered over the contestants like a referee, gun in hand, unable to identify them. Then suddenly one of the wrestlers broke loose and lunged at the Captain, only to be deflected by the interposing thrust of his opponent's body. A loud groan was punctuated by the crack of Prem's automatic. An eerie silence settled on the compound. Two bodies, almost side by side, lay motionless on the ground. Prem fell on his knees beside one. As I approached he looked up at me.

"The assailant...he's dead," he muttered in cold fury, pointing at the other form.

I bent over Prem just in time to hear him moan under his breath. The words spilled out in anguish, "He deliberately took the knife blow intended for me. Raj, he's...he's badly wounded..."he choked into silence. All the while his hand tenderly brushed the hair from David's clammy, perspiring forehead.

In that instant I became a doctor responsible for the care of a critically injured patient. Emotions were brushed aside lest they impair clinical judgement. This transfer to an alter ego, like a tranquilizing drug, eased my heartsick pain. Rapidly opening the bloody shirt, it was obvious that immediate surgery was essential. David was critically wounded and rapidly deteriorating into shock.

"Get an ambulance and alert the hospital," I urged Pratap, who was looking over my shoulder.

Surjit Singh, Professor of Surgery, met us at the emergency entrance and took over. I declined the invitation to scrub on the case. Pratap, Prem and I waited in the doctor's surgical dressing room. We said little and glanced superficially at some of the medical journals lying about. A large percolator, half-filled with cold coffee, sat on the table, surrounded by dirty cups. Prem alternately sat and stood, chain smoking. His eyes were tired and drawn with worry. Two hours passed at a crawl as we kept our silent vigil.

Surjit Singh stepped into the room under the intense scrutiny of three pair of eyes. He untied and removed his outer surgical gown and snapped off his rubber gloves before sitting down. Surveying each of us individually, he confided, "His vital signs are barely stable and in all honesty the chap's condition is critical."

"Massive internal bleeding?" I asked.

He nodded. "Used five units of blood besides the electrolyte fluids. Barely able to maintain his pressure. A large liver laceration and the portal vein was partially transected."

"Any visceral perforations?" I questioned.

"Bowel injured, duodenum and transverse colon, with substantial peritoneal contamination." Surjit Singh's eyes signaled to me the gravity of the situation. He went on to say, "We're loading him with antibiotics, slow i.v. drip, and the lab's doing a total blood volume on him now."

"The bloody bastard!" Prem muttered. "If only I could have gotten my shot into the cad a few seconds earlier."

"Join me for some toast and coffee?" Surjit Singh rose and beckoned us to follow. Outdoors the dark of night was yielding to the first light of dawn. The dining room was empty except for two nurses sitting at a table in the far corner. A resident surgeon, one of the doctor's assistants, brought a tray with toast and a pot each of tea and coffee. The pleasant smell of food and drink began to ease our tension. The sharp edge of our apprehension was blunted somewhat by the familiar acts of buttering, creaming and sugaring. My thoughts flashed back to the Los Angeles County General Hospital and the hundreds of times at all hours of the night our exhausted surgical team had rejuvenated frayed nerves and jaded bodies over hot cups of coffee.

"Does David have relatives who should be notified?" I asked, looking across the table at Prem.

"I know of none. His family was annihilated in Delhi back in the partition." He paused thoughtfully a moment. "Ahmed Kahn was married in Bombay about three years ago. I attended the wedding but there were no relatives. Lovely bride, and they were very happy together. She died in childbirth a year later. The infant also died at birth."

"Oh, dear God!" I choked. He had never mentioned the tragedy to me, even after I shared the story of Pat's death.

"Ahmed was extremely depressed for a time after this double sorrow." Prem hesitated and looked down at his hands folded on the table before him. "You know he considers me his father."

My throat tightened painfully and I bit my lower lip to control turbulent emotions.

Our conversation was interrupted by the hurried approach of a nurse in surgical scrub dress who called Surjit Singh to the recovery room. Prem turned toward me questioningly and for the first time I saw the unmistakable look of fear in his eyes.

I caught my breath as Surjit Singh re-entered the dining room. He carefully worked his tall angular frame into the chair and, scanning our faces, said, "He went into irreversible shock, a sudden turn for the worse...he never regained consciousness..."

Prem's face turned ashen and his hands folded on the table before him clenched tightly until the knuckles blanched. We all sat in silence for a moment, then Surjit Singh rose and wordlessly extended his handshake to each of us. He and his surgical team walked away. I tried to reach Prem, but his eyes stared beyond into his personal tragedy.

Shafts of morning sunlight, intensified by haze and dust, cut through the shade trees and focused down on the road over which we drove from the hospital. We rode in silence, each afraid to break into the others' thoughts.

"Ahmed Kahn should be buried here in Amritsar, where he died," Prem said, ending the brooding silence. "Doctor Pratap, will you help us make the necessary arrangements?"

Pratap Singh, obviously relieved by this evidence of easing tensions, responded quickly, "Yes, yes, let me handle it. There's an ancient Muslim cemetery here in Amritsar and a dear friend of mine, actually he's also my patient, is a highly respected Mohammedan *imam*. I'll get hold of him immediately."

"Of course I shall attend the funeral," I interjected.

"Leave the changing of our travel schedules to me, Raj. I'll do the necessary," Prem offered.

The telephone connection to Nilapat was delayed but finally came through. I gave the news of David's death to Joan who cried quietly. Jay would meet me on the following day at the station. Biba, for reasons of her own, wanted to wait for me in the privacy of the bungalow.

Imam Muhadin, his kindly face framed in a full white beard, sat quietly as Prem narrated the story of Ahmed Khan. I interrupted to describe the Delhi episode in which the Captain had saved the lad's life. It was evident that the Imam was touched by the deep friendship between the Hindu Captain and the young Muslim. I watched the emotion-charged eyes of the priest as he heard the story of David, culminating in his supreme sacrifice for the man who, many years ago, had risked his life to protect him.

"Tell me of the murderer, the one who killed Ahmed?" the Imam asked.

Prem picked up the conversation. "The assassin was a Naya Ghadrite. He was avenging the death of one Prakash Singh, a Naya Ghadr leader."

As the story ended, there was a prolonged silence in the room. We all watched the Imam slip his feet out of the delicately hand-tooled leather shoes with pointed and curled toes. He wiggled his feet briefly, then drew his legs up under him in the chair. Long closefitting white cotton pantaloons were hidden at the waist by the free-flying tails of a white collarless shirt, buttoned in front with gold studs linked together by a continuous chain. The outermost garment was an open black silk vest, weighted down in front by various objects crammed into the pockets. His head of white hair, closely cut, was crowned with a low flat-topped round cotton hat, whose sides were brightly embroidered with flowers and leaves.

Imam Muhadin squinted and surveyed the audience solemnly, ducking his head and looking over small silver-rimmed glasses. "The funeral of Ahmed Khan will be held at nine o'clock tomorrow morning in the Muslim cemetery. I shall arrange for the grave, the simple wooden casket, and I personally shall perform the burial ceremony. My community will accept no recompense for these services and we shall care for the grave as we do the others."

With these words, spoken in a very precise but accented English, the Imam uncoiled his legs from under him, slipped on his shoes, walked around the room to bid each of us farewell and left.

"I offered to drive him home," Pratap said, "but he would have none of it. Imam Muhadin is a very influential man in these parts, both in the Muslim community and in the other religious sects. As you are aware, we are very close to the Pakistan-India border here in Amritsar. At the time of partition with its murder and terrorism, the Imam refused to leave India. He remained, under great personal danger, and worked with Sikh and Hindu leaders here to protect the persecuted of either side. At the risk of his life he organized the smuggling of Muslims to Pakistan and Sikhs and Hindus to India. You can understand why he is respected by all elements of our society."

That afternoon Prem and I drove down to a shop recommended by Sundar and I outfitted myself with a suit and other necessary items. Returning home we found that our hostess had called in a *darzi* or tailor who made the necessary alterations on the spot. He brought with him his own hand-driven sewing machine, and sat on the floor of the bedroom, ripping apart seams to readjust them for perfect fittings. Once again I felt adequately dressed to move about comfortably in society.

It was a brisk and sunny November morning as the three of us drove out to the cemetery. We parked the car outside the walls and walked through the gate and on to the far side where several people were gathered about an open grave. As we approached the site, Imam Muhadin stepped forward to greet us. The plain and unpainted wooden casket rested by the burial site.

As the Imam chanted the rituals, my mind turned back to my many days with the young man whose life had just ended. He who appeared to love life so fully now lay a corpse in that wooden box. His had been the supreme sacrifice, given unflinchingly, the repayment in full of a debt incurred at Subzimundi. As I stood reflecting, a consuming sadness overwhelmed me and uncontrolled tears coursed down my cheeks. A hand sought and grasped mine. I looked up into Prem's face, also wet with tears. We stood weeping quietly as the casket was lowered into the ground.

Driving back, Pratap reflected out loud, "A most unusual funeral. A Hindu, a Christian and a Sikh as the chief mourners at the graveside of a Muslim. And all four of us the products of this great Asian sub-continent."

As we climbed the front steps of the bungalow, another car pulled up into the driveway behind us and Imam Muhadin got out. Pratap invited us all into the house where, as on the day before, we sat down to converse over cups of tea.

"Captain Narayan, should you ever find relatives of Ahmed Khan or have any reason to contact me, here is my name and address." The Imam handed him a calling card.

"You must realize I am deeply indebted to you," Prem said quietly.

"I've a special request to make of you, Mr. Muhadin," I said.

"Yes?" The Imam squinted at me over his glasses.

"Do you place any kind of an inscription on the headstone?"

He studied me thoughtfully for a moment. "Our graves are simple and austere. Nothing resembling living forms lest they be considered as idols. But why do you ask?"

"Perhaps I'm presumptuous, and if so excuse me. I would like to suggest a few words to be placed on the marker at the gravesite."

"And what might those words be?"

"'Greater love hath no man than this, that a man lay down his life for his friends.'"

Imam Muhadin sat in silence a moment, his eyes closed. Then he murmured, "How very appropriate. I am truly touched by your selection."

"Thank you. I'm glad you like the verse," I offered quietly.

"Doctor, I am sure you must know the source of those words?" There was the faintest of teasing twinkles in the Imam's eyes.

"They're from the Christian scriptures." I replied, adding quickly, "but possibly not proper for a Muslim grave."

"Tut, tut, my young friend. Truth is truth and beauty is beauty, wherever one finds them." He smiled puckishly and shook his finger at me. "You see, I wrote my religious thesis on the comparative studies of the Koran and your New Testament." He leaned forward to say in a stage whisper heard by all the room, "You will find the quotation in the fifteenth chapter of the Gospel of Saint John. The words will be inscribed on the headstone."

"Thank you."

The Imam continued, "I was moved deeply by the funeral service. Having lived through partition and its aftermath of hatred and evil, all vented solely on the basis of religious differences, I felt the warmth of a benediction settle over the grave this morning. The three of you joined in mourning over the death of Ahmed Khan, yet each of the four, three living and one dead, were of different oriental faiths." He paused to scan our faces. "I observed the tears of sorrow and prayed that Allah would accept them as an expiation for the hellish animosity that tore our land apart a few short years ago."

We all sat in silence for a moment, broken abruptly when Imam Muhadin jumped to his feet, bidding us farewell and exiting hastily.

Expressing our appreciation to the Pratap Singhs for their gracious hospitality, Prem and I drove to the airport, where the Captain would catch his flight to Delhi and I would pick up Lieutenant McVey, who was to act as my personal bodyguard from this point until I left India.

On the way to the railroad station, at my request the driver detoured to permit me a look at the Golden Temple. I had hoped to visit inside this shrine of the Sikhs, but there was no time. The Temple was smaller than I had expected, but more than made up in beauty for what it lacked in size. Like a golden lotus, it rose out of the center of a small lake. A short causeway, beginning in an ornate arch on the shore side, led across the water to the Temple. The building was crowned by a central dome surrounded by four minarets, one at each corner. Bordering the esplanade about the shrine were several smaller canopied minarets raised on supporting pedestals. I stood in reverent silence and watched the still water mirror the golden beauty of the spiritual home of the Sikhs.

Chapter Twenty-One

It was dark when the Delhi Express pulled into Nilapat. The platform lights outlined Jay, cowboy hat tilted back on his head and arms folded across his chest, leaning against the station signpost.

"Raj, you maverick son of a gun!" Jay's enthusiastic bearhug actually hurt.

"How're the gals?" I asked as my breath returned.

"Great, both just great! Man, that Biba's going to eat you up alive. She's been as excited as a coyote dancing on a rattler."

The Gurkha saluted as the jeep swept through the gate and into the compound. Samuel, the cook, Ganga Ram, the sweeper, and Chotu, the gardener, fell upon us almost before the vehicle had come to a stop. Handshakes and greetings made the rounds. Again I felt the deep sense of David's loss.

I barely had stepped into the front room before Biba was in my arms. Her warm lips and the softness of her body against mine wrenched me out of the unpleasant recent past into the exquisite joy of the present. We clung together for a moment, lost in our own little world of ecstasy. "Feel like an intruder," Joan said, putting her arms around my neck and kissing me.

Jay joined us, rubbing his hands briskly before the burning logs. "No need to tell you, this place has been like a morgue these past few weeks. Raj, for God's sake let's quit this cops and robbers business, O.K.?"

"Not my doing, you old cowpoke," I countered, grinning sheepishly.

"Same room," Joan announced. "Chotu just put your bag in there. Not much luggage this time, eh?"

"Left in a hurry. No time to pack." We laughed.

"Let's wash up and meet here in a half hour for some drinks before dinner," Jay proposed, waving his hand in a sort of benediction.

A hot bath and a change of clothes further improved my outlook on life. I returned to sit alone before the crackling flames. The soft moonlight flowed in gently through the windows. The pacing footfall of the guard on the verandah offered sober evidence of the continued security. My thoughts returned to the darkness of that early dawn, which seemed so long ago, and the first ride from the Nilapat station with Jay. Vivid memories persisted of the shifting lights and shadows as our vehicle turned into the compound. I had experienced an unexplainable revulsion, a feeling that evil stalked the grounds. Tonight a twinge of that same nagging fear was compounded with worry for Biba's safety. But why worry, I thought. The Naya Ghadr leadership is broken up and Prakash is dead. Of the two who escaped, only one survives. However, the fact that one *goonda* was free preyed on my mind.

In the midst of my reverie, Biba came up from behind and put her hands on my shoulders. I looked up and our eyes met. Her long black hair tumbled free to frame the beauty of her face. Moving around, she sat on my lap and I breathed deeply of the fragrance of jasmine.

"Biba, our wedding..." I began.

"It's all set," she interrupted.

"What do you mean by that?"

"Joan and I started planning again the moment we got the telegram from Srinagar."

"And when's the day?"

"Day after tomorrow."

I broke out laughing. "Biba, how in the world did you do it so quickly?"

"Alexander Graham Bell's great invention, the telephone. Just called up our old guest list. Raj, everyone's delighted."

"I can't believe it."

"You'd better believe it because in two days we'll be married." We laughed together.

"Darling, I've a couple more guests to add to our wedding list. Doctor and Mrs. Pratap Singh and Imam Muhadin, all three from Amritsar." I told Biba about the three new guests.

"How can I contact them?"

"I pulled out a card from my wallet. "Here's Pratap's address and phone. They can get us in touch with the Imam."

Biba held her wrist down toward the fire to see the time. "It's not too late, I'll try and get them now." She jumped off my lap and headed for the phone.

Ian McVey sauntered in from the verandah where he had been checking with the guard. Sitting beside me he quietly began filling his pipe. Neither of us spoke at first, but I noticed him looking at me mysteriously several times.

"What's on your mind, Ian?" I finally broke down and asked.

"I've an announcement to make when we all get together," he replied.

Jay joined us before the fire, sinking into his chair with a loud yawn.

"Where's Joan?" I asked.

"Oh, she's checking the laundry with the *dhobi*, you know, counting off the items, six shirts, four sheets, thirteen towels," he broke off with a laugh. "What was it Mark Twain wrote? Something about the *dhobi* breaking rocks with shirts."

The electric power went off and Samuel began lighting and setting up the kerosene lamps.

"Sorry about the electricity," Joan apologized, walking into the room.

"Same problem in Chandigarh, electric power failure," Ian commented. "The power plant, Bhakra Nangal right north of us, just can't meet all demands. Delhi uses too much, particularly in the hot season."

"Imam Muhadin and the Pratap Singhs are coming to our wedding," Biba called out from the dining room. "They'll be down on the morning train on the day of the wedding."

Biba joined us in the circle of chairs about the fireplace. Ian relighted his pipe and drew on it vigorously, then rose from his chair and walked over to lean against the mantel beside the fire. We all sensed that he had an important announcement to make.

"A few minutes ago I had a call from Captain Narayan in Delhi." The Lieutenant paused dramatically. "He'll be arriving tomorrow afternoon to attend the wedding, and the Captain will be bringing a guest."

"Who?" Biba and Joan asked in unison.

Ian slowly and tantalizingly tamped down the tobacco in his pipe bowl. He looked around and muttered, almost to himself, "A bit strange, I must say."

"Ian, for God's sake, man, quit stalling. Who is he bringing?" Jay exploded in exasperation. We broke out laughing at his outburst, easing the building tension. Then all eyes focused on Ian.

"Tara Kaur, Bubli," he announced in a low voice.

A stunned hush followed the statement. We all stared at Ian in astonishment.

"It's cruel, absolutely cruel!" I broke the silence. "Why harrow the poor woman now. My God, she's sick, mentally ill."

Ian again waved us to order and we sat waiting for him to continue. "Bubli was the C.I.D. undercover agent with the Naya Ghadr."

"Then Bubli wasn't an anarchist," Biba whispered.

After the first shock wave of his announcement had subsided, Ian continued, "Tara Kaur infiltrated the Naya Ghadr about three years ago. By the sheer force of her bravery she fought her way to the top of the organization. Before joining their ranks she met with the Director of the C.I.D. and informed him of her plans. He tried to dissuade her because of the extreme danger."

"Poor Bubli," Biba murmured. "She's been through hell."

"Ian, why did she do it?" I asked.

"The Naya Ghadr was destroying something very precious, her husband and her family name."

"God, what a gal!" Jay broke in.

"The identity of Tara Kaur was a well-kept secret known only to a very few of the people in the C.I.D. Of course Prakash knew who she was but did not realize—at least not in the beginning—that she was an agent of the C.I.D. For three years now, at the daily risk of her life, she's been feeding us invaluable information about the Naya Ghadr."

"But Ian, her psychotic role playing?" I asked.

He took a couple of leisurely puffs at his pipe before replying, "Over the past several months, and increasingly so since your arrival, Bubli's cover was becoming precarious. And during the past fortnight, while you've been a captive, Prakash has definitely suspected her loyalty to the cause. Bubli was fully aware of this change and informed us of the added danger, not only to her but to you as well." The Lieutenant aimed his pipestem at me.

"Let's get back to her schizophrenic symptoms" I persisted.

"Realizing this critical change in her position, our medical consultant advised her to feign psychotic episodes and play on the superstitions of certain members of the Council. She was given explicit instructions on the symptoms of schizophrenia. In this part of the world there are those who consider insanity as a touch from the Gods."

"What about Gurdial's murder? Bubli couldn't have sanctioned that, could she?" Biba asked.

Ian shook his head. "No, she had nothing to do with his murder. We now know that Prakash, in a test of strength, contrived and ordered Gurdial's death."

"That varmint Prakash got what was coming to him," Jay muttered.

"Gurdial had guts of a sort," Ian continued, "and secretly kept undermining certain of the anarchists efforts. This was his way of getting even with them for the blackmailing. Bubli knew nothing of her husband's murder until it was done. Obviously, she was grief-stricken, but didn't dare strike at Prakash lest it precipitate an immediate showdown. Such a crisis not only would have jeopardized the success of the Ladakh raid, but probably would have resulted in her and your deaths."

"Where is Bubli now?" Biba asked.

"In Delhi. Under cover and well protected. Remember that there's one anarchist still free and Bubli's become a prime target."

"But Ian, won't this be dangerous? Exposing her at our wedding?"

He looked at me thoughtfully. "She wanted very much to see both of you. Then too there was. . ." he seemed to run out of words.

"There was what?" I persisted

Ian chewed soberly on his pipestem before responding, "She has other reasons. . .very definite reasons. But then you'll all find out later." It was evident that he wanted to drop the subject.

Biba turned to Joan, "Bubli will be one of my matrons of honor."

"That'll leave Jay and me against the three of you," I said in mock fear.

"That's all been taken care of," Biba said with a mischievous look. "Prem will make a good addition to the wedding party, and that'll make three of you."

Noting a pull of apprehension about Joan's face I asked her, "You worried about something?"

She laughed self-consciously. "Oh, probably nothing really, but the dhobi appeared a bit absent-minded as we went through the laundry just now."

"So?" Ian perked up.

"Well, it seems the regular rickshaw walla whom he uses to bring our washed clothes here, couldn't be found this morning, and a stranger sort of insisted on being used as a substitute."

"Why did he tell you this?" Ian pressed.

"Ganga Ram had just told him there were goondas about."

Ian jumped up. "They're still here, the Dhobi and the rickshaw walla?"

Joan nodded. "Haven't paid them yet and they're both waiting behind the kitchen."

Samuel came in with a log for the fireplace and after stirring the embers, producing showers of sparks, he laid the wood down on the coals. We watched in silence as the flames leaped up into the chimney.

"The wedding plans are moving along well," Joan interrupted our thoughts. "Most of the guests will be arriving tomorrow or early the next morning."

"What about the cooking?" I asked.

"Samuel and his wife will have help for the 'wedding feast' as he calls it. The meal will be served after the ceremony outdoors under the shamiana tent."

"Those shamianas," Jay broke in, "wild, wild colors. Looks like a huge patchwork quilt. Really quite attractive."

"How many guests?" I asked.

"About forty for the meal," Joan replied. "We've broken them down to thirty-two non-vegetarians, five vegetarians, and three strictly vegetarians."

Ian stepped back into the room and stood by the fireplace knocking out the ashes from his pipe bowl. "Silly bounder, that rickshaw walla, too damned smooth-tongued. Dhobi chap sounds honest."

"We've had the same dhobi from the time we first arrived here," Joan volunteered.

"I've let them go but, as you Americans say, we'll be tailing them."

"There's something about that rickshaw fellow that's vaguely familiar."

"His dress?" Ian asked.

Joan shook her head thoughtfully. "No. Something about his looks and voice, but then it's probably my imagination." She shrugged.

At dinner that night a happy banter pervaded our conversation. With the electricity still off, the soft lights of kerosene lamps lent a casual atmosphere to our meal. After some urging, Ian sang a Scottish ballad in a good baritone voice. The camaraderie spilled over into the front room where we gathered before the crackling fire and shared personal tales of the past, running the gamut from humor to pathos. Finally the party broke up and Biba and I were left alone sitting on a sheepskin rug before the fireplace.

"Darling," Biba said softly, "I know you're worried about my safety, but...well in the first place I've a sort of inward assurance that we'll return to America together. Sort of a woman's intuition, if you will." She looked into my eyes for understanding.

"I'm with you, hon."

"In the second place, let's not forget that I'm the one who proposed that we be married here in India."

"Getting back to your woman's intuition, I wouldn't think of disregarding it."

"Even though it can't be proven by the yardstick of scientific investigation?"

"Darling, the dearest and most profound treasures of our lives will fall into that category, those things that can't be proven scientifically."

"You're so right," Biba sighed. "How does one prove things like love, hope, faith...?" She turned on the rug and laid her head on my lap, looking up at me. "Raj, when did you first fall in love with me?" Her voice was quiet and serious.

"At our first meeting. That night on the Frontier Mail." I leaned down to kiss the tip of her nose. "And what about you?"

"That same night."

The fire burned low. Outside, the intermittent barking of village dogs and the steady monotonous beating of a lone drum were the only sounds. The soft rays of an almost full moon fell as a benediction on the trees in the compound.

Chapter Twenty-Two

The roar of the jeep motor brought a sudden end to my sleep. It was still dark outside and I remembered that Doug Gordon, arriving on the Frontier Mail, was due to be picked up at the station. I followed the sound of the vehicle down the driveway, through the compound gate and on into town, finally losing the harsh sound in a distant purr. The bungalow and its environs fell silent again but, unable to sleep, I lay quietly in thought.

Bubli would arrive this afternoon. What utterly different circumstances would surround our meeting today as compared with our last confrontation in Ladakh. In a sense it seemed preposterous that Bubli would be one of Biba's bridesmaids. Certainly her own emotional adjustments must be difficult in the extreme. But then, as only women knew how, Biba and Joan would temper the trauma of recent events. Bubli's immediate personal danger must have been clear to her and the C.I.D. Perhaps she was functioning as a lure to any remnants of the Naya Ghadr. What bitter gall it must be to the anarchists to discover that she, their leader, was an undercover agent. This fact would place her life in even greater jeopardy than either Biba's or mine. Paradoxical as it might be, here we were, the three of us, and each a prime target. Was it wise, or even reasonable, for us to gather like this? It was too late to change plans. The die was cast. Shedding my grim thoughts I jumped out of bed to prepare for the day.

As usual the Frontier Mail was punctual. I heard the jeep arrive, its lights searching through the window as it turned into the driveway. Soon Doug, all smiles and hand outstretched, stood in the doorway. Jay brought in his suitcase and I helped Doug settle in.

Dressing quickly, I stepped into the front room to relish the cheery warmth of the fire. An early dawn was erasing the ill-defined shadows about me. I could hear Jay singing happily, although a little off key, in the Clemens' room. There were stirrings in the kitchen presaging breakfast. I rotated, like a chicken baking on a spit, warming all sides of my body.

"What a fire!" Doug exclaimed, walking up rubbing his hands vigorously. "The Punjab in November's hard to beat. I'll bet we'll see snow on the Himalayas when the sun rises."

"Doug, before I forget, thanks so much for keeping my folks informed. Biba wrote them regularly but your notes were thoughtful."

I saw Biba step into the room and turned to greet her. She was wearing a black pongee suit with a white silk shirt, the tailored coat edged with white braid. No Parisian collection was ever modeled with greater distinction or grace. She put both hands on my shoulders and raised her lips to mine.

"Biba, this is Doug Gordon," I presented her proudly.

Biba shook his hand and, tipping her head coquettishly, said *"Namaste, ji, ap kaise hai*—Greetings, sir, how are you?"

"Mai bahut accha hu, dhanyavad—I am very well, thank you," Doug responded without batting an eye.

We all laughed, for Hindustani was a second language to all three of us. It seemed incongruous somehow, two of us of Indian heritage but born and raised in the West, and Doug, of Western heritage born and raised in India.

"I apologize for not being quite authentic, I mean for shaking your hand rather than placing my palms together in obeisance. Call it a compromise, if you will, of the East and West," Biba said.

"After meeting you, Biba, if I may call you that, my regard for Raj's judgement has risen a hundredfold." Doug complimented. "We three have much in common—I also am a compromise of the East and West."

"Please do call me Biba and I shall call you Doug," she replied, her eyes laughing.

Samuel vigorously rang a hand bell announcing breakfast. The sun shafted its slanting rays through the compound trees. Spirits were high as the six of us gathered about the table. Doug had met the Clemens at Landour and the McVeys at Woodstock, so no introductions were needed. The conversation turned to plans for the day. Ian would meet the Captain's and Bubli's train at around two in the afternoon. Jay was to supervise the setting up of the shamiana with its tables and chairs. Joan would have her hands full overseeing the preparation of all meals, not to mention the conversion of the front room into a wedding chapel. Ian expressed his firm orders that Biba and I remain indoors.

As we all rose to leave the breakfast table, Ian raised his hand for attention. "Just a couple of words about security. Only two doors in the bungalow will remain unlocked, the main entrance and the kitchen. A guard will be at these doors at all times. As you know each of the four bathrooms has an outside approach. These will be kept locked, barred from the inside."

"But Ian, what about hot water brought in by Ganga Ram?" Joan pled.

"Clearance for entry into the bungalow has been given Samuel and his wife, Ganga Ram and Chotu. These people will enter the building only through the guarded kitchen door. If problems arise just let me know."

"Good plan, Ian," Jay nodded, "but tomorrow's going to be a sidewinder. All those people in the compound. How in blazes can you keep up security?''

"Captain Karan Singh of Ambala has promised me some men from his police force. Prem and I'll have four C.I.D. men besides ourselves. All transportation except ours will remain outside the compound."

While Jay, like a circus roustabout, struggled outside with the shamiana, Joan and Chotu, with the indentured services of Biba and me, were reconstructing the front room. Shortly after noon the transformations, indoors and out, were complete. The many-colored shamiana stood on the front compound like a circus tent, all set for the wedding dinner. The front room had been converted into a lovely wedding chapel with rows of folding chairs, and an improvised lectern almost hidden in the foliage of potted plants and paper bunting.

"Raj, you look a bit tired. Why don't we take a short nap before Bubli arrives." Biba and I had just finished a light lunch.

"Sounds like a good idea for both of us." I concurred with a yawn. "I'll wake you up in time."

I found Doug stretched out fast asleep. The bungalow seemed exceptionally quiet, but then I realized that most of us were enjoying that delightful Indian custom of an afternoon rest. Against this noiseless background, I heard voices, low and earnest, just outside the bathroom. Intrigued by the apparent seriousness of the conversation, I stole to the window and listened. Two men were speaking in Hindustani. I could see neither one of them. "*Phir jaldi milege*—We'll meet again soon," were the only words I heard. The men must have moved away. By the time I had opened the door to look out, they were gone. Such easy access to the edge of the bungalow would mean that at least one of them was a recognized servant.

As I knocked on Biba's door she opened it and stepped out. She had changed into a light blue sari of Banaras silk.

"Raj, you're staring," she said with a laugh.

I took both her hands in mine to say, "Sweet, I just can't keep up with you. You're a woman of many changes, a gorgeous chameleon."

"I hope that's a compliment," she grinned.

Ian joined us just as Prem and Bubli stepped through the front door. Biba engulfed Bubli in an embrace and Prem moved toward me with a broad smile and a prolonged handshake.

"Gentlemen, it's most important that Bubli, Raj and I have a short private meeting...a family affair," Biba announced, waving the two officers off with one hand and taking Bubli in tow with the other.

The three of us stepped into the master bedroom and I closed the door behind. Biba and Bubli fell into each other's arms and tears flowed freely. Slowly the weeping subsided to a few catchy sniffs and sighs. We talked then, talked of recent sorrows, present fears and future hopes.

"Thanks for the bracelet, Bubli," I said, exposing the silver amulet. "It probably saved my life more than once. But now's the time to return it.''

She stared past me for a moment as if in another world. Biba gently touched her hand and she focused her eyes on mine, studying me thoughtfully. "It's yours, Raj. It has your name inscribed on it.''

"Mine?'' I said in surprise.

Bubli's features softened with a smile and she nodded slowly. "Please keep it and don't remove it until you're out of India.''

Biba and Bubli sat side by side on the edge of the bed while I rocked in a rattan chair. The two were so much alike. Even their voices carried the same vibrant qualities. Both were beautiful, with finely sculptured features. The past three years had taken their toll on Bubli. Harsh lines spider-webbed her forehead. Prematurely gray streaks ravished her raven-black hair. Under her gentle smile, I saw a granite firmness.

"Raj, I was worried sick over your safety,'' she confided, drawing a deep sighing breath. "When I realized that my leadership over the Naya Ghadr was being challenged and because of this your life was jeopardized, well, I almost lost my mind. Then came the blow with Prakash ordering Gurdial's murder... it...'' she broke off and buried her face in her hands to weep silently. Biba placed a comforting arm around her shoulders until the heaving sobs quieted. "Sorry,'' Bubli murmured. "The tension just caught up with me.''

I moved over to sit on the bed beside Bubli. Taking her hand in mine, I asked, "Why didn't you let me know that morning in Ladakh when you came into my room?''

"Let you know what, Raj?''

"That you were an agent of the C.I.D.''

"It would have been sheer suicide, death for both of us, if I'd tried to communicate with you. Prakash was listening to every word and probably wishing we would try to do just that. In fact at one point you scared the hell out of me.''

"When I tried to tell you about the C.I.D.?''

Bubli nodded. "I thought you might give everything away, ruining the chances for a successful raid. That was when I started ranting, remember?''

Sensing the need for a change of topic, Biba jumped off the bed to announce, "I almost forgot, you're to be one of my matrons of honor.'' The look of utter surprise on her face sent us into gales of laughter.

"I take it that saris will be in order. Any particular color scheme?'' Bubli recovered quickly.

"We'll talk it over with Joan,'' Biba suggested.

The buzz of conversation in the dining room came to an abrupt halt as we stepped out of the bedroom, I with a lady on each arm. Jay and Joan joined us, and Bubli was introduced to those who had not met her.

"Gosh, you sure look alike. Like two fillies from the same mare,'' Jay said, grinning broadly.

"For goodness sake, Jay, your cowboy language might not be understood in..." Joan broke off and started laughing in spite of herself.

Bubli laughed until the tears came. "Well, we are cousins, you know, Biba and I," she said when she could speak again.

"No offense intended, ma'am," Jay apologized with a twinkle in his eyes. "In my country that would be a compliment."

The three ladies left the room together, absorbed in plans. I joined Prem and Ian who were engrossed in serious conversation in one corner.

"How's Bubli adjusted since the Ladakh raid?" I asked Prem.

"Far better than I'd expected," he replied, removing a cigarette from the cloisonne case.

Both men listened closely while I recounted the conversation outside my bathroom.

"They spoke Hindustani, you're sure?" Prem asked.

"Yes, but why?"

"Usually the Sikhs will converse among themselves in Punjabi. I would conclude that probably one of the men, and possibly both, were not Sikhs."

Ian agreed that at least one of them must have been some person accepted by the guards and with free access to the bungalow. Prem suggested that Sergeant Major Sardar Khan check the matter out immediately, and Ian left to carry out the order.

Prem glanced around self-consciously and asked, "Raj, about this best man thing, just what am I to do?"

I chuckled and slapped his back. "So Joan got to you. Great! No problem, really quite simple."

"*Accha.*" He looked relieved.

"Your being my best man will mean a lot to us, Prem."

Joan was ringing the hand bell to get everyone's attention. The guests, minus Ian McVey, gathered to hear the announcement.

"We'll all meet in this room for the rehearsal in an hour, that is, all the members of the wedding party. Of course all of you are invited to watch, if you wish." Jay leaned over and whispered in Joan's ear. She smiled and added, "Oh yes, the rehearsal dinner at eight o'clock includes all of us."

Ian joined Prem, Biba and me shortly after. "Sardar Khan's checking the servants. Should report back soon."

Biba surveyed me suspiciously. "Have I been left out of something?"

"Sorry, sweet, didn't have time. Bubli's arrival and all that." I related the incident of the conversation outside the bungalow.

"Raj, I want you to carry that automatic at all times," Prem said, scanning the bulge under my coat. "I understand you're quite proficient in the use of small arms."

"Oh, fairly good, considering..." I began.

"An understatement if ever I heard one," Biba broke in with a chuckle. "Raj was on the Stanford competitive team and has a shelf of trophies at home for his marksmanship. Jay told me."

"*Accha.*" Prem nodded and changed the subject. "You know I'm to be best man at the wedding, do you not?"

"Yes, Joan just told me, and I'm so glad, Prem."

Samuel stepped into the room and whispered in Ian's ear. He excused himself and followed the cook into the kitchen. Bubli and Joan wandered over to join us.

"Captain Narayan will be my escort to Bombay. We'll be leaving tomorrow evening, and from there I'll be flying to Canada." Bubli gave Prem an appreciative look.

"She'll be living with an uncle of ours in British Columbia and that means we'll be seeing each other from time to time," Biba interjected.

Prem drew deeply on his cigarette and exhaled slowly, watching Bubli closely. He stabbed his cigarette in her direction and said quietly, "Tara Kaur, our country, yours and mine, is greatly indebted to you."

Ian walked into the room followed closely by Sardar Khan. The latter continued to present a faultless military bearing. Prem introduced him to the ladies.

"Looks like a conference and time for me to leave," Bubli volunteered, glancing at the Captain.

"No, please remain, we're all involved." He waved us over to a corner of the room.

At a nod from Prem, Ian began his briefing. "The cook's wife hired a rickshaw to bring back the marketing from the bazaar this afternoon. They unloaded at the kitchen door. After the rickshaw walla was dismissed, no one of the servants knows for certain just when he left the premises..."

"Damn it!" Prem cut in, "that's poor security."

Ian continued, "The *chowkidar* estimates the rickshaw was in the compound not more than half an hour."

"Is this the same man who ran the rickshaw yesterday afternoon?" Prem asked.

"The servants think so. Is that right?" Ian shot a quick glance at the Sergeant Major.

"Yes, sir. That is correct." He nodded.

"Another item of significance is that the timing of his presence in the compound coincides with the conversation outside your room," Ian paused for questions but there were none, and the three men left the room.

The rehearsal for the wedding moved smoothly under Joan's quiet direction. Lighthearted bantering soothed our tensions. I left Biba and Bubli at their room and stepped into mine.

"How went the rehearsal?" Doug asked.

"Without a hitch."

"Raj, you've won quite a few Brownie points with the C.I.D." Doug was struggling with his tie before the mirror.

"Really?"

"Your ears should have burned more than once over the past couple of weeks. Messages from the C.I.D. have come to our Embassy in Delhi with copies to the Bombay Consulate."

"Thanks," I said self-consciously. "And you know, Doug, Biba's played a significant part in this drama."

"She's not in my bailiwick, Raj. Biba comes under the protective arm of the Canadian High Commission."

"That's right, she does—until we're married tomorrow."

"We're proud of you both."

Chapter Twenty-Three

The rehearsal dinner was a tribute to our fast friendships. Each person around the table seemed to have accepted a responsibility for the whole party.

Joan announced after-dinner demitasse in the front room by the fireplace. We drifted in that direction and arranged chairs around the blazing logs.

"I knew I'd forgotten something," Doug exclaimed, jumping from his chair. "My camera. Brought it just for this." He dashed off.

Biba sat next to me and I reached for her hand. She rested her head on my shoulder and whispered, "Raj, I just couldn't be happier!"

"Good God!" Doug's voice resounded through the bungalow. I instinctively pulled Biba closer. Prem and Ian sprang from their chairs and ran toward the bedroom, drawing their automatics. Doug was standing in front of the almira, clutching the door he had just opened. On the floor within, between hanging clothes, was a man, his bent head resting on flexed knees. All eyes focused on the knife handle protruding from his back. Fresh blood was dripping down onto the bedroom floor, its distinctive odor pressing on our senses. For an instant we stood still as the macabre scene was imprinted on our minds.

"Saw the blood trickling from under the almira door, and when I opened..." Doug groaned suddenly and coughed into his handkerchief, then turned quickly toward the bathroom. Prem grimaced at the unpleasant sounds of retching that followed.

Waving us all back a few steps and looking toward the ladies gathered just outside the bedroom door, Prem suggested, "Better not come in. Please go back to the fireplace. We'll keep you informed."

Under the Captain's quiet but firm supervision, we did the necessary. I checked the victim for signs of life and found none. Ian was dispatched to fetch the Sergeant Major. Doug, pale but recovered, photographed the deceased and the scene. Ian returned with Sardar Khan and they immediately identified the dead man as the rickshaw walla, the one who had brought the dhobi into our compound on the day before. As we worked at removing the body from the closet a dagger fell from his pocket and clattered to the floor.

"Vicious weapon, eh? Intended for one of us. Bloody bastard got his just deserts he did." Prem spat.

The murder knife was photographed in position before it was

removed, carefully, to preserve fingerprints.

"Looks like a kitchen tool," Ian said, inspecting it closely. "I'll check it out with Samuel."

Prem nodded and turned to the Sergeant Major, "Sardar, you will interrogate the three adult male servants, singly of course."

After a final flash of the camera, a sheet was thrown over the body and we joined the ladies before the fireplace. For a moment Prem stood quietly in thought, his arms folded across his chest and lips pursed tightly. The scar on the left side of his face, animated by the fluctuations of the wood fire, portrayed an unusual harshness. Joan moved about quietly pouring coffee in our diminutive cups.

Turning back to pace back and forth before us, Prem fell into a monologue. "A man is murdered in this bungalow, a relative stranger, not known or seen by us until just yesterday..."

"I've seen him before," Joan cut in. "He's the same fellow who tried to get a job here as a cook and brought messages from Ambala scaring our servants."

"You're certain?" Jay interjected.

"He's done something to his face, a mustache or something, but the rickshaw walla and the would-be cook are one and the same."

"Good. That clears up one point, the whereabouts of the bugger who brought those Naya Ghadr notes. In all probability they used him as a hit man. Motives for his murder? Actually, several of us right here might have good reason to destroy a man of his ilk. This murder may have saved one of our lives. After all, he was out to kill one or more of us." Prem threw his cigarette stub into the fireplace and lit another. "The killer must have had access to the inside of this building. Probably slipped into the bathroom, unbolted the door, smuggled the victim into the almira then rebolted the door to the outside."

Ian stepped into the room to report, "No one saw the victim, sir. He must have had an accomplice within the compound."

"Agreed." Prem waved the Lieutenant to a seat. "Someone had to help the victim get inside."

"Then you think the assassin is still within the bounds of the compound?" Doug asked.

"Definitely. The blighter must be someone known to us all. Of course, we can't take it for granted that the one who admitted the man was the murderer. They need not be the same person. However, at present it appears that the rickshaw walla was smuggled into the bungalow by an accomplice, carefully hidden in the almira and then murdered by his supposed confederate."

Joan handed the Captain a cup of coffee while Jay stirred the logs in the fireplace.

"Time of death? Very recent, a matter of minutes. There was blood running from the wound. It would appear that death followed close on the stabbing. No signs of a struggle."

"Ugh!" Joan expressed her distaste.

"As to the motive, who knows?" Prem threw up his hand.

The sweeping lights of a car approaching the bungalow flashed through the window. The Captain excused himself and stepped past the guard at the front door.

Captain Karan Singh had arrived from Ambala. He stepped into the room with Prem and Ian. After a brief greeting, they moved to the bedroom.

"What a helluva way to end a rehearsal dinner!" Jay exclaimed, pounding his fist in the palm of his hand. "Let's forget the whole caboodle of damned cattle rustling thieves and move on."

I agreed. "Look, folks, let's not get morose. This has been shocking to us all, and we can't just ignore it, but life goes on. Biba and I are getting married tomorrow morning, just don't forget! As for the Naya Ghadr, let's leave that problem in the capable hands of Prem and his staff."

"Agreed." Biba sang out, standing beside me. I lifted her chin and kissed her resoundingly. The fireside group applauded. Jay even let out a Sioux war whoop. Tensions eased and soon we were conversing without restraint. Joan called Doug and me over to explain that the sweeper's wife was cleaning our quarters. She questioned our willingness to sleep in that particular room. We both assured her that we had no qualms about it. She was relieved.

The jeep engine growled and moved out of the compound, taking Captain Karan Singh back to Ambala. Shortly thereafter Prem and Ian joined our party again.

"Ladies and gentlemen," Prem addressed us formally, raising his hand for attention, "please be assured that even tighter security will now be maintained. As of now, no servant may enter the bungalow without the approval of a guard. Under no circumstances shall any of you leave the building during the night. The bathroom doors shall be bolted at all times."

Ian picked up the report, "Samuel has been interrogated and, in our estimation, he's innocent. This holds for his wife as well."

"Oh, what a relief," Joan sighed. "That takes a weight off my shoulders. I mean the wedding preparations, food and..." she frowned and looked embarrassed. "I really didn't mean that to sound so callous."

"The gardener and sweeper are being questioned now," Ian continued, "and the body has been removed to Ambala where further identification procedures will be carried out." He looked around to see if anyone had any questions. We all remained silent.

"Folks, please listen," Joan announced, standing to face us. "Breakfast's at eight in the morning."

The group began breaking up. Out of the corner of my eye I watched as Prem slipped an automatic into Jay's hand. They conversed in low voices for a moment before separating.

After the others had left, Bubli, Biba and I remained in the front room. Although the flames were low, the embers continued to radiate warmth. We turned out the light and sat on the floor before the fireplace. Biba nestled on one side of me with her head on my shoulder. Bubli sat on the other side, serious and pensive.

"Sort of a recurring nightmare, isn't it?" Bubli whispered.

Biba leaned forward to see past me. "Yes, but nightmares pass. They don't last forever, do they?" Reaching over my lap to squeeze Bubli's hand, she continued, "You know, all three of us could have avoided this whole mess. But we chose to stay. I don't know about you two, but I'm proud of us. I mean it!"

We sat quietly for a few moments, the soft moonlight flowing over us like a benediction.

Again, Bubli spoke. "I'm so happy for the two of you, so happy for..." she broke off with a catch in her voice. I encircled her with my arm and drew the three of us close together. Bubli cried softly on my shoulder. Biba and I said nothing.

"I'm sorry to break up this way." Bubli wiped her eyes. "Jolly long time since I've enjoyed the luxury of crying. Life over these past three years has been..." she groped for a word, "been so loathsome. Wonderful to be human again, to be with friends," she murmured.

"Bubli, dear, you'll have a good life in British Colombia," Biba consoled. "Life can begin again, you know."

"Thanks, you're dears. I shan't forget your friendship." She leaned over and kissed each of us, then hesitated as if wanting to say more.

Biba and I waited.

"I've something to finish tomorrow, if plans work out," she dropped her voice to a whisper.

"Meaning?" I asked.

"Oh, a matter to settle..." A cold bitterness crept into her voice. I chose not to press her further.

"We're turning in, sweetheart," Biba proposed, nudging me gently with her elbow. I appreciated her sensitiveness to the fact that Bubli should not retire by herself. Bubli discreetely went in to their room while Biba and I lingered at the door.

She snuggled close, her head resting under my chin. The faintly perfumed scent of her body thrilled me. An exhilarating warmth flowed in sensuous currents through us.

Doug was fast asleep when I entered our room. An incandescent reflection from the moonlight outside softened the darkness within. The outline of the almira stood ghost-like against the far wall of the bedroom. There was a slight odor of phenol about. I shivered as I pulled up the covers, whether from the cold or the grim memory, I could not say.

Chapter Twenty-Four

I awoke early on our wedding day and watched the first rays of dawn's light creep stealthily into the bedroom, like a cat stalking his quarry. It was cold and clear outside. A gentle knocking on the outside door interrupted my shaving. Walking over to the window and pulling aside the curtain, I could see Chotu's face outlined by the bathroom light, and beside him the turbaned head of a guard. They both entered and the gardener deposited a bucket of steaming bath water inside the shower stall. Chotu's eyes were drawn with worry.

"*Sub thik hai*—Is everything alright?" I asked him.

"*Ha ji, sub thik hai*—Yes sir, everything is alright," he replied with a sober nod.

Barring the door after the two men, I walked back into the bedroom and paused to scan the floor in front of the almira. The sweeper's wife had cleaned up all evidence of the killing. A faint odor of carbolic still pervaded the area. Leaving Doug lying fast asleep I ventured out into the front room, now our wedding chapel. I paused in front of the lectern and its banks of potted plants. Before noon Biba and I would be standing in that exact spot taking our marriage vows. My lips moved in a silent prayer that God would bless our marriage.

Samuel came in to light the morning fire and we made light conversation. His voice sounded tired and his smile was forced. With roaring flames in the fireplace, he excused himself and left for the kitchen. I pulled a chair up to the hearth and sat down, stretching legs and hands toward the warmth. The wood burned with zest, sparkling and sputtering, soon dissipating the chill of the room. Through the north window, I could see the craggy and snow-crested Himalayan ranges pinked by the morning sun.

"Darling, our wedding day!" She had come up from behind and kissed the top of my head. "I know it's supposed to be unlucky for the bride and groom to see each other just before the wedding, but I'm not a true traditionalist."

I rose to put my arm around her waist and we stood at the window, drinking in the sheer majesty of the scene.

"And how's Bubli?" I broke into our reverie.

"You know, she's doing well considering her statement last night. I was worried..." she sighed. "I'll not feel easy about her until she flies out of Bombay. Good thing Captain Narayan's taken her under his wing.''

Conversation around the breakfast table was restrained. As the meal drew to a close, Prem stood and grasped the back of his chair. He cleared his throat and began, ''There are two matters I must discuss. First, security at the wedding. The guests will not be permitted entrance to the chapel until ten minutes before the ceremony. The two ushers will be Mr. Gordon and Lieutenant McVey. Guests will be passed through the door by the guards one at a time to the usher who will accompany each one individually to a seat.''

We all knew that the second subject would relate to the almira assassination. As tension spread about the table, we were surprised to see Prem sit down and Ian stand to take his place.

''The Captain has asked that I brief you on the matter of last night's homicide.'' Ian looked tired. ''We have a confession by the alleged killer, who is at this moment in the Ambala jail.'' There was a collective sigh of relief. Ian paused and frowned. ''Ganga Ram, the sweeper, has confessed.''

Joan and Jay must have been privy to this information, for they evinced little outward reaction to the news.

''Captain Narayan has asked that I summarize the facts of the case for your information.'' Ian drew heavily on his pipe. ''Just a few weeks ago, while Doctor Singh was a guest here, Ganga Ram's son was killed by someone in league with the Naya Ghadr. The boy, Ramdas, was the apple of his father's eye.''

''Poor little kid died in David's arms,'' I murmured.

''Three days ago the victim rickshaw walla came to Nilapat. At this point we can't be certain as to whether he actually was a member of the anarchist group or a hired killer. Both Ganga Ram and Mrs. Clemens have identified him as being the same person who applied for the position of cook and carried threatening letters to the servants a couple of months ago.''

Joan nodded her agreement with Ian's statement.

''We do know that he gained entrance to this compound with his rickshaw on two different occasions, once with the dhobi and then yesterday afternoon with the cook's wife. At that time he contacted Ganga Ram...''

''The talking outside my bathroom,'' I interjected.

Ian nodded and continued, ''The victim offered the sweeper a substantial sum of money to smuggle him into the bungalow. Ganga Ram agreed but without actually accepting the bribe which later was found on the person of the murdered man. According to Ganga Ram, he met the man after dark at the compound wall and hid him in the servant's quarters while Ganga Ram entered the bungalow and unbolted the bathroom door. Still using the darkness as a shield, the two men slipped inside, all while the rehearsal dinner was in progress.''

"Where in hell were the guards?" Jay asked bluntly.

Ian looked at him wearily. "The killing was made possible by the fact that Ganga Ram had clearance and full access to the premises."

"I understand," Jay said impatiently, "but the whole damn thing's so fouled up. The bad guy gets his proper dues. Just what he damned well deserved. But the good guy who saved our lives goes to jail. That's a helluva note!"

Prem explained, "Although I agree with you, we do have laws in this land which must be followed." He nodded at Ian to proceed.

"On gaining access to the bedroom, Ganga Ram hid the victim in the almira and then, with cool precision, plunged the blade into his back. He waited a moment to be certain of his accuracy, then slipped out through the front door past a guard. Samuel recognized the murder weapon, a long thin-bladed butcher's knife, which had disappeared from the kitchen sometime yesterday afternoon." Ian relit his pipe and puffed smoke up at the ceiling.

Doug asked, "Why did the sweeper go through all of this dangerous maneuvering to get the chap into the bungalow when he could have disposed of the man elsewhere, say out in the compound?"

"Ah," Prem picked up the conversation, pointing his cigarette at Doug. "You'll remember that the lad Ramdas died in that very same room. What a stroke of poetic justice to avenge his son's death at that very spot!"

"So you believe the motive was revenge?" Joan asked.

Prem nodded. "Primarily. Yes, I believe it was revenge. Obviously he was crushed by his son's cruel murder. However, I find it quite difficult to disassociate the act from a sense of loyalty to some of you. One can't forget that Ramdas dearly loved David and you, Raj. The luring of the victim to the bungalow might very well have been a desire on Ganga Ram's part to destroy what he considered to be a common enemy, common to him and to us, and triumphantly leave the evidence here at our feet."

"Do you think the rickshaw walla was the same person who accosted little Anandi outside the hospital?" Biba asked.

Prem shook his head. "Doubt very much if he was the chap."

Bubli, who had been stirring her cup of tea, held the spoon up for attention. Prem waved her on. "How did Ganga Ram react to the interrogation?" she asked.

Captain Narayan pointed to Ian for a reply. "He was the last of the three men brought in for questioning. We had considered him to be the prime suspect. But to answer your question, he was calm and confessed fully without hesitation."

"Can't we do something to help him?" Joan asked, looking around the table. "It's hard to believe..."

"Mrs. Clemens," Prem broke in, "there are some highly mitigating circumstances in this case and I feel quite certain the court will take these into consideration. Please be assured our reports and depositions will support him in every way possible. After all, he did away with a would-be assassin.''

"We'll take care of his family. They can remain on the compound," Jay volunteered.

"Raj and I would like to contribute to a defense fund," Biba announced, throwing me a quick look for approval.

"Absolutely," I nodded my agreement.

"Why did the rickshaw walla specifically contact Ganga Ram? He must have remembered that he killed the lad, wouldn't you think?'' Doug directed his question to Ian.

"Ever since Ramdas' death, Ganga Ram has been waiting patiently for an opportunity to avenge him. He told us during the interrogation that he was suspicious of the rickshaw walla from the time he first came into the compound with the dhobi. He also recognized him as the would-be cook and note bearer from Ambala."

"Why in hell didn't he tell us that he recognized him?" Jay asked.

"We put the same question to Ganga Ram and he stated quite frankly that he wished to be avenged by his own hands. But to continue, the sweeper then deliberately placed himself in positions of easy accessibility. The bait was taken." Ian paused thoughtfully before asking, "And what was the second part of your question, Mr.Gordon?''

"Did the victim know of..."

"Oh yes, I remember. Either he did not know that Ramdas was the sweeper's son or became overconfident, most likely the former."

Prem stood and announced, "All of us will gather here after the wedding for instructions before we move out to the shamiana to eat." We separated, each to our own preparations.

The large clock on the wall tolled eleven, and before the echoes had died, the Reverend Masih and Taran Singh, the Sikh priest were seating themselves behind the lectern. I led Prem and Jay around the screen to stand with me before them. The Captain slowly scanned the audience. Joan and Bubli paced down the aisle to stop across from us, then Jay reached down to switch on Mendelssohn's *Wedding March*.

I shall not soon forget the picture of Biba's entrance into the chapel on her father's arm. She seemed to float alongside him in gossamer detachment. She had chosen to wear a turquoise sari, and a bouquet of red roses lay in the crook of her left arm. Balak Singh was the epitome of the elderly Sikh gentleman, dignified and proud. A profuse silvery beard aproned his long black woolen *acckan*. A neatly and firmly applied white turban crested his head. Biba had told me that relatives referred to him affectionately as "The Patriarch." The designation suited him.

The short sermon by the Reverend Masih on the sacredness and responsibilities of marriage was simply but beautifully presented. On the completion of the wedding vows, the minister called the Sikh priest to his side. Taran Singh quoted briefly from the *Granth Sahib*, the Holy Scriptures of the Sikhs, consecrating the ceremony.

Joan, in her unhurried but effective way, grouped us for the reception line. We all stood in a semi-circle in the dining room. The entrance from the chapel was controlled by Ian, while Doug saw to it that the people kept moving. At one point, Prem stiffened and his hand reflexively slipped inside his coat. Samuel had suddenly stepped between Bubli and Joan to ask a question.

I took particular pleasure in introducing Biba and her father to Imam Muhadin and the Pratap Singhs. As they prepared to move on down the line, the Imam dropped his voice and confided, "The words you suggested have been inscribed on Ahmed Khan's gravemarker." He paused to survey Biba and me closely. "Doctor Singh, cherish your beautiful bride, for her price is far above rubies. Incidentally, you will find these words in the Book of Proverbs of your Holy Scriptures." His face wrinkled into a puckish smile.

"Far above rubies," I heard Biba repeat as she smiled up at me.

Our little Anandi Khosla, the Nilapat Wonder, moved up the line of greeters, bursting with energy and hardly able to contain herself. With me, she was able to restrain her excitement, but exploded into a mixture of laughter and tears as she clung to Biba. Balak Singh surveyed the confrontation between his daughter and the diminutive nurse with a broad and tolerant smile.

Chapter Twenty-Five

The last guest had been shepherded out of the dining room. Prem stepped out before us, surveying us with a good-humored smile, and said, "We must all meet here and proceed to the shamiana together. We have a contingent of guards, police from Ambala. Unfortunately, or perhaps fortunately, the compound looks like an armed camp. Word of the murder last night has gotten around the countryside, so we've a crowd of the curious gathered outside the compound gate. This has added to our security problems. Lieutenant McVey will continue the briefing."

Ian changed places with Prem and announced, "There is a special table at the front of the shamiana for the wedding party, including Mr. Gordon, Mrs. McVey and myself, a total of twelve. Four other tables have been set up for the guests. Incidentally, the buffet includes vegetarian and non-vegetarian dishes, all clearly marked. No one will be served food or drink by another person, either guest or servant." He paused for emphasis and repeated, "As a matter of security this must be a self-service meal. Any questions?"

"Why self-service?" Jay asked.

"A bit more difficult to poison an individual dish," Ian replied matter-of-factly.

Stepping out onto the verandah, our party of twelve followed Captain Narayan down the bungalow steps on into the shamiana. Lieutenant McVey brought up the rear of our procession.

"Bubli's carrying a gun," Biba whispered, leaning over toward me.

"How do you know?"

"I saw it when we were dressing for the wedding."

"Biba, you know that Jay and I are both carrying guns."

"But Raj, Bubli? It seems so out of place for her." She groaned and made a wry face.

Our seats at the table were marked with place cards. After all of the guests had been positioned, Ian led the wedding party to the buffet. Police stood around the periphery of the shamiana. After we had helped ourselves and returned, the others lined up along the tables. I watched for anything unusual. I spotted no irregularities. Our security appeared to be tight. It seemed that a Naya Ghadr infiltration would be nearly impossible. I squeezed Biba's hand under the table.

Leaning over toward me, she sighed, "Darling, this seems like a dream. Am I really your wife?''

I chuckled happily. "If not, my sweet, there's been a terrible mistake somewhere.''

"Raj, kiss me. Please, kiss me right now.'' Her voice was urgent.

"Here in public?'' I searched her eyes. "Darling, you really do mean it, don't you?'' She nodded and, oblivious to the surroundings, our lips fused in a lingering embrace.

A trembling hand grasped my elbow from behind. I turned quickly and found Anandi staring up at me. Her whole being betrayed a naked fear. On her knees beside my chair, she crouched as if hiding from the others in the shamiana.

"I saw him, Doctor. I saw the man!'' Her voice quavered with agitation. "He was just now inside the room, but has gone out.''

I turned partially in my seat and held her hand. "You mean you saw the man in the sari? That man who...''

"Yes, yes, that man,'' she cut in excitedly.

Both the Captain and the Lieutenant were watching closely. I nodded them over. Biba exchanged places with Prem. Ian kneeled behind us.

"You're certain? You know this man?'' Prem questioned the nurse quietly.

She nodded emphatically. "He is with a lame foot.''

The Captain shook his head in disbelief and muttered, "How could the bugger have broken through?''

Anandi's flashing eyes surveyed the three of us in one rapid sweep as she exclaimed, "He is one of you!''

"What in God's name do you mean, child?'' Prem burst out.

"He is a guard,'' she replied in a hoarse whisper.

I shot a quick glance at Biba. Bubli stiffened in her chair and her hand felt searchingly under the fold of her sari.

Quickly recovering, Prem asked, "Did he recognize you?''

Swallowing forcibly, she replied, "I do not know. Perhaps, my nursing uniform...'' her voice drifted off.

Prem gently assisted Anandi into his empty chair. She reached for my hand and grasped it firmly, her fingers still trembling.

"*Sardar Khan-ko ek dum bulao*—Call Sardar Khan at once!'' Captain Narayan whispered to a guard. In a matter of seconds the Sergeant Major joined us. Ian summed up our dilemma, his voice sharp with concern, "The bloody intruder's exploited the fact that we have two groups of guards, dressed very much alike, but one detachment can't identify the members of the other. So he has a built-in camouflage.''

Sardar Khan suggested, "Sir, let me check immediately with the leader of the Ambala squad so I can identify their men, and knowing our men, I can identify the bugger.''

Prem nodded his approval, but added, "You'd better hurry Sardar. We might not have much time.''

Perched straight-shouldered and upright in her chair, Anandi's eyes oscillated back and forth like miniature radar screens, maintaining a constant surveillance. She was the only one who could identify the assassin. The Captain and the Lieutenant squatted quietly at either end of the table, keeping a critical watch. I stared at Biba and Bubli, both of whom had turned their chairs to face the center of the shamiana. Time dragged as we waited.

Anandi jumped to her feet, pointing unsteadily at a uniformed man who had just entered the rear of the tent. Her mouth opened but no sound came out. With a second try she produced words, mechanical and faltering, "*Wo admi! Wo admi!*—That man! That man!"

The anarchist, who knew he had been recognized, glared about wildly for a couple of seconds, then broke into a limping run toward our table. He waved a gun. Instant pandemonium broke loose inside the shamiana as guests fled the path of the killer. Jay and I sprang to our feet and drew our automatics. Prem and Ian both stood and covered the charging assailant with their weapons. The rest of the wedding party sat frozen in their seats.

"Don't shoot!" Captain Narayan called out sharply. With the milling guests as background, he was an extremely hazardous target. My heart tightened as I saw Biba and Bubli directly in the path of the oncoming madman. He ran with a slight limp, hoarsely shouting unintelligible slogans. I tried to swallow, but my throat had gone dry. Good God, I thought, someone must shoot! My finger began squeezing the trigger.

Suddenly, Bubli's hand rose from her lap, hung poised in midair for an instant, then exploded with the report of a firearm. We all watched in stunned silence as the killer pirouetted crazily and slumped to the ground, almost at her feet. In the instant of death his expression changed from one of hellish hatred to astonished surprise. Bubli stared down at him for a few seconds, then rose from her chair and slowly approached Prem Narayan.

"I shan't need this anymore," she said in a tired voice, handing him her automatic. Prem reached out just in time to catch her in his arms as she fainted. We carried her to the bungalow and to the master bedroom. Biba maintained a bedside vigil until Bubli regained consciousness a little later.

Doug, Prem and Bubli were catching the evening train to Delhi. Biba's father and Karan Singh joined Doctor and Mrs. Masih who were driving to Ludhiana. Ian was seeing Joyce off in the family car heading for Chandigarh. The exodus was in full swing.

"A damned sticky wicket," Prem admitted, shaking his head. "Jolly good marksmanship, don't you know." He was chatting with Jay, Doug and me.

"I'll never be the same again," I confessed. "That horrible tension of waiting for someone to stop that man. My Biba was directly in line..."

"You can say that again," Jay cut in. "My finger was squeezing down on that old trigger."

Prem nodded. "Cool nerve and jolly fast thinking, waiting that long, right to the last second, before shooting. The closer the target, the more accurate the shot and also the higher the trajectory. Less danger to the guests, don't you know."

"Who was he?" Doug asked.

"Lower echelon Naya Ghadr...last of the bloody bastards. Delhi telegraphed me the specifications from their files this morning. You'll never believe how he came by his limp—a camel stepped on his foot a few weeks back."

"Good old camel," Doug muttered.

Prem lit a cigarette, blowing a large smoke ring above our heads. "We were expecting the bloke. He damned near fooled us. Clever bastard he was. The bait, Bubli, was displayed in as enticing a manner as we dared. That little nurse gave us the clue, thank God." He sighed with relief.

"Why Bubli?" Jay asked Prem. "With all of us here, why should she have to do the shooting?"

"Bubli insisted on having the opportunity to destroy this man if possible. She surmised, and rightly so, that she was his prime target. There was a reason for her wanting to be his executioner. He was the man who actually carried out Gurdial's death sentence.

Joan, Biba and Bubli came out of the bedroom, followed by Chotu carrying the suitcases. Bags were packed into the jeep, leaving just enough room for the four to sit. Bubli embraced me warmly, saying that she already had said her farewells to everyone else. Prem and Doug extended their welcomes to visit in Bombay on our way out of India. With a roar of the motor, Jay drove through the compound gate, leaving a cloud of dust and fumes hanging about the Gurkha *chowkidar*.

The afternoon was taken up bringing the bungalow back to normalcy. Captain Karan Singh arrived from Ambala to confer with Ian on the removal of the body. Jay supervised the dismantling of the shamiana. Joan, Biba and I changed the improvised chapel back into a front room. With the work completed, Biba and I strolled on the verandah. Ian joined us and suggested a libation.

"Hold everything. Let me forage. I know where the stuff is kept," I volunteered.

The portable bar moved easily into the front room and I filled the orders. The afternoon shadows were stretching out and a noticeable chill infiltrated the bungalow. Samuel started a fire and the three of us moved chairs in front of the fireplace. Ian eased himself into his chair and heaved a long sigh. Pulling out his pipe he started the ritual pipe-lighting. Holding aloft his glass, he proposed a toast, "To a wonderful couple. May your marriage be one of utmost joy."

"Oh, thank you, Ian." Biba responded. "You know you're one of the most romantic fellows I've ever met."

Almost unnoticed, dusk had quietly changed into darkness, throwing a curtain of intimacy around us. The ruthless world outside, for the moment at least, seemed far removed. Jay and Joan joined us around the fireplace and we all sat watching the flames dance over the logs. I clasped Biba's hand in my lap, holding firm to a reality of love in a happiness tempered by the violence of the past two days.

Jay sighed and stretched his arms, finally rising to lean against the fireplace mantel. "I'm hungry," he announced. "Hardly ate a bite in the shamiana. Too damned many interruptions."

This threw us into gales of laughter. The pent-up tensions broke loose spilling over into relaxed and animated conversation.

"Where in tarnation did this frail little chick, Bubli, learn to shoot?" Jay asked Ian.

"Before infiltrating the Naya Ghadr, she was given an intensive course in survival by the C.I.D. Small arms marksmanship was a part of this instruction."

"Are Biba and Raj safe now?" Jay pressed.

Ian stepped over to the fireplace and banged the bowl of his pipe on a log, knocking out the tobacco ashes. "Today Bubli removed the last Naya Ghadrite not in jail. But we still must maintain a degree of security. Tomorrow I'll be going down to Bombay with them as a precautionary measure."

Samuel announced dinner. For the most part, around the table, we conversed quietly, all of us wrung out emotionally. Toward the end of the meal I raised my wine glass in a toast. "Biba and I can never repay the host and hostess of this bungalow for their warm and loving hospitality. They have shared our dangers and our joys. Here's to a wonderful couple, Joan and Jay."

"Here, here!" Ian boomed.

Not to be outdone, Jay pushed his chair back and stood to say, "I'd actually given serious thought to entertaining you all with my Sioux war dance..." he grinned and looked around the table for approval.

"Oh, Jay, this just isn't the time!" Joan protested, pulling at his sleeve.

"But in deference to my dear wife, and because this is a marital rather than a martial occasion, here's a toast to the honeymooners. May their lives be as happy as Joan's and mine." Taking a sip from his glass, he stooped down to kiss Joan.

"Breakfast at seven and then the Raj Singhs will be heading for the station on their way to Bombay," Joan announced.

To the enthusiastic applause of our audience, I took Biba in my arms and carried her across the threshold into our bedroom. She closed the door behind us and turned the key in the lock.

Chapter Twenty-Six

Our friends welcomed us on the platform of the ornate Victoria Terminus in Bombay. Soli and Indira Dorabji embraced us warmly. Prem greeted us, then singled Ian out for a private conversation. Prem was to drive us to the Taj Mahal hotel where we would stay until our boat sailed in three days.

Biba took Ian's hand and led him over to me. We had become quite fond of the Lieutenant, through whose veins flowed the blood of our oriental heritage as well as that of our adopted occident. We put our arms around each other and Biba, to his surprise, kissed him soundly.

"Give our love to Joyce," I called as he walked away. He turned and waved, then disappeared into the platform crowd on his way to catch a train back to Delhi and on to the Punjab.

Soli and Indira confirmed the time of our party in the Gateway Room of the Taj. "See you tomorrow night," they called in unison, heading for a taxi waiting impatiently.

Prem beckoned and we followed, spearheaded by two coolies carrying our bags. At the station entrance a uniformed driver led us to an official vehicle and directed the loading of the baggage.

Because of arrangements made by the C.I.D., our signing into the hotel was quite perfunctory. We were soon settling in to our quarters at the end of the fourth floor corridor. Prem entered with us and remained until the bellboy had left. He surveyed the suite, peeking into all the closets and out each window.

"Rather lavish," he admitted, "but the best room for security purposes."

A look of concern crossed Biba's face. "We're still in danger?"

Prem smiled reassuringly. "Doctor Biba, in my estimation there still is a degree of danger, but much less than before. Although the Naya Ghadr is accounted for, we still have this damned R.S.S.S. to keep in mind. Don't forget that Raj overheard a conversation between Prakash and Shivaram when he was imprisoned in Dharamsala. They were trying to fix up some kind of affiliation. Shivaram's headquartered here in Bombay."

"I'm sorry. You'll have to excuse my worrying," she said, a little plaintively.

He reached over and took her hand in his, patting it with affection. "No excuses, my dear. The two of you have contributed much toward the liquidation of the Naya Ghadr and I find it difficult to express the appreciation of our Department...and at great personal risk. Then comes another complication for you, the R.S.S.S. This situation is nothing of your doing, but unfortunately both of you now are exposed to this danger by virtue of your association with the C.I.D.''

"What are our limitations?" I asked.

"One of our men has been assigned to you. He will keep a close surveillance. I've deliberately not had him meet us here. Being anonymous, at least in the beginning, will contribute to our security measures. For all practical purposes he will be just another hotel bearer.''

"And how do we identify him?" Biba asked.

Prem leaned over to flick the ashes from his cigarette into a tray. "You will match two portions of a couplet. The first half is, '*Jab ag jalti hai—When fire burns.*' The counter to this is '*Tab dhua hota hai*—There is smoke'." He moved to the door, turning to call back, "I wish you both a good rest.''

We began unpacking our bags into closets and drawers. "I'm going to wear a sari tomorrow night to the party," Biba mentioned as she watched me pull out my wrinkled suits.

"Indira mentioned black tie or regimentals for the men,"I complained, holding up my soiled tuxedo. "Better get these to the cleaners. You have anything to go, hon?"

Biba checked over her clothes and segregated a small bundle which she tossed on the bed in front of me. We ordered an Indian dinner and sent our clothes to the hotel cleaning establishment.

A tapping on the door heralded the arrival of our evening meal. The bearer brought in a large tray from which he selected the settings and food for a most attractive table. As a final touch, at my request, he carefully positioned two rather ornate candelabra, one at each of our places.

"Madam, shall I light them?" The bearer pointed at the table, matches in hand.

"Please," Biba replied, turning to whisper, "Raj, how romantic.''

With the lights turned out the candles cast a living glow over the room. The bearer left us to the intimacies of a night alone.

Morning sunlight was filtering through the window curtains when our bearer, the same one who had served us the night before, knocked on the door and took orders for breakfast. Biba and I let our breakfast extend over a good part of the morning. The leisurely pace seduced us into reminiscences. We relived in their relating the past few weeks, and filled in the details of our adventures during the separation from each other. Our talk was interrupted by a phone call from Balak Singh, who had just arrived in Bombay by plane from Delhi.

"We'll be seeing you at the party tonight, Dad," Biba said, hanging up the receiver.

She was bathing and I was browsing through *The Times of India* when I remembered that our clothes had not been returned. The telephone rang for some time before a voice said, "Cleaning."

"This is Doctor Singh, room four hundred. Is my cleaning ready?"

"*Main Angrezi nahin samajh sakta*—I cannot understand English," a man replied in a muffled voice.

"*Ya Doctor Singh hai aur mera kamra-ka number car sau hai*—This is Doctor Singh and my room number is four hundred."

"*Ha ji. Apka cleaning tyar hai. Abhi milege*—Yes sir. Your cleaning is ready. You will get it right away."

Surprised that a hotel with a cosmopolitan clientele should employ someone who spoke no English, I hung on to the receiver a moment. Then just as I was about to put the phone down, a voice in the background mimicked, "*Main Angrezi nahin samajh sakta*," with a loud guffaw. I barely picked up the two words, "Sewak Sangh," just before the communication line clicked into silence. I dialed Prem's emergency number, and had him on the line in a matter of seconds. I related the incident.

"Sewak Sangh," he muttered, "the last two components of R.S.S.S. Raj, you're certain these were the words?"

"Not the least doubt."

"We'll treat this as a matter of immediate priority. My men will be checking the cleaning shop within a few minutes."

"Biba's taking a bath and knows nothing of this." I could hear the water splashing into the tub.

"Don't tell her, and remain in your room until I pick you up for the party at seven-thirty."

I sat on the davenport trying to collect my thoughts, but was interrupted by a knock on the door. The same bearer who had been serving our meals now stood in the corridor with our cleaned clothes. I studied him closely and he responded promptly with a reassuring smile.

"*Dhanyavad*—Thank you," I addressed him, turning to lay the clothes on a chair. "*Apka nam kya hai*—What is your name?" I continued in Hindustani.

"*Ji, mera nam Gaikwad hai*—Sir, my name is Gaikwad."

I listened carefully to see if there might be any characteristics which could link the voice with that of the cleaner. There were none. Placing a finger on his lips, he stepped into the room and closed the door behind him. Slipping a hand inside my pocket I released the safety on the automatic.

"*Jab ag jalti hai*," he whispered, flashing me a broad grin.

"*Tab dhua hota hai*," I responded, relaxing.

Stepping out into the corridor, he turned to say in a low voice, "I also speak some English."

Biba came out of the bathroom with a large towel wrapped around her head and whistling happily. At least she needn't be bothered by this recent miserable development, I thought, feeling just a little conscience-stricken at withholding the matter from her.

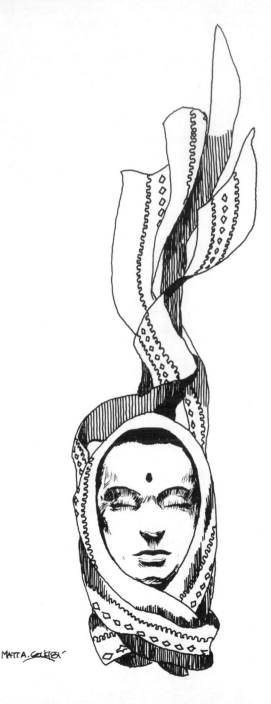

MATT A. GOLETSKY

Chapter Twenty-Seven

Captain Prem Narayan, dressed in his regimentals, ribbons and all, stepped into the room and stopped abruptly to stare at Biba and me with an expression of surprise and pleasure

"Something wrong?" I asked, perplexed by his silence.

"A bit rude I am..." he grinned at both of us. "Such a splendid looking couple, and...and frankly I'm enjoying what I see."

Biba broke out into a laugh and then whistled as she closely scrutinized the Captain from head to shiny boots. "Impeccable!" she murmured in awe.

Prem grinned shyly.

Stepping out into the corridor we headed for the stairway, following Prem. I heard him mutter under his breath that the lifts could not be adequately secured. At the stairwell landing on the second floor Gaikwad joined our entourage. We entered the smallish dining room through a side serving door, avoiding the hotel lobby. I saw that Prem was disturbed by the number of people milling about in the adjacent corridor. A single long table, seating eight, stood in the center of the room. Floral arrangements, with a bouquet of red roses in the center of the table, created a gala atmosphere. In one corner a small bar had been set up with a bartender ready to serve. Prem nodded to the man and informed me on the side that he was a C.I.D. employee. A quick survey of the room revealed no windows and only two doors, the one for serving through which we had just entered and the one connecting with a short corridor leading directly to the main lobby. It was evident that the setting for our dinner party had been planned with care. As yet none of the other guests had arrived.

"The Dorabjis were planning a large party, including not only many of their friends but also members of the American Consulate, certain of the Parsi and Sikh communities as well as quite a list of others," Prem confided with a wry smile. "They had reserved the large Gateway Room for tonight's festivities...orchestra and all the trimmings.'

"And?" Biba questioned.

"They're not all that keen about my decision." He shook his head with a dour look. "My ultimatum was that the party should be for twelve or less, otherwise no party. I think the Dorabjis would like to have me sacked."

Biba patted his arm. "Oh, Prem, I'm sure they'll understand."

"Jolly well hope so."

The Dorabjis handed their coats to the bearer at the door and came in. Indira was wearing a royal purple sari trimmed in silver, arranged in that slightly different fashion peculiar to the Parsi women. Soli in tuxedo and black tie looked the part of an affluent Bombay business man. They waved and came toward us, faces wreathed in smiles. "How exquisite you look!" Indira exclaimed as she embraced Biba.

Soli engulfed me in a bear hug and turned to survey our wives. "Lovely gals, eh? We're just plain lucky, Raj."

"Captain, those are handsome regimentals," Indira complimented Prem.

Further conversation was interrupted by the arrivals of the Gordons and Biba's father. This made the party complete. Drinks were served as we broke up into smaller groups. Prem ordered a carbonated orange drink which he sampled occasionally without particular enthusiasm. Biba and Sharon Gordon sipped sweet vermouth, while Doug and I opted for scotch and soda. The Dorabjis drank a red Goanese wine. Balak Singh, disdaining a drink of any kind, engaged in an animated discussion with Doug.

As we found our places at the table, I watched Prem converse briefly at the service door with Gaikwad. Both men appeared to direct their attention to the kitchen. Gaikwad disappeared for a moment and then returned to join the Captain. "*Batti thik hai, ji*—The light is alright, sir," I overheard. Prem stared out into the hall a moment before rejoining the party.

The individual place cards were fitted into slots cut into the domes of miniature ivory Taj Mahals and the napkins rolled into ivory serviette rings on whose margins strutted peacocks carved in bold relief. Soli and Indira sat at opposite ends of the table with Biba on his right and me on Indira's right. Doug and Sharon were directly across from Biba and me respectively, Balak Singh between Doug and me, with Prem seated across from him separating Sharon and Biba. The service door was behind Indira while the entrance toward the hotel lobby lined up directly behind Soli. This seating arrangement, obviously engineered by Prem, gave him a good view of both doorways.

When we were seated, Soli asked the bearer to bring in the champagne. He ceremoniously popped the cork and personally poured the bubbling drink into each of our glasses. He lifted his goblet, proposing a toast, "To Raj and Biba. May their marriage be 'a thing of beauty and a joy forever'."

"Thank you," we responded in unison. While the rest still stood, I glanced diagonally across the table and lifted my glass in a personal toast to my wife. She responded with an intimate wink. At that moment I fell in love with Biba all over again.

A noisy group of partying people moved through an adjoining

corridor and I noted that Prem seemed tense. He beckoned Gaikwad over and had further conversation with him.

Rising to my feet, I waved across the table for Biba to stand. Jointly we proposed a toast, "Gold is tried in the heat of fire, friendship in the stress of need."

A light behind me suddenly went out, darkening the service doorway. Prem jumped from his chair to grab frantically at Biba and pull her down into his lap. Gaikwad leaped toward the service entrance. A high-pitched sound whined past my left ear.

For a matter of two or three seconds there was an unnatural stillness throughout the room. Then the sudden splintering of a champagne glass on the floor was magnified a hundredfold.

Biba had collapsed in Prem's lap, head hanging limply and arms dangling grotesquely to the side. With a reflex surge, born of the discipline of a surgeon, I moved into action. A process of self-induced psycho-surgery severed my emotions from the intellectual demands of professional judgement. In retrospect, many of the details of that night escape me.

Prem and I laid Biba on the floor, his coat folded under her head. Rising, features distorted with anguish, he dashed off, automatic in hand. The remaining guests gathered around as I knelt examining my patient. Someone was crying softly. Two spots of crimson outraged the pure white of the sari draped over her shoulder.

"Soli and Doug, listen, call an ambulance and contact a neurosurgeon." My voice was firm. "Notify the University Medical Center that we're bringing in a brain injury...gunshot wound." They both ran out.

Biba was unconscious but responding to my pain tests, a favorable sign. The only external injury was a small puncture wound in the right temple which oozed a slight trickle of blood. The pulse rate and respiration were stable, greatly to my relief. Her reflexes, except for pupillary reactions to light, were fairly normal. She moaned softly as I moved her head during the examinations.

Prem returned, out of breath. "Bloody bastard escaped in the crowd but we found his gun in the hallway. German make...handgun with silencer...small bore and high velocity." He paused to catch his breath. "Ambulance is on its way. My man's at the entrance to direct them here."

Doug and Soli hurried back into the room together. "We've decided on Doctor DeSa, the neurosurgeon at the Medical Center," Soli announced. "Fortunately he was still at the hospital making final rounds for the day. Doug and I both know him well. We're fellow Rotarians."

"You spoke to him in person?" I asked.

"Yes," Doug assured me. "He's making all arrangements and will meet us in the emergency room."

Gaikwad led in two men with red crosses emblazoned on their sleeves, carrying a folded stretcher. Prem invited Balak Singh to ride with him to the hospital. I sat in the ambulance with Biba, holding her hand and monitoring her pulse and other vital signs. As we sped through the dark city, my heart groped through its own black night.

Doctor DeSa, a man perhaps ten years my senior, grasped my hand with a reassuring smile. I gave him the salient points and my initial physical findings while Biba was being transferred from the ambulance to the examining table. There was a small waiting room adjacent to Emergency and I found Prem, Balak Singh and the Dorabjis waiting there. Sitting down in one corner, I buried my face in my hands. "Oh dear God," I groaned softly in a prayer of bitter desperation.

In a few minutes Doctor DeSa stepped into the waiting room. "Surprisingly stable for an intracranial injury of this nature. We've cut down on an ankle vein for rapid fluid or blood replacement if and when needed."

"Very good," I responded, reaching out desperately for signs of reassurance.

"We're sending your wife to x-ray and from there on to Intensive Care..." He studied my face closely. "My assistant will be with her. A good lad, just completed his M.S. in surgery."

"Vital signs stable?" I asked hopefully.

DeSa nodded. "Quite satisfactory at the moment. We'll keep an eye on the hemodynamics for evidence of increased intracranial pressure. Shan't be gone long and then we'll take a run upstairs to check over the x-rays."

"Soli and Indira, why don't you both go home," I suggested, walking over to them huddled together on a bench as if in mutual support. "It's getting late and the girls will miss you. If there's any change, I'll call."

Soli shuffled his feet. "You're sure, Raj?"

I nodded. They stood and Indira embraced me with tears running down her cheeks. Soli gave me a hug in silence.

Biba's father sat alone, brave but disconsolate and unable to comprehend fully the tragedy engulfing us. I moved over beside him and took his hand. I recognized heartache and fear in his eyes.

Prem stood at a window, looking out into the night. Stepping to his side I placed a hand on his shoulder. He turned and faced me, his teeth clenched tight, afraid to trust his own voice.

As the immediate protective numbness following physical injury permits survival, so does the initial dulling of emotions after severe psychic trauma preserve sanity. As the numbness wore off, flashbacks to the instant of the shooting circled cruelly. I saw her crumpled in Prem's grasp, like a cloth doll draped over a little girl's arm.

"Let's take a walk up to x-ray," DeSa suggested, beckoning me to join him in the hall. We climbed a flight of stairs to the viewboxes where the technician had set up Biba's films. DeSa interpreted them in a running commentary, "Bullet entrance right temporal...now lodged left temporal just under the surface of the bone...so far so good. Appears to be minimal bone splintering at the site of implosion, probably due to the high velocity as well as the small size and steel jacketing of the bullet."

The technician positioned a stereoscopic set of films which we both studied. I noticed a shadow of concern cross DeSa's face.

"Trajectory just posterior to both orbital sockets..." I began. It seemed as if someone outside of me had been speaking.

"Those stereos do disturb me a bit," he commented quietly.

The surgical assistant stepped up to brief us on Biba's immediate condition. "Blood pressure rising and pulse slowing, sir."

"Better check that out," DeSa proposed. "Like to come along?"

I shook my head. "Experience has taught me that relatives, particularly professional relatives, should keep out of the way."

He was obviously relieved. "As you wish, Doctor Singh. But do use my office. It's just outside I.C.U."

Accepting his offer, I sat at his desk and listlessly thumbed through medical journals. Time dragged heartlessly. Finally he returned, his face sober.

"Intracranial bleeding. Not much doubt. Her blood pressure's rising steadily, with a decreasing pulse rate."

"Probably the middle meningeal, torn by a bone splinter. No time to lose," I said quietly.

He walked down the hall toward the operative suite, where swinging doors swallowed him up. God be with you and your patient, I prayed silently as a sickening hurt spread through my body.

Balak Singh bore up well under the news of impending surgery. As promised, I put in a call to Soli and advised him, against his wishes, that Indira and he remain at home. Again I promised to call after the surgery. Prem had left for a few minutes. Out in the shadows of the hallway, I caught a glimpse of Gaikwad leaning against the stair rail.

Unable to sit in the waiting room, I paced back and forth in the corridor. I wrestled with the clinical analysis of Biba's condition. The immediate hurdle was controlling the intracranial hemorrhage, technically not too difficult a procedure if in fact it was the middle meningeal. But the trauma from the bullet probably damaged other vessels as well and bleeding, severe bleeding, was a stark possibility. Desperate measures to control the hemorrhage could in themselves inflict serious neurological injury. If she lived, Biba's eyesight most certainly would be compromised. The stereo films haunted me. How could the bullet have avoided the optic nerves?

Prem came in from the stairway. "How is Doctor Biba?" he asked.

"She's in surgery."

"May the gods protect her," he said, his voice husky with emotion.

Dawn was lifting the blanket of darkness from over Bombay and the noises of a large city awakening filtered up from the street. I looked at my watch. Biba had been in surgery almost five hours. I stepped out into the corridor. Prem and Gaikwad were conversing quietly. As if by prearrangement, Doctor DeSa came into the hall just as I did. The familiarity of the rumpled green scrub suit, cap and surgical mask hanging around his neck was a stabilizing influence on me.

A flicker of a smile touched his tired face. "She's doing alright."

"Thank God!" Only two short words, but a prayer of profound gratitude.

He led me down the hallway to a small verandah and stood in silence a moment looking down on the stirrings of the city.

"Sorry it took so long, I know you've been through hell. We had to move slowly."

"I understand."

"Hemorrhage controlled without too much difficulty, the main source of bleeding."

"Middle meningeal?"

He nodded. "Some of the smaller vessels along the trajectory were buggers, but metal clips and the coagulator did the trick. Had to be damned cautious moving through the traumatized tissue, the debriding, don't you know. Removed a few bone splinters."

"Much blood loss?"

He shook his head. "Minimal, really. No transfusion needed."

With Biba's life assured for the time being, we both recognized the question now uppermost in my mind. But I deliberately postponed the confrontation and temporized, "Were you able to remove the bullet?"

"Yes, rather simple, really. Lay just under the left temporal bone plate."

The issue had to be faced. "The optic nerves?"

He fixed his eyes on mine. "Cleanly transected, both of them."

I caught my breath. "Total, permanent blindness."

DeSa nodded, sadness lining his face. "The optic nerve just doesn't regenerate." He stepped over and placed his arm around my shoulders. A shadow of a smile replaced the sadness around his eyes. "Yes, she'll not see, but let's look on the other side of the coin. Unless unexpected complications arise, she'll live, with a normally functioning brain and without paralysis."

My tears began to flow and I wept unashamed. The hot tears, an extraordinary blend of joy and sorrow, streamed down my cheeks unchecked. Biba would be blind but she would live. Our lives would go on together.

"I say, old chap, come have breakfast with me, will you?" DeSa's invitation pulled me back into the world of immediate realities.

I nodded, drying my eyes. "Thanks, but first let me pass the word on to her father and Captain Narayan."

"Jolly good. I'll wait."

I turned to leave, then paused to whisper, "Let's not say anything about the blindness to the others, at least not at the moment."

"Righto."

Prem stood in the doorway of the waiting room. He had changed from his uniform into mufti. We wakened Balak Singh and gave him the news of Biba's favorable status. Both men were delighted, each manifesting this in his own quiet way. Biba's father handed me a card with a telephone number and left.

"What about security for Biba?" I asked Prem.

"Must be maintained for both of you. I'm placing a special operative on your wife, a nurse. And Sergeant Gaikwad is assigned to you until the day you leave India."

The dining room was quite busy, at the nurses' shift change. DeSa nodded pleasantly at the cashier and whispered a message concerning Gaikwad, who had been instructed by the Captain to remain close but not as an obvious member of our party. The two of us took a booth in a corner while the Sergeant seated himself at a table nearby. A waiter served coffee and took our orders.

"I find it difficult to express my appreciation for what you've done..." I began.

"Please," he broke in with a wave of his hand, "this has been an honor. I only wish I could have saved your wife's sight."

"Well, do accept my gratitude."

"So you're a Stanford man. Almost went there for a course last year."

"Really."

"Course in vascular microsurgery."

"Where did you do your graduate work in neurosurgery?"

"London. Bart's."

"St. Bartholomew's. Oldest medical college in the British Isles. I visited Bart's on my way out here, not far from Saint Paul's Cathedral. A great painting, that one of the Good Samaritan at the medical center on the wall above the stairway."

DeSa was pleased that I had visited Bart's. We exchanged information on our backgrounds, mine in California and his in Goa, which used to be a colony of Portugal on the west coast of India.

My host stood, stretched his arms and suggested, "Let's see how things are going. I know you're anxious to take a look at your wife."

We walked to the end of the hall and climbed two flights of stairs with Gaikwad following close behind. Biba was the only patient in Recovery. A nurse was aspirating her intratracheal tube as we entered. Seated at a desk charting notes in a record was a young man whom I assumed was the anesthesiologist. He rose to report, "Patient's condition is stable,

Doctor DeSa. Vital signs are remarkably normal.''

I picked up Biba's left hand—the other one was taped to an arm board with tubing and needles for parenteral fluids. Both eyes showed the black and blue secondary to retrobulbar hemorrhage. She looked relaxed and peaceful. I swallowed hard and agonized over the moment when Biba would first open her eyes and realize that they were sightless.

Stepping up to my side, DeSa proposed, "Both of us need a couple of winks. I've a wet clinic demonstration for the senior medical students in a couple of hours. A little rest would do us both good."

"Good advice," I replied, turning to follow him out of the room. Suddenly I felt very tired.

Prem and I rode in the back seat of the official car with Gaikwad in front beside the driver. There was an unusual hardness to the Captain's expression. His narrowed eyes stared out into the passing traffic.

"Damn that bloody bastard!" He muttered through clenched teeth.

"This may sound strange but I've lost the capacity to hate the man. Perhaps I'm just too exhausted to hate."

Prem chose to make no reply. We rode in silence for several minutes, each of us buried in our own thoughts.

"Must have been Shivaram of the R.S.S.S." I turned to stare at Prem.

He nodded. "Raj, I was the target last night. Trying to pull her out of danger, I placed her directly in the line of fire. That bullet was intended for me."

I put my hand on his shoulder. "Prem, please listen to me. There's no way you can blame yourself for what happened last night."

He looked at me in silence for a moment before breaking into a wan smile. "You're most understanding, Raj, most understanding." The steely severity of his expression had softened slightly.

Arriving at the hotel, Prem urged in a voice heavy with fatigue, "Have a good rest. Gaikwad will be your shadow from now on."

My first duty was to contact the Dorabjis and the Gordons. I made no mention of the blindness. I placed a call to the Clemens, then bathed. While I was shaving, Nilapat responded, with Joan on the line.

"This is Raj in Bombay, Joan. Is Jay there?"

"Hi Raj. Jay just left on his regular village survey trip."

"Joan, can you hear me clearly?" The connection had deteriorated.

"Pretty well. Raj, what's wrong?" She had heard the tension in my voice.

"I know of no way to cushion this news, Joan. Biba was shot in the head at our dinner party last night by an anarchist gunning for Prem. She was in surgery five hours."

Except for a faint mechanical hum over the telephone line, there was total silence for several seconds. Then I heard a gasping sob. "Oh my dear God!"

"She came through surgery alright and is stable at the moment, but...but..." my voice failed me. I could feel my lips moving but they produced no sound.

"Raj, please. I can't hear what you're saying."

"Joan...she's...Biba's going to be blind."

"Oh...no...no!" I heard her sobbing.

After a moment she controlled her crying enough to listen.

"Tell Jay the bullet cut both optic nerves but no critical brain damage."

"Raj, for God's sake how can you be so matter-of-fact about this?" She sounded angry.

"Joan, please. My emotions are wrung dry. I've almost passed the point..."

She began to cry again. "I didn't mean that, Raj. You must forgive me."

"Biba's blind, but Joan she's alive and normal in every other way." My voice choked, but I cleared my throat and went on, "You know I came close to losing her."

"You're so right Raj. When Biba comes to, tell her we love her, and you know she has our prayers."

"Thanks. I'll tell her. Be calling you tomorrow, Joan." I hung up and sat down, dry-eyed but torn apart inside.

Chapter Twenty-Eight

Prem joined me for lunch in my room at the hotel. Sergeant Gaikwad hovered in the background, tending to our needs. The raid on the cleaning shop had netted two suspects, both identified as members of the R.S.S.S. According to the Captain, there was only one more anarchist of any substance still unaccounted for, Shivaram. As long as he remained free security was essential.

Prem Narayan was unusually tense for a man reputedly circulating ice water rather than blood. Biba's wounding had disturbed him deeply. As I listened to him he spoke with a quiet reserve, but his words were honed to the cutting edge of steel. When he was not speaking the muscles of his jaw clenched intermittently, bulging out as knots on the sides of his face.

"Aren't you quite vulnerable?" I broke the silence. "You're exposed daily to this assassin."

He nodded and shrugged.

"It seems a bit odd that Shivaram would go to all the trouble and risk of shooting at you at a dinner party," I observed.

"They probably considered it a dramatic coup," Prem said reflectively.

Luncheon completed, we moved over to the lounge. Prem lit a cigarette.

"Sergeant Gaikwad is a damned good man." He lowered his voice so that only I could hear. "Trust him. He was born and raised in Bombay so the city is very familiar to him." He drew deeply on his Camel then blew a burst of smoke from his mouth and nostrils. "An official car and driver will be at your disposal."

I understood why Prem wanted to have lunch with me. He needed the emotional support that I could share with him.

"Cheerio." He stood and shook my hand. "Have to muck about the office a bit."

Gaikwad and I headed for the hospital. Biba had been moved from Recovery to Intensive Care. A nurse who introduced herself to me as Sister Lakshmi, handed over a chart. All appeared quite satisfactory. She was beginning to respond, stirring and moaning a little. There was no evidence of increased intracranial tension or pulmonary congestion. Her temperature was elevated less than a degree, which would be normal under the circumstances.

I moved to the side of the bed and Lakshmi thoughtfully gave us privacy behind a moveable screen. Biba looked so fragile and pale, her eyes surrounded with black and blue. I leaned over and kissed her cheek. Pulling up a chair, I sat down and reached under the covers to find her hand, slowly bringing it out to hold in mine. There was a response. Her fingers flexed as if trying to reach me. Then she stirred both legs and the other arm. My heart pounded. She had just demonstrated normal motor function of the brain. I heard her moan softly as if in distress and her lips moved ever so slightly.

"Biba, I'm here beside you," I bent forward and whispered in her ear. Her eyelids fluttered slightly but did not open. Again her lips moved soundlessly as if with great effort and her fingers tightened on mine. The tip of her tongue swept over her dry lips. Then she became quiet and seemed to fall asleep, breathing a slow rhythmic pattern.

"A cup of coffee, Doctor Singh?" Sister Lakshmi stood behind me with a small tray.

"Please," I turned and smiled at her in appreciation.

Handing me the cup, she whispered, "*Jab ag jalti hai.*"

I whispered back, "*Tab dhua hota hai.*"

So Sister Lakshmi was with the C.I.D. I wondered why Gaikwad hadn't introduced us, then realized that our security would be enhanced if others didn't know of the association.

For several moments I sat quietly sipping the coffee, my eyes caressing Biba's face. She was beautiful in spite of the head dressings, the pale face and black eyes. She began to moan again. I stroked her free arm with one hand and held her fingers with the other. She appeared to relax until I released my grasp on her to move the chair closer. Her hand slipped across the blanket, fingers spread out searchingly, and on touching mine, clasped them firmly. Her lips struggled to speak. Even this much seemed an extreme effort.

"Biba, this is Raj." I enunciated slowly. "And please do one thing for me, sweet, squeeze my hand."

Scarcely daring to breathe, I waited for the signal. The barest flicker of a smile touched the corners of her lips. Then, there it was, a tightening of her fingers on mine.

"Once more, Biba, just once more," I urged, fighting to control my voice.

For the second time she came through with the signal. We had communicated. I lifted the palm of her hand against my lips and wept quietly.

Balak Singh stopped at the entrance to Intensive Care and peered about hesitantly. His face was etched with concern. Seeing me, he smiled and came to the bedside. He gazed silently at his daughter for a moment, and, after patting her arm affectionately, strode out of the room.

That night, from my hotel room, I placed a telephone call to my parents. It was around noon in California. Mother answered the phone—Father had driven that morning to Pasadena on business. Painstakingly I recounted the story. Mother listened in silence. It had not been my intention to tell her of Biba's blindness for the time being, but on impulse I changed my mind.

"Mother, the bullet...it..."

"*Ha, kahte jao*—Yes, keep on talking," she urged gently.

"Mother, Biba's going to be blind," the words rushed out.

"*Mujhe thik thik kahani sunaiye*—Please tell me the story exactly," she urged.

"She should be well in every other way, no brain damage or paralysis."

"Thank God," I heard her whisper. She added in a firm voice, "Take courage, son, Biba will have our every support."

"But Mother...why..." the dam on my emotions broke and I wept.

"*Mera bacca, mera chota bacca*—My son, my little son," she consoled in words so familiar to my childhood. These simple words, carried twelve thousand miles over oceans and continents, eased the gnawing hurt. I slept through the rest of the night soundly and dreamlessly.

The hospital was relatively calm after the flurry of the morning routine. Surgical rounds were completed. Medications had been disbursed and vital signs recorded. The major concern of the moment seemed to be bed baths. Student nurses in their colorful uniforms, under the direction of supervising sisters in white, wielded washcloths and towels on faces, necks, backs, chests, and stiffly extended extremities.

Sister Lakshmi was all smiles. "Doctor DeSa has left orders for Mrs. Singh to be transferred to her private room at noon today," she announced. A private room would make her job easier, I was sure.

I pulled a chair up to the bedside. Reaching under the covers, my hand touched Biba's and our fingers entwined. Fascinated, I watched tiny wrinkles of a beginning smile play about her mouth and then grow like a time lapse picture of an opening flower to touch all her face.

Biba slowly moistened her lips with her tongue and murmured thickly, "Raj...I...I know you're there..." she squeezed my fingers. "Don't worry about me, darling...I'm doing alright."

Fighting to control my voice, I said, "Superb, Biba, you're doing superbly."

"How long..." she licked her dry lips again, "...how long have I been here?"

"Since night before last."

Letting go of my hand she gingerly felt the dressing about her head. "Surgery?"

"That's right, hon."

Her lips moved but no words came out. She swallowed and tried again. "My head feels...so big."

"Probably the medication and an anesthetic hangover."

"Raj, my memory's blanked out a bit. Can't quite remember what..." She reached for my hand, "what happened."

"Biba, let's not worry about that just now. I'll tell you everything later. How about that?"

"Alright." She released my hand again to feel her eyelids with the tips of her fingers. "My eyes feel like lead balls. They must be swollen."

"You really should see them..." I forced a laugh. "They're the prettiest black and blue."

"Not going to try them out just yet," she confided quietly.

I suddenly felt sick. I dared not speak—my voice would have rebelled. There must be a way to ease and share her hurt, her hurt when she opened her eyes only to look into a fathomless darkness.

"Sister told me I was being moved to a private room this noon," she smiled.

"She gave me the same news." I patted her hand reassuringly.

"Darling, if you don't mind I think I'll rest for a while...."

"Please do, sweet." I kissed her cheek. She reached up to touch my face with searching fingers. Tucking the sheet around her shoulders, I whispered, "Biba, I love you so dearly...."

A faint smile passed over her lips. She drew a sighing breath and turned her head to the side.

Sister Lakshmi took me upstairs to see Biba's new room. It was the last room at the end of the corridor. A large window overlooked a garden, beautiful with bright marigolds and pansy beds, a riot of color which my wife could never again enjoy.

"If you don't mind I'm going to relax here." I sighed and sank into an upholstered chair, stretching my legs out before me.

She smiled sympathetically. "Sergeant Gaikwad will sit in the hall just outside the door."

In the quiet isolation of the room I thought over Biba's situation. Her thought process appeared to be functioning properly. The major muscle actions were natural. Stable vital signs indicated no further hemorrhage. It was too early to be certain, but the normal temperature and pulse belied any serious infection. A bullet wound is always considered to be contaminated, and particularly dangerous when it invades the central nervous system and its covering cerebrospinal fluids. Heavy doses of a broad spectrum antibiotic were being administered intravenously as a protection against this potential complication.

I decided that Biba's progress was encouraging. We had much for which to be grateful. Having come to this happy conclusion, I promptly fell fast asleep.

Chapter Twenty-Nine

When I awoke, an entourage of orderlies were shuffling furniture about the room. Waiting in the corridor outside was Biba in her bed which had been rolled up from Intensive Care. Like a ship sailing through narrows into the safety of a harbor, the hospital crew navigated Biba through the door. Completing their mission, the staff disappeared, leaving our room quiet. Gaikwad and Lakshmi sat just outside in the hall.

"Hello, Raj," she whispered as I picked up her hand.

"Hi, darling. How are you?"

Her face crinkled into a smile. "Doing just fine. Feel a lot stronger since my nap."

"Good start on a rapid convalescence."

"Raj, just what am I convalescing from? I don't have the vaguest idea, except that there was surgery."

Drawing a deep breath, I said, "Biba, you were shot by an anarchist...a member of the R.S.S.S."

She reached up and felt her dressing cautiously, "In the head?"

"Uh-huh."

"Guess I'm pretty lucky, eh? My mind's clear and I can move my arms and legs."

"Very lucky, my dear."

"The dinner at the hotel...last thing I remember."

"Yes, darling, it happened at the party."

"Anybody else hurt?"

"No."

"Thank God for that!"

Biba withdrew her hand from mine and slowly investigated the bandage about her head. Then she ran her fingers over her face, touching the closed eyelids. I watched the inspection, holding my breath. Finally, heaving a sigh, she clasped her hands before her and lay back on the pillow.

"Darling," she spoke in a low voice, scarcely above a whisper.

"Yes, Biba?" I watched as her hands unclasped and one of them moved across the bedspread in search of mine. Our fingers locked in embrace.

"Remember our promise? We shan't hide anything from each other, shall we?"

"Yes, sweet. We must be honest." I felt caught in a current of unfolding events moving toward a climax over which I had little control. Biba's fingers tightened on mine.

"Raj, you know something..." she paused, her lips trembling, then cleared her throat to continue, "Raj, I'm blind."

I bit my lip and tasted blood. My chest tightened until I couldn't speak. We held hands in silence, each appreciating the agony of the other.

"Yes, Biba, I know," the words finally came out, so strange I hardly recognized them as my own.

There was another pause before she asked, "Is it...is it permanent?"

"As scientists we can hardly use the word permanent, can we..." I began.

"Sweetheart, remember your promise."

I recited slowly, "Biba, the optic nerves were transected by the bullet."

"Then it is permanent. Optic nerves don't regenerate...no regeneration," she whispered.

We sat in silence. Uncertainty, that nagging destroyer of endurance and creator of eroding fear, no longer stalked our minds. As cruel as the truth might be, we now stood on a common ground of understanding.

"Raj," she broke the silence.

"Yes, Biba."

"I knew this morning. Peeked and saw nothing, not even light." She straightened her shoulders and breathed deeply. "Listen, darling, let's take this a little at a time. Want time to think things over." She sounded surprisingly matter-of-fact.

"I'll leave the proper timing to you."

A glistening tear poised briefly on her left cheek, then scurried down to her chin. Smiling bravely, she brushed the moist path with the tip of her finger.

Sensing her need for quiet and reflection, I softly kissed each eyelid and her lips before rising to leave. She rewarded me with a smile. Stepping out into the corridor, I picked up Gaikwad and Lakshmi took my place in the room. I lunched in the hotel, then stretched out on the bed. A tangle of questions fought for my attention.

Biba was right. She must not push toward immediate resolution of all the problems that would attend her blindness. She needed to adjust to her new limitations a step at a time. Her life would change from one of carefree independence to partial dependence. She must not succumb to self-pity, and she would have to learn to accept with good grace the humiliating condescensions of thoughtless well-wishers. And in our own particular situation, she must never fear that she was cheating her new husband of a complete bride. She had to be convinced of the truth, that blind or not I was deeply in love with her.

Telephone calls to Prem, Balak Singh, Indira and Sharon brought them up-to-date on Biba's convalescence. Knowing that now her many friends would be visiting, I was forced to tell them of her blindness. Prem Narayan's moan of torment I shall not soon forget.

Dusk had blanketed the city as Gaikwad and I rode over the crowded thoroughfares. The driver deposited us at the front of the hospital. A faint medicinal odor permeated the hallways as we climbed to the fourth floor. The door to Biba's room had a sign outlining visiting limitations. Knocking softly, I stepped inside to find her, with headrest partially raised, eating from a tray. Lakshmi was standing by, assisting as needed.

"Hi, Raj." Biba turned to face the door and waved a spoon at me.

"And what's for supper?" I asked, kissing her.

She grinned up into my face and warily reached out to touch my cheek. "Surgical soft diet. I've just graduated from the surgical liquid. Doesn't taste all that bad, and believe it or not, I've a wee bit of an appetite."

Lakshmi excused herself and stepped out of the room.

"Good lord," I exclaimed. "I wonder how many times I've ordered surgical diets." We both laughed.

"Darling, I'm going to need some help with this custard dessert," she confided with a smile. "I know where my mouth is, but could you direct my spoon at the loading end?"

My immediate impulse was to take her in my arms and hold her close but instead I guided her hand toward the dish.

"Called our friends this afternoon," I reported.

Biba hesitated, a slight frown on her face. "Did you tell them everything?"

"Everything."

A smile replaced her frown. "Good. Now none of us need ...well...what I mean is the matter is all out in the open now. There's no need to pretend." She sounded relieved.

"You know something, sweet, I'm delighted with the way you're convalescing." I kissed the tip of her nose playfully.

"How soon do you think we can leave...leave for the States?"

"Oh, I'd say in a couple of weeks or even sooner."

She sat quietly a moment. "I still would like to go home by boat."

"First thing in the morning I'll check on sailings." I squeezed her hand. "We'll finish our honeymoon on the high seas."

Her face broke out into a radiant smile. "You're a romantic character, Raj, and I love you for it," she said, reaching out to find my face and explore its contours. "Those weeks on board will give me more time to master this disability," she added soberly.

"You'll never have a more attentive physician," I promised.

Biba slowly turned her face in my direction, her open eyes staring sightlessly at me, and burst out, "Oh, Raj, I'm going to need an awful lot of patience and..." her voice trailed off into a sob.

I drew her into my arms, holding her close while she cried softly against me. "My precious...my very precious wife," I whispered in her ear.

Freeing her hands, she wiped the tears from her face. "This blackness...it's so pitch black...can be overwhelming. But I'm climbing out of it."

I gently laid her head on the pillow. The crying had subsided. Turning the lights down low, I stroked her shoulder and arm until she slept. I kissed the back of her hand and stepped out of the room. Calling Lakshmi to take my place, I joined Gaikwad in a brisk walk through the hospital corridors and into the quiet night. As we drove out through the hospital gates, a lone *chowkidar* waved us on with his staff. Prem joined us in the hotel lobby.

"Haven't had dinner—how about joining me?" I asked.

"For that matter, neither have I."

"Then you'll join me?"

"*Accha*. My pleasure."

The three of us climbed the back stairway to my suite. Gaikwad left to fill our orders. Prem, restless and troubled, paced the floor smoking heavily. Suddenly he stopped short and asked, "How's Biba?"

"Doing surprisingly well. DeSa says her recovery's ahead of schedule."

"That...that which you told me over the phone this afternoon...I mean the matter of..."

"Yes, Prem. Biba's permanently blind." I broke in, mercifully helping him come to the point.

He groaned and dropped his head to stare at the floor. Slowly the words came. "Raj, I'm not one to weep easily, but after you told me that Biba had lost her sight, I locked the door to my office and wept like a child."

"The tragedy wasn't of your making, Prem. There's no way under God's sun that you could have altered the circumstances."

He shook his head sadly a moment, then looked up at me. The hurt was reflected in his eyes.

Gaikwad returned with the dinner tray and we sat down to eat, our conversation meager.

As Prem stepped out into the corridor, I urged, "Be sure and come to the hospital tomorrow. Biba wants to visit with you."

Later I was able to contact Nilapat and bring the Clemens up-to-date on Biba's progress. Their words of encouragement raised my spirits and I found myself humming a tune in the shower. At Prem's insistence, a cot had been set up in the room for Gaikwad.

Sometime late that night, the telephone rang harshly, waking me from a sound sleep. Turning on the bedside light, I grabbed up the receiver.

"Doctor Singh?" It was a man's voice.

"Yes," I responded sleepily.

"Please come to the hospital immediately. Your wife has taken a turn for the worse." His English was heavily accented and he seemed short of breath.

"Oh my God!" I exclaimed. "Be right there."

Gaikwad was sitting on the edge of his cot watching and listening. I told him of the message. He shook his head, frowning. Reaching for a slip of paper in his pocket, he handed it to me and suggested, "Sir, here is the hospital phone number. Please call and talk to the floor sister."

My heart pounded its way up into my ears as I placed the call. The very calmness of the hospital operator's voice was exasperating. At last the quiet response of the desk nurse came through, "Medical Center, private floor."

"This is Doctor Singh," I said, struggling to control my words. "How is Mrs. Singh, Doctor Ranjit Kaur, doing?"

There was a pause and conversation in the background before the reply came through, "Mrs. Singh continues to do well, doctor."

"You're quite certain?" I asked with an overwhelming sense of relief.

There was more talking at the other end of the line, before the voice came through again, "Yes, doctor, she is quite well and sleeping soundly." She hesitated, "Is anything the matter, sir?"

"No, nothing and...and thank you." I replaced the receiver with a sigh. My palms were clammy with perspiration.

"May I use the telephone, sir?"

"Certainly. But Sergeant, what made you suspicious of that call?"

He smiled enigmatically and shrugged. "*Pakka nahi hai*—Not solid." In a few seconds he had Prem on the line.

"Raj, sorry about the bloody bastard!" the Captain exploded.

"It's alright. A bit of a shock, but thank God it was false," I responded with all the calmness I could muster. "Incidentally, Gaikwad's to be credited for spotting the phony situation. He saved us from a wild goose chase."

"Possibly much more. That bugger could have ambushed you somewhere between the hotel and the hospital."

"That serious, eh?"

"Raj, did you recognize the voice? Possibly like that of Shivaram whom you heard in Dharamsala?"

"The voices in Dharamsala that night were muffled. But I can say this fellow on the phone just now was short of breath...possibly emphysematous."

"I'm sure it was that bloody cad Shivaram," Prem muttered bitterly.

Chapter Thirty

Biba's convalescence progressed rapidly, beyond our fondest hopes. Ten days after her surgery, she was up and about her hospital room, painstakingly adjusting to the loss of her sight. Lakshmi, her shadow, hovered about always ready to help. I was proud and delighted to watch Biba's intellectual and emotional adjustment to her handicap and found myself intimately sharing her joys of accomplishment as well as the heartaches of failure. Every day she made progress, past mishaps becoming the successes of the present. She was pressing her four remaining senses to accept the responsibilities of the one so cruelly destroyed.

The discolorations about Biba's eyes were barely evident. Doctor DeSa had called in an ophthalmologist to survey the results of the injury and outline rehabilitative exercises, if necessary.

"You are fortunate, my dear, that the extrinsic muscles to the eyeball are functioning normally." She nodded reassuringly at me and added, "By looking at you, no one need ever know that you are blind."

"Thank you. Thank you so much," Biba murmured, reaching out to grasp the doctor's hand. "And...and they'll maintain their size? They won't atrophy...won't shrink?"

The opthalmologist impulsively reached over and took Biba's other hand as well. "No, there should be no atrophy. I anticipate a continued normal intraocular tension in both eyes."

"Should there be any exercises?" I asked.

She shook her head. "None that I can think of."

I watched Biba's face light up. Almost to herself she whispered, "Normal. Thank God, normal!"

That night I turned in early and slept soundly .

"Good morning, sweetheart. Doctor DeSa just told me I am to be discharged tomorrow." Biba sat in a chair eating breakfast. The window was open and the usual noises of the awakening city flowed in from outside.

"Now that's what I call good news!" I exclaimed.

Lakshmi excused herself and slipped out of the room, closing the door behind her. Biba lifted her lips to mine and clung to me for a moment. Pulling up a chair beside her's, I watched as she demonstrated her ability to eat unassisted. Finishing the cup of coffee with a flourish, she turned to me with a satisfied smile.

"Gee, hon, you're really something."

"Not all that hard," she confided proudly. "First thing is to identify the positions of the various dishes, then move slowly. The right hand wields the fork or spoon while the left becomes the eye... *presto digito*... touch replaces sight."

"You make it sound easy."

"Put on my own make-up this morning with a little help from Lakshmi."

"No kidding!" Tilting up her chin with my hand, I inspected her face. "Looks great, lipstick and the whole works."

Biba found my hand and pulled it over into her lap. Unable to see me, physical contact had become a means of closer awareness of my presence.

"What do you think of my hair?" she asked, patting her head gingerly with the palm of her hand.

I felt the short crop of hair, black and thick. All the sutures had been removed days ago and the operative scars, which had been made within the hairline, had disappeared into the new growth. "At this rate you'll have a short bob before we get back to the States," I assessed with a chuckle.

A knock on the door and Lakshmi admitted Prem Narayan. He had been a daily visitor. The first time after the shooting, he had slipped into the room on tiptoes and stopped to stare silently at the patient propped up in bed. She called out his name and without speaking, he walked over to take both her hands in his. Tears had filled his eyes. Visually unaware of the emotional tensions, she carried on an animated conversation, easing Prem's heartache. Her facial expressions were warm and sensitive, giving out generously that which she could not see in return.

"I'm to be discharged tomorrow," Biba sang out happily.

"*Accha*. Jolly good. Jolly good I must say." He repeated. "What time shall I pick you up?"

"About midmorning? Say around ten?" I proposed.

With a wave of his swagger stick, Prem left us smiling broadly.

The day of discharge dawned clear and cool with a smell of seaweed in the wind wafting from the Arabian Sea. Gaikwad moved about in an air of excitement preparing for Biba's arrival. His cot was taken from the room. In celebration of the special occasion, I planned a formal dinner in our room, complete down to the candles.

"Sergeant Gaikwad," I said, breaking into his frenetic preparations.

"Yes, Doctor?"

"I would like a bouquet of red roses, about a dozen, for the table tonight... a surprise for my wife." I winked at him. "In fact, why not have them here when she arrives."

"*Bara lal gulab-ka phul*—Twelve red roses," he responded, grinning.

Biba's move from the hospital to the hotel was remarkably easy. Prem functioned as the major-domo, radiating a benign but firm authority. Holding my arm, she walked erect and unafraid, a bright bandana attractively tied around her head. I watched heads turn in evident admiration as she passed by.

Leaning toward her, I whispered, "Darling, you're stunning. Wish you could see people watching you." She squeezed my arm to her side.

Prem and his cohorts stared with interest as I lifted Biba over the threshold into our room. "An American custom," I explained over my shoulder.

"You'll both need some rest, so I'm going to leave you alone," the Captain suggested as he checked out the closets and the bathroom. "Just a couple of days until you sail. Let me ask that you be particularly security conscious. Gaikwad and Lakshmi will handle any outside needs." Stepping into the hallway, he turned to add, "I'll drop in to see you tomorrow."

We unpacked her things. "Raj, help me orient myself, would you?" she asked, standing in the middle of the room and looking around as if trying to visualize her surroundings.

We spent the next hour going from object to object, repeatedly identifying distances and positions, until Biba could get about the room confidently. She studied the sound of my voice coming from various places. Her increasing accuracy in these estimations surprised both of us. Biba suddenly began sniffing the air.

"Oh you darling!" She almost strangled me with her entwining arms. "Roses, you got me roses."

"They're red."

"You lover, you. My special color...and you surely know that red is for passion," she teased.

Pulling out a single rose from the bouquet, I placed it in her fingers. She smelled its delicate fragrance and lightly caressed the red petals with her lips. Finally she held the flower at arm's length, staring in silence as if trying to visualize its beauty.

"Dinner for two and in candlelight," I announced with a flourish.

"Ah, my darling, you must come up and see me sometime," she mimicked in a low throaty voice.

Changing into lounging pajamas, we stretched out on the bed. Biba lay with her head in the crook of my arm. "I've so much to learn," she sighed. "But you know something, Raj, I'm not afraid of the future. I'm grateful that I knew the world by sight, that I can always relate to a visual world. Now that red rose I held was vivid. I could see it from memory, every petal."

We lay side by side in silence for a few moments. Biba suddenly raised up on her elbow to look down into my face. Her fingers gently explored my ears, eyes, nose and lips. Almost self-consciously, I stared back into the depths of her sightless eyes. She lay back.

"Over the past few days I've been wrestling with the problem of salvaging my professional life. All those years of medical education just can't be wasted, my specializations in pediatrics and pediatric psychiatry. Suddenly a possible solution came to me."

"Let's hear it, sweetheart."

"I could make a career with adolescents...primarily counseling."

"Terrific idea, honey. The teenager's become the forgotten patient. They're too old to feel comfortable with squalling babies in the pediatric waiting room and too young to feel at home with adults."

"You really think I'm on the right track?" she whispered.

"Absolutely. I'm delighted, Biba."

Gaikwad phoned, asking when he might set the table for dinner.

"Six-thirty would be a good time, Sergeant, and you have the candles?"

"Oh yes, Doctor Singh, very lovely ones from the hotel dining room."

Biba excused herself and soon I heard bathwater running. Dozing off, I awoke just in time to watch her sit down at the dresser. She arranged the cosmetics before her with careful precision. I watched closely as she made up her face. She followed each move with turns of the head and eyes, as though she were watching the entire process. Touching up her lips, she leaned forward, focusing on the mirror.

"You're amazing."

"In what way?" Biba turned and looked at me directly.

"Oh the perfectionism. The way you're disguising the fact that..." I broke off uncomfortably.

"That I'm blind?" Her voice was matter-of-fact.

"You're uncanny."

"Worked out my approach in the hospital. Checked over a list of things which tend to identify a blind person."

"Go on, I'm fascinated."

"One of the most common problems is that they fail to follow the action with their eyes, with their attention. For instance, they often just don't look at the person they're addressing. Again, they rarely follow their hands even in such simple motions as reaching for an object."

"I'd really never thought of that."

"Raj, you've never been blind," she pointed out with a grim laugh.

"You're right," I conceded, kissing the top of her head.

Gaikwad, with Lakshmi in tow, arrived on time. The two of them went about their duties arranging a table setting which had the intimate decor of an exclusive restaurant.

Biba put the finishing touches on her sari and jewelry. Long golden eardrops and wrist bangles set off the royal purple sari. She left her head uncovered, contributing to a surprisingly chic look. Lakshmi exclaimed, "You are very beautiful!" I could have hugged her.

"Thank you, Lakshmi," Biba responded shyly, beaming.

"Shall the candles be lighted?" Gaikwad looked expectantly at me.

I nodded, then took Biba's hand and led her to the table. The dinner was superb and she demonstrated a surprising mastery of the art of sightless eating. The process was slow and painstaking, requiring the recognition of the shape and consistency of the food. She creamed and sugared her tea with confidence and accuracy. The dishes were removed and our tea replenished before Gaikwad and Lakshmi bade us goodnight.

"The candles are flickering," she said softly, "and the shadows are dancing on our faces. I can smell the burning tallow and wicks and I can hear the soft sputtering of the flames."

"You know, my sweet, you can sense things I can't."

Biba undressed while I showered. Her singing and humming were contagious. We sang together, popular songs, and when we ran out of words we just continued the tune.

I stepped out of the bathroom to find Biba hanging up her clothes. The room was almost dark. "Honey, don't you need more..." I suddenly realized that she no longer needed the light.

"Need more what?" she asked, shutting the closet door on her carefully arranged clothes.

"Nothing hon," I answered lamely.

"Raj, are the lights turned low?"

"Yes, Biba, but why?"

"Oh, I've got to learn more about those switches," she laughed. "Don't like to undress in a bright light. Have to at least make a show of modesty."

"The light is low."

In the dusky room Biba slowly dropped her negligee on the floor and started toward me, stately and unabashed.

Chapter Thirty-One

The dinner party at the Dorabji's was constrained at first, what with the memories of the last such gathering, and everyone's uncertainty about how to comfort Biba. The tension dissipated quickly, though, as Biba's skill in handling her handicap became apparent. Farewells were in order because Captain Narayan had passed the word around that shipboard leave-taking would be discouraged as not in the best interest of security. With a round of warm good-byes, the party broke up.

We rode back to the hotel in silence for the most part, reflecting on our evening. I sensed that Biba was tired. She had exerted herself in an effort to put the guests at ease. Prem, who was riding in front with the driver, was unusually quiet.

Biba woke up first in the morning and shook me out of a sound sleep. "Raj, we're sailing tomorrow and I'll have to give some attention to my packing," she reminded me happily. In short order she was dressed and packing her saris. While I shaved, Gaikwad and Lakshmi set up breakfast.

As we sat over our coffee, Gaikwad called me to the phone. It was the American Express office, asking for signatures on documents which had been delayed because of the last minute rush on our bookings. I checked with the Sergeant, who suggested that he pick up the papers and bring them to the hotel. Time was short, though, and I didn't want to compromise our sailing, so I decided to drive to the office. Lakshmi would remain with Biba and Gaikwad go with me.

Soon after our departure, Lakshmi excused herself to run down to the lobby and mail some letters I had given her earlier. She instructed Biba on the security of the door and told her there would be no need to open it until she returned. Hardly had the nurse guard stepped out of the room than there was a knock. Biba hesitated, wondering if Lakshmi had forgotten something, but discounted this because there was no identification signal. The knocking persisted, so she called, "Who is it?"

"Telegram for you, madam," a man's voice replied. "It is marked 'urgent.'"

"Who is it from?" Biba tried to draw out the conversation in the hopes that Lakshmi would return.

"It does not say, madam."

"Please slip it under the door." She heard the rustling of paper below her and stooped to feel for the telegram.

"It does not pass under the door. If you will open a little I can give it to you."

"My maid will be coming shortly."

"No madam, I cannot wait and I must have your signature before leaving the envelope."

Biba thought a moment about the security of the door and decided that the protection of the chain night latch would be adequate. Carefully she slid the bolt open, taking care to keep out of reach of any hand that might be thrust through the narrow space. She waited for the telegram to be slipped into the room. She heard a quick metallic crunch...an instrument cutting the latch chain...and the door was shoved against her and then closed.

"Who are you?" Her voice was disdainful and showed no fear.

"You will find out," he mocked.

"Let's not play games. I am blind and do not recognize your voice."

"I am aware of your blindness. In fact, I am responsible for your blindness."

"The Rashtriya Swayam Sewak Sangh?"

"Yes."

"And your name must be Shivaram?"

"Yes."

"Now that we know each other, just what do you want?" Biba demanded, folding her arms across her chest defiantly.

"To bring shame and discredit upon the Criminal Investigation Department."

"And how do you plan to accomplish that?"

"By destroying you."

"Your bravery astonishes me," she spat.

She heard him walk toward the window sounding as if he were out of breath. "Your maid will not be returning soon," he wheezed.

"You didn't hurt her?"

"No. Merely detained her until my task is completed."

"Thank God for that," she sighed.

"Of course you know that bullet was intended for Captain Narayan, not for you."

"Poor marksmanship," she taunted.

"The Captain saved his life trying to protect you."

"Probably not within the range of your understanding, but that was a brave and noble act."

"We consider our aims noble. We fight for a pure India, ethnically and religiously."

"And to accomplish this you assassinated Mahatma Gandhi?"

"The end justifies the means. We are India's true patriots. Gandhi was a pacifist coward and tried to accommodate the Muslims."

Biba listened carefully to his labored breathing. His intermittent spells of coughing and wheezing indicated advanced emphysema. Shivaram was a sick man. Was he mentally deranged as well, she wondered?

"Why don't you sit down?" she suggested after one of his severe bouts of coughing. Moving slowly toward the dresser, she indicated a chair. He made no reply, but she could tell that he sat down by following the sound of his deep breathing.

"No sympathy, please," he coughed out the words one by one and eased himself into the chair with a sigh.

There must be a way out of this, Biba thought. I've not come through all that I have just to be done away with by a physically and mentally ill anarchist.

"And what are your plans?" she asked.

"In due time, young lady." He paused to catch his breath. "Don't press for an answer to your question. Just enjoy every second of the present."

Biba felt a chill flush through her body. He was playing with her. "I...must...not...panic," she counted off each word under her breath. Suddenly a plan came to mind. Her antagonist was helpless during his bouts of coughing. From the variations in the sounds, she knew that during these attacks he doubled forward and gasped for air. She must exploit this. Shivaram probably considered her quite helpless and she could play on this misconception. Cautiously moving closer to the chair, she deliberately stubbed her toe against the dresser.

"Clumsy of me," she muttered, pretending to be embarrassed. "Can't see a thing. I feel so feeble."

His reply, if he intended to make one, was interrupted by another siege of coughing. Again Biba listened intently and decided that during the seizure the man bent over toward her.

"Have nothing...against you Americans...but you have...become important to us...because you...are important to the C.I.D.," he wheezed.

He definitely plans to kill me, Biba thought, but found to her surprise that she was not afraid and was thinking clearly. He began shifting uneasily in his chair. There was a limit to his time as well as hers. A weapon, I must find a weapon, she thought. The candlesticks, she suddenly remembered. Gaikwad had placed them on the dresser where she had felt them the night before. Her hand started to explore carefully and unobtrusively. There they were. Her pulse began to pound.

"You're a sick man, you know that," she said, trying to distract him from her manipulations.

He merely grunted.

Now to wait for an episode of coughing, she thought. She shuddered at the thought of what she was about to do. She must succeed. There would be no second chance.

"Your husband's efforts, with the support of the C.I.D., all but destroyed the Naya Ghadr, did they not?" he gasped.

"We hope so."

The chair squeaked as he shifted his weight. "Good riddance. They were not real patriots," he said disdainfully.

"No worse than the R.S.S.S.," she taunted, hoping to goad him into another fit of coughing. It worked. He tried to reply but broke into a moist cough which grew into strangling paroxysms. Moving quickly, Biba picked up the candlestick with both hands and paused an instant until she was sure of the position of his head. Then she brought the heavy weapon down with all her strength. The sickening sound of metal against skull proved her accuracy. She heard his body sprawl heavily to the floor, sliding forward to rest against her legs. Still holding the cudgel in one hand she knelt and grasped his hair firmly with the other, ready to deal another blow. She waited patiently for the return of her nurse. Finally the prearranged signal sounded at the door.

"Lakshmi, is that you?"

"Yes."

"Use your key. The night latch is broken."

Lakshmi cried out and rushed to Biba's side.

"I'm alright. There should be a weapon on the floor somewhere. I heard it fall."

"An automatic with a silencer, beside the chair."

"Anything else?" Biba asked, rising to her feet.

"Heavy metal cutting shears on the floor just inside the door."

"Is he dead?"

Lakshmi knelt and checked his vital signs.

"He is dead, Mrs. Singh."

"I killed a man," Biba whispered. Turning to Lakshmi, she asked, "What detained you?"

"In the lift...he stopped the lift between floors. Cut some wires."

Biba phoned Prem Narayan. "I just killed a man," she announced.

"Good God! You what?"

Biba explained briefly.

"Be right over. You weren't hurt?"

"I'm fine, except...I'm not used to killing..." her voice faded.

"Have Lakshmi bolt the door and for God's sake stay in your room!"

Prem, Gaikwad and I showed up at the same time. "Biba...." I began.

"Oh, Raj," she started toward me, "I just killed a man." I took her in my arms and felt her body go limp. She had fainted. Placing her on the bed, I bathed her face with a wet towel. She came to with a start and sat upright, reaching out her hands to identify her surroundings.

"Darling, I'm right here sitting beside you." I put my arms around her.

She smiled wryly. "Things happened while you were gone, Raj."

I could only laugh in profound relief.

With the four of us listening, Biba pieced together the story. Prem took her hand. "My dear, what you've done here...it's unbelievable! My God, what courage and resourcefulness!"

Gaikwad answered a knock on the door. The Bombay police had arrived to take a deposition and remove the body. Prem guided Biba through the procedure. In order not to delay our sailing, he assumed responsibility and promised the interrogators that the C.I.D. files on Shivaram would be made available to them.

"I'll be checking with you around ten in the morning," Prem announced, waving his swagger stick at us from the hall. "Have your baggage ready to go."

We ordered a light dinner that night. Biba had been tense, haunted by the fact that she had killed someone. I reassured her that he was evil and steeped in hatred, and had broken in with one purpose in mind, to murder her. She relaxed as the evening wore on.

"Guess Bubli and I are in the same boat now," she reflected over her tea.

"Sweetheart, go in and take a hot bath, fill the tub and just soak for an hour. It'll do wonders."

She took me at my word and soon I heard her humming as she lay soaking in the water. She came from the bathroom wrapped in a large towel. I pulled her down into my lap and held her tight.

"Doesn't take as long to get ready for bed," she laughed.

"How come?"

"My hair—don't have to comb it out or braid it."

"You know something, hon, I can almost see it grow and at the risk of sounding trite, your short hair looks downright cute."

Turning the lights low, we stretched out in bed. I cradled her head in the crook of my arm. She searched for my hands and drew them to her breasts, lifting her face to mine. Her body trembled and responded to the delicate ecstasies of our tender love. We fell asleep in each other's arms.

The sun rose bright on our last day ashore in India. The Captain was on time as usual. Under the direction of Gaikwad, all the bags were sent to the *M.S. Silver Bear*, an American freighter bound ultimately for Oakland, California. Balak Singh had been invited to accompany us to the docks. We had agreed, for the time being, not to complicate things by telling him about Shivaram.

"Your ship sails early this afternoon," Prem told us. "There are ten other passengers, all Americans save one Dutch couple. The captain's name is Hansen."

"Did you tell them that I'm..." she broke off.

"Yes. They're aware of this."

The *M.S. Silver Bear* stood out trim and newly painted, with the Stars and Stripes floating at the stern. Winches rattled and jittery derricks lifted the last minute freight. A ferment of men and motorized trolleys wrangled on the dock.

Balak Singh hugged Biba and said his farewells at the end of the gangplank. He promised to visit us soon in our new home. Gaikwad saw to the transfer of our baggage. Prem accompanied us into our cabin. After looking about the quarters, he paused, his dark eyes studying us.

"You two are an extraordinary couple, and you have paid a dear price..." his voice broke and he bit his lower lip.

Biba reached out until her fingers met Prem's and she threw her arms around his neck and embraced him, crying silently.

"I shall always miss David..." my voice trembled, "he was like a brother to me."

"Ahmed Khan was a son to me," Prem whispered, then throwing his shoulders back, he shook my hand and stepped over the high cabin threshold onto the deck. With a twinge of sadness I watched him walk down the gangplank and turn at the far end to raise his swagger stick in salute.

Biba and I strolled the decks, watching those myriad things that go on about a ship preparing to sail. I described everything to Biba, who correlated my narration of the visual with her senses of sound, touch, smell and even taste.

Soon we felt the vibration of the ship's engines, and heard the winches rumble as they pulled in the hawsers. Just over the rail below us, a tug struggled to move us away from the dock, its powerful propellers stirring up whirlpools of muddy water from the floor of the harbor. Buildings and cranes on the wharf slipped away as we eased out into the channel.

Dinner that night was a pleasant affair. Biba and I were seated at the Captain's table. In his faultless English, heavily tinged with a Norwegian accent, Captain Hansen put us all at ease. Word had been passed around that Biba and I were on our honeymoon. Bottles of champagne, nestled in buckets of cracked ice, appeared on the tables. The tinkling of glasses being set out by the stewards made happy music, punctuated by the popping corks. Mr. and Mrs. Wormerveer, the Dutch couple, presented us with a bottle of Vandermint, a Holland chocolate liqueur. Captain Hansen rose and proposed a toast, "May your love be eternal."

I took Biba's hand and we smilingly accepted the well-wishes of the ship's officers and our fellow passengers. My wife was radiant. Impulsively I put my arms around her, drawing her close, and we kissed to a crescendo of applause.

The Captain was handed a note during the main course. It was addressed to me so he passed it over. The radiogram read,

TO THE DOCTORS SINGH STOP CRIMINAL INVESTIGATION DEPARTMENT SUBMITTED RECOMMENDATION GOVERN-

MENT INDIA YOU BOTH BE AWARDED HIGHEST CIVILIAN
DECORATION FOR EXCEPTIONAL SERVICE TO YOUR ANCES-
TRAL HOMELAND STOP BUBLI JOINS ME INVITATION TO
OUR WEDDING VANCOUVER NEXT JUNE STOP PREM
                              NARAYAN

I slipped the communication into my pocket to share with Biba in the
quiet of our cabin.

After dinner we promenaded briskly on deck. The cold night wind
precluded loitering. The ocean air was fresh and our lips soon tasted of
salt.

Our cabin was cosy. The porthole glass was frosted with spray.
Somewhere a lanyard, goaded by wind, snapped nervously against the
ship. Increasing swells made it difficult for Biba to maintain her stance.

"Something I hadn't really thought about," she said with a laugh. "A
rolling floor complicates things a bit."

Sitting on the edge of the bunk, I pulled her into my lap. "Now we'll
roll together," I whispered in her ear.

"M-m-m, you taste salty, and I'll bet I do too." She was nibbling on
my cheek.

"You sound happy, hon."

She laid her head on my shoulder. "I've not really been discouraged
since I left the hospital. . . because then I was convinced that you loved
me. Nothing else really mattered."

I took her face in my hands and kissed her firmly. She relaxed in my
arms with a deep sigh.

"Biba, a radiogram came during dinner. It was from Prem."

"No kidding! What did he have to say?"

"The C.I.D. is submitting our names to the Government of India for
their highest civilian award."

"Well I'll be! Our folks will certainly be happy."

"You aren't kidding."

"Was that all of the message?"

"Now what makes you ask that?" I asked in mock surprise.

"Woman's intuition, I guess."

"Actually, there was something else in the message. Prem invited us to
Bubli's and his wedding in Vancouver next June."

Biba laughed happily and threw her arms around my neck. "Oh, Raj,
how wonderful. You know they've been through so much."

We sat in silence for a moment, our arms around each other. "Raj, I
hope you'll understand what I'm about to say. It's very important to
me."

"Yes, sweet."

She took my hands in hers. "Darling, don't ever pity me, please. I can
adjust to my blindness, but pity can rob the birthright of love. Do you see
what I'm trying to say, Raj?"

I pulled her against me. "I do understand, Biba. What makes you so important a part of my life isn't pity, it's love. I'm head over heels in love with you."

"Thank you, Raj," she whispered. "I'll never raise the subject again." Her smile was soft, almost shy.

I awoke from a sound sleep, confused for a minute as to time and place. The muted hum and steady vibrations of the ship's engines gave me my orientation. I felt a surge of elation. We were headed home, my bride and I. The heady jubilation was touched with sadness at the separation from those citizens of that great Indian subcontinent who had won their way into our hearts.

Biba lay in the crook of my arm, fast asleep. A shadow of a smile played across her face. Slowly I disengaged my arm from under her head and rearranged the pillow, pulling the blanket up around her shoulders. Placing a kiss in the center of her forehead, I took the two steps that separated our bunks and climbed into the other.

MEL

It happened at a cocktail party!

Among the generals and admirals that night, I searched out a doctor who had attained a high place in the officialdom of Washington. He was a wise man, and I trusted his wisdom.

We talked of many things, as one does at such functions, but uppermost in my mind was one thing: *another move*. Another change faced me and my family.

So many times I had tried to put down permanent roots!

"Doctor," I said, "Mel and I are approaching mid-life. We have had so many moves in and out of several professions. Is he doing the right thing?"

"My dear Olivia. Where do you suppose I would be today had I refused to change jobs? I'd be back in the little town where I landed after graduating from medical school."

The encouragement from that man has remained with me these many years, as I followed my man around the world and throughout the States in thirty major moves.

He walked with ease among queens and presidents, with prime ministers and governors general—and with leading doctors and educators, here and abroad.

He was "Father/Dean" to many medical students, including the late Tom Dooley.

He gave comfort and new life to the sick.

He had time for the beggar and the leper.

At commencements, at convocations, and in medical classes I have witnessed his challenge to youth. There has never been anyone more at home on the platform. His "everyday" language is transformed when he stands at the podium.

Every institution with which he has been associated has been bettered for his touch: clinics, Pentagon office, medical school, mission hospital and university.

With a group of medical deans in India, he helped organize the first Indian Association of Medical Colleges. He assisted in getting their Journal started, and he served on their editorial board.

For his services to N.A.T.O., in France, he was awarded the French gold Medal of Honor.

They loved him in China. He joined the guerrillas in World War Two as liaison between the U.S. Armed Forces and the Chinese Communists.

He walked hundreds of miles, lived in their caves with them, starved with them, patched up their wounded, and helped to organize the medical services of the famous 8th Route Army.

Loyalty has always been supreme in his life: To his family...To his country...To his God!

At Westminster College, where Winston Churchill made his "Iron Curtain" speech, he was given an honorary Doctor of Law degree.

At one time in our lives, I really didn't know how to introduce him. "Shall I call you 'Your Honor,' 'Dean,' or just 'Mr.' (in India and England often used to designate a surgeon)?" Mel only smiled.

Yet through it all there has always remained a genuine humility. He was surprised when he was asked to become the Dean of a university medical school, or to help Harry Truman and Dwight David Eisenhower.

Coming home from India, already past fifty, he helped to organize a clinic of some twenty doctors, all of them specialists. He became Chief of Staff in the local hospital, while the prestigious Los Angeles Academy of Medicine elected him its president. The Los Angeles Surgical Society made him a life member.

At 65, he shut his office door at the clinic, donned his cowboy hat, and became a "gentleman farmer." The hard work of landscaping our acre took off twenty pounds. Tanned and strengthened by his labors, he escaped that heart attack so common to doctors.

At long last freed to pursue another dream, he is now an author; not of medical or philosophical or religious articles...of which he had already written more than 150...but of mystery and adventure. From the land of his birth...from the India he knew for 23 years.

On the morning of my 72nd birthday I opened my eyes to find on my pillow the following:

> trod the market place in search of fitting
> pronouncements, but finding none, the inner
> recesses of my heart I probed
> discovering countless jewels of tender love
> for one who on this date of her birth has reached
> the sweet and mellow age of seventy-two
> Furthermore, the coming first of June
> marks the passage of two-score and ten years
> since our exchange of nuptial vows

In choosing the jewel to tender in return, I pondered deep and long. Finally, I selected one, worn smooth by its oft use; words simple and devoid of sophistry, but how all-encompassing:

I love you!

Olivia Casberg
Solvang, California
1982

MATTEOLIG 81´